wearing
the **spider**

wearing
the spider

susan schaab

Galavant Press, LLC
New Canaan, Connecticut

Published in the United States of America
by Galavant Press, LLC.
First Printing.

Galavant Press, LLC
P.O. Box 636, New Canaan, Connecticut 06840
www.galavantpress.com
1.800.886.1802

Library of Congress Control Number: 2006910989

Publisher's Cataloging-in-Publication
(Provided by Quality Books, Inc.)

Schaab, Susan.
    Wearing the spider / by Susan Schaab. — 1st ed.
        p.   cm.
    LCCN 2006910989
    ISBN-13: 978-1-934291-05-4
    ISBN-10: 1-934291-05-6

    1. Women lawyers—Fiction.   2. New York (N.Y.)—
Fiction.   3. Legal stories.   4. Detective and mystery
stories.   5. Suspense fiction.   I. Title.

PS3619.C295W43   2007   813'.6
                                        QBI07-600001

To my loving husband
who opened the creative door for me
and encouraged me to walk through it.

And to my amazing son
who blesses me with inspiration and joy.

wearing the spider

the

PROLOGUE

I didn't guarantee it would be *paperless*, my friend," said a man's voice speaking into a wireless headset. His secretary appeared in the doorway with coffee, and he waved her in. Following his gesticulating index finger, she placed the cup and saucer carefully in the small clearing on his desk and left the room.

"No, it's a twelve to fifteen year proposition on average, from petri dish to market. Only a few thousand *ever* get the green light. It's more than just a red-tape issue," the man said into his headset.

As he spoke, he toyed with a brass figurine of a female. After a few seconds passed, he took his first sip of the Kopi Luwak brew and rubbed his chin with his thumb and forefinger.

"Oh, hold on." The man pushed a button on the telephone. "Yeah?"

A woman's voice came through the speaker. "That reporter's calling again. Line two."

"Let him wait," said the man. He pushed the button to resume his conversation.

"Sorry for the interruption."

He opened a drawer, pulled out a Redweld and extracted a bundle of papers clipped together. "Yeah, just think of me as an alchemist turning dross into gold." He chuckled. "We can arrange for the results to show a seventeen percent relative reduction. Data's inherently malleable."

He flipped a page and listened, as he took another mouthful of coffee, swirled it over his tongue and swallowed.

"No, that's the beauty of it," he paused. "I'm not a gambler. I'm a *creator* of wealth. Value at the close of the transaction, not dependent on any uncontrollable variable."

He smiled to himself. The computer screen on his desk glowed with a webpage of statistics.

"Two billion at least. That's worth a few dead people, right?" He laughed into the receiver and then fell silent for a few minutes. His email inbox had replaced the Internet browser window on his computer screen and he typed electronic messages as he listened to the voice in his ear.

"Oh, come on, Chuck. Corporations make product line decisions every day based on the cost of potential wrongful death suits as a debit against profit. Whether or not a few side-effects show up is really inconsequential to the bottom line. You're trying to play in the big leagues, my friend, but you guys want to keep using an amateur's playbook."

He fell silent again. "Yeah, that's right," he said after a few seconds. "That's all it is. Just a cost of doing business."

He slurped the steaming liquid. "Okay. Will do," he paused. "Done. We'll talk next week." He yanked off the headset, pushed the blinking button on his phone and spoke openly into the air of the room, "Mad Max! What can I do for *you?*"

"I have a question," a male voice sang out of the telephone speaker. "Yep."

"When I ran into you last week and you bought me a drink, did you slip me a mickey or something? I had some crazy hallucinations that night and the mother of all headaches the next day."

"Don't blame me if you can't hold your liquor," the man said, as he drained the last drops of dark liquid from the cup.

"C'mon, man. That whole conversation was off the record. You didn't have to *drug* me."

"*Maaaax,* amigo, you insult me. You really think I'd do something *that* pathetic?"

"Okay, right. Never mind. Now, *on* the record. Gimme your reaction to Newspan's cover story. You know. The one that claims the FDA lets scientists from the big drug companies serve on advisory committees. The guys that dictate drug policy."

The man stayed silent as he stood and stuffed some items into a leather portfolio.

"C'mon, man. They're talking about Congressional hearings. Don't you have *any* comment?"

"Why would I comment on that?"

"You represent Finley Regent, don't you? And, other pharmaceutical companies?"

"Yeah, that's public knowledge."

"What about these allegations of *'conflict of interest?'* Some of these scientists are making big bucks from their recommendations to the FDA. Any of Finley Regent's scientists under investigation?"

"If you think I'm going to answer that, you must still be under the influence of whatever was in your drink the other night," the man said as he disconnected the line.

A few minutes later, he was standing on Park Avenue hailing a taxi, another headset in his ear, this one attached to a BlackBerry. A taxi slowed and approached the curb where he was standing.

"No, she won't. I *know.* Field research," he said into the receiver. "And, even if she does, it'll fall on deaf ears."

A few seconds passed. "The brass ring. Partnership," he said.

Pulling open the passenger door, the man scanned the backseat. He frowned and turned back toward the sidewalk, nodding to a smartly-dressed elderly woman who had approached, also seeking transportation.

Surprised, she walked slowly toward the taxi and he ushered her into the backseat to the sound of her expressions of gratitude. The person on the other end of his cellular conversation, an audio bystander, commented on his act of chivalry.

"Yeah, okay, so sometimes I'm a gentleman," replied the man. "There's another one right behind it." He waved down a second yellow cab that followed the curbside ritual.

"Actually, that taxi was a tar pit. I'm wearing a five thousand dollar suit," he said, as he inspected the seat of the second taxi and slid inside. He slammed the car door and grumbled directions to the elderly Hispanic gentleman behind the wheel. "God, I miss my car and driver," he said into the headset.

For the next several minutes, the man sat silently in the backseat listening to the voice in his ear. The taxi turned into a side street in pursuit of the destination he had announced. After a second turn, onto Broadway, a loud popping sound could be heard, followed by a swoosh as the vehicle began to rock rhythmically to the left rear, in an awkward tri-tire waltz.

"Blowout," said the driver as he guided the taxi to a nearby curb.

"A fuckin' blowout," repeated the passenger into his headset. "Can you motherfucking believe this? Goddamned third-world transportation. Gonna be late. Call you back."

He ended the call and opened the passenger door. Jumping from the backseat, he stood on the sidewalk, looking for another cab as he began to rant at the driver.

"Don't you people inspect the *tires* before you start a shift? What kind of bullshit service is this? If you think I'm gonna pay the meter, you're . . ."

The Hispanic man had knelt down to inspect his damaged tire and was ignoring the tirade.

"*Santa Maria!*" said the driver, his eyes wide and his face flushed as he made the sign of the cross and ducked down next to the fender of the car. He began breathing rapidly and squinted, inspecting the busy, traffic-congested street and across the upper sections of the surrounding buildings.

"Thaz NO *blowout*," he shouted in accented English as he pointed to the destroyed tire. *"Thaz a BULLET HOLE!"*

chapter

1

T he sound of four voices undulated in tandem during a pre-dawn
conference call on the fourteenth floor of a midtown Manhattan
office building.

"So, you're saying you don't think we could register *any* of these
trademarks?" asked a participant from a remote location.

"I'm just saying you run an acute risk of challenge," said Evie Sullivan, rubbing a new hue of redness into her eyes. "Once we file, the
application can be opposed by other trademark holders. If their claims
are valid, they can prevent the ultimate registration of your mark."

"*That's just great.* We've . . . we've already invested significant capital
in start-up costs. The timeline's been set."

"I'm sorry about that. I only received your email yesterday and I
ordered immediate searches. It was what I saw in those search results
that made it important that we speak so early this morning."

"So, you think Pharsalus could block our application?"

"It's a strong possibility. There's a likelihood of confusion with similar marks they own. As we've discussed, they have over thirty marks registered in Classes Three and Five. I don't think we could get a registration through for any of these." Evie sipped from a steaming paper cup and scribbled on a stack of Official Gazette copies from the U.S. Patent and Trademark Office.

"We've got our hottest product of the decade about to be introduced with no name," said a voice from among those murmuring over Evie's speakerphone.

"So, you have your FDA approval in hand?" she asked.

"Yes. All the bureaucrats are cooperating except those in the Patent and Trademark Office."

"I'm sympathetic," she said. "Howard, Rolland & Stewart is on call to file an expedited application when you come up with a new product name."

"Okay, we'll have to go back to Marketing," came the dispirited response. "Please tell Alan what we're up against."

"Absolutely. I'll keep him informed."

As Evie disconnected the line and took a bite of a cinnamon muffin, she glanced down at the *New York Law Journal* on her desk, dated August 24, 2005, a Tuesday. A headline grabbed her attention, so she took a second look at the front page:

Finley Regent Acquires Wagner Zeus
Closes Deal with Record Speed

She knew that the deal was being helmed by a partner at her firm. The same partner who would have participated in the early morning conference call if he'd met her at the office that morning as promised.

The Finley Regent acquisition had apparently proceeded to closure within weeks, which was unusual for a deal in the hundreds of millions. *Alan will come in here all full of himself,* she thought. *His ego will have gained ten pounds.*

She sorted briefly through the stack of mail that had accumulated while she'd been away, but because of the early hour and a dissipating caffeine haze, her thoughts drifted and she succumbed to distraction, allowing herself to relive the prior day's flight.

She had boarded an afternoon flight home from Los Angeles and expected to surrender to exhaustion after working through the weekend. As she approached her third row business class seat, she noticed a man seated on the aisle who was devoted to the stack of reading material in his lap. He had wavy dark hair with strands of early gray at the temples, and she saw in his face a tanned serenity. His herringbone sports jacket was flush with the contours of his shoulders and his slacks were defined by the thighs of an athlete.

She politely declined his offer of assistance with her suitcase and deposited it in the overhead compartment herself. When she moved across him to take her seat, she held only an airport-bought copy of the *Wall Street Journal*.

"Are you planning to read all the way to New York?" he asked. She noticed his eyes move from his reading material and rest on her newspaper.

"The headlines . . . if I can stay awake," she said while fastening her seat belt and turning her gaze toward the window. The ground crew was completing its pre-flight preparations and the airplane engines were purring. She felt the man's eyes on her so she turned toward him and asked, "Why? Want to borrow it?"

"I'd rather have you *read* it to me," he replied.

Evie then focused on the man's face, without the cool displeasure she often felt at unexpected male overtures.

"I read the front page while standing in line," she said. "An article on prison reform. Guaranteed to soothe you to sleep. Or, there's an Op Ed ranting about the Enron case. A chorus of corruption."

"A friend of mine reads the *Wall Street Journal* religiously. Claims everything in his life depends on it."

"Many people consider it required reading."

"Joe Barton," he said, extending a hand.

"Evelyn Sullivan," she paused. "Evie." After shaking, she asked, "You from L.A.?"

"Just north of Malibu. Got a meeting in New York." His voice was a rich baritone, but he spoke softly.

"Buy you a drink?" he asked.

"Are there any worthwhile choices?" She glanced toward the flight attendant taking orders a row away.

"I can offer you something a bit more interesting." She watched Joe reach under the seat in front of him and extract a bottle of a Veneto Amarone and a corkscrew from a leather bag.

"I see you don't need anything but glasses," the attendant said as she deposited two airplane-issue wine glasses on his tray.

"Thanks, Irene." Joe had either noted the woman's nametag or had taken the flight frequently enough to become acquainted with its attendants.

"To illusions," he said, raising his glass in Evie's direction.

"Thanks for the wine," she said. "But are you going to help me out with the toast?"

"Ever heard the theory that positive illusions about oneself can cause a person to be more successful? There was this study. It concluded that people who allow themselves to hold a few exaggerated perceptions about themselves may have more success than those who are strict realists."

"What kind of success?"

"The study didn't specify," he said with a slight grin.

"Hmmm. And what sort of self-deception do you engage in?"

She remembered Joe's laugh as he ignored the question. "The theory is based on the fact that memory is organized egocentrically—the more self-descriptive something is, the more memorable it is. And the more it affects behavior. So, since those distorted perceptions are at the forefront of a person's memory, the more positive they are, the more they may motivate that person."

"For example?"

"For example, a man thinks of himself as a professional-level golfer. As long as he believes that, he might actually play a round at a level worthy of a pro." Joe smiled and she noticed that he had charming little creases at each end of his smile. She remembered thinking he must smile often.

"So, you're saying that living in a fantasy world might improve a person's performance? Sounds like a re-hash of 'the power of positive thinking,'" she paused. "May I ask what sort of exaggerated self-perceptions you allow yourself?"

"The whole process depends on keeping those perceptions to oneself. If they're revealed and reality sets in, well then, their effect is lost." His smile was contagious.

"I'll try not to let mine show. Okay . . . to illusions," she agreed as they clicked glasses.

"So you have business in New York? Or is it home?" he asked.

"New York's home. I'm returning from a meeting in Los Angeles."

"In the interest of someone else?"

"I was negotiating with the owner of an office building downtown. His company was bidding on a license to a work of art created by one of my clients. A sculptor."

"Yeah?"

"It's a stunning piece called The Solitary Lady."

"So, you're a lawyer?"

"Yes. I counsel clients on intellectual property rights."

"Copyrights and trademarks. Uhmmmm. All your clients artists?"

"No. Mostly technology clients. More software deals than anything, but my passion is representing artists—protecting their reputations and trying to control the unauthorized use of their work."

"And I evaluate technology projects for patent potential. We're always at the negotiating table granting licenses to patented property. I could be a future client."

"Or adversary."

"Or *adversary*."

"You're a consultant?"

"No. I run the project development division of a software company." He handed her a business card.

She remembered her first impression of his card. It presented in small italic font: Joseph A. Barton, Parapier, followed by an email address and telephone numbers. It was as enticing as he was, she thought—minimal information mysteriously presented in a classic, welcoming format.

"A French company?"

He nodded and said, "I'm the executive vice president of the U.S. subsidiary."

"Pleasure to meet you, Joe. Perhaps we'll sit at a negotiation table sometime."

~

Evie's reverie was interrupted suddenly with a knock on her office door. Her secretary, Helen, bounced through the portal like a three-dimensional color wheel.

"Good morning," greeted Helen with a parade of waving fingers.

"Hi Helen. You're here early." Evie smiled at the plump dark-haired woman with blue-framed glasses, fire-alarm red lips and a flower-print dress in an abundance of reds and yellows.

"You have that meeting with Senator Arbeson, and I didn't want you to forget."

"Forget about a meeting with the firm's most powerful client? Have I been that distracted lately?"

"Well, I know you were working sixteen-hour days last week. I was just worried that you'd—"

"I appreciate it, Helen. I'm on top of it."

"Did you end up with the quiet room away from the elevator?" asked Helen.

"Yes, but I didn't spend much time at the hotel. For most of those sixteen hours I was at Percunico's office or in a conference room with opposing counsel."

"I hope you got some sleep."

"I'm getting used to the absence of it. I'm okay. Just sitting in this morning. It's Hanover's meeting. And after that, I have to go over to Seth's office. You got me a ticket to that Thursday night auction, right?"

"Yes," Helen said. "Yes, I did. Anything else?"

"You know, you could really help me out by organizing the Roma Sori file. I had a message from Hanover that they'd like to meet sometime this week, and I've been sticking email printouts and correspondence in there randomly over the last few weeks. It's a mess."

"That's the perfume company, right?"

Evie nodded.

"Don't they have a new fragrance?" Helen grinned.

"Priori." Evie extended her arms toward the ceiling and leaned her head back, stretching her neck muscles.

"Oh yeah. Isn't that the one they're testing in that contract you have on your desk?"

"Right." Evie reached into a desk drawer and tossed a small plastic container of clear liquid to Helen. "Here. See what you think. I'm sure Adam would welcome your feedback."

Evie's telephone display blinked with an internal call. Helen gestured toward her desk outside Evie's office.

"That's okay, Helen. I'll get it." Evie picked up the telephone receiver, surprised to see her fellow associate's name in the small digital window. Helen fingered the tiny perfume vial with the look of a mouse just given an enormous wedge of cheese, and made a quick exit.

"Jen, what are you doing here this early?" Evie spoke into the receiver.

"Never left," Jenna said in a coffee-stained voice. "My third all-nighter in a week. If this deal doesn't close soon I may resort to physical violence."

Jenna was an associate one year senior to Evie who had already been up for partner the previous year. Known to be smart and attentive to clients, Jenna had nonetheless been passed over. The rumor was that she tended to interject herself too directly into clients' politics. Jenna believed she was overlooked because of her gender, an opinion she had shared only with Evie, and unofficially with a sex discrimination attorney who was a friend at another firm.

"Client or partner?" asked Evie.

"Both."

"I wish I could offer some great advice, but—"

"I know. You've had your share."

"Reminds me of a dream I had a few nights ago," said Evie. "I'm working under a tight deadline, researching case precedent for a client memo. In my dream, all the resources I need are located in this group of buildings . . . in one location . . . like the Smithsonian. I'm trying to walk from building to building gathering what I need. But there's all this scaffolding in front of the buildings I have to crawl through and it's all spider-webby and I get caught up in it. And my legs. It's as if I'm crawling through thick mud. Something's sucking my legs down. They get heavier and heavier and it's taking all my energy just to lift them. So ironic. All I need to write my memo is right there, I just can't seem to get to it."

"Hmmm. An allegory for this firm," Jenna said as she smacked her lips. "Speaking of sucking . . ."

Evie laughed.

". . . did you get rid of that new matter Alan was trying to stick you with?" asked Jenna.

"Oh, you mean that patent licensing deal."

"You make it sound so dignified," snorted Jenna. "How many partners have clients who want to license vibrator technology?"

"Yeah, well, yeah."

"What was it again? Personal pleasure devices?"

"They do make, well, adult toys and they had a tentative deal to license their technology to this children's toy manufacturer."

"Can't make this stuff up. I wonder if the parents buying those 'playthings' know that the toy's mechanics can be found in bedside tables across America?"

"I guess technology is technology."

"There's just something about it being used for children's toys . . ."

"I agree, but just working with Alan is always enough of a demoralizer. Fortunately, the deal fell apart. I sometimes wish the others would, too."

"You know you have to be able to work with *all* the partners if you ever want to make partner yourself. Where does Alan get these clients?"

"Why knows? I'm just tired of being at the top of his assignment list."

"No mystery there. Simple attraction."

"Okay, stop. Why did you call me?"

"I've forgotten. *Oh!* You never worked on that Gooseneck-dot-com agreement with Reyser, did you?"

"No, but I assume by the question that someone in the firm did."

"I knew you couldn't have negotiated such a crappy deal. Have you ever seen it?"

"No."

"Unbelievable. I hope whoever worked on it kept good documentation."

"Why? What's wrong with it?"

"It's terribly one-sided and it puts all kinds of nightmarish restrictions on Gooseneck that software developers never agree to. The code they wrote for Reyser can't be used for any other client. You know the typical language we're always fighting against. And, of course, the code they *delivered* to Reyser includes their core stuff. The stuff they routinely license to clients all over the world."

"Standard sink hole. Most associates I've worked with know to negotiate their way out of traps like that."

"Alan was the supervising partner. I don't know who took the laboring oar. Probably somebody who doesn't work on software deals too often."

"That could be sticky for the firm if there's ever a dispute. Not to mention the political minefield because Alan's involved. What brought your attention to it?"

"Litigation. Brad told me that Reyser's making noises like they might sue if Gooseneck designs a system for their competitor."

"And the firm hasn't provided a very good foundation for their defense."

"I know. Their goose is cooked!"

"Not funny."

"Definitely not the best legal advice we've ever dispensed. Unless someone has some thorough documentation showing that Gooseneck overruled the lawyers during the negotiations, the firm could be facing a malpractice claim."

"Better alert Hanover, but choose your words carefully. Partners do stick together."

"Yeah, *the brotherhood*. As soon as he gets in. He's been out a lot lately."

"See ya."

Evie hung up and sifted through an assortment of folios and pulled out her notes for the meeting with Senator Arbeson. A consulting agreement between the Senator and an actuarial firm. It was a bit odd that the Senator hadn't delegated this transaction, or at least the mundane details of it, to an aide, but she surmised that the meeting was part business and part camaraderie. The Senator counted several of the firm's partners among his close personal friends.

With the planned luxury of an hour before the Senator's arrival, Evie allowed herself to resume the mental playback of yesterday's conversation on the flight home. Evie recalled losing any desire to sleep on the plane.

"I'm intrigued," Joe had said. "Tell me about this sculpture negotiation."

"Are you sure?" she'd asked. "You really want to hear about my meeting?"

"I welcome any chance to learn your secrets before I sit across from you at that negotiating table."

"Okay. My client told the story in an interview he gave to an art magazine, so I can tell you." She shifted in her seat to face him. "One of the more unusual clauses in the license agreement given to us by the building owner was the right to destroy or alter the sculpture. Sculpture is unique in that sense. After a work is designed and installed, it stands, representing its creator, in the negotiated location. In this case, the lobby of an office building. Anyway, over time, it sort of becomes a part of the personality of the building. If the owner of the building at some point decides he wants to renovate the property, he often mistakenly believes that he can freely destroy or alter the sculpture, sort of the same way he can move walls around."

"You mean take an ax to the Solitary Lady?"

She remembered smiling at his flippancy. "Well, as it happens, the rights of a visual artist are unique. His works are protected under a legal principle called moral rights."

"Extraordinary . . . the law recognizes morality?"

Okay, she thought. *He hates lawyers.*

"Because my client is a sculptor of some note, his reputation is considered to be part of the work he creates and the moral rights laws prevent deliberate destruction of his work without his knowledge. But the building owner was represented by savvy counsel. He negotiated for the right to destroy or alter the sculpture if he wanted to, without notifying my client. It then became a matter of money."

"Isn't it interesting in a negotiation how one ultimately attaches price tags to rights requested by the other guy that neither knew existed at the beginning of their meeting?"

"Yes, I suppose that's true. But, when an artist has made a name for himself against the odds, that's worthy of protection."

"Is there a frustrated artist behind the advocate?"

"Oh, no. I wish I was, but no. I'm not a creator, only an admirer."

"I'm an enthusiastic admirer myself." His gaze distracted her for a moment.

"Have you ever noticed the insight you can gain about an artist by careful examination of his art?"

"And what did you learn about your client from the Solitary Lady?"

"As you probably imagined, it's his conception of an ethereal, naked, beautiful woman with an introspective sort of look on her face."

She remembered the intensity of Joe's eyes as he'd listened to her words.

"I think he admires women who are independent and beautiful and not afraid to be alone," she'd continued. "Maybe *he* is afraid to be alone, and by creating a being who is not, he conquers his own fear."

"With all due respect, he may have just seen a beautiful girl on Madison Avenue, fantasized about her and decided to create a replica so he could pretend to touch her."

"Well, even if that's true, isn't that a stirring thought? To be so moved by another human being that he invests the time and energy to capture his memory of her in a work of art?"

"You've got me there."

After pulling out a photograph of the sculpture from her suit pocket, she passed it to Joe and watched him study it carefully for a few moments.

"Not a bad attempt. I've seen worse. Even on Madison Avenue."

"His work has been displayed in galleries all over the world and brought top dollar at auctions. Are you creative?"

"I'm not sure if anything I've ever produced could be described as a creation, but I've been a weekend photographer. I actually still have a dark-room covered in cobwebs in the attic. Digital photography just doesn't do it for me. So, what was the outcome of that discussion?" he asked. "Did you manage to thwart the efforts of the presumptuous landlord?"

"The client was pleased."

She remembered feeling him watch her as she sipped the wine. Neither of them seemed to notice the absence of conversation for a minute or two.

"Did you meet any interesting people in L.A. besides Mr. Real Estate and his attorney?" he asked.

"Not this time. I have to say, I've rarely enjoyed trips to L.A. The geography is beautiful, but the beaches are overrun or overly commercial, and I never seem to stay around too long."

"How often do you fly to the west coast?"

"Two or three times a year. On a trip last year, I did meet someone I thought was interesting. A woman playing a beat-up guitar on Venice Beach. She was singing the most incredible blues with one of the most amazing voices I've ever heard. Sort of Aretha Franklin, but with an injection of sadness."

"Did you speak to her?"

"Well, that's the interesting part. I'd just finished eating at one of my favorite restaurants in Santa Monica, The Ivy, and I was carrying a doggie bag full of leftover grilled shrimp salad. A man standing nearby told me the woman was homeless so I offered it to her, but she politely declined saying that she didn't need any food. Can you believe it? I mean, think about it. This was someone living off emotion, spirit. It was as if the song was the only nourishment she needed. The man said he'd never seen her eat anything, but she was known to sing for hours on the beach never taking a break."

"Some people seem to live in a parallel universe," said Joe. "No schedule. No need for social contact. No concept of what it's like to chase any sort of career goal. Sort of a wake-up call for the rest of us. To leave time for feeding the spirit, whatever that may consist of."

At that moment in the conversation, Evie recalled that the Fasten Seat belt sign had illuminated, and the captain's voice had announced the approach to New York's LaGuardia Airport. When Joe returned from the lavatory, the airplane abruptly jolted downward, shaking the fuselage and vibrating the passengers.

"I told him not to take his hands off the throttle," Joe smiled at her, noticing her white-knuckled grip on the armrest.

The captain announced his apologies over the airplane audio system and assured the passengers that the unexpected wind gust was an isolated one and the airplane was well under control.

"Are you free for dinner tonight?" he asked. "It's Monday, so even with no reservation, we've got a decent chance for a table."

She declined, saying she had to prepare for a client meeting, but to keep the conversation going, she told him about the auction she was supposed to attend Thursday night to gather "intelligence" for an artist client.

"Need an escort?" he asked.

"An escort?"

"To the auction. Would you like some company? To complete your disguise, of course."

Evie smiled to herself as she recalled that exchange. In those final moments, she'd handed him her business card. Thinking back on it now, she couldn't remember the last time she'd offered her card to a man without the stale repartee of concluded business in the air. Before they had deplaned, her last words to him were: "If you're planning to be in New York on Thursday, give me a call."

She shook off the daydream and checked her email, not really expecting to see a message from him, but there were a few new ones. A subject line, *Trademark Search,* caught her eye. She glanced at the clock. A few minutes after nine o'clock A.M. Over twenty minutes until the Senator's scheduled arrival. She clicked open the message, thinking it might be related to that morning's conference call, but it wasn't. It was from a username she didn't recognize and had been sent around six o'clock A.M. It was short and direct:

> *Evie—Please do prelim search RE: Neolactin,*
> *Class: pharmaceuticals plus other standard classes.*
> *Beth Hoffman, paralegal, Your Client Number 1270,*
> *charge to general matters*

The number 1270 she recognized as Finley Regent, the company that had been granted front-page coverage in the current *Law Journal,* but it was unusual for a client employee to refer to an internal firm tracking number. Now that she saw the full name, Beth Hoffman, she thought she remembered seeing it before.

Evie forwarded the Finley Regent message to Helen with a request to create a new file to initiate the matter. Its content reminded Evie that she needed to inform Alan about the trademark discussion she had concluded that morning.

She began typing an email message addressed to him:

> *Discussed prospective product names with Neully this morning as planned. Can't recommend any of their current choices as trademark-worthy. They said they plan to go back to their Marketing Department to come up with something more unique that won't be too similar to any Pharsalus mark. They said they already have their FDA approval and that the name issue was the only thing holding up product launch. Are we handling anything else for them that I need to coordinate?*

After hitting SEND, she gathered a notepad and correspondence relating to the Senator's matters, and stopped briefly in the restroom to make sure there were no remnants of breakfast on her mouth. Frowning at her long, straight hair, she swept it back into a loose French twist.

As she was walking out the door, Helen caught up with her.

"Evie, the Senator's here, but he's making the rounds to say hello to a few of the partners. Hanover said to meet them in Conference Room B in about fifteen minutes."

"Okay, thanks Helen."

"Since you have a few minutes, could we go over a problem Accounting discovered in last month's expense report?" Helen asked, walking with Evie toward the receptionist's desk.

"Sure. What's the problem?"

"Natalie said there were some inconsistencies in the paperwork."

"Which trip was it?" Evie said, stopping to face Helen.

Helen looked at the first page of a stapled report. She had inserted the words *"see attached"* in the blank for hotel on the face of the form. As she lifted the first page, she said, "I always keep your receipts in a file until I finish submitting the expense report. And I know you always leave your travel file in my inbox when you return. I found your L.A. receipts when I came in this morning."

"I hope you can make some sense of them. Sorry I didn't have time to organize them."

"No problem. I'll put them in order," said Helen. She looked back at the flagged expense report. "Here's the problem. It was that trip to Dallas last month," she said. "The receipt that's attached says you had a room at the Colonial Court Hotel. The reservation confirmation I included with the expense report isn't here. But, I remember that trip. I booked you at the Windham, but I remember you sent me a message saying they'd had some sort of plumbing problem. Didn't you end up staying at the Euphorion?"

"Mmmm. Let's see . . . I'm trying to remember. Oh, yeah. I think you're right, Helen. I took a taxi to the Windham, but when I got there they sent me over to the Euphorion. There has to be some mistake. Can you call both hotels and try to find out what happened?"

"Sure. I'll do it right now," said Helen, turning back toward her desk.

Wrong hotel. Somebody else's receipt. Expense Report Hell. With notes in hand and her mind a controlled clutter, she started down the hallway toward Conference Room B. Jenna appeared from around the corner with the pace of someone chasing a thief. She was searching as she jogged and she wore an urgent expression, stopping short when she saw Evie.

Jenna's eyes darted as she whispered loudly to Evie, "Alan's new secretary, Mary, told me *your* name was in her records as having negotiated that Gooseneck agreement."

"You're kidding!"

"No, afraid not."

"Great. Faulty records *everywhere*."

chapter

2

W hen Evie entered the wood-paneled conference room, Senator Winston Arbeson was already there, standing in the corner, smoking cigars with Alan Levenger. No one was going to tell a United States Senator, the firm's most important client, that it was illegal to smoke in the building; even Alan defied the city's smoking laws. As she approached, both men turned in her direction, causing Alan's last few words to spill out toward her: *"Like I always say, if you're going to shoot at me, you damn well better hit me."* Evie could not help hearing the phrase, but it meant nothing to her so just smiled. He was wearing his recent victorious closing for Finley Regent, just as she predicted he would.

"Evie!" The Senator greeted her as if they were long lost friends.

"Hello, Senator," she answered. "I hope I'm not intruding."

"No, not at all," he said. "Alan and I were just finishing up."

Alan, whose glare felt to Evie as if he were inspecting a potential purchase, walked toward the door without a word, wearing a jackolantern smile.

She watched him leave and then turned to Senator Arbeson. "Senator, I'm not sure when—"

"We don't need Jack. I'll tell you what I want."

"Okay. Is this about the actuarial consulting firm we talked about?"

"No. I don't care about that. Someone with my campaign will follow up with you on that." Senator Arbeson walked to a sideboard where the aroma of fresh coffee danced on a spiral of steam. He poured a cup and took a hearty sip. "I need some tax advice. Jack said you'd be the one to ask."

Evie clenched her teeth, but maintained a calm outward countenance. Tax law was an area largely foreign to her. She wondered why Jack would've suggested her for answers, unless the tax issue was within a small section of regulations relating to art, the only tax law with which she had any familiarity.

"I have an art collection."

Evie relaxed.

"I'll see to it that you get the help you need, Senator. What's the situation?"

"I want to deduct appraisal, storage and other expenses associated with a collection that includes Picassos, Renoirs, a Gauguin, a Degas and a Warhol. My understanding is that I can do it if the collection passes muster as an investment."

"Well, that's true, but that's just the first hurdle," Evie said while a chill reminded her that she was running the meeting with one of the firm's most important clients. "A taxpayer who holds art primarily for its appreciation income, *can* deduct certain expenses associated with the collection."

"What proof's required?"

"There are a number of qualifications." Evie struggled to remember a list of criteria she'd read in a case summary. "The artwork must've been *acquired* principally for investment purposes as opposed to personal enjoyment. I'll have to do some research to be sure, but the context of your consultations with appraisers may help us establish that you viewed your purchase primarily for investment value. Also, maintenance-type attention and any public display of your collection may support our contention that you considered it an investment because you were intent on enhancing its value." Evie paused. "I assume you've kept formal records of the purchase, maintenance and expenses."

The Senator nodded and gulped his coffee.

"How much expense money are we talking about?"

"Thirteen million and change."

That's a lot of expenses. Client perception was an important part of her job, but not a client in the process of committing tax fraud. *Not even a senator.* What could he have spent thirteen million dollars for in the maintenance of an art collection anyway?

"It's typically an uphill battle to prove investor status, but it has been done in certain cases. Then, the expenses in question must be 'ordinary and necessary.'"

"Well, you should have no problem establishing my case. An aide will send over the specifics. Take care of it, okay?"

"I'll have to look over your paperwork, but we'll try to make a good faith argument. Is this in response to an IRS inquiry?"

"No, part of a required public disclosure that nobody but the press even takes a look at, but no doubt the IRS will take notice once it's out, so I want it to be airtight. You'll fill in the blanks with the necessary bulk. Understood?"

"Let me review the matter and I'll let you know where we stand."

"Stalwart. I'll talk to Jack. You should be a partner if you're going to be working on my matters."

"Mmmm. Well, thank you, Senator. I appreciate all votes of confidence, but I haven't done any work for you yet."

Senator Arbeson said nothing more, offered a conspiratorial smile and shook her hand before he left. Evie stood for a moment and let the conversation hang in the air. Was Senator Arbeson asking her to bolster the facts in his favor? She mulled over his words. Did she just receive a directive to manipulate his tax information? Or, was he just expressing confidence in his case and suggesting she do as aggressive a job as legally allowable? *I want the partnership, but for the right reasons. Not for manufacturing a taxpayer status that can't be reasonably argued from the situation.* "Even if it means keeping a senator happy," she said under her breath.

Ten minutes later, she was in her office preparing for her next meeting.

Oh . . . Alan. She dialed his extension.

"Evie?" His greeting served double duty, asking the question: *"What do you need?"*

"Alan, did you get my email about Neully? They were not too pleased about the news I had for them this morning."

"Don't worry about it. They're supremely disorganized. I agree with your analysis of the marks and I'll tell them so."

"I don't understand why their email didn't show up in my inbox until yesterday."

"Computer glitch probably. I'll call them and apologize for missing the call this morning."

"Okay, Alan. Oh, there's one other thing. I'm afraid there's a mistake in some of your record-keeping. Your secretary has me listed as the associate who negotiated a recent agreement for Gooseneck-dot-com. I never worked on that matter."

Evie glided around her office as she spoke. A Redweld file reclining on a chair opposite her desk fattened as she loaded files into its opening.

"Evie, that matter's closed. Why are you concerned about old records?"

"Well, it's important to me that the firm's trail of my work is accurate. Reviews are coming up and I wouldn't want there to be any confusion."

"Ahh. Understood. You're gunning for partnership. Okay, I'll check into it."

"Thank you, Alan."

~

The humidity bathed Evie's face as she walked through the streets of midtown after an afternoon of client meetings. She could not avoid breathing in the dense odors that were transported on the moist summer air of the City. As she walked at a brisk pace, the welcome aroma of fresh fruit from a street vendor's cart was replaced by the mildewy spittle of a window-bound air conditioner.

She wove her way through the crowds of people blanketing the sidewalks, pushed open the doors to her building and ran for the elevator to the fourteenth floor. After ducking into the restroom to freshen up, she heard Jack Hanover's booming voice behind her in the hallway so she turned around and smiled at the firm's managing partner.

"Evie. I was planning to stop by your office. Thanks for handling Arbeson this morning. I knew he'd get good advice from you."

"No problem." *I wonder what he told Hanover.*

"It's just that kind of client service that makes a well-rounded lawyer. And it's *that* type of lawyer that we look for in our partnership decisions."

Before she could say anything more, the acclaim was followed by the inevitable demand.

"Before I forget, retrieve my Roma Sori Blueline file from Liza and put together a summary of the issues for me, cross-referencing your notes. Please have it for me by noon tomorrow."

"Of course." Evie suppressed a sigh as she shook hands with Hanover and walked past him toward her office.

Another night at the office. All things personal will have to wait. Again.

Evie finished drafting comments on a trademark license agreement at around 7:45 p.m. and turned to the matter Hanover had requested. Helen had not only organized the file but also created a chronology of her correspondence and telephone notes. The Roma Sori Blueline memo for Hanover would be easy. *Helen, you're a lifesaver.*

At 9:20 p.m. she took a break to walk down the hall for a cup of coffee. The office was quiet, although she counted four glowing valleys of light under the office doors of other senior associates, one of them Jenna's. Evie knocked, opened the door, and leaned in.

Jenna had already been staring in that direction, apparently deep in thought, and spoke before Evie could issue a greeting.

"What are two beautiful single women doing in a place like this with all that nightlife happening a few hundred feet south?" said Jenna.

"That is the question, isn't it?" Evie stepped into the room and stifled a yawn.

"Are you leaving soon?"

"Yeah. I'm finishing up some revisions to a draft, but I should be ready to leave in about twenty minutes. Want to grab a late dinner?" asked Evie.

"If alcohol is involved, I'm there."

"I'll buy you one."

"Meet you at the library door in twenty."

∽

"Any partnership news?" asked Jenna over a frothy chocolate martini at Capers, a trendy bar near the office.

"Hanover dangled a carrot today, but I'm not going to bite. Awfully coincidental. It was right after I'd met with Senator Arbeson who asked me to handle something for him."

"If he wants you to be made a partner, you *will*."

"We'll see how he feels *after* he receives my memo. I'm not comfortable pushing to the point he seemed to suggest."

"That's the problem with V.I.P. clients—they can make your career *or break it*."

Evie and Jenna both pleaded exhaustion after two drinks and an assortment of appetizers so they hugged and departed for their respective apartments at 11:40 P.M., leaving a crowd just beginning to churn.

"Finally made an escape from d'office, Miss Sullivan?" greeted Fred, the doorman at Evie's apartment building at the corner of 65th Street and Central Park West. She gave him a generous smile as he opened the door for her.

"Night, Miss Sullivan. Oh, almost forgot . . . d'ere's a package for ya over t'the front desk."

Evie nodded. The concierge handed her the usual collection of bills, catalogs and junk mail, then reached under the counter and retrieved a porcelain vase that held one dozen red roses.

"Somebody sure likes you," he said.

"Thanks." Evie smiled and lifted the vase to walk to the elevator. She decided to read the card once she was in her apartment where she could shed her shoes and lay down the heavy briefcase and collection of mail.

Could it be? How would he have been able to find out where I live? As she hurried to her apartment door and opened it, her eyes focused on a white piece of paper that had apparently been delivered under her door. She deposited her gatherings on the console in the foyer, bent down and grabbed the handwritten note.

Hello, love. Haven't seen you in awhile. Miss your smile.
Can we have a drink and catch up on gossip?
Or how about brunch on Sunday? Love, Ralph.

Ralph Crosby was her neighbor across the hall and a trusted friend. He had donated a washer to her one laundry day in the basement, and they had become acquainted during simultaneous spin cycles. Ralph was an import from Great Britain who had attended law school in the United States and had established himself in New York as a partner in a small litigation firm.

Evie smiled as she read Ralph's note. She then searched for a card attached to the roses. There wasn't one. She looked around on the floor and shuffled through the mail to see if the card had fallen or had mixed in with the envelopes and magazines. Nothing. She dialed the concierge.

"Ellis, was there a card? Did the roses come with a card that might have fallen off behind the desk?"

"Uh, well, I don't . . . let's see. I honestly don't remember seeing any card. Hold on." She heard him put down the receiver. In a moment, he returned. "Sorry, Miss Sullivan. No card anywhere here."

Evie hung up. She was too tired to go back and search the elevator so she collapsed on her bed, intending to sort through the stack of mail, but falling asleep with an open telephone bill in her hand.

During her Wednesday morning commute, she thought about the roses that had greeted her the night before. *It must've been Ralph.* No card, but their delivery had coincided with the note he deposited under her door. She made a mental note to telephone him later from the office.

There were two scheduled client meetings for today in addition to the pile of work that she knew waited on her desk. She had to stop by her office to gather some files and check her messages before taking the subway to Wall Street where the first client would be waiting for her.

~

Alan Levenger lit his fifth Camel of the morning, walked to his desk and sat down. He leaned back in the tufted-leather chair like a land baron contemplating newly annexed acreage. As he spun his reclined throne to starboard, the edge of the neck-rest brushed an asymmetrical stack of old newspapers that had balanced itself for months on an overburdened credenza. The movement disturbed multiple copies of an old issue of one of New York's tabloids, *Spellbound!*; they fell at Alan's feet.

He retrieved one of the copies. His eyes focused on the front page containing a tease for a story about a sex scandal at a Manhattan investment firm. He flipped over to the society page and his face reflected his self-amusement, recalling the moment that the *Spellbound!* photographer snapped a particular photograph.

It showed a nameless female in a strapless dress on his inebriated lap in the company of one of the firm's prominent clients. Fortunately, the photographer had not captured the moment when Alan had slipped his hand around the client's surprised wife. *What was her name? Carol, Cathy . . . I don't remember. It doesn't matter. Some just have something to trade for power and then actually believe they're powerful.* The sound of an email arrival drew his attention to the computer screen and he opened the new message:

Prepare the Docs. Arrange TC. Closing 9/20.

As he read, Alan blew out a lung's worth of smoke through puckered lips and licked away the dry after-effects. He closed his eyes and leaned back against the leather upholstery. His blood surged. Everything he'd predicted was falling *right into place.*

chapter
3

One of the firm's most senior partners, Paul Wayford, appeared in the firm's kitchen on Wednesday morning, as Evie was supplementing the milk in her café latte.

"Morning, Evie," he said. "Don't forget that we'd like you to say a few words about that moral rights matter at the partner's meeting this afternoon."

"I remember. Is a brief summary okay or do you want something more formal?"

"That's fine," he said pouring coffee into his cup. "Nothing elaborate. We just want to hear about the highlights of the negotiation. The deal closed, did it not?"

"Yes, it did."

"Terrific. Few partners in the firm have had exposure to . . . shall we say, such arcane issues."

"I understand. No problem. I'll be there."

"Great. See you at four."

After a late morning meeting on Wall Street, Evie took the subway back to midtown. She deposited her briefcase and jacket on a chair and opened plastic containers of miso soup and vegetarian spring rolls, positioning them on her desk between stacks of files. Flipping through the bundle of written messages Helen had left on her chair, she came to a note requesting her to see Alan in his office immediately upon returning.

She sat at her desk and played her voice mail messages while she dipped a spring roll into the soup and took a few bites. No message other than Alan's seemed urgent so, on the assumption that his summons related to a matter that she knew was active, she grabbed the VelloPro file.

Until the end of last year, Evie had not consciously held any opinion of Alan Levenger. It was an encounter during a November client visit in Chicago that had left an indelible stain on her perception of him. Even though she'd been aware of his propensity toward roguery, she'd been shocked when he followed her back to her Chicago hotel room, kissed her and tried to force his way into her room. After his vehement apology and a pledge not to repeat the behavior, she had agreed not to report the incident, but the wisdom of that compromise had haunted her ever since, especially after confiding in Jenna.

She walked down the hall to Alan's office with her defenses on alert.

"Sit down and put your feet up for a conference call." He greeted her allowing his eyes to travel freely around her person for several seconds. "You're an art historian, aren't you? A question," he said. "Who was it during the Renaissance Period that said: *'If only man had fifty senses, since five give such pleasure?'*"

"Lorenzo Valla, but he said it a bit differently." She looked past him. "So, you corrected those records on Gooseneck, right?"

"Yeah, yeah. Absolutely. Honest mistake."

"Thanks. Okay. Will this call be on the VelloPro matter?" She met Alan's gaze and regarded him for a moment. His strawberry-blonde hair, its earlobe-length and layers a contrast to the legal establishment, hugged his head in a thick collection of gelled strands. His overly tanned skin camouflaged the light-colored clusters of facial hair on his upper lip and made his eyebrows barely visible. The texture of his skin spoke of a lifetime of sun and his cheeks were speckled with a constellation of freckles. He had a well-tended physique and a ready smile full of milk-white veneers that he often flashed to further an agenda.

"Okay. VelloPro," he said, as he removed a fresh cigar from his pocket, cut the end and struck a match. "You should listen, learn and take notes."

Evie pointed at the cigar, but he ignored her. She looked to her lap, reviewing the open file. It had been three weeks since she'd handed Alan the final draft of the VelloPro memo for his review, and he had not said a word about it until now. She knew he had not even read it, as it was still in the sealed envelope in which she had delivered it to him, laying in the center of his desk, partially covered by a jumble of papers. Alan rotated his chair tossing papers from one pile to another. As she sat there, he telephoned to arrange a group of guests for a black tie charity dinner.

Evie could see a red light blinking on another line and concluded that the conference call had already been initiated.

Finally, VelloPro executive Frank Mueller was summoned from telephonic limbo and announced himself. Alan pitched around some polite conversation and asked Frank to summarize his concerns.

"Have you been able to put something together yet?" Frank asked with no apparent frustration at the delay to which he had been subjected.

"Well, as a matter of fact," Alan began, "I have a copy of a draft review that was submitted yesterday by my dutiful associate, Miss Sullivan, who is sitting in my office right now." Evie suppressed a frown at the misinformation.

"Well *that's* reassuring. I asked you the question a month ago. Well, forget it. Gimme a summary of the content." Frank now seemed reluctant to waste any more time.

"Certainly," Alan said, with no effort at an explanation.

Evie moved forward in her chair, poised to take notes with a stoic facial expression.

"Well, I've heard that you're a bottom line man," Alan began. "The bottom line is that we believe you're certainly within your rights to exercise the option in section 13(b) of the agreement to sublicense the modified software."

Evie gestured silently to Alan. She hastily scribbled on a notepad the contractual prerequisites, or the actions the client would have to undertake prior to exercising the "13(b) option," and slid the pad in front of him. Alan paused for a sip of coffee and glanced over the penciled points.

"Of course, there's a troll under the bridge," Alan added.

"So it's not a clean right under the contract?" Frank asked. "What are the implications for us if we go down that path? Are we gonna be liable for any additional royalty or license fees?"

Alan did not respond and seemed to be looking for something on his desk. He looked impatiently at Evie and gestured toward the speaker on his telephone.

Evie began to speak. "Frank, this is Evie Sullivan. To answer your question, there are several issues that you should be aware of if you decide to sublicense. Let me try to summarize them for you."

Alan interjected, "Frank, I'm going to let Evie answer your question." He repositioned his cigar in his mouth and nodded at Evie, leaning back in his chair and extending his arms in a backward stretch as puffs of cigar smoke formed a cottony cocoon around his head.

Evie leaned toward the speaker, described the constraints she saw in the contract language and suggested a strategy to operate within them.

When she finished and looked up, she noticed that Alan was staring at her, the cigar held firmly between his teeth. She looked away and her eyes fixed on a golf club that was leaning against Alan's bookcase wearing a Yankees cap covered with blood-red lipstick kisses. She imagined that there must be a story associated with that collection of objects, but she found herself thinking that she wasn't the least bit interested.

"Okay, Evie," said Frank.

Evie started to speak again, but Alan held up his hand to stop any further contributions from her. He disengaged the speaker to privatize the remainder of his conversation with Frank, repeating a few of the points she'd made, as he manipulated the remnant of the cigar, now smoldering in a gold-embossed ashtray. Evie stared at the ashtray.

"You know, coincidentally, Evie had just asked me those very questions before you called and we discussed the issues. We apologize for the delay. She's been busy, but I'll have her re-prioritize," Alan added, grinning boldly at Evie as if she was in on his charade.

"We'll revise the memo for you and have it out by the end of the day," said Alan into the receiver. He turned his attention to the window as if Evie no longer existed. "Hey, you know I tried to make that tee time last month, but work intervened . . . Yeah. Absolutely. Yeah, we can do that . . . That's right . . . Yeah, private cigar party at Louis Penchman's penthouse. Park Avenue at 73rd. Hope you can make it. Great. Wonderful. See you there."

Alan wore an enormous smile when he hung up the phone and rose from his chair.

"*That's* how you handle a client," Alan muttered as he mouthed a fresh cigar. "I think you need to re-write this memo. It needs some work. I hope you learned something about fielding client questions." Alan allowed his cigar to float at the corner of his mouth as he spoke. "I need the re-write as soon as possible so I can review it and send it out today. I also want to speak to you about this revised version of the Sangerson-Zoomhelix agreement."

Evie suppressed another frown and swallowed a series of adjectives and adverbs that would undoubtedly have had a sour taste. "Yes. Okay. But I don't have that file here with me."

"Well, I don't think you'll need to *refer to a file* while we're speaking."

"Okay. Sure." Evie shifted her weight in the chair. "I made minimal changes to Zoomhelix's license agreement, just as you said. I only made changes I felt were absolutely necessary and they're noted in red."

"Yeah, I saw. The problem is that this Zoomhelix agreement is pathetic." Alan removed the cigar from his mouth. "There are parts of it that are just illogical. For example, this section on warranty is at the beginning of the agreement before any software delivery has been described and the definitions are in the middle of the document. What kind of form agreement has the defined terms in the middle of the document after many of the terms have already been used in the text?"

"Yes. I know. We spoke about this when you assigned it to me. We agreed that the form was terrible. And we talked about the order of the sections. You said you knew it was unusual, but your instructions were to leave the agreement intact."

"I never would've said that," he said as he re-inserted the cigar at the corner of his mouth.

"You specifically said not to rewrite it and to only add provisions that were absolutely necessary to protect the client. You said because the client's new, you didn't want to overwhelm them with a complete rewrite on their first deal with us."

"Are you sure that Buniker didn't tell you that? Sangerson is the first client he's brought to the firm, ya know. He might be a little paranoid."

"No. Alan, with all due respect, it was *you* who gave the instructions and told me to limit the revisions. We've seen badly worded agreements before, but you said this should win some sort of prize. You even joked about the pretentious type font that Zoomhelix used and the copyright protection extending to the *'ends of the universe, including without limitation all undiscovered galaxies.'* Don't you remember?"

"Well, I don't recall that conversation and it's irrelevant. I think you've shown a serious lack of judgment here, Evie, and I have to say that I'm very concerned about it because you're a senior associate. You should be much more savvy at this point in your career." He laid the cigar in the ashtray and walked over to a wooden cabinet, reaching behind a door and pulling out a golf glove. "This agreement should've been re-written. I can't send this embarrassing document to a client."

"Well, I agree, but my instructions were to—"

"Stop being so defensive. It's not professional."

Evie bit her lip and fell into a contemplative silence.

"Forget what you may have concluded from any prior conversations. Rewrite it. Use one of our standard forms. And write a cover letter to the client explaining in a diplomatic way why we felt it should be rewritten. We don't want to insult the software vendor our client has chosen to do business with. Email both documents to me. I don't want them to go out until I've seen them."

Evie felt a hot bubble of rage churn upward in her stomach, but she swallowed, took a breath and said, "Okay, Alan. I'll rewrite it. I kept my reading notes so I can do a completely new version. Who'll call Zoomhelix? Doesn't someone need to prepare them since the contract they sent Sangerson for review will now be returned to them in an unrecognizable form?"

"Don't worry about that. Just do it. I hope they're good notes because you have to turn it around quickly."

"How quickly?"

"By the end of the week."

"*Alan.* That's going to be difficult. Today's Wednesday. There'll be many hours of work here, I—"

"Well, unfortunately, because we've had the agreement for two weeks, Sangerson's getting a bit anxious. And they *are* a new client, after all. We don't want them to get the impression that we're not responsive, do we?"

"No, of course not," Evie's pencil moistened with her perspiration and swam invisibly between her hands in her lap.

"Okay, *andale.* Let's just get to work."

"Wait a minute, Alan. What about this VelloPro memo? I don't think we clearly agreed on what's to be done. The points we discussed on the phone are already in it. When you say 'it needs some work,' exactly what do you mean?" Evie asked, determined to clarify *these* instructions.

"I don't like its flow. I think the paragraphs are in the wrong order." Alan grabbed the unread pages and tossed them back down.

"If you're just concerned about paragraph order, can't you have a secretary clean it up? I have two other matters to finish this afternoon, besides the enormous amount of work to be done on this Sangerson document."

To resist supporting a partner was unlike her and she felt a knot form in her stomach. She was having difficulty neutralizing her disgust at Alan's farce. His accusation that she had acted irresponsibly was unwarranted. As if she'd been force-fed a bite of hot red peppers, her mouth was burning to refute the implication that she had mismanaged the matter.

"Well, that's gratitude for you," Alan snapped. "You know, I didn't have to include you on that call. You *are* still an associate, Evie. Before I made partner, I put in the time for much less money. It's amazing to me that we pay you what we do and we get this unprofessional laziness in return."

Evie did not even try to suppress the third frown. "Wait a minute. I gave that VelloPro memo in draft form to you three weeks ago. No response from you. You misled the client to cover the fact that you've spent zero time on it, but I was happy to step in on your behalf. I'm even happy to re-write the memo if you have substantive problems with it, even though you promised to send it out today without checking with me to find out if I could meet that deadline," she paused and licked her lips.

"And, *then,* you reprimanded me for following *your* instructions because you decided you couldn't send that Zoomhelix form agreement out once you focused on how poorly written it is. And because *you've* neglected to re-direct the review until now, there's suddenly time pressure for me to turn it around."

Alan was focused on her, grinning. Then he turned and walked back around behind his desk.

She continued. "You promised to meet me here yesterday for that conference call with Neully. You know I've never worked with that client before. You didn't even bother to let me know you wouldn't be able to make it. And, you expect me to be grateful? Exactly *what* am I supposed to be grateful about?"

Alan's mouth was open, poised to respond when Mary buzzed him with a call from a woman named Cheryl. Immediately his demeanor changed. As if suddenly injected with adrenaline, or perhaps testosterone, Alan raised his palm toward Evie and picked up the receiver. His face animated. Evie collected her papers and was out the door before Alan's first words to Cheryl echoed around his office.

A few moments later, Evie dropped into her desk chair with a sigh and pulled a bag of peppermint tea leaves from a drawer, dropping it into a cup of hot water she'd retrieved from the kitchen. She inhaled the fresh fragrance as she listened to voice mail messages. The VelloPro file flew through the air and collided with an empty chair opposite her desk.

The recorded succession of voices resonated in the small room. She paused as she heard her client's announcement that he had changed his mind about attending the Thursday night auction. A confirmation of the receipt of a document followed.

Then there was a message from Joe Barton. The first time she listened she was preoccupied by the sound of his voice.

"Evie, I'm in town through Friday and I'd love to see you. Still need some company for tomorrow night's auction? Call me at the Plaza Hotel."

No longer having a business reason to attend the auction, should she call him and suggest something else? They could have dinner instead. Would spending an entire evening with him be a good idea? What would be the purpose, anyway? *He lives in California,* she thought. *California. Three-hour time difference. A different world.*

She sipped her tea, dug around again in her top desk drawer and found a small sample bottle of body oil from Roma Sori. She massaged it into her arms and hands. It was a combination of lavender, marjoram, ylang ylang, patchouli and blue chamomile. A brief serenity.

Joe's card was still in that same desk drawer. She pulled it out and studied it as if it might hold further hidden information about the man it represented. She dialed the Plaza. The hotel operator answered, and she gave his name and asked the operator to ring his room. She felt a peculiar sense of melancholy, but shrugged it off, brushing away a strand of hair that had worked its way free over the course of the day.

A second or two passed and she was connected to his room. After four rings she heard the hotel voice mail pick up, but it announced only the room number. She hoped she was leaving her message in the correct electronic box. *"Joe, I got your message. The auction plans have been cancelled. It's likely that I'll be working late instead."* She paused. *"It's possible that I may be free for an early breakfast Friday morning if you're so inclined. If we miss each other, have a great trip back to California."*

She replaced the telephone receiver. A melancholy flooded her spirit. It was as if she had closed the door to a place where she might have belonged. She raised her cup to her lips, sipped her tea and returned Joe's card to the drawer. As she closed the drawer, her eyes focused on a newspaper clipping she hadn't noticed before that was hidden under the jumble of tea bags.

chapter
4

The article profiled the troubled marriage of Senator Arbeson and a recent public argument with his Latin wife that had been dissected for weeks in the tabloids. She wondered who had clipped it out of the newspaper and deposited it in her drawer, but concluded Helen had deemed it useful information, given that Evie was now working on a matter for the Senator. Each quote from the wife had been underlined in red ink. She threw it in the trash and answered some client email. A glance at the clock reminded her of the commitment to address the partners so she searched for the file with her moral rights research, flipped through the printouts from LEXIS and gulped the remaining few swallows of tea.

Although she had spoken at legal seminars with audiences of hundreds of people, she was not as comfortable speaking to the partners of her firm. They held her career in their hands, as their judgments about her would determine whether she someday joined their ranks. It was considered an honor to be invited to attend a partner-only meeting, whatever the purpose. Most associates used such opportunities to showcase successes or campaign for political juice—a pronouncement of his or her longitude and latitude on the firm's navigational chart.

Paul Wayford opened the door to Conference Room A with a greeting. She entered and nodded to the eighteen partners seated around the table.

"Evie recently completed negotiating an agreement for a sculptor that involved a moral rights issue few attorneys in this firm have encountered," Paul addressed the room. "I've asked her to brief us on the law involved so that we'll have a general awareness of the issue should it arise again."

Evie walked to the head of the conference table and deposited her folder on the lectern.

"Good afternoon, everyone," she began with a smile and nodded to several of the faces, subtly avoiding Alan's. "In the interest of full disclosure, the bulk of my experience with the Visual Artists Rights Act arises from the client matter I've just concluded, so my conclusions may be somewhat client-specific. Instead of spending time relaying the details of case precedent I discovered, I'll just briefly mention one of the most well-known cases, as I describe the client's situation. I'll provide a copy of the full research file to anyone who requests it."

She walked out from behind the lectern. "As you all know, federal law protecting works of art was drafted with the intent to encourage artistic endeavors. In symmetry with that objective, VARA, an amendment to the federal copyright law, placed certain restrictions on the use of acquired visual art. An artist who offers a single copy or limited edition of a painting, drawing, print, photograph or sculpture can prevent any intentional distortion or mutilation of that work that would be prejudicial to his or her reputation." Evie paused and her eyes traveled around the room.

Hanover beamed at her as if she were his accomplished daughter. Alan coughed and seemed to be drawing pictures on the side of his paper coffee cup. Sam Lewis, one of the youngest partners, took notes on a yellow legal pad.

"Unless negotiated terms dictate otherwise, such an artist can sue the collector for damages for simply tiring of the work and disassembling it, as long as the work is one of recognized stature."

She was relaxed now and she ignored the crunch of the paper cup being crushed in Alan's hand. Hanover glared at the disruption and its source, but Alan's gaze rested on Evie as she continued speaking.

"In *Carter v. Helmsley-Spear, Inc.,*" she continued, "the Southern District of New York interpreted 'recognized stature' to mean that the work must be perceived as meritorious by art experts. This standard is still the precedent."

Evie smiled at the eyes attentively watching her as she retrieved a photo of a sculpture from a folder and displayed it, advancing the photo in a slow waist-high arc in front of her to allow viewing by each side of the room. "This is a work called *Solitary Lady* sculpted by our artist client. Because he has mastered his medium, according to certain respected members of the artistic community, and the *Solitary Lady* was arguably consistent with his signature style, we had a good argument that the Visual Artists Rights Act was applicable."

Alan was now staring with a mischievous grin and Evie was actively forcing herself to look beyond him. She fought off a sudden shiver with the realization that his expression seemed to be accusing her of posing nude as a model for the sculpture. As she was nearing the end of her commentary, Alan leaned back dramatically in his chair, distracting her. She took a breath and managed to regain her thoughts.

"The final agreement included supplemental fees for the liberty to destroy, distort, mutilate or remove the work and the right to combine the sculpture with other artistic works," she said. "It was truly a case of intangible rights dictating their monetary value."

Hanover's secretary appeared in the doorway, but had to make her way around the back of the room to wrestle away Hanover's attention. She whispered in his ear, and he rose to leave the room. As he stood, he gave a final nod to Evie and then disappeared through the door. Some part of Evie's subconscious noted that he was walking slowly, but she kept her focus.

After Hanover departed, Evie finished her chronicle of the negotiation and opened the floor for questions. As she answered inquiries, she noticed that Sam Lewis continued to take copious notes. Partners offered thanks or nodded and began to leave. She bent down to retrieve a pen that she'd dropped and sensed Sam walk out. Evie looked up, expecting to see an empty room, but met Alan's stare. He was sitting quietly, frozen in place. She decided that this time she would just stay silent and leave. Her annoyance was palpable as she leaned over the front of the lectern to gather her materials.

As she turned to leave, she saw that he had moved between her and the door. No one else was in sight. Evie sighed and psychologically braced herself. With Alan, anything could come out of his mouth. Especially now that there were fresh angry words between them.

"That was very interesting," he spoke in a low animated voice. "Although, you know, I had a bit of difficulty focusing on your words. All I could think about was what color underwear you're wearing."

Evie rolled her eyes and shook her head in disgust, her resolve to stay silent abandoned. "Harassed anyone *else* lately, Alan?"

"I *know* you. I know you very well." Alan's pursed lips curled confidently, and his eyes pulsed with arrogance.

"And you're willing to bet the other partners won't be offended by your behavior?"

"You're too smart to start making allegations. You know how many natural barriers there are to female partnerships and your *performance* has been substandard."

The oblique reference to their earlier exchange was not lost on Evie. She moved to his right to try to slide past him, but he shifted in front of her.

"Can I quote you on that?" she snapped. "The 'natural barriers' part?"

"Running to my partners with a sob story could be a fatal obstacle." He put his arms up on each side of the opening so she couldn't leave.

"You can't deny a poor overworked colleague a bit of levity, now can you?" He grinned. "What color underwear *are* you wearing? Mine are black silk."

"I'm not wearing *any*," she half whispered in a flash of anger as she pushed by him and headed back to her office. *Not that you'll ever know.*

Damn it. I can't believe I let him get to me like that. How could I have said something so stupid? She rubbed her forehead and grimaced to herself. Somewhere in her office was a mini digital recorder she'd used for client meetings. She took a look around, but it was not in any logical place. *If only I had recorded that initial set of instructions about Sangerson.*

Sitting down at her desk, the pile of work there discouraged her from spending any more time searching for the recorder. She responded to an email from one of Hanover's clients, Meter Beverage Company, about a trademark-protection policy. Despite growing vexation, she dutifully opened the VelloPro file and took out the draft memorandum that had been the subject of the conference call earlier. She brought up the file on the computer, rearranged the order of the paragraphs to create a flow that she thought Frank would find more logical, re-read the document once more and emailed it to Alan. *He can't say I didn't follow through. I'm done. He can take it from there.*

She purged some unnecessary emails, opened the electronic Sangerson file on the system, found her notes and began a rewrite of the document, drafting in a form consistent with the contracts she usually produced. At 8:15 P.M., she closed the document, copied it from the firm's electronic library to her laptop's hard-drive and loaded her notes into her briefcase to continue work at home.

Oh . . . that expense report. Evie took out the report and its attachments and began to review the typed text Helen had inserted. A Post-it note stuck on the first page indicated that Helen had made calls to the hotels, but no one had offered an explanation as to how the paperwork mix-up could have occurred. Evie's hotel stay at the Euphorion had extended from a Monday night through a Thursday afternoon. Evie flipped through the receipts attached and came to the computer print-out with the logo of a hotel at the top. Just as Helen had said, it was not the logo of the Euphorion Hotel or the Windham, it was the letterhead of the Hotel Colonial Court. *That IS really strange. I didn't stay at the Colonial Court.* She looked back at the first paragraph of the printout. It *did* contain Evie's name and the firm's address, so it was not someone else's bill. The date of arrival in Dallas was correct.

She read down through the paragraphs grouped by date. The days were correct, Monday through Thursday. There were meals listed, but she honestly couldn't remember how many times she had ordered room service or eaten at the hotel breakfast buffet. There were other charges, telephone calls. Oddly, the outgoing calls were almost exclusively to a series of related numbers with an international dialing sequence. There was a separate listing of telephone numbers from which calls had been *received* for the stated room number. She didn't recognize the country code that preceded each of the international numbers. Some of the incoming calls matched those outgoing numbers, but there were still more incoming calls from local exchanges.

How could this have happened? She tried to remember that particular check-out experience. No clear recollection of reviewing the bill before leaving the Euphorion Hotel on that Thursday materialized in her mind, but she had to have at least glanced at it. That was her normal practice.

Evie thought about that trip to Dallas. She had been representing Green Tree, a client from Philadelphia that had enlisted her services to negotiate a license grant for a squirrel cartoon character to a Texas children's clothing manufacturer. It had been a lengthy but fairly smooth negotiation that had culminated in a celebratory cocktail party on Thursday before Evie left to catch a flight back to New York. She tried to remember the series of meetings that had taken place over the several days, but it was all a blur. So many other clients' needs had received her attention since her return.

As was typical of any associate of the firm, she had taken the work of other clients with her on the trip and had spent some downtime in her hotel room on those matters, but she couldn't recall making or receiving any international calls. She wrote a note to Helen, *"Please call one or two of these telephone numbers and say that you are cleaning up some administrative paperwork. Try to identify sources without alerting them that we don't know who they are. I guess it's possible that these calls could be calls to another room charged to me by mistake. Also, look up my billing records for those dates and make a list of client matters I billed time to. See what you can find out. Thanks!"*

Evie left the note and the expense report on Helen's desk and checked the clock. Before she left the office, she would have to wait for a telephone call. One of her more disorganized clients on the west coast was scheduled to call any minute for a consult that she knew they considered urgent. And the time difference meant that they expected her to be available for the remainder of the *California* business day.

The office was unusually quiet. She needed coffee. Evie rose from her desk and walked out into the hallway to refill her coffee cup. As she walked past Jenna's office she noticed that it was dark. She glanced back toward her own office to confirm that she'd left the door open to enable her to hear the telephone. Evie walked into the kitchen, slid her coffee mug in place, pressed the "with milk" button and stood watching for the liquid to flow into her cup.

Evie thought about her earlier exchange with Alan and wondered whether she should have held her tongue. *I've never spoken to a partner that way . . . even if he or she deserved it.* Nothing seemed to be happening with the coffee machine, so she fumbled with its buttons, but it refused to cooperate. The lower drawer revealed raw sugar packets and Evie added milk manually from the refrigerator. She could hear the sound of a muffled voice in the small conference room adjacent to the kitchen. It would never have entered Evie's mind to eavesdrop, except for the fact that she heard her name mentioned.

chapter

5

*E*vie Sullivan . . . I told you . . . won't be a problem . . . *"The door between the kitchen and the small adjoining conference room was ajar. She moved slightly closer to the door and strained to hear more, but the voice was purposefully muffled. There was only the one voice, though. A man's voice. Whoever it was must be speaking to someone on the conference room telephone.

> *". . . sufficient . . . schedule . . . show the deal take shape . . ."*
> *". . . paper trail . . . . acted alone . . ."*

Nothing else was intelligible except that some words sounded like Spanish or some Latin-sounding language. Evie stood silent and did not breathe. The cup holding her coffee became very heavy and started to slide from her weakening grip. She focused on the voice coming from the next room, speaking at a low pitch and with an artificial cadence. It sounded familiar. Who *was* that? The voice came from Conference

Room C, often used by Steve Buniker because his office was just next door. But the voice was not Steve's baritone.

It sounded like Alan, but she couldn't be certain. Why would someone choose to place a call from a conference room telephone extension instead of from the privacy of his office? She knew that the firm tracked calls made from each attorney's office extension for client billing purposes. *Was this person making a call that he did not wish to be attributed to him?* She took a breath and recognized a familiar odor wafting through the tiny opening, a *cigar* smell. *Alan.*

Evie moved in a trancelike state toward the hallway door, coffee in hand. She walked the length of the hallway in the direction opposite Conference Room C, turned the corner, and took the long way around toward her office. She put the cup of coffee on the corner of her desk, grabbed her briefcase, stuffed in her BlackBerry without thinking and switched off her desk lamp.

When Alan had mentioned her name, the words he had spoken told a chilling story. And who would he be speaking to in Spanish? She felt a sense of dread . . . her defensive instincts had awakened. There was a sudden realization that she was being isolated, targeted. *What could he have been referring to? "Paper trail . . ."* Was he saying that I acted alone? And what sort of action was he talking about? What did he mean by 'problem' and what was sufficient about a schedule? What deal taking shape?

As she turned to leave, she heard two male voices, the volume and clarity increasing as they approached. She froze, but could not make out the words. The steps quickened and she suddenly realized that they were headed right toward her door. As quietly as she could, she vaulted back to her desk, flipped on the desk lamp, flung herself into the desk chair and assumed a natural slump over the desk with her acute attention devoted to a series of pages in the center of her desk. She was staring solidly down toward the second page of a confidentiality agreement when the two men passed in view of her open door.

They were still talking, but she could hear that the conversation had turned to an armed robbery that had occurred on the adjacent street the week before. One of the men was indeed Alan and the other was a younger partner, Lance Warren, who had not been at the partner meeting earlier in the day. Two feet beyond her door they stopped and abruptly ended their conversation.

Evie concentrated on relaxing her facial muscles as she felt Alan enter the room and approach her desk.

"You're here awfully late," he said flatly.

She looked up. "Don't you remember that you asked me to finish work on Sangerson by the end of the week?"

"Are you always here this late?"

"Depends." *No more details. And no more reactions.*

Alan walked slowly around Evie's office, straightening a crooked picture, studying each book title as he made his way around to where she was sitting. He turned his eyes toward the page beneath her hand, his eyes traveling along the desk to the cup of coffee still perched on the corner of her desk. "May I get you a fresh cup of coffee?" he asked, as he suppressed a yawn. "That must be cold by now."

"No thanks," she said calmly. "I'm on my way out in a few minutes." Evie suddenly, horribly, realized that the coffee cup was full and had been standing awkwardly on the edge of her desk untouched while she and Alan were avoiding each other's gaze.

She nonchalantly picked up the full cup. She wanted to go back to the kitchen and pour it out, but she didn't want to leave Alan in her office unsupervised. Her every instinct screamed out not to trust him. She placed the cup on the other side of the desk and sat down again in her desk chair. She pretended to organize some papers and then looked up at Alan. "Is there something you wanted to talk about?" she asked.

In his full regalia of artificial charm, Alan sat down in the chair across from her and began recounting anecdotes about his years at the firm as if reminiscing with a long-lost friend. He propped his feet where the coffee cup had been on the edge of her desk. He seemed unaffected by Evie's expressionless gaze and preceded as if they were two jovial colleagues sharing a beer. After a few moments he finished with a "Well, see you tomorrow."

She watched him leave, feeling sick to her stomach. *What the hell was he up to?* With a shiver she tried to imagine the portion of Alan's conversation in Conference Room C that she had *not* been able to hear. There might possibly be plausible and benign explanations, but she couldn't stop herself from thinking that he was arranging something manipulative. She suddenly felt certain that he was capable of more than abuse and sexual misconduct. She wondered how ruthless he could really be.

She looked at the clock and realized that the gallery from the west coast had not called so she checked voice mail once more and then looked over at the computer screen for any new email. She noticed one electronic message that read:

> *Go ahead with the deal we discussed in Dallas.*
> *Adinaldo, Gerais Chevas*

What? She had no idea who Adinaldo was and she had never heard of Gerais Chevas. She drafted a reply.

> *Dear Adinaldo—Your email was received by Evelyn Sullivan of Howard, Rolland & Stewart instead of your intended party. You may want to try re-sending it to its rightful recipient.*

She had a thought. She right-clicked on the sender's email address. ARafael@gchqt.br. A Brazilian extension to the domain. *I wonder . . .* she retrieved the Dallas expense report from Helen's desk and looked at the international country code listed by the international telephone numbers on the telephone call list—55. They were all from the same country, but with several different city codes. She dialed 00 for the international operator and asked for Brazil's country code.

"*Dial 011 55, the city code and the number you are trying to reach.*"

"What city would be associated with the city code 21?"

"That's Rio de Janeiro."

"Thank you." Evie again looked down at the expense report's attachment. *The country code matched. These calls were communications with someone in Brazil.* According to this hotel document, she had made and received telephone calls to several Brazilian telephone numbers. And now someone named Adinaldo was sending her email from a location in Brazil. And she had just overheard Alan saying something about her in a Latin-ish language. It could easily have been Portuguese. Her blood ran cold.

On impulse, Evie rose from her chair and walked out into the hallway. She walked around the east end of the building past Alan's office. It was dark. Only a couple of offices appeared to be occupied at this hour, but with doors closed, the hallway was vacant and quiet.

She arrived at Conference Room C. When she got to the door, she looked around and confirmed to herself that no one was around. She walked into the small conference room. *I'm just going to check.* She opened the door to the kitchen and confirmed that it was empty. Then she approached the conference room telephone. She knew that it had a memory feature and retained telephone numbers that had been dialed from its base. It was a last-in-last-out technology that stored only the five most recently dialed numbers. She pressed the buttons to cycle through the five currently stored. There were two New York numbers, a number that she thought might be a Philadelphia area code and then an international number.

A Brazilian number! She had no proof that the telephone call Alan had conducted earlier from this room was that specific call, but what were the odds that the call was unrelated to the email she had just received?

The firm's practice was international, but before now she had not heard of any South American clients. Alan had never mentioned a Brazilian matter to her. He was certainly capable of extreme disorganization and even calculated mischief. It was very possible that he could have planned to involve her in a matter and then neglected to tell her. If that was the case and he *had* made that call, why would he not mention anything about it to her *after having just completed a discussion about it?* She struggled with that thought as she walked to the subway with the Sangerson file in her briefcase. She was so distracted, she almost missed her stop.

Once home, Evie settled into her favorite upholstered chair with a glass of wine and closed her eyes. Rosemary Clooney sang *More Than You Know* from a docked iPod.

All her protective instincts were now on full alert, but she couldn't organize her thoughts. Could this have anything to do with her rejection of Alan's overtures toward her last November in Chicago? Was this some sort of retaliation even after she made it clear she would not pursue any redress within the firm? They had agreed to forget it. Why would he set her up now when she had in effect given him a break? *Am I handling this all wrong? Am I handling this at all?* A knock on her door interrupted her deliberation.

Ralph entered the room in a steel-colored Armani windowpane suit with a crisp white shirt and his signature tie that looked like a Picasso painting. His wavy hair was brushed back and forced into obedience by a shiny gel. His blue-green eyes sparkled and he seemed to be smiling with his entire body.

"You're looking at a courtroom conqueror," he said carrying something behind his back. Evie returned the smile and pretended not to notice, playing into his unfolding melodrama.

"Not to dull your sword, but you look like you just walked off a runway during fashion week." Evie kissed his cheek. "Want a drink?"

"Love one. *You're* looking a little dodgy, but I intend to cheer you up."

"I'm afraid you've caught me at a moment of self reproach." She walked to the kitchen to mix the drink for him.

Ralph stood just outside its swinging door and as she came through, he presented her with a four-color bouquet of tulips. She stopped and gasped, holding his gin and tonic.

"I don't know what I did to have a neighbor like you." She traded the drink for the flowers and managed a half-baked smile. Evie turned and again pushed open the door, bouquet in hand.

"The second bouquet of flowers from you in a week," Evie spoke over her shoulder as she walked, her words riding the arcs of the rocking door. "Do you know something I don't know?"

"What do you mean, second?" he said in a distracted voice. In surveying the state of her apartment, Ralph failed to notice that his question was unheard, falling against the door, now at rest in a closed position. Evie's briefcase lay open with papers spilling onto the floor, an assortment of unopened mail littered a table and a wrinkled suit jacket seemed to have been tossed in a dispirited heap on a chair.

Evie selected a thin fluted vase from a kitchen cabinet, filled it with water, and returned to the living room. She began detaching each stem for submersion. Ralph took a sip of the gin and tonic and scowled. "You never *could* mix a proper drink." He put down the glass and grinned at her.

"You look knackered. Law firm fatigue?" he asked.

"I guess you could say that."

"Hey, didn't you tell me your firm does work for Senator Arbeson?

"Yeah, some."

"I heard a rumor about him today. I think the feds are going to investigate that blighter on a backhander charge."

"A what?"

"Bribery. Word is he was caught bang to rights."

"Oh wow, really? Are you sure?"

"A bloke in the U.S. Attorney's office told me. Usually a fairly straight-up source."

"Hmmm. The good Senator has been dominating the news lately, hasn't he?"

"I also heard that his wife is planning to chat up the talk show circuit. Now *that* will be interesting. Whoever's representing him should pay close attention."

"Well, we wouldn't be handling that. We don't do white collar defense."

"But you've done *some* work for him, haven't you?"

She nodded.

"I'd stay clear of him, if you can. Never know what bloody mess they'll be creating out of his life. And that fiery South American wife will look to cause him any sort of trouble she can. Could drag in any part of his dealings. And shag a few of his attorneys to generate some investigative pressure."

"Yes, well, I'm sure he'd scream attorney-client privilege in every language he knows." As she answered, Evie simultaneously remembered reading about Senator Arbeson's dramatic delivery of campaign speeches in Portuguese to encourage joint business development between certain New York industry leaders and those of South American countries. *Is there a Brazil connection? Is this Adinaldo who emailed me somehow associated with the Senator or his wife? Could Senator Arbeson have something to do with Alan's paper trail?* Her mind flashed on the cordial ambience when she'd entered the conference room on Tuesday morning. She struggled to remember that last bit of their conversation she'd over-heard, but it was lost to her memory. Her imagination began to conjure up a scary scenario.

"Evie, sweetheart. Are you listening to me?"

"Sorry, yes. I'm listening." She shook off the thought and studied Ralph's expression for more information. "Do you know any more about what the investigation might consist of?" she asked.

"No, but I'll chat up my source for you. C'mon. Let's go get a *real* drink. I'm spittin' feathers."

"Oh Ralph. I'd love to, but I'm tired and I wouldn't be able to keep up with your celebratory mood tonight. My turn to buy dinner tomorrow night. I promise to be a more lively companion then."

After Ralph left, Evie fluffed a few pillows on her bed, nestled in and flipped through *New York Magazine* in an effort to induce sleep. Reading the *Intelligencer,* her eye fell on a photograph of Senator Arbeson taken at a recent fundraising dinner. He was seated with his arm around a woman whose face caused her to take a bewildered second look. The woman looked almost like a mirror image of *her*. She studied the photo more closely, but the caption failed to identify the Senator's companion by name.

On impulse, she decided to cut out the photo and she opened her bedside drawer in search of a pair of scissors she kept there. Sorting through the drawer, she stumbled on a man's gold cufflink. It had been years since a man had spent the night in her bedroom and she had no memory of this particular item, but she decided it must be leftover from her days with Julien, her last relationship of any depth. Still preoccupied with her look-alike, she returned the cufflink and located the scissors. She cut out the quarter page, slipped it under the base of her bedside lamp and hit the off switch. Sleep came, but it was not restful. When she woke the next morning with a jolt, her sheets were wet with perspiration and her lungs felt heavy, as if she'd been struggling to breathe through an asthmatic slumber.

chapter

6

E vie arrived at the office at seven o'clock A.M. and logged onto the shared network where the firm's active files for current clients were stored. She had decided that it wouldn't hurt to check around in the generally available portion of the firm's server, avoiding any electronic avenue that would capture her user name and draw attention to her inquiry. She would limit herself to viewing the system-stored documents, searching for any files created within the prior six months under the client name "Gerais Chevas."

That was the company name in the signature line of the email from Adinaldo—Adinaldo from Brazil. She had to find out if it was a firm client. Her office door swung open abruptly, startling her. It was a relief to see Jenna enter, carrying white bakery bags and balancing a cup of amaretto coffee on a cardboard file. She carefully cleared off a space on Evie's desk and arranged the breakfast in the opening.

"Hey," replied Evie, "please go close the door." Evie looked at the paper bags. "Cinnamon muffin?"

Jenna nodded and obediently closed the door to Evie's office. She brushed some imaginary street dust off her jacket and walked over to a side table where she noisily emptied the contents of her purse, apparently looking for something. "You would *not* believe what I just went through," she began. "I just spent an agonizing twenty minutes waiting in line at the pharmacy while this woman had a meltdown over a refusal to re-fill her Wellvex prescription. Obvious addict. Then, this guy next to me painstakingly read every label on every brand of condoms at the checkout. He kept bumping into me to reach for each one and looked to see if I noticed him. Who in the hell needs condoms at eight o'clock in the morning?"

"Maybe he was trying to send you some sort of message," Evie laughed.

"Well, I hope he got *mine*. I finally tripped him."

"I would think that a woman who had paid her way through law school selling her eggs would be a bit less disturbed by such things."

"Hey, that was free enterprise at work, babe. A woman should be entitled to exploit the few advantages she has over men in this disgustingly male-dominated marketplace. And hey, I'm *still* selling'em. I get this sort of male-inspired thrill spreading my seed around. I think I'm addicted to the fertility drugs they give you to increase egg production. And anyway, it has supplemented my income quite nicely, thank-you-very-much," said Jenna as she dumped sugar from a packet into her coffee.

"Speaking of addiction. I read about Wellvex. There've been calls for the FDA to pull it off the market. It's been blamed for some nasty side effects."

"That's not one of Finley Regent's is it?"

"No. Thank God."

Evie and Jenna's friendship had preceded their present co-employment by at least ten years. The two women had met in a coffeehouse in Boston while pursuing law degrees at separate universities. Jenna, who attended Boston University, had been perfectly comfortable living in a dangerous part of town in a boarding house known to harbor drug dealers. It was all part of embracing life, she had explained. Jenna became adept at dressing to blend in with the neighborhood, wearing torn jeans and army-issue jackets. Evie attended Harvard in Cambridge and had chosen to live on-campus to save money, but often felt the need to escape to surrounding environs. She admired Jenna's passion, and had once described her as capable of donning a tattered tenth-generation vinyl raincoat acquired at a Brooklyn garage sale while acting as if she was wearing a black mink from Saks Fifth Avenue.

As she stirred her coffee, Jenna glanced around Evie's office.

"Whatever happened to that picture of Julien?"

"I took it home and put it in a shoebox under my bed."

"Well, that'll teach him."

"It's over."

"Yeah, but you keep that picture of Mireille on your desk," said Jenna as she picked up the small framed photo on Evie's desk, took a glance and returned it to its resting place.

"Well, I guess I formed a relationship with Mireille that survived the breakup with her dad." She paused. "You know, I found a gold cufflink in my drawer last night that I think must've been his. Should I return it?"

"Forget it. Have it melted down and sell it."

Jenna ignored Evie's scowl and walked to the window. She opened the blind and the sun lit up her face.

"Isn't there anything else you'd like to talk about this morning?" asked Evie. "Any more news on Gooseneck?"

"No, they're still posturing. I told Hanover about what I found in the final contract and he's looking into it."

"Did you find out which associate worked on it?"

"No, but you said that Alan corrected his records, right?"

"He told me he did."

"You sound like you don't believe him."

"Well, I'm not so sure I do."

"Okay, different subject," Jenna finished the last sip of coffee and crushed the cup. "I finally convinced Stephan to go back to Louisiana and settle things with his old girlfriend."

"That's great. I know you'll be in a much better place with him when he comes back."

"*If* he comes back."

"You know he will."

In Evie's view, Jenna was and would always be one of those naturally persuasive people who manages to coax everything and everybody into doing her bidding. *Even her own reproductive system.*

"Speaking of ambiguous male behavior." Evie turned from her computer and faced Jenna directly. "Can you keep a secret?"

Her eyes locked on Jenna's.

"Well, now that's a suspense-builder," said Jenna. "What's up?"

"I think I uncovered something yesterday, but I'm not sure."

"Is this a confession or what?"

"No seriously, I think Alan is . . . I think he may be setting me up."

"*Tell* me." Jenna's expression registered concern. "What happened?"

"Accounting sent back an expense report for a hotel bill. It attributed to me some number of international telephone calls to and from Brazil *that I never made.*" Jenna wore a puzzled ambivalent look as if she was thinking "*what does this have to do with Alan?*"

Evie continued. "After that, I was at the coffee machine around eight last night. Someone was in the conference room next door. I *know* it was Alan. I think he was speaking with someone from Brazil. He was talking about something involving a paper trail and the deal taking shape. And something about somebody acting alone. He mentioned my name and then he said '*won't be a problem.*'"

Evie looked directly at Jenna, but ignored the premature verdict apparent on her face, continuing her story. "And *then,* I noticed this email in my inbox. It was from somebody with a Brazilian domain name extension. The author of that email told me to *proceed* with some deal. I have no idea who he is or what he was talking about."

"Wait! Assuming it *was* Alan you overheard, how do you know he was talking to someone in Brazil?" Jenna sat on the desk and leaned forward. "Are you sure you're not imagining things because he's such a prick?"

"I know it sounds crazy, but I checked the telephone memory. He was calling from the conference room phone. Next to the kitchen."

"EVIE! My God! Are you sneaking around keeping notes on him? I thought things were resolved between the two of you. I really think that Gooseneck thing was just a record-keeping mistake. What's gotten into you? Have you become completely paranoid?"

"I *heard* him. He said something about . . . that something or somebody wouldn't be a *problem* and then . . . he said something in *Spanish* or some Spanish-like language. He was keeping his voice down. And, I had this odd feeling. You know. When you get an uneasy feeling that something just isn't right."

"Oh. Okay, so maybe Alan selected you as the preferred associate to work on a new deal. Maybe you were being singled out as an associate who has the talent to salvage a deal gone bad. Maybe he thinks you can handle it alone. That it wouldn't be a *problem* for you. That's a *compliment.* Maybe he was talking about the paper trail you would need to get up to speed on the deal. *Maybe he just hasn't gotten around to* briefing you on it yet."

"Well, but then *why* was he calling from the conference room telephone?" She shook her head and squinted. "Okay, Jen, maybe you're right, but isn't it coincidental? I mean . . . the firm . . . it's not like the firm has a roster of Brazilian clients. It's just . . . Oh God, maybe I've really lost my mind." Evie rubbed her eyes. "Maybe it's just like *Julien* said. Maybe I *am* imagining things that aren't there. I just have this *feeling.* Maybe I'm working too hard."

"Did you *see* Alan after you overheard what he said?"

Evie nodded slowly. "He showed up at my office afterward."

"It figures. He always tries to assign matters to you first."

"He didn't say anything about assigning me anything. It was odd. We're not on the best of terms. We had *words* yesterday. And then, he shows up in my office and starts telling me firm war stories like we're old friends."

"And he didn't mention anything about the Brazilian deal he had *just discussed* on the telephone? He didn't describe it to you or ask you to be available for it?"

Evie shook her head at a solemn slow tempo.

"Okay. Okay. Maybe he *is* up to something. I think we should have him knocked around."

"Jenna, be serious."

"I *am*. I would confront him immediately." Jenna placed both hands palm down on the desk and looked directly at Evie, her dark irises dancing with intensity. "No offense, but that's what a *man* would do. Ask him what the hell he's up to. Be blunt. Make direct reference to this Brazilian matter. You may be able to tell something from his reaction. If there's no monkey business going on, he should have no trouble explaining this deal to you. If he *is* up to no good, no matter what he says, at least he'll know you're on to him."

"Yes, but he'll also be in a position to cover his tracks more carefully and make it harder for me to investigate what he's up to."

"True. The element of surprise is a useful weapon."

"I can't *believe* after all the work I've done, I have to worry about being set up by a partner. You know, I actually made him look good in a conference call with a client *yesterday*. You know how nonchalant he can be with the details of a transaction. You'd think I could expect some professional courtesy for at least a *few minutes* afterward."

"Alan doesn't think that way. He's a man without conscience. A socially savvy psychopath, in the reality gala. He feels no appreciation or remorse and takes no prisoners no matter what the circumstances. You really expected him to be a decent human being after he tried to put the moves on you in Chicago?"

"Well, yeah, that was despicable, but you know, aggressive arrogant men are like that. They always try."

"I never thought I would hear a boys-will-be-boys argument from you."

"Yeah, I know. I'm not excusing him, but *those* kind of moves you expect. You can usually see them coming and they're easily deflected. If he's setting me up for some kind of professional trap. *That's* really different. Careers should be equally vulnerable. Gender shouldn't be an advantage or *disadvantage.*"

Jenna sat back down in a chair, shook her head and rolled her eyes. "You just don't get it, my friend. You let the statute of limitations run on *that* one. You had a gender card to play and you failed to play it. Now you're back against the glass ceiling, only it's more like a one-way mirror."

Evie leaned forward and rested her head on the palms of her hands, her elbows braced against the surface of the desk. "You know, before we left Chicago, I actually told the jerk that I wouldn't report him for grabbing me and kissing me, as long as he never let the lines of professionalism blur again."

"I still think you should've at least talked to Hanover about it. That's the advice you would've given me. Even if the firm only gave it lip service, you would've put his dirty laundry out there where it needs to be. I mean, what if he's doing it to some other less-prepared female in the office? You know how you felt about Julien's brother and the moves he put on Mireille."

Evie rose from her seat, stretched her arms backward and grabbed at the strands of hair streaming down her neck. Then she covered her face with her hands. "I can't even *think* about that right now."

"Sorry. I shouldn't have brought it up."

Evie walked around to the front of her desk and began to straighten piles of opened mail. "I think the other partners know him for what he is. I didn't want them thinking about *me* in that context—that I was some sort of overly-sensitive, complaining bimbo looking to cash out on a sexual harassment claim."

"Well, have you ever thought about how a man with that kind of profile reacts to rejection? Maybe he *is* setting you up. Maybe he's got a plan to get back at you for failing to swoon after he tried his best swash-buckling maneuver on you."

"No way. Could he be that vindictive? Do you really think—"

"No. I don't. I think you're imagining something sinister when it's probably just him being an inconsiderate ass. I think he has assigned a new matter to you and has failed to alert you or give you any background. Or maybe he thinks he already *has*."

Evie sighed and sat down again in her chair.

"But then . . . there's something else."

"I'm listening."

"I found out Senator Arbeson may be facing a bribery investigation."

"Oh my God. Where did you hear that?"

"It doesn't matter. It just occurred to me that there might be some connection. You know, because Arbeson is married to a Latin woman and has all those Latin associations. By the way, I saw a photograph of him in *New York Magazine* last night with a woman who was not his wife."

"So, what's your point?"

"The spooky thing was that she looked like *me*."

"That's icky."

"*Yeah.* Anyway, getting back to Alan. On that call, he was speaking partly in Spanish or Portuguese and he's tight with the Senator. And this strange email—"

"You're *really* starting to sound paranoid."

"I knew I could count on you for support."

Jenna stood and popped a pinch of apple pastry into her mouth. "You're going to drive yourself crazy with this. It may amount to nothing. Even if there's something sinister going on, you can't do anything about it until you have some proof." Jenna swallowed and grabbed a second bite of pastry. "I know what you need. Come out with me to Biko's. I'm meeting Melanie, Hannah, Lisa and Amanda at one fifteen for lunch and I think you could use some time with some female energy. We deserve a leisurely lunch to make up for the fact that we have no life in the evenings."

"I don't think I'd be very good company."

"Bullshit. There's always lots of interest among these girls to support fellow femme fatales on that ever-turbulent voyage to professional nirvana. You will enjoy yourself. It won't do any good to sit in your office worrying about this. You need to relax and collect your thoughts."

"Okay. I'll go. I'll meet you in front at one."

Jenna waved her index finger at Evie in a friendly scolding exit.

Evie returned her attention to her computer screen. *Jenna was probably right.* She *was* becoming paranoid. Despite Alan's insolent tendencies, she really had no concrete evidence of any surreptitious, unscrupulous undertakings in connection with this client from Brazil. *Suspicions.* Even though there was some feeble basis for them, they were still just suspicions. *Why am I always so suspicious?*

She picked up a client file and opened it to begin working, but her mind wandered back to that confrontation with Alan in his office. He had implied that her work was deficient. He reprimanded her for following directions he had given her, saying that she had *"shown a serious lack of judgment."* Those were the kind of comments that could undermine a bid for partnership. And all partners with whom she had worked would be asked to opine on her performance. *Maybe he's laying further groundwork to sabotage my partnership chances. Maybe he's trying to destroy my reputation. But why? Could it really be because I rejected his sexual advances?* She brought up the firm's general directory for the electronic document library. Alan had accused her of being defensive, but he was *forcing* her to think defensively.

If Gerais Chevas was a client of the firm and files existed for any of its matters the firm was handling, those files would likely be stored in the electronic library. The stored version of a file was considered the official version, even if multiple attorneys within the firm working with that client had copied the file onto his or her own laptop computer. If an attorney needed to alter the official version of the file, there was an electronic procedure he or she would follow to "check out" that file. It would then be announced to any subsequent person accessing the file that it had been copied off the system for editing. The system then prevented any access other than *read-only* for that file until the person who had checked it out had re-stored the file to the system in its updated form.

The system had been purposefully set up so that everyone in the firm had at least read-only access to all files, but that at any given point in time only one person had editorial control over a particular file. Any deviation from that system might result in multiple versions receiving simultaneous edits. Then no one would be able to determine the version that contained all of the official mutually-agreed changes.

No one would question an associate looking up files on a client even though that associate had not been assigned to work on that client's matters. Associates were actually *encouraged* to seek contracts and documents existing in the system for examples of proper format and structure. It saved time to tap into the collective firm knowledge when drafting a particular type of document. To that end, the system automatically stored the names of the most recent five people who had accessed a particular file in what was called a *Hit History* so that the associate could ask questions of those persons who created or edited that file.

So Evie knew that her name in the *Hit History* for any Gerais Chevas files *should be* considered inconsequential. She had no idea what dates to look for, but she could do a general search under the Gerais Chevas client number. Since all client files were stored in the library by client number, she had to first find Gerais Chevas's client number. *If there was one.*

She brought up the electronic firm-wide client list, which was arranged alphabetically. She scrolled down to the "Gs" and read down the list: Gabriel, Byrd & Baker client number 11950, Gafferty Corp. client number 12220, *Gerais Chevas, client number 13606.* Okay, this Gerais Chevas *is* an existing client of the firm.

Then she entered 13606 in the field for client number and executed a search for all files stored under that client number. Four electronic document names popped up on the screen. She clicked on the first one which was entitled "Neon One." A window appeared with the message: ACCESS DENIED. SECURED DOCUMENT. *Okay . . . this is interesting . . . I don't even have read-only access to this one. It's only readable by some group of designated people.*

Denying any type of access to certain files was not uncommon in law firm protocol. Because the library of client files was generally available to *all* lawyers in the firm, measures often had to be taken to restrict access to highly confidential or sensitive files. Under conditions where a potential conflict could arise from a certain lawyer's exposure to non-public information about a particular client, perhaps because of some other matter that lawyer was handling, he or she had to be screened from all files and discussions relating to that particular client. It was also common to restrict access to the files for a certain matter where the client was highly sensitive about the *confidential nature* of a particular transaction, and in such cases the deal was often given some sort of code name like "Project Neon," so that the transaction could be referenced in conversation without revealing the identity of the parties. *The deal documented by these files must then be highly confidential . . . or controversial.*

She knew that her user name had been checked by the electronic library software and she was being denied access because her name was not on the permitted access list. She was *not* among those who were assigned to this deal. *At least not officially.* Since Gerais Chevas was actually a client of the firm, it might be as Jenna said. Alan may have forgotten to assign her or may have the mistaken impression that he already did. If this *was* a case of Alan's neglect or oversight, even though other questions would remain unanswered, the situation would certainly be less troubling than the conclusion that he was intentionally planning a trap for her.

Fresh from the controversy over the Sangerson matter, there was new urgency in documenting all instructions and matters involving

Alan. If she could *print* the page with the ACCESS DENIED message, it would shield her from any accusation by Alan that she was somehow responsible for some aspect of this deal. *At least it would support my claim that I haven't been assigned.* She pressed print and quickly walked down the hall to the printer to retrieve the hard copy. When she picked it up off the printer tray, she noticed to her chagrin that only the message box printed. Nowhere on the page was identification for the file or client for which access was being denied. She suddenly felt the need to distance herself. She resolved to forget about the Gerais Chevas matter.

She tore up the page and dropped it into the wastebasket beside the printer. As Evie arrived at her desk, her telephone began to ring. Helen was not around to answer it, so she picked it up herself.

"Evelyn Sullivan."

"Hello Evelyn Sullivan. This is Joe Barton."

chapter
7

J oe. *Joe.* Yessss, hello. Joe, how are you?" Gerais Chevas was now
momentarily forgotten.

"Terrific. You know, I was supposed to go to an auction tonight
with this beautiful girl I just met, but her plans changed. Is it possible
that she might be free for dinner?"

Evie smiled audibly into the telephone. "Well, my instinct would be
to say yes, but I promised to take a friend to dinner tonight to celebrate
a courtroom victory."

"I knew I should've called you yesterday." Joe's tone turned surprisingly
somber. "I've been involved in some intense corporate gamesmanship
which dominated the day and spilled over into the evening."

"And did the best man win?"

Evie could hear Joe sigh on the line, but she felt his mood lift. "We
agreed on some key terms, but there are some crucial details yet to be
worked out. That means that I will be in town through tomorrow at
least. Please don't tell me your weekend's all booked, too."

"No. I thought I would be working this weekend, but I really don't feel much like it. What does your schedule look like tomorrow?" Evie ignored the voice in her head that reminded her to proceed with caution.

"Unfortunately, I can't meet for breakfast and I won't be able to make any plans for the evening until this meeting gets underway and I can see where we are. I know I'm sacrificing any chance at chivalry here, but may I call in the afternoon and suggest a meeting place and time for a spontaneous dinner?"

"No problem, that's fine. But we should probably make a reservation now even if we have to change it. Where's your meeting taking place?"

"An office building at Madison and 62nd. But, I can't ask you to spend an evening with me until I've showered off the residue from battle. I'm staying at the Plaza. If you like Greek food, I'll see if I can book a table at Molyvos on Seventh Avenue. You know it?"

"I love that place, but I don't think I've ever ordered off their dinner menu. I never seem to have an appetite after eating too many of those wonderful Greek appetizers."

"Well, have a light lunch and we'll see what we can do to change that. How about we meet at the Oak Room at a time to be determined tomorrow?"

"Great. I'll see you tomorrow."

Evie hung up the telephone. *Okay, I need the diversion.*

The computer screen still wore the ACCESS DENIED error message and the cursor blinked obediently as she picked up the telephone receiver again. *I'll just check one more thing . . .*

Technical support answered on the third ring. "Marcus?"

"Yeah. Oh, hey Evie," Marcus must have glanced at the caller identification window on his telephone.

"Hey. Listen, Marcus, is there a way to bring up on the screen the list of attorneys who are on the access list for a particular group of secured files in the database?"

"Well, yeah, but only us Tech Support people can pull them up. The partners wanted it set up that way."

"Is it difficult to do?"

"No. Takes two seconds. If you tell me the name of the client and matter, I can print out one for you."

"Would it be something you would have to keep a record of?"

"Well, we're supposed to keep track of all requests in the log, but—"

"You know what? I have to take a call on the other line, but I'll get back to you. Thanks a lot."

Something caused her to glance at the clock. Eight minutes after one o'clock! She almost forgot her lunch plans with Jenna! Evie logged off her computer, grabbed her jacket and sprinted down the hall to meet her.

～

"You remember Evie, don't you?" Jenna was saying to Melanie as they sat down at the table she'd reserved.

"Yes. I do. Evie, very good to see you again."

Three other women approached exchanging greetings and everyone sat and pulled their chairs up to the round table.

"I'm so disgusted," said Hannah as she opened her menu.

"All men or a man in particular?" asked Jenna with a knowing smile. The other girls looked up from the descriptions of pumpkin penne and bell pepper risotto.

"Okay, some time ago, I was at my dentist's office. He had to delay my appointment for an hour because he had an emergency, which turned out to be a client of his who'd broken one of her bright-white veneers. She was close to hysterical because she was going on a date with Donald Trump that evening. This was while he was still single, of course." Hannah rolled her eyes and continued, "So, anyway, this femme fatale was a supermodel and her money undoubtedly spoke much louder than mine, so she bumped me. Anyway, I told this story to a guy I just went out with and he said he wished he could demand such perfection. Can you believe this? Is this truly pathetic? Our mothers worried about getting their hair done before a date, we have to worry about our teeth being perfect?"

"Well, very few of us will ever have to worry about meeting Trump-like standards," said Amanda.

"Yeah, but New York men are so spoiled. All these supermodels walking around."

"I dated a guy who wanted to trade resumes before we arranged a second date," said Evie.

"Well, I just met an interesting man at, where else, a gallery opening, and he has possibilities," said Amanda.

The waiter appeared and scribbled notes as each woman made her selection from the menu.

"What is his personal capital quotient?" Lisa asked Amanda, adding her menu to the stack the waiter was accumulating. After depositing a basket of bread on the table the waiter disappeared into the controlled roar beyond their table.

"His *what?*" asked Amanda.

"You know. The collective appeal of his looks, education, social status, any sort of unique first name, like *Truman,* his family name, degree of career success, the cachet of his chosen profession, his net worth and the location of his season tickets at the Met."

"Lisa, you're just as bad as the guys," said Jenna.

"Well, let's be absolutely clear here. A high personal capital quotient equates to enormous power because of the universal appeal to women and because men who score high in multiple categories are so rare."

Lisa drank from her wine glass and continued. "The only real power women have over men is sex. Men can't do without it and women decide with whom it happens and when, if ever."

"So how many dates should a woman wait before having sex with a man she really likes?" asked Jenna.

"It's not so much the number of dates, it's the degree of sexual tension she should allow to accumulate before she gives in. And there should be some discernable attachment that develops and coexists with the sexual yearning." Lisa retrieved her velvet-rose lipstick from her purse and applied a stroke to her bottom lip with her gaze fixed in the tiny compact mirror she held in her left hand. She looked up from the mirror, gesticulating with the lipstick wand, as she continued her answer.

"Before she gives in, he should've spent substantial amounts of money on her, sacrificed something important to him like courtside tickets to a basketball game, introduced her to his mother or taken a trip with her requiring a passport. Or any combination of the above."

Evie and Jenna exchanged smiling glances. Melanie almost choked on her olive bread as she tried to suppress a laugh.

"Men do have the power. The sex scenes in movies written by men almost always portray sex as a *'wham-bam'* blast of sexual energy. It's symbolic. Through brute physical force the man is shifting back the balance of power," added Lisa.

"Yeah, I know what you mean," said Amanda. "And a man's portrayal of good sex seems to always include extremes and rarely takes into account the real needs and perspectives of a woman. What do you think, Evie?"

"Have any of you ever been sexually harassed at work?" asked Evie as she looked around the table. There was a deafening silence for a few fleshy seconds.

"You really know how to change the subject."

"I'm sorry," said Evie, "but I need some help with a situation at work."

"I had a bad experience with a peer," said Lisa. "He tried to grab me and pull me into a stockroom. After I told him where to get off, he started teasing me in front of other people. There was a group of us in a room on a video conference. He positioned the camera to look right up my skirt."

"That sounds like what they call a 'hostile' environment, even though he wasn't your superior. Did you report it?" asked Evie.

"No. Nobody saw the grab and the teasing was just in front of a few guys—all his buddies. There was nobody to corroborate my story."

"That seems to be a common problem," said Evie. "There's this partner who kissed me and tried to push his way into my hotel room on a business trip. Nobody else was around."

"Oh my God! He kissed you?" asked Amanda.

"Yes. And I've waited too long to report it, I'm afraid."

"Why do you think that?"

"Well, you know how people become suspicious if time has passed," answered Evie. "It'll look like I have some new motive to drag him through the mud."

"Do you?"

"Yes. He's toying with me."

"What a nightmare. What are you going to do? Are you going to leave the firm?"

"Doesn't it suck that women always feel like it's up to us to exit?" said Lisa.

"Well, I've thought about it, but I have a lot invested. My track to partnership would be so much longer if I switch firms. So difficult to get full credit at another firm for my record. It could be like starting over."

"I know what you mean," said Hannah. "My former manager put his arm around me and tried to put his hand up my shirt. The company officer I went to didn't believe me at first, but then he ultimately fired the guy. I was actually promoted after that, but I never felt like I was treated the same. I never felt trusted or part of the inner circle. I was so uncomfortable, I finally quit. Lost all my tenure. So just reporting it and eliminating the offender doesn't necessarily end the problem."

"Did you consider suing?" asked Jenna.

"Based on what? They fired the guy and promoted me, so they did everything they could to correct the problem. I didn't think I could make much of a case just based on feeling left out. It's not illegal to have an almost all-male management team."

"Men are such a pain in the ass," said Jenna. "I wonder what it would be like to work in an all-female law firm. You never know when that testosterone is going to boil over."

"I went out with this guy once," said Melanie trying to lighten the mood. "He took me to Disneyworld. I thought, okay, I'll go with this. Maybe he loves kids or something. He ended up picking a fight with Mickey Mouse."

Everyone laughed.

"A fist fight?"

"Yeah. It was so embarrassing. He had words and started trading punches with the guy who was wearing the Mickey Mouse costume. We got kicked out of the park."

"I wish I had some advice for you, Evie," said Amanda. The other girls nodded solemnly.

"I'd still report it, if I were you," said Lisa. "My situation was a peer. You're stuck with working in a subordinate position to this jerk."

"I'm thinking about it, but I appreciate all your input," said Evie.

Amanda looked at her watch and shrieked. *"EEEeeeoo.* I'm late for my salon appointment. I hate to piss off Gerry when he's about to stand over me with a pair of scissors."

Melanie counted out the contributions and handed the check to the waiter. Melanie and Jenna walked arm-in-arm, and Hannah, Lisa and Evie gathered their things and walked behind, promising to get together again soon.

Evie almost gasped when she walked back into her office and saw Alan Levenger sitting in her chair.

chapter 8

He *must have timed us.*

"You're working on Collburn Regan, right?" Alan said in greeting. "There'll be some changes. The deal may not proceed." He rose from her chair and walked slowly around her office as he spoke.

"What kind of changes?"

Alan avoided eye contact with Evie, but he seemed to know that her eyes were glued to him. He paused beside her desk to pick up the framed photograph of her and Mireille, which he studied as he continued to speak.

"Farraway."

"The executive vice president we're working for?"

"Yeah."

"What about him?"

"I'm going to get him fired."

"Why would you do that?"

"He crossed me."

"How?"

"Not important. He's in way over his head anyway."

Evie stared at Alan with nothing to say. *Arrogance. How does he think he's going to convince a client to fire an executive?* Alan looked at her as if he expected her to vocally join his campaign. She moved around her desk and sat in her desk chair, which she noticed was quite warm. She wondered how long Alan had been sitting there.

"How's work going on Sangerson?"

"Wait, Alan. Just to be clear, you *don't* want me to do any further work on Collburn Regan, correct?"

"Yes. We need to get that Sangerson contract out. How's it going?"

"It's going." *Now he DOES seem to remember I'm working on it.*

"Just a reminder. Don't send it out until I've seen it. Email it to me first."

He winked and smiled as he left her office.

She inspected the clutter on the surface of her desk, trying to determine what he might have been looking at while sitting there, but there were only client files and notes. Nothing personal and no evidence that she had been investigating the Gerais Chevas matter. *This is not going to go away. It's a lot easier to get ME fired.* She retrieved a file from her briefcase and the next few hours evaporated as she continued drafting a new agreement for the Sangerson-Zoomhelix deal. Alan's presence seemed to linger in the air like rotting cheese, but she forced herself to ignore it.

Her telephone rang once indicating an intercom inquiry from Helen.

"Yes, Helen?"

"Adam Peyton, from Roma Sori, on line one, and by the way, thank you for the lovely flowers. You are *such* a dear."

"Oh, you're very welcome. Just wanted you to know you're appreciated. Thanks, Helen." Evie pressed a button on the telephone. "Hello, Adam? This is Evie."

"Evie! How are you?"

"Fine, thanks. Hey, Adam, I read that you have a nine percent growth expectation for the third quarter. Congratulations. You and your management team are an impressive group."

"Thank you, Evie. Who was it that said *'No one rises so high as he who knows NOT where he is going?'*" He laughed. "I'm never one to succumb to the illusion of my own success. I have to admit, though, it's always easier to market a winning product."

"I've actually become a customer myself after Pavi gave me that box of product samples. I love the body oil and that jasmine-based fragrance."

"Well, you're definitely the demographic we're chasing. Now that I think about it, you would make a great model for our new television spot." He laughed.

"I'd better stick to lawyering, but I appreciate the thought."

"Well, you have plenty of legal talent, for sure. The purchasing division is really pleased with the database system deal we negotiated for them. Even the rollouts went smoothly. The contractual terms have really kept the techies in line. It seems that we found a software vendor who actually paid attention to your explanation of how the development process should work. I have to tell you, I enjoyed working with you so much I think I'm going to do a deal with SerosaSoft."

"You know you could do these deals yourself with one hand tied behind your back."

Adam chuckled into the telephone, "Hey, don't let your billing partners hear you say things like that." He paused. "Seriously, I need your input. I want you to work with me on it."

"Are you serious? So you really have been negotiating a deal with SerosaSoft? What about Blueline?"

"That one hasn't taken shape yet. But SerosaSoft is moving faster than I expected. We're interested in licensing their supplier management software. They've proposed customizing it for us. Peter and Tate have unfortunately already seen a demo and agreed on licensing fees. As usual, you and I have been brought in after the systems people have been psychologically seduced and after the business dialogue has progressed to courtship."

"What does the timeline look like?"

"Well. That's the bad news. Their form agreement is being sent, as we speak, by email, to you, me, Peter and Tate, and those two have cleared their afternoon schedules to review it. They said they will have their comments to us by end of business and they want us to have our initial issue discussion with SerosaSoft tomorrow morning."

"No problem." Evie solemnly glanced at the Sangerson file and an evergreen list of personal *To Do's* sticking out of the side pocket of her briefcase. "Do you want Hanover to set up a new matter for this deal?"

"No, you can just use the general matter number for software transactions. Thanks for meeting such an unreasonable deadline. You are hereby nominated for attorney of the year."

"I'm not letting you off *that* easy, Adam. You owe me."

Adam laughed. "And I'm sure you'll collect! Hey, call me at home tonight if you have any questions. If I read it this afternoon, I'll send you my comments by email."

"Thanks, Adam. Talk to you in the morning."

He hung up. Evie sighed to herself at the sacrifice of another evening, but that thought quickly dissipated. She didn't mind working tight schedules for grateful and respectful clients like Roma Sori.

A glance through her email inbox yielded the expected SerosaSoft document, which she downloaded to the printer. Another new email emerged from the list of titles representing the day's electronic communications. It was an internal message from Hanover requesting her to contact him about a team of attorneys he was assembling to fly to Florida for a contract negotiation next week.

She had been the contract draftsperson on that Florida deal, but had been pulled off of the assignment due to her other commitments. Hanover was personally requesting that she reinsert herself into the matter and take the lead in the negotiation. *Well, at least I know its specifics. And to travel with Hanover might present an opportunity to talk to him about Alan and see if he knows anything about the Gerais Chevas matter.*

It would also present an occasion, albeit a bit late, to tell him about Chicago, but she had no idea how to characterize it or how much she should say. *Plenty of time to think about that before next week,* she told herself. She responded to Hanover's email that she'd be happy to work with him on the Florida deal and would instruct Helen to coordinate arrangements with his secretary. She cc'd Helen on the message as was her usual practice when she needed travel assistance.

The rest of the afternoon was quiet, so she was able to finish Sangerson and start her review of the SerosaSoft document. She emailed the completed Sangerson-Zoomhelix Agreement to Alan with a draft cover letter addressed to the client, as he had requested. At 6:30 P.M., she downloaded emails onto her local hard drive, then gathered her pages of notes, the SerosaSoft form agreement and her laptop computer to meet Ralph for their planned dinner to celebrate his court victory. She would have to finish her work on SerosaSoft tonight after going out with Ralph.

The outside air was cool and welcoming this evening as she walked toward her apartment. The humidity and heat of the day had succumbed to a weather front blown in from Long Island Sound. She hurried to the desk in the lobby of her building, and as the concierge simultaneously gathered mail for two other residents, he handed over a note that had been left for her. It was from Ralph and was full of apologies. An urgent family matter had required him to suddenly travel to London. A question emerged in her mind: should she call Joe? *No, he'll think I'm crazy. It's too late to make a plan for tonight.*

She left her computer and briefcase with the concierge to run out and pick up some food for dinner. Her favorite Chinese restaurant was three blocks away and she decided to walk instead of dialing for takeout, to enjoy the cooler evening weather. When she left with her bag of sesame chicken, she looked back briefly and noticed a man in a gray suit standing alone looking off into space.

As she walked, she was aware of the man behind her and he seemed to be in step with her for a few blocks. She focused on the sidewalk ahead, but listened for the sound of his footsteps as she dissected his appearance in her mind. It was the end of a business day, but his suit was crisp, his grooming was fresh and he was holding no briefcase. She visualized him again. His hands had been completely free. As she crossed the street to her block, she increased her pace and heard him lag behind, continuing on the same path she had. She glanced back and noted that he looked away a bit too mechanically. Slightly spooked, she walked quickly toward her building and its front door, held open by Fred with his friendly smile. She stood in the foyer just inside the door for a few moments to see if the man followed, but he was nowhere in sight. For an instant, she considered alerting Fred to watch for the Gray Suit, but there was nothing distinctive about him and she decided he was probably just a typical pervert looking for a conquest. She shrugged it off.

~

Friday morning began with a conference call between Evie and the Roma Sori executives in preparation for their discussion with Sero-saSoft, during which they all agreed on the numerous problems with the document.

As they waited for the remaining voices to chime in, she sorted through layers of papers on her desk. Buried under yesterday's *Wall Street Journal* was a press release she had found the day before from LEXIS/NEXIS, but had not had time to read, *Gerais Chevas Industries Accepts Bid for Software Giant*. She had printed it out to see if it might be related to the Gerais Chevas deal referenced in the unexpected email from Adinaldo, but in her haste had forgotten to slip it into her briefcase. With a shudder, she realized it was buried here when Alan was seated at her desk when she returned from yesterday's lunch. *Had he seen it?*

A voice captured her attention as one of the executives announced that everyone who was to participate on the call seemed to now be connected. She placed the press release on top of the stack of paper. Each participant offered introductions and the SerosaSoft sales machine began to churn with Roma Sori as the intended target. After about an hour, the discussion concluded and Evie disconnected her line.

The pace of the conference call had prevented her from reading the press release, but now there was nothing else to distract her. While there was no real depth to the release, it did contain interesting information.

> *BUENOS AIRES, ARGENTINA, 17 April, 2005—Gerais Chevas Industries, a Brazil-based software development powerhouse, has announced that it has accepted an offer to sell the Company's statistical software division, GC Quadra, to Argentina-based Romez Nuevo for US$179 million in cash and securities. After aggressive early growth, GC Quadra struggled through a widely reported strategic miscalculation to become a recognized worldwide leader in the development of software for statistical analysis. Gaining a respectable market share in corporate planning, its Quadra Numbers software has been successfully implemented by a number of governmental agencies worldwide, to produce a statistical basis for the allocation of government funds to population-dependent expenditures. The transaction is subject to regulatory approval and is expected to close in the third calendar quarter of 2005.*

A sell-off of a software division. One of the division's software products had reportedly become established in the government market. The transaction to close at the end of September. *Was this the deal to which Adinaldo's email related? Was this the deal discussed in Dallas by some unknown person in all those Brazilian telephone calls? The one she'd over-heard Alan talk about while on the telephone in the conference room?*

She looked back at the article. It was a transaction between two South American companies. Could her firm have been retained to handle this deal? *Why would a New York law firm be chosen to handle a deal between two South American companies? What was the U.S. connection? A $179 million deal. Nothing obviously untoward. Nothing unusual on its face.* She stuffed it into her briefcase for later re-examination.

Helen had deposited a short stack of mail in her inbox during the conference call, and Evie sorted through it, looking for items that required priority attention. In the stack was a note *from* Helen, written after she had dialed some of the telephone numbers on the Colonial Court hotel receipt, at Evie's request. It read that each number seemed to be associated with a company called Gerais Chevas and that two of the people with whom she connected spoke English, and claimed to have had numerous conversations with Evie. Her note concluded, questioning whether she should add Gerais Chevas to the billing records because it appeared that it was a client Evie had spoken to at length about some matter. Helen had obviously decided the whole series of calls had simply been forgotten by her overworked boss. Evie sat for a moment lost in thought. *Why do I have no memory of these conversations? Why would these people say they spoke with me if they hadn't?*

While Evie continued to sort through the pile of mail, she played back a voice mail that came in while she was on the conference call.

> *"Evie, it's Joe. I made a dinner reservation. How about meeting me at the Oak Room at six thirty? I was given some tickets for a concert at Carnegie Hall, if we decide to go. Let me know if you get held up at the office. Plans are flexible."*

She dialed Alan's office to ask him whether he had finished reviewing the Sangerson-Zoomhelix Agreement so she could send it on to the client, but he was out. She drafted an email to him, again attaching the agreement and cover letter, asking him to review them and send them out if he was satisfied. In her message, she highlighted her planned departure time from the office and added that she would be unable to send out the documents herself until Monday if she didn't hear from him before five o'clock.

The contents of Helen's note plagued her. Maybe she'd been mistaken somehow. It was not like Evie to forget a conversation with a client, but then she had been working so many hours, servicing so may clients that it was not impossible. Perhaps it had been a routine inquiry that had required a brief answer and she'd simply forgotten the context. But a client from South America? She would have remembered a Latin client simply because it was unusual.

As she clicked on SEND, she saw a hand-addressed letter that she'd missed in the stack. There was no return address, but the penmanship was quite elegant. She opened it and was shocked to see the printed photo of Senator Arbeson with the female companion that she herself had clipped from *New York Magazine* two nights before. The cutting was accompanied by a note on twenty-pound linen paper bearing no logo or name and displaying no other identifying features. It was written with the same elegant penmanship, but the curvy script seemed an eerie contrast to the message:

Are you having an affair with our Senator?

chapter
9

H ello, Evie."
"Hello," she extended her hand. Joe kissed it and stood
regarding her. Her hair was straight with the shine and color of
liquid chocolate; her skin creamy, fair and translucent. She wore no lipstick, but her lips were moist and she wore a simple black dress. A glass
of wine sat in front of her on the table at the window of the Oak Room.

"You are stunning," he said.

"Thank you." Evie smiled, testing the visual image before her against
her memory of the man on the plane. He was dressed in a dark blue
Brioni suit and a tie patterned with muted golds and auburns over a
starched white shirt. He seemed freshly shaven and radiated the same
wonderful aftershave she remembered from their shared row on the
plane. His wavy hair was still slightly damp and his eyes sparkled.

"I'm so glad you were free tonight." He surveyed the room. "Would
you like to stay here for awhile and have another drink," he paused, "or,
have a drink at Molyvos?"

"Let's go to Molyvos," she said, glancing at the rapidly growing size of the crowd in the bar. "I just have to pay the house," she added as she rose from her chair and retrieved her wrap from the back of the chair.

"You relax. I'll take care of it," he said before weaving his way through bodies in the direction of the bar.

Evie sat down again and allowed her eyes to follow Joe. She watched him as if observing the difference in the movements of men and women for the first time. His body displaced air with the gracefulness of a practiced athlete.

He returned quickly and guided her to her feet, holding her hand while pulling her chair out. He draped the wrap around her shoulders, gently took her hand and used his body to part the crowd leading to the exit. When she joined his rhythm, her movements seem to tap the same source of energy and she felt invigorated.

On the walk to the restaurant, Joe's arm encircled her several times as the sidewalks presented various Manhattanesque obstacles: street performers, open delivery chutes, street elevators and dumpster-overflow along the sidewalks. Evie found herself anticipating each touch even though she recoiled slightly each time out of reflex. *What a relief it would be to relinquish control for awhile.*

She noticed the soothing Greek music immediately upon arriving at Molyvos. The hostess escorted them to their table, which Evie noticed afforded privacy, tucked away from the crowded bar. After helping her into her seat, Joe slid in across from her and smiled broadly.

"I didn't notice the wine you were drinking at the Oak Room," his eyes searched hers. "Or, do you have a favorite Greek wine?"

"I usually resort to random selection, so I'll let you choose."

Joe summoned the waiter and ordered a bottle of Thalassitis Gaia Assyrtiko, a white wine from the island of Santorini. Evie had nodded at the waiter's description of the Psari Plaki fish entrée, so Joe ordered two and surrendered the menus.

"You know, I would have never guessed you to be the Plaza Hotel type," Evie said, her eyes sparkling.

Joe laughed, "You already read me well. A colleague made the reservation."

The waiter appeared with the wine and proceeded to extract the cork as Evie fell into a contemplative silence, distracted by the hand-written note and the identity of its writer. He poured wine and prepared portions of complimentary hors d'oeuvres on each plate with choreo-graphed precision. After depositing the bottle of wine in a bucket of ice, he left.

"Evie, are you okay?"

"Oh, yes. Fine. Just having a little trouble leaving the office behind."

"Understood. Work long hours every night?" Joe asked.

"Many nights."

"And you travel a lot?"

"Several times a month, typically. I seem to have the disposition for it and at this time in my life, I like the change in scenery. How much of the time do you travel?"

"About half my time, on business. I also tend to travel quite a bit in my down time, though."

"Where do you go? In your down time, I mean?"

"Well, my father fancied himself a big game hunter and used to take me to Kenya every few years. I kind of continued the habit as an adult."

"Mmmm. You continued the habit? To hunt?"

"No. I never developed the hunter's instinct, but the high coun-try of Kenya—that really stayed with me. I've been on a number of safaris—everything from the primitive torch-lit camp to the firm-mattress gourmet excursion catered by international chefs."

"So you have a special affection for Africa. Why do you think that is?"

"I'm sure there's some psychological connection to those times with my dad, but beyond that it's simply that the land is so beautiful and enriching. It's as if your soul is let out to play like nowhere else in the world," Joe sipped his wine and his eyes took on a slight glaze as if he was traveling in his mind. "You're reduced to your instincts, and survival in the wild is a refreshing change from the politics of career navigation."

"Mmmm. *Oh yes.* I understand absolutely. I can only imagine what it must feel like." With a welcome relaxed breath, Evie found herself becoming lost in Joe's anecdotes.

His voice softened as if he was a storyteller under a listening moon, "There are moments in the night there when you sense the vastness and the endless numbers of different species alive, living . . . all around you. You can hear them—the baboons, the wildebeests, the hippos, zebras, crickets, birds and the occasional rustling of an elephant or lion. But you can also *feel* them. It's heady. All that raw survival instinct walking around at night with no rules, no schedules."

"Hmmmm. I never really thought about it. You make it sound inspiring . . . it sounds . . . like a wonderful experience." She studied him for a few seconds in silence, with genuine interest in joining him in the memory. "You know, I find it fascinating that with such a love for the wild you chose a high-tech corporate career for yourself."

"Yes. I guess I'm an odd combination of corporate yearnings and wilderness nostalgia. *Actually,* while I was spending one of those summers in Kenya with my dad, I invented something that I was ultimately able to patent. I guess that exposure to the corporate machinery awakened another part of me. Anyway, I went to college at Stanford, graduate school at MIT, and I ended up returning to San Francisco, where I was born. Then I moved down the coast for my job."

"What invention did you patent?"

"It's a device for purifying drinking water; it's used in parts of South Africa. A mechanism that uses sedimentation, absorption, straining and biochemical processes to remove impurities. Unique, I suppose, because it can purify while it maintains the balance of certain beneficial elements in the water. It was adopted for use by one of the humanitarian organizations over there, and they helped me apply for the patent."

"Your father must've been very proud of you. Is he still alive?" She tasted a spanakopita and sipped her wine.

"Yes, but he's not well. He buried my mother a long time ago and he lives with a number of ailments near Santa Barbara . . . with a collection of birds he breeds."

"Ummm . . . the undercurrent of nature. I suspect that you are from a long line of rugged explorers who can truly understand the animals," she smiled. "And you travel exclusively to Africa for pleasure?"

"Well, I have a feeling that trips to *New York* will now be more pleasurable," he said grinning. "Now, Evie, it's my turn to ask questions." The waiter appeared, deposited the aromatic fish entrées and replenished their glasses with wine and water.

"So, Evie. How did you come to be a lawyer?" inquired Joe as he took a bite of fish.

"Well, I guess my journey wasn't as targeted as yours. I applied to law school at the suggestion of a college professor. He taught a pre-law course that I scored well in. I always enjoyed logical reasoning, so practicing law seemed a natural next step. And when I was awarded a scholarship, my life seemed to plan itself." She took a bite of fish. "I can't say that I really made a choice to be a lawyer, but once I started practicing intellectual property law and working with artists and creative types, I really began to enjoy it."

"Ahh. Such as your representation of the sculptor who created *The Solitary Lady* that you told me about on the plane."

"Yes. Exactly. Although, I think my ratio of artistic clients to software-related clients is about forty-sixty."

"And so confirms my initial suspicion about you—that you are an artistic soul that has not yet found a satisfactory avenue of expression."

"Possibly. And what else does your suspicion about me tell you?"

He swallowed another bite. "That you distrust men. Maybe you've had a few bad experiences with men?"

"A few. Yes. Am I that transparent?" she felt herself blush slightly.

"No. I'm good at reading people." His eyes softened, and their expression sliced through her and comforted her simultaneously. He kept his eyes on her as he collected the delicate fish on his fork.

"What would you have been had you not become a technology executive?" Evie changed the subject. *He IS good at reading people. He's some sort of scary contradictory force. Elusive but available. Unfamiliar and foreign, but there's an invitation to trust.*

"Probably a photographer for *National Geographic,* but *wait* a minute," his smile revealed well-entrenched lines around his eyes. "You reclaimed the line of inquiry here—*I'm* not through asking questions yet."

Evie chewed another bite of her dinner and her fork played with an olive on the plate as her eyes registered his answer.

"Evie, how is it that a beautiful, intelligent young woman like yourself is not being pursued by a string of adoring men?"

"And how do you know I'm not?" she smiled.

"Okay. You're just adding me to the list then?" his dimples reappeared.

"No. Actually, I'm not," she laughed. "I haven't had a succession of dates with any one man for over two years. And lately, with work, if I do manage to go out, it's usually sporadic, impromptu or tortured by time constraints."

"Well, then, I'm all the more grateful I have you to myself this evening."

Evie extended her fork for a stuffed grape leaf. Joe suppressed an urge to touch her. He'd accurately sensed her wariness when he was escorting her on the street, but he wondered what made her so cautious.

"So," she said. "Let me see if I understand correctly. You're an executive who guides the technological direction of your company, but . . . you're not the Chief Technology Officer?"

"Yeah. That's right. I evaluate patent potential, establish research agendas, negotiate technology purchases and help to chart the strategy of developing product lines. The company's vague about titles."

"And how does a technology executive evaluate the patent potential of an idea?" Evie smiled, enjoying the fact that she had once again garnered the role of questioner.

Joe licked his lips and took a drink. His eyes twinkled in play. It had become a game, and he could see the reluctance in her to share too much about herself. He decided to be patient, let her set the boundaries.

He smiled and said, "When a new product or idea is conceived, one of our engineers, usually the developer, puts out a spec sheet that describes the product or process. Something like the spec sheet that a pharmaceutical company issues with a new drug. It's packed with information not only about the product or process itself, but about its potential with other products and its ability to solve a problem or meet a perceived need. And, of course, its uniqueness in the market. Other engineers in the company then comment on it and there are discussions. Problems are worked through and then a decision is made about its future."

Evie watched his mouth as he spoke. It was as if he tasted each word.

"And what is the reaction when one of these spec sheets comes out and it has a lot of problems. Do you consider it an obstacle or a challenge?"

"Good question. It really depends on the degree of the problems and the perceived value of the product, but we've found that this process is an invaluable way to refine and perfect the product. Prior to market testing." Joe deposited another forkful into his mouth.

"Interesting. You must be one of those people who are very comfortable moving around in the underbelly of a computer system." She hesitated and asked, "Do you know a lot about file systems and file security?"

"Some. Why do you ask?"

"Just curious," Evie looked down at her plate and finished off the last bite of fish.

"Tell me about your family," he said.

"My family. My parents are both dead. My father died in a car accident when I was seven years old. My mother died of pneumonia she contracted when she was in the hospital during my second year of law school."

"Oh, I'm sorry."

"It's okay. I've long since worked through my feelings, but I do miss my mother from time to time."

"Were you able to spend time with her before she died?"

"Yes. Fortunately, I did. I was with her when she died. Are you close to your father?"

"He's very independent despite his various ailments, but I do speak to him by telephone at least once a week."

"Do you have sisters or brothers?" she asked trying to imagine Joe as a young boy.

"I have a sister, Ariel, who lives in Connecticut with her son. She and I have a closer relationship than either of us have with our father."

"So you see your nephew often?"

"I try to see them each time I'm on the East Coast. But it's not ideal. I miss them."

"Have you ever been married?"

"No. I've been a slave to my career."

"I don't believe that."

"Well, I guess I never found the right girl."

"So, what do you *do* when you're in Africa?" she asked.

"Take photographs mostly."

"Do you track animals?"

"Only until I can get them to pose."

She smiled, "Have you ever had a close call . . . a dangerous encounter?"

"Not on the African continent."

After a moment, Joe said in a mellifluous voice, "I've walked a lot of trails, logged many miles in Kenyan wilderness. I've seen a few lions, but was always lucky enough to be downwind and between meals."

"Did you have native guides go with you?"

"Yes, sometimes. But I was often wearing the spider."

"Wearing the spider?"

"Yeah. That was what we called the lead. The person in the lead always cleared the trail. Walked through the spider webs. Sometimes the spiders rode along for a bit."

"You *wore* the spider? You let it crawl around on you while you walked?"

"Well, most of the time they were pretty good at staying put where they landed."

"Why would you not just brush it off?"

"And let it land on your mate who was following close behind?"

"Oooohhhh. I'm not sure I'd be good at wearing the spider."

"I'm kidding." He smiled again, "Spiders *always* get the brush-off. It's just a matter of technique."

"I guess that takes some skill, not to *mention* consideration for your mates."

"Another chance for chivalry," he laughed.

"You'd wear the spider for me?" she asked.

"I'd wear whatever you asked me to."

Evie reached for her water glass and took a slow drink. She glanced down at the empty plates as the busboy appeared to clear the table.

"Joe, that was a lovely meal. Thank you."

"There are these tickets to the Vienna Philharmonic at Carnegie Hall, but if you prefer, we can go to Doubles."

"That club at the Sherry Netherland?"

"Yes. A friend who's a member invited us to go as his guest. It's a quiet place where we can have some dessert and coffee."

Evie nodded and smiled, prompting Joe to waive at the waiter and ask for the check. They walked out into the warm night, up Seventh Avenue and along Central Park South toward Fifth Avenue. A soft breeze waltzed through the horse chestnut trees in the park, muffling the sounds of the taxi-dominated traffic. There were mostly couples and groups of tourists at the edge of the Park and their conversations rode the wind, disguising their origin.

Joe's voice had become a whisper, and as they walked he told Evie stories of prior visits to New York when he was young and reckless. The horse-drawn hansom cabs lined the north side of the street as the drivers, like actors on a sidewalk stage, mingled, dressed in everything from top hat and polo attire, to what appeared to be nineteenth-century British military uniforms. Most of the horses, clad in their colorfully decorated tack, stood head down, buried nose-deep in buckets of water or oats. One bay gelding looked toward Joe and Evie as they approached; Joe stopped.

He whispered to Evie, "Do you know how to greet a horse?"

"Other than the usual pleasantries, I'm afraid I'm at a loss," Evie laughed.

Joe grinned, removed his jacket and placed it neatly over her arm, with a dramatic display. He then asked her to watch.

After gaining permission from the horse's owner, he walked slowly toward the bay gelding, his eyes fixed on the horse's gaze. Joe's movements were gradual but decisive, and he began to lean his head slowly toward the gelding's head as if bowing to a stately gentleman. Without further explanation, he gracefully positioned his mouth at the level of the gelding's nostrils and blew a short blast of air toward the gelding's right nostril. When the horse felt Joe's breath, he shivered and nodded as if in recognition of an old friend. His eyes flashed, he snorted a return greeting and then seemed to study Joe, like an embarrassed acquaintance trying to remember where they had met previously.

Joe reached out and gently caressed the head of the gelding, lightly massaging behind the horse's ears. The gelding submitted calmly, nodded again and turned toward Joe in a blind admission that recognition was futile, but with the willingness to make a new friend. Evie laughed from her place of observation some four feet away. Joe bowed to his new friend, bid him adieu and turned toward Evie with a broad smile.

"A blast of air in the nostril is their form of greeting. It's as if I was speaking his language, and he was appropriately taken by surprise."

"Well, perhaps you should exchange business cards," Evie said laughing as she nodded to the gelding's handler, who laughed with her.

When Joe returned to her side, he retrieved his jacket and took her hand in his, squeezing gently. As they continued their walk toward Fifth Avenue, Evie felt as if she was standing on the edge of a cliff admiring the view, contemplating a dive into a crystal blue sea of emotion.

They disappeared from view through the revolving door of the Sherry Netherland Hotel. After floating down the crimson steps into the hidden sanctuary of the private club, Evie and Joe shared a strawberry pastry, sipped coffee and danced for over an hour to Frank Sinatra.

As they moved slowly around the dance floor, Evie felt an internal war brewing. Part of her was enjoying being swept away, but there was a persistent voice chanting caution. Joe could have easily been a manufactured image in a dream. Maybe she *was* dreaming. Maybe she would awaken with a flush in her cheeks and a lilting afterglow. He held her close as they danced and traded tactile messages. Afterward, she was glad to sit down at their table and sip a glass of water.

He walked out to the hotel lobby to check his voice mail, leaving her in a state of reflection. *This man is dangerous. He is too good to be true.* When he returned she was extracting a red rose from the vase on the table. She held it to her nose.

"So you *do* like roses," he said.

"Yes, very much," she paused and suddenly remembered the beautiful bouquet that had been waiting for her Tuesday evening at her apartment building. She had thought that they were from Ralph, but had failed to confirm her conclusion. "This is embarrassing, but did you send me roses earlier this week?"

"Yes, but I was afraid you didn't like them since you hadn't said anything."

"Oh, God, I'm sorry. There was no card ... except there was a note under my door from my friend Ralph across the hall. I ... well. I thought *he* sent them. It was really a lovely thought. You must think I'm so *rude*."

Joe didn't answer at first, but then said, "Well, Ralph owes me then." He laughed and asked, "Do you want to know what the card said?"

"Definitely."

"Let's pursue this."

"You wrote that on the card?"

"Yes."

"How did you sign it?" she asked.

"The man on the plane."

Evie smiled and thought for a moment. "How did you find my address? I'm unlisted."

"Information like that's fairly easy to obtain," Joe grinned. "I also know you were born in 1972 in New Jersey, an only child, that you financed your liberal arts degree from Columbia and that your law degree is from Harvard, which you completed with honors. You were at Harvard three years after I finished at MIT and left Cambridge, so we missed an opportunity to meet. I know you lived briefly in Paris, I'm assuming you were interning, perhaps as a legal clerk, and then you worked for Marvyn & Goldstein for a year or so prior to your present firm, where you're a senior associate in the corporate department."

Evie stared at him.

"I . . . uhhh. Is all this published somewhere?"

Her first thought was that she should have been flattered that this man had been interested enough to seek out information about her, but it made her uncomfortable nonetheless. The voice of reluctance in her head returned and chanted more loudly now its message of caution.

"Well, it's like a puzzle. A little determination is all that's necessary to assemble the pieces."

A stab of uneasiness pierced her stomach. She smiled, excused herself and went to the ladies room to verify that the growing anxiety she was feeling was not visible in her face. She sat on a vanity stool and looked at herself in the mirror. A wave of some insistent sensation rushed over her. She felt chilled and feverish and her hands were moist with sweat. Her stomach was tightening and she felt light-headed. Her heart pounded and she had to force air into her lungs. She was afraid for a moment that she was going to cry. She took a few slow deep breaths and felt a little better. She dabbed at a tear in the corner of her eye with a Kleenex.

Why do I feel so violated by Joe's information gathering? Am I just tired? Tired of being tired. She hadn't thought about Alan all evening, but maybe she was more fearful about the potential career harm Alan could inflict than she had let herself believe. Could he be behind the handwritten note? *Maybe she was having a full-blown anxiety attack.* She combed her hair and powdered her nose. *Pull yourself together, Evie.* She closed her eyes for a moment and forced her mind to quiet itself. Although she had genuinely enjoyed the evening, she suddenly felt the need to go home.

When she returned to the table, she saw that Joe had left the table and was standing at the bar chatting with a man dressed in a tuxedo, who seemed to be the evening steward of the club. She approached the two men, and Joe put his arm around her, carefully, so as not to disrupt the placement of her wrap perfectly draped over her shoulders. Joe introduced her to the man and after a few polite words, the man excused himself and disappeared behind a door.

"Are you ready to go?" Joe asked, stepping with her to a side area near the coat room, away from the path of traffic.

"Yes. Thank you. Joe, I really had a lovely evening."

"Well, I hope this is not goodbye. I intended to walk you home."

"If you don't mind, I'm a bit tired. I think I'll just grab a taxi."

"I'll go with you."

"Please don't be offended, but I would prefer to say goodnight here," she said.

"Evie, did I say something to upset you?"

"No. Definitely not. You're the perfect gentleman. Truly. I just have a lot on my mind, and I'm exhausted from the week."

"May I see you again?"

"Aren't you leaving town tomorrow?"

"Yes, but I'll be back soon."

"Joe. I uhhh . . . Okay. Yes, sure, of course. We can get together again when you're back in the city."

"Are you sure you're okay?" Joe asked, searching her eyes and noticing for the first time a growing distance there.

"Yes. I'm fine," she smiled and kissed him on the cheek. "I'm really useless when I get tired. Please forgive me."

"There's nothing to forgive," he said, "but at least let me put you in a taxi."

"Okay."

With his arm around her more firmly now, he guided her up the stairs to the hotel lobby and through the revolving door, nodding at the doorman, who whistled at a taxi parked to the right of the hotel awning. The taxi moved toward the center of the hotel entrance and waited. Joe escorted Evie to its door, opened it, but before helping her inside he turned her body toward him and placed a soft kiss on her forehead. She smiled up at him and slid into the seat. He shut the door and leaned in the window of the front seat and handed some bills to the taxi driver. "That should cover it," he said as the driver nodded.

Evie opened her mouth to object, but instead smiled broadly at Joe, mouthed *"Thank you"* through the window and waved as the taxi moved away from the curb.

On the ride home, Evie retreated to her thoughts. *I met this man four days ago.* To anticipate a date and actually leave the office early was a rarity for her. She had enjoyed herself more tonight than any other time in recent memory. It was as if she was standing on a beautiful beach just feet away from a beckoning ocean that she knew was denominated by an invisible, life-claiming riptide, only the strength of the riptide was unknown. Was it that she was simply afraid of becoming close to a man, afraid of getting hurt? Was it something specific about Joe himself or the fact that his life was based on the opposite coast? There was something about him that made him seem unreal and confidence-worthy at the same time.

Or maybe her anxiety attack had not really been about him at all. Maybe it was her sense that she was on the cusp of a real career battle, and she wanted to travel light when it came to relationships—they always seem to absorb so much energy. She sighed and returned her thoughts to the more urgent situation at the office, and a male figure who seemed much more clearly defined.

chapter

10

On Saturday morning, Evie woke early and dialed her office voice mail before her first cup of English Breakfast tea. Not sure what she would hear, she felt compelled to check, as if the act of listening would magically prevent any bad news. No new messages. She made the morning's pot of tea and took a cup into the bathroom, showering and dressing in less than twenty minutes.

With the clarity of thought that followed a good night's sleep, she was more confident this morning in her memory that Gerais Chevas was not among the clients she'd spoken to in the prior month. There had to be a mistake that was not hers. Or, was the false hotel receipt part of the *"paper trail"* to which Alan had referred?

She left her apartment and walked south on Seventh Avenue, thoughts flowing freely. Despite waking up with the same set of indigestible facts she had faced yesterday, the unsolved puzzle seemed less debilitating this morning. Whoever had sent that handwritten note would be peddling a lie if he or she published the accusation anywhere;

it was not Evie in the photograph. No threat had been made anyway. She decided to forget it. And as for Alan, she decided to plant herself in front of Hanover and tell him everything. Jenna and Lisa were right. She should describe her history of encounters with Alan, including the incident in Chicago that she had failed to report. Despite the passage of time, the circumstances of that night had not grown stale in her mind; on the contrary, they sometimes tormented her like a recurring dream.

After running some errands, she stopped in a *Frozen Willy* yogurt shop and ordered a couple of coconut scoops on a multi-grain cone. She crossed 53rd Street and walked north. She found a small outdoor pavilion and sat in the sun listening to the manmade waterfall and engaging in full-frontal people-watching. Mentally, she began thinking through a list of details she wanted to cover with Hanover. She would be as objective as possible and let Hanover react. As the managing partner and head of the firm, he would be compelled to at least investigate. In theory, Hanover's involvement should make it much easier to find out what was really going on.

She finished the last bite of yogurt and walked the remaining blocks to her building. When she arrived at her apartment door and turned the key in the lock she noticed that her door was already unlocked. *Did I forget to lock the door?* She pushed open the door and, before walking through the threshold, studied the interior. There was a stack of twenty dollar bills visible on a side table, just the way she'd left it when grabbing some money for her errands. *An intruder would have taken that. I must've left the door unlocked. How careless.* The thought ended there.

She settled into her chair with a large envelope Helen had left for her. It contained the expense documentation for Senator Arbeson's art collection. From the date of purchase, most of the paintings had been displayed in his Upper East Side apartment. However, there was a series of rental payments on a climate-controlled warehouse for a period of time and a package of invoices for cleaning, removing contaminants, repair of scrapes and flaking, re-varnishing. There were invoices for appraisals on several different dates. There was an additional storage fee for a period of time when the paintings were placed in another art collector's apartment. How did these paintings suffer so much abuse? And why would someone have an expensive art collection stored away after displaying them in one's apartment? Odd.

She found nothing in his documentation unequivocally supporting the notion that any of the paintings had been acquired as investments. Other than the repetitious appraisals, one would have a difficult time establishing a tax-friendly motive. As she flipped through the documents, she found an itemized document that looked to be an inventory from a divorce settlement with the paintings highlighted and some of the restoration expenses charged back to his ex-wife's share. *Ahhh.*

Evie remembered reading about wife number one—a hotheaded woman who had claimed marital abuse, sold her story to a tabloid and sucker-punched the Senator's initial senatorial campaign. No one had given her story much credibility, but perhaps there'd been some truth to it. Maybe the paintings suffered some of the damage during one of those violent arguments. From the recent news stories about his current marriage, it was apparent that his relationships were fraught with rancor. In any event, there was clearly not enough documentation to establish ordinary and necessary business expenses totaling thirteen million dollars in connection with an investment. Senator Arbeson would likely change his mind about supporting her quest for partnership once he received her memo.

She put the envelope back in her briefcase, booted up her laptop and dialed into the firm's network system. The CPU hummed its startup tune and the modem issued its series of tones to establish communication. She worked all afternoon, drafting the memo to Senator Arbeson and creating a timeline of her work over the summer to show that Gerais Chevas had not been among the clients she'd served.

When she was finished with her timeline, the resulting document was a voluminous, convoluted monologue on overworked law firm associates. *A controvertible alibi.* She knew there could be electronic or other evidence to contradict her claimed workflow, but it was her best attempt. A pitiable house of cards, there was no way to prove absolutely that she didn't help on a particular deal—she worked on too many of Alan's matters and her name had now appeared, at least electronically, in connection with this Brazilian contact. And, honest mistake or not, she'd been listed as working on Gooseneck when she had not. *Where else would her name show up?* While her inability to access files ostensibly provided current proof of her lack of involvement, she knew passwords and access parameters could be changed in seconds, erasing a history of inaccessibility.

She reluctantly deposited the drying roses in the garbage, the roses that she now knew had been from Joe. As if he was telepathic, the telephone rang and his voice greeted her.

"Evie, glad I caught you home. Feeling better today?"

"Yes, Joe . . . thank you. I'm fine. Listen, I want to apologize for last night. And I want to thank you for a really wonderful evening. I didn't even realize how much time we had spent together until I got home."

"I'm glad. I called because I wanted to tell *you* how much I enjoyed spending time with you. I really want to see you again."

"Okay. What did you have in mind?"

"Well, as a matter of fact, it looks like I might be on your side of the continent again this week."

"*Oh*. I have to be in Florida this week. I'm leaving Monday night and I don't know how much of the week I'll be there."

"Mmmmm. Okay. Well, then there's another option. Two weeks from tonight there's a charity event in New York I was considering attending. One of those *I-wish-I-ate-before-I-came* sort of things. My sister, who I told you about last night, is on the board of this charity and is threatening me with all sorts of mayhem if I don't show up."

"It's black tie?"

"Yes. But *you* don't have to wear one."

"Very funny. Is it a sit-down dinner?"

"Yes. Dinner and dancing and the usual sort of award presentation to some honoree."

"Are there horses involved?"

He laughed, "No, not this time."

"What's the charity?"

"It's called 'Women and Children First.' It's a caretaking organization for abused women and children."

"Hmmm. How interesting. I know it."

"You do?"

"Yes."

"Would you like to go with me?"

"Let me just check . . . okay, I'm completely open. Yes, I think that would be very nice."

"Great. I'll get back to you with the details. I may fly in the day before, but I'll let you know. Do you like champagne?"

"Yes, if it's dry."

"Duly noted."

"Will you be at the Plaza again?"

"No. Probably the Four Seasons. I've got to go. Don't get sunburned in Florida."

"I'll sit *away* from the window. See you in two weeks."

"Bye."

"Goodbye."

She hung up. *Well, he seems to be undaunted by the challenge of a long distance pursuit.*

After another hour of working on her computer, she felt chilled and remembered that she'd left all the windows open. She trekked around the apartment closing them, but the one over her bed didn't cooperate. It was a tilt-out window design with a metal crank and latch. The frame on the window was warped and the resulting curvature kept the crank from returning it to its closed position.

As she fought with the hardware, Evie noticed a woman standing at the corner looking up toward her building. She could see that it was a female with dark hair, but she couldn't make out any more detail, other than the woman's hands appeared to be holding binoculars or a camera or other type of small object up to her eyes. *Tourists,* thought Evie. *They'll photograph anything.*

~

On Monday morning, she checked her voice mail first thing, out of habit. All three messages were about the same subject although left by different people. Hanover had been admitted to the hospital to undergo some tests. Something about potential heart blockage. The last message, from Paul Wayford, asked her to proceed with her plan to attend the client meetings in Florida. She would be handling the entire negotiation without Hanover, but a junior associate would be accompanying her to assist.

She flashed on the image of Hanover walking slowly out of the room during her presentation the other day. And Jenna had said he'd been out of the office more than usual.

She dialed Paul's extension, but he wasn't in his office. She left a message acknowledging his request and said that she would take care of the client. She busied herself preparing the paperwork for the trip and at 9:45, Paul called back.

"Evie, could you come to my office please?"

"Sure, Paul. I'll be right there."

When she walked through the door, she noticed Steve Buniker sitting in one of the chairs at the small table in Paul's inner office.

"Evie, take a seat," Paul indicated a chair next to Steve and came around the desk, taking a seat in a third chair at the small table.

"Is Hanover okay? What's happened?" asked Evie looking from Paul to Steve and back to Paul. The tension in the air offered no clues as to its origin.

Paul took a slow breath, glanced at Steve and turned his gaze to Evie. "Hanover had triple bypass surgery last night. He'll be in the hospital a few days."

"Oh my *God.* Is there anything I can do?"

"No, his prognosis is good, but that's not why I asked you here." Paul looked down and then looked directly into Evie's eyes. "Did you send out an agreement to Sangerson on Friday?"

Evie glanced at Steve and her eyes fixed on Paul. "I sent it to *Alan*. He told me not to send it out to Sangerson until he'd seen it."

"Did you draft this?" Steve broke in, raising a stack of paper stapled at one corner. He handed the document to Evie who scanned the first page and felt her blood pressure begin to rise. She was looking at the *original* Zoomhelix agreement that she had labored extensively to re-work. *How did he get this?*

chapter
11

S he began speaking while still flipping through the pages. "This was the form of the agreement we *received* from Zoomhelix. My initial instructions were to minimize the alterations to it. Last week, Alan asked me to change direction and re-write it, which I did. I sent the *re-written* version to *Alan* on Friday. I haven't sent *anything* to Sangerson yet."

Steve looked at Paul. Paul reached for the document, glanced at a few pages and returned his gaze to Evie. "Do you have a copy of the re-written document you could show me?"

"Sure." Evie started to rise, but Paul motioned for her to sit down. "Not just yet—"

Steve interrupted, "Alan said that you were to send it out on Friday to *Sangerson*. He promised them they would have it on Friday. He said he didn't hear from you and he assumed that you had sent it out as agreed. Sangerson called this morning and they said that *this* was the document they received." Steve pointed at the document that had now fully made the rounds at the small table. Steve rubbed his chin and with squinting eyes added, "Alan said this morning that you sent a 'cc' of that Friday transmission to him. He forwarded it to me. It was *this* document that was attached."

Evie's mind raced and she felt her hands become sweaty. *WHAT? He's lying. He's lying. He knows that's not true.* "I don't know how Sangerson received *this* document," she said. "I sent the *re-written* version *only* to Alan. I had to leave early on Friday . . ." She suddenly shivered at what must have transpired while she was enjoying her evening with Joe. She shook her head and looked directly at Paul with determination. "Paul, I can *prove* it. I can print out the email I sent to Alan on Friday. I can print out the attached document . . . the *re-written* contract."

"Okay," Paul stood. "Go and get the copy of the re-written agreement and the email you sent to Alan on Friday.

Evie stood and felt the blood rush to her head. She ignored the subsequent dizziness and quickly exited the room, unaware of the faces she passed in the hallways back to her office. It was as if they were strangers ignored while running to catch a subway train. She hurriedly docked her laptop and booted it up. She logged into the firm's system, brought up her email and clicked on the file of sent messages to view the list of emails she had sent on Friday.

To her horror there was an email sent out from her username *to* Sangerson *with a 'cc' to Alan!* The listing indicated that it was sent at 6:08 P.M. Friday. That was *after* she had left the office to get ready for her date with Joe. Her mind raced . . . could she prove that? She tried to remember if anyone saw her leave. But how would she prove that the email was not sent by *her* from a modem-connected remote location? *How can I prove that my username has been hijacked?*

She brought up the message. It was a brief announcement to Sangerson that the revised agreement with her revisions was attached for their review. She clicked on the icon for the attached document with her stomach churning. It *was* the original Zoomhelix Agreement! She looked down the list of sent messages to find the *actual* message she had sent to Alan. It was not there. How could he have pulled this off? *Erasing all evidence of the message I sent him, fabricating a message with the wrong document attached, sending it from my username after I left . . . I didn't know you could send messages from someone else's username. And how did he get my system password?*

She quickly exited email and brought up the firm's electronic database of client files. She pulled up the document that she had created and saved to the system containing the re-written Sangerson-Zoomhelix Agreement. The file contained the original Zoomhelix Agreement! He must have saved the original over the rewritten version she had created. *Why is he doing this?* It would have taken quite a bit of time to create this fraudulent electronic trail. *What is he trying to do to me that is more important to him than a happy client?*

She brought up the history of the saved file to show the names of those persons who had most recently accessed the file. Her name was listed repeatedly with the last timed access Friday evening. *He was thorough, wasn't he? And he's apparently quite astute with the computer. How did he manage to replace my re-written version with the original and avoid adding his name to the Hit History for this file? He must've been working from my network address for some time . . . he must've logged in as me using my username and password . . . but how did he get my password? What in the hell is he trying to do to me?*

The minutes ticked by and she searched the system for any other documentation that might prove that she was telling the truth. Suddenly she thought to search her own hard drive located on her laptop that was *independent* from the firm's networked drives. She found her re-written document in a draft form. It was not the final version that she had saved in the firm's electronic database, which had been overwritten, but it was some proof that she had re-written the agreement. She printed it out and walked back to Paul's office wondering how she was going to convince two partners that she, an associate, was being set up by a third partner. To what possible motive could she point?

When she reappeared inside Paul's office and explained, Steve Buniker lost his temper and began to yell. "My client deserves better from you, Evie! I can't believe you would send out the wrong document and then try to make up some story to blame a partner! So you left early! What was it, *a hot date?* It's obvious that you couldn't finish re-working the document by the time you wanted to leave, so you just sent out the original."

Paul raised a hand to calm Steve, and Evie simply stared. *He's doing it,* she thought with a chill. *He's really doing it. He's going to get away with it.*

"If I was going to send something unfinished, why wouldn't I send this partly-finished draft? At least it's better than the original," she said depositing her printout on the table.

Evie turned again to Paul. "You believe me, don't you, Paul? I can't explain how the email was sent out under my username. I can't explain what happened to my re-written document that I saved in the system library. All I know is that I re-worked it, saved the final version on the system, attached it to an email addressed *only* to Alan and left at five fifteen. I also left voice mails for Alan, but I wouldn't be surprised if they have been conveniently erased. I can't explain how at eight minutes after six, someone pretending to be me sent out the old version to Sangerson under my name. I know it's hard to believe, but *I'm being set up.* And yes, I was at a social engagement and can prove I wasn't sending emails last Friday evening."

"Yeah, right. I'm sure whoever you were out with would say anything you wanted them to about your whereabouts," said Steve.

"Why is it so easy for you to believe that I'm a liar?" Evie said staring at Steve.

Paul looked concerned but not convinced. He picked up the document she had dropped on the table and flipped through it. As he walked back around to his desk chair, he seemed to be deep in thought. At the start of each of Steve's insistent supplications, Paul held up his hand to wave it away.

"Where is Alan, anyway?" Evie asked, feeling slightly emboldened by Paul's disregard for Steve's interruption attempts.

"On a plane. Left this morning to meet with a client in London," he said.

Steve continued in his half-whispered rant of reproach and insisted that Evie be removed from the Sangerson matter. Evie stood her ground, but said nothing. She didn't have any interest in continuing her work with Sangerson. Her schedule was uncomfortably crowded with matters from other clients. She *did* have a significant interest in her reputation and her mind raced with what she could say in her defense, but she knew anything she offered would be misinterpreted as a desperate attempt to deflect the blame for this mess. Her face was calm but interested, as if she was observing an incident of road rage on the highway.

"I'm going to look into this with a little more depth," said Paul finally. "In the meantime, Evie, attend to that Florida matter and leave Sangerson to me."

It was far from a satisfying outcome to Evie, but she knew instinctively it was the best she was going to get. *How odd,* she noted to herself, *just a week ago Paul was cheering me on as the champion of moral rights . . . and now . . .* Steve paced and grumbled in the background, but his mumbling failed to distract Paul as he continued speaking to Evie. Steve threw down the original document and picked up Paul's side telephone, dialing with angry fingers.

Paul, with a myopic focus on future client business, promised to have Hanover's secretary forward some emails and other information to give Evie the necessary background for the upcoming Florida meetings. He added that if she needed to ask any questions to contact him because Hanover might not be interacting with the office for a few days. She thanked him and excused herself. *That certainly changes the forecast.*

Back in her office, she sat fuming. It was clear to her that Alan was targeting her, falsifying interactions with her, setting her up for firm reprisals. She didn't know if Paul really believed her and she knew now that her actions would be closely watched by the partnership. *And Alan may have already set other traps. It will be good to get out of town for a few days and work for a client unrelated to Alan.* She emailed the Florida client, Martini Investments, that she would be supporting their negotiation efforts solo.

The telephone rang with an internal call and she picked up the receiver when she saw on the digital display that it was Jenna. "Hey!" said Jenna.

"Hey, Jen," said Evie.

"I haven't had a chance to talk to you," answered Jenna. "Did you hear about Hanover?"

"Yes, I know. Kind of shocking. Although when I really thought about it, he hasn't been his normal energetic self lately."

"Definitely not, and he just hasn't been around that much. I tried to see him several times and he wasn't taking meetings or was out of the office."

"I hope he's okay."

"Yeah, me too. I hate to think of someone else at the helm; in fact I can't think of anyone worthy. Anyway, how're you doing? Any new developments with our favorite dickhead?" asked Jenna.

"You don't want to know . . . I feel like the character from that Alfred Hitchcock movie, *Stranger on a Train,* who's been unwittingly recruited into a sinister plan, but the delegated part of the plan remains unknown," she sighed. "So, what's going on with you?"

Jenna sneezed into the telephone and apologized, then said, "I was in D.C. yesterday and I have to go back tomorrow for Breckenridge. They are outsourcing their entire data processing function to Emerson Data Works. It's going to be an enormously complicated transaction. Lots of deployment phases and performance standards."

While organizing the contents of her Martini Investments file, Evie spoke into the telephone speaker, "That sounds like a good time. Hey . . . y'know, I've got some really good performance-standard schedules you could use as a guide, with very precise language and good benchmark formulas. I'll email them."

"Great. I hate to re-invent the wheel. Thanks ... uuhhh ... wait, someone just came into my office," said Jenna in a professional tone. "Hey, if you need to talk, call me tomorrow at the Capitol Hilton—it's that hotel where we stayed last year near the White House."

"Okay. Thanks, Jen. Good luck."

They hung up and Evie looked up to see David Hadelman in her doorway. David was a litigator who had switched to the corporate department to do transactional work. A thirty-something, Brooks-Brothers type, he was tall and pleasant looking with a square jaw, burr-cut, jet black hair and deep set, penetrating eyes.

"Have you actually returned to the office or am I seeing things?" he asked with an amused air as he leaned against the doorframe, balancing a mug of coffee and a donut in one hand.

Evie looked up and smiled even though she felt that she had no time to chat. "David. Hi. Uhhh ... how are you?"

"Great. Living large is the best revenge, I always say," he took a bite of the donut, leaving chocolate traces at the corner of his mouth.

"Did your divorce become final?"

"Yes. She's calling it a 'starter' marriage. I'm calling it an education. And even though I have no money left, I have my Jaguar, my guitar and my books. When are we going to get together?"

"I'm not in a position to plan anything. I'm about to leave on another trip."

"My band's playing around the city. I would love for you to come to one of our gigs. This week we're headlining at The Turquoise Bar. Can you make it?"

"I don't know. I'm in Florida all week and I'm not sure what shape I'll be in by the weekend."

"Well. I'll leave your name on the guest list at the door."

"Thanks, David. That's very kind of you. I'll see how I feel." She glanced down briefly at the stacks of paper on her desk. "Sorry to be abrupt, but I have a lot to do before I fly out in a few hours."

"Your frequent flyer miles must be some sort of firm record. Hey, before I go, do you have the Collburn Regan file? Alan said you were the last one to have it."

"Yes, I do. Why?"

"Well, I guess Alan wants me to take it over. He must think you have too much on your plate." *I'll bet. Well, anything to get rid of an Alan matter.*

"Oh. Okay. No problem," she said as she searched for the file. "You in touch with Mike Farraway?"

"Who?"

"Mike Farraway. He's the Executive Vice President at Collburn Regan we were working with."

"Oh. No. Farraway got axed Friday morning. Apparently it was pretty sudden. Stan's going to put me in touch with his replacement in a few days."

"Fired? Wow. That *was* sudden." Evie's mind flashed on Alan's promise the previous week regarding Mike Farraway's future. She felt a sudden cold shudder, but managed to hold her expression to a mild look of surprise. "Do you know why? I mean what caused such a sudden decision?"

"No clue. I guess he had a falling out with the wrong person."

No kidding. She reached for the file and handed it to David. "That's really too bad," she said.

"Yeah. Tough break. Oh well. Hope to see you Friday or Saturday night."

She waved and managed a smile as he turned and disappeared from view.

Oh my God. Was Alan responsible for that? The timing's just too coincidental. Mike held that position for at least three years. How could Alan have managed to convince Stan and the board to fire him? Client management firing an executive at the request of their lawyer? *Maybe Alan made up some sort of lies about him. I guess I'm not the only one.*

On impulse, she dialed the number for Stan Miller at Collburn Regan. His secretary answered and Evie asked to speak to Stan.

"He's on another line, no . . . hold on . . . Okay, I'll put you through."

"Stan?"

"Yes. Hello, Evie. How are you?"

"Fine, thanks. I wanted to let you know that I regret not being able to continue working on your behalf, but I understand that David Hadelman has been assigned. He's a very good attorney."

"Thanks, Evie. Those are good words to hear. Sorry to lose you, but Alan assures me that David will do a good job for us."

"Yes, I'm sure he will. By the way, I understand that Mike Farraway has left the company. Is that true?"

"Yes. I'm afraid so."

"Oh. I'm sorry to hear that. It was so sudden. I hope that his departure didn't create any problems for you."

"No. Actually, it solved some problems."

She waited for further details, but none were forthcoming so she decided to leave it there and said, "Oh. Well, all my best."

"Thanks, Evie. I hope we get the chance to work with you again. And thanks for calling."

"Absolutely. I hope so."

"Bye."

Okay. I have to assume that Alan orchestrated his firing. Apparently, he doesn't mind crashing people's lives if doing so suits his purposes. I wonder if I'm next.

chapter
12

Evie began to collect her files for the trip to Florida and her thoughts wandered to Hanover. Even if he had returned to the office by the time she got back from Florida, there was a good chance he would be too weak to help her out with a problem she wasn't even capable of documenting. It was all still largely not provable on her part. *And becoming even more unbelievable all the time.*

"Evie," said Helen over the intercom, "the car's here to take you to the airport."

"Thanks, Helen. He's early. Ask him to wait. I need a few minutes."

Evie sped up the loading of her briefcase, while wondering what she would say about the harassment incident. *Will it seem like a desperate attempt to deflect blame from myself?* It could be interpreted as a concocted charge to marginalize Alan, given the Sangerson contract debacle. But she had to be able to offer her rejection of Alan's advances as the probable motive for these retaliatory frame-ups. *Is he trying to prevent my partnership chances or get me fired? Would he also try to end my career?* She needed to be able to produce some evidence to prove that he was actually engaged in a retaliation and intimidation effort against her. Otherwise, he just might succeed.

After stacking her briefcase on her suitcase by the door, she decided to take a few additional minutes for some quick research. She turned to her computer and brought up the firm's document library. Her hands were surprisingly steady as she squinted at the screen and entered 13606 in the field for client number. The same four Gerais Chevas document names appeared. She had a premonition that this request would yield more than the familiar ACCESS DENIED response, but she didn't know what to expect.

She clicked on the first file, and for the first time since she had discovered the existence of these files, *the text of the document appeared on her computer screen.* The reality of what had happened didn't register for several seconds. Then she stared at the screen with perspiration soaking through her clothes.

This must mean that someone - *Alan* - had added her name to the electronic list of persons who were able to access the file. She closed the file. She clicked on the second document, named "Neon Two." Again, she was allowed into the file and the screen was filled with the contents of its first viewable page. When she tried to open the third and fourth files, she was provided with an introductory screen seeking a password. Alan had apparently decided that she was now part of the Gerais Chevas team, but he had shielded the contents of two pertinent files under password protection. She went back to the contents of the first file, which was entitled *Neon Term Sheet.*

She needed to know if this was the transaction described in the press release she'd found and why Alan might want to involve her surreptitiously. As she watched the text of the first document re-appear on her screen, she realized that her username would now be stored in the electronic *Hit History* for these documents as the last person to have accessed them. Anyone accessing the files after her would be able to see that *she* had looked at them. She didn't care anymore. There was now a more urgent need to know.

She studied the contents of the *Neon Term Sheet.* There were numbered paragraphs containing the salient points of the deal. It *did* seem to be the $179 million deal she had read about. It appeared to be a standard sell-off of a business unit of Gerais Chevas to a company called Romez Nuevo. *If Alan wanted to involve me in this deal, why would he not openly do so?*

After glancing at the clock, she concluded that she still had ten minutes before she had to leave. She downloaded the Neon Term Sheet from the firm's document library to her laptop's hard drive to preserve her own copy.

She opened the second file, "Neon Two," and saw its internal title, *Neon Purchase Agreement.* She downloaded the file and quickly scanned the text. As seller, Gerais Chevas was making certain representations and warranties to Romez Nuevo about the business unit being sold for the purpose of assuring Romez Nuevo of its quality, including specifics regarding its properties and assets and the scope of its business. Nothing patently improper here.

She knew that these types of assurances were common in any buyer/seller relationship and not unlike the representations about the condition of a house that are made by the seller in a real estate transaction.

She continued reading, but her pace slowed as she read:

> *Seller warrants that as a condition of closing, Seller shall secure Project Neon, as evidenced by the delivery to Purchaser of a duly executed binding agreement ("Sub Agreement") which shall include without limitation the obligations set forth in Schedule B7, and shall be consistent in form and substance with the language set forth in said Schedule B7. The performance of the obligations in such Sub Agreement shall be the responsibility of Seller's legal counsel. This contract shall not be binding*

on Purchaser until such time as such counsel's signature
shall have been electronically affixed to Schedule B7.

She read it again. The Gerais Chevas lawyer was becoming a party to
the Agreement. Romez Nuevo was requiring the Gerais Chevas *lawyer*
to *himself* or *herself* agree to perform certain obligations, in Schedule B7,
as a prerequisite to completing the deal. *What?!!* Evie was incredulous.
This could be a legal land mine. A gas leak waiting for a lit match. Potential career suicide for a lawyer, not to mention the monumental personal
liability to which the lawyer would be subjecting himself. *Why* would a
lawyer ever agree to become a *party* to the transaction?

She dialed Jenna. "Hey Jen, I couldn't wait until tomorrow. Can you
talk for a minute now?"

"Yes, of course. Want to come to my office?" Jenna recognized tension in Evie's voice.

"I have to leave for the airport in a minute, but let me just ask you
something over the phone. In a sale of a business unit, how common is
it for a contract to include the seller's legal counsel completing some set
of tasks?"

"What kind of tasks?"

"I don't know, but can you imagine any circumstance that would warrant an attorney becoming a party to the transaction? You know, assume
responsibility for any of the binding obligations of the core deal?"

"Well, sometimes a lawyer can be contractually obligated to facilitate
the deal, like being in charge of holding documents or escrowed funds.
Or to offer a formal legal opinion or act as the official communicator
between the parties, but I've never heard of a lawyer taking on a primary
part of the core deal. You'd have to know the context."

"It has something to do with a lawyer agreeing to perform some set
of obligations in the future to secure some project. The seller is warrant-
ing as a condition of closing that his lawyer will do this."

"That's pretty vague. I guess if the buyer's due diligence uncovers
something—"

"Due diligence is pretty open-ended usually, isn't it?"

"Well, I don't know if you'd call it open-ended. The buyer is entitled to a cursory investigation of the business records—whatever is mutually agreed—to try to minimize the great unknown for the buyer. But even a fairly thorough due diligence leaves big voids. Things like historical facts and market interdependencies don't necessarily shake out from looking at a bunch of archives. That's where the reps and warranties come in. To add some certainty for the buyer about the quality of what he's buying."

"In this case, the seller is promising to secure some sort of project that's apparently described in a schedule. The lawyer has to sign up to the obligations in a sub-agreement and delivery of that signed document proves that the seller has secured this project."

"Sounds like the obligation to secure this project, whatever it is, is being delegated to the lawyer."

"That's what it sounded like to me, too. Can you imagine any type of project being secured by a lawyer?"

"Well, that's still pretty vague. I guess it could mean that the lawyer is agreeing to serve one of those functions I mentioned, 'securing' the transaction, or it could mean that the lawyer is acquiring a project of some kind. Hey, does this have anything to do with that Brazilian transaction you think Alan's pinning on you?"

"Yes, but discretion, okay?"

"Absolutely. Anyway, getting back to your original question, it's definitely risky for a lawyer to agree to any significant obligations as part of a deal."

"And, we're not stating the obvious."

"Yeah. At worst, a lawyer agreeing to perform some unknown set of actions . . . the actions could be illegal. So, you think Alan is setting you up to be this lawyer?"

"I think it's entirely possible. The lawyer's obligations and, I assume, the description of this project are in some hidden schedule."

"Can you get your hands on that schedule?"

"It's on the system, but accessible by a select group and it's password protected."

Just then, Evie flashed on something she had overheard Alan say while on the conference room telephone. He'd said something about a "schedule" and showing "the deal take shape." It was starting to appear that the evolution of this elusive schedule was intended to be the final nail in her coffin.

"Damn, there's complex security on this deal. I think you're right—there's definitely something suspicious here. Even the most *confidential* matter I've worked on for the most *paranoid* client was more loosely handled than this."

"I was thinking. How could Alan even pull off something like this? Putting me in the driver's seat and binding me to perform some role in a deal I would be completely ignorant about."

"He could always claim your denials were lies. All he would have to do, really, is put your name on record as the responsible attorney for the matter, destroy all evidence to the contrary, paste your name all over the paperwork and get the crooked client to cooperate. He could even pull some electronic shenanigans with dated documents for credibility. Sounds like he's already started *that*. Hell, he could even go so far as to plant some incriminating paperwork in your office."

Evie glanced around her office thinking how vulnerable she was while traveling, and said, "But why would a client agree to something like that?"

"Who knows?"

"And what about the fact that I'm not a partner? Why would I have been trusted to handle such a large transaction alone? Do they ever truly trust an associate with a deal over a hundred million?"

"Well, you *are* one of the senior associates and aside from what propaganda Alan may throw around, I think the partnership considers you to be among the best. In fact, if you let me eighty-six Alan, you may make partner before me."

Evie stuffed her laptop in its carrying case while she listened.

"Anyway," Jenna continued. "I know they typically assign a really difficult or stamina-inducing assignment to an associate as a kind of test before they seriously consider them for partnership. They could certainly demonstrate that such a practice would've supported assigning this matter to you. I'm not sure anyone would believe that the partnership had no knowledge at *all* of the deal, but they could screen out any controversial part, claim ignorance and pin it on you."

"Thanks for the comforting theory. You know, if I'm right about this and Alan follows through with this plan, I'll be forced to deny involvement in something I had no part in and no knowledge of. And whatever it is, it's apparently *not* something one would put on a resume. Forget partnership. And if it turns into anything media-worthy, I'm dead. Not to mention the damage to the firm. You know the impact it could have even though the story wouldn't be true. I would never be able to clear my name. My career would be over."

"Okay, *hey*, why don't you just go to the source? Call up these people in Brazil and ask them direct questions about this transaction?"

"I had Helen call a few of them who claim to have spoken to me on a number of occasions. What can I say to these people to get them to betray Alan?" Evie continued after a beat, "And anyway, the information I need, the specifics of this attorney obligation and whether there's any illegal aspect to it, won't be easy to extract in a telephone conversation. Even if my name has been circulated as the attorney taking the lead in contract drafting or negotiation, I don't know who knows I'm not really involved and who doesn't. In fact, the people within the company who *have* been involved will wonder why I don't already know the terms of the deal if they are *not* in on the set-up, and will continue to conspire to keep me in the dark if they *are*."

"Good point."

"Listen Jen, I've got to go catch my plane. Thanks so much for your advice."

"I still say you should confront him."

"I'll consider it. Bye, Jen."

"Have a good trip."

Evie grabbed her things and sprinted for the elevator. During the ride to the airport, she tried to imagine how the language she'd discovered could have an innocent, deal-enhancing purpose. There was still the possibility that this was a straightforward arrangement, but the heavy security on these files suggested otherwise. If the intent was for the lawyer to *obtain* a project instead of guaranteeing that the transaction would run smoothly, then it would be crucial to know what type of project was targeted. Schedule B7 should provide some answers and it was most likely included in one of the remaining files. *How could she get those passwords?*

E vie, how was Florida?" Joe asked. His was the first call she was returning after arriving home from the airport Friday evening and checking her messages.

She had read and re-read the two Gerais Chevas files she had downloaded to her laptop's hard drive before leaving for Florida and had not found anything else as troubling as the reference to the mysterious contents of Schedule B7. It still seemed likely that Schedule B7 was housed in one of the two password-protected files—the files that were named generically "Neon Three" and "Neon Four." At odd opportunities during the Florida negotiation, she had logged onto the firm's network to feed various passwords into the interface for the two elusive files, but all her attempts had so far been unsuccessful.

She settled into a comfortable position on her bed. She was determined to hide her growing anxiety.

"It was strange," she began. "We were taken to one of the houses of this technology multimillionaire who'd been trying to negotiate a joint venture with our client. We discussed the terms of the proposed transaction over a three-course lunch with his trophy wife, dressed in Dolce and Gabbana, who flirted with everyone but me," Evie laughed and continued. "We sat in this enormous opulent dining room overlooking the ocean surrounded by nude photographs of his wife. Cigar smoke everywhere. It was one of the oddest negotiations I can ever remember. He *did* provide a furnished office on his estate where we drafted the agreement, but he probably had the room bugged. The deal was basically completed in one week."

"Sounds like a man who knows how to use psychological cues," Joe laughed. "I guess he didn't count on having to negotiate with a female."

"No, he definitely did not. And I don't think he enjoyed it much, either."

"That's my girl."

"Joe, mmm, I hope you don't mind me asking, but I was wondering if you could help me with something."

"Sure, anything."

"There are two files related to a client that I've got on disk that I can't access because they're password-protected. There has been some mix-up, and I haven't been given the password. Do you happen to know if there is any way I can get them open?"

"What do you see on the screen when you try to open them?"

"It asks for a *Private Password.*"

"Well, it's possible the files are encrypted using some sort of asymmetric encryption protocol."

"What's that? Consider me technology-challenged."

"Sorry. The prompt may be asking for part of a pair. Okay, let me explain . . . A file can be encrypted using a public key, or *password*, which is made public so many people can use it to encrypt multiple files. Only people with the private key can decrypt the files."

"So files could be created by different people, encrypted with the same public key that is generally available, and be accessible only by a select few who have the private key."

"That's right. You said there were two files, right? My people some-times send me confidential files in pairs. The use of one password opens the first file which contains the password to access the second file."

"Oh. Hmmm."

"It allows that second file's password to be randomly changed and provided only to people who have access to the first file. You can't con-tact the client and get that Private Key?"

"Well, because of exigent circumstances, I can't wait for an exchange with the client."

"And you checked your email for any other messages that might include a password?"

"Hmmm. Okay. I'll do that. But, if I don't have it and I can't get it in time, is there any software program that I could use to discover the password? I've heard of these programs that hackers use that try every possible combination and break the code?"

"There are any number of what they call brute-force algorithms out there that claim to be able to try billions of passwords per minute, but their speed depends on the number of key bits, which is the number of digits in the key. I could probably come up with a program for you, but they do require a substantial amount of RAM—*memory*—to run."

"Oh. I guess just getting the password from the client would be faster."

"Well, let me know if I can help further."

"Thanks, Joe. Hey, were you in New York this week while I was gone?"

"Yes. Turned out my business concluded quickly this time, so I took Bradley, my nephew, to the Big Apple Circus. A Connecticut preview performance."

"Now that sounds like fun. Much more fun than living out of a suit-case," she said sighing.

"Tired of traveling so much?"

"I had this friend who was living off her trust fund, and she trav-eled constantly—and to more exotic places than I usually go. Anyway, I asked her why she traveled so much and she said she was trying to find herself," she paused. "I always thought that was so odd because the more time I spend traveling, the more I feel like I'm *losing* myself."

"Hmmm."

"But, maybe that's because my travel is always a business necessity and rarely offers any opportunity to just *absorb* a place."

"How would you feel about spending a few days in California with me?"

"Well, I don't know. I'm not sure that it's such a good time for me to be taking off."

"I doubt you ever give yourself enough time off," he said.

"Well, you're taking me to a charity ball next weekend, aren't you?"

"Yes, but I'm talking about sunshine and relaxation. After the ball, I might just kidnap you and take you back to California on Sunday."

"And I might let you, but let me think about it."

"Okay. Get some sleep."

"Take care, Joe."

They hung up.

A separate email that might contain the private password. That's what she needed to look for. Alan was the only person she felt certain was privy to the deal and its files. How could she manage to get into Alan's electronic mailbox? *Did she really want to take that drastic of a step?*

She looked at the clock, 8:30 P.M. She hadn't even unpacked her luggage yet. She was exhausted after sleeping only sporadically while in Florida. A trip to the office tonight had definitely not been the plan. She shrugged, Friday night after eight o'clock P.M. is probably the best time for a surreptitious visit to Alan's office. After washing her face, she changed clothes and grabbed a light jacket. She carried her leather briefcase full of the files she'd brought back from Florida. If anyone thwarted her intended agenda she would simply pretend to have returned to the office to finish up some work. She knew it was unlikely that she could successfully infiltrate Alan's email, but she had to try.

The night was balmy and the streets were filled with weekend revelers mostly moving to or from Times Square. Ironically, partly due to the reduced crime rate that New York had enjoyed over the past years, Evie felt very safe weaving her way through the noisy crowds of people on the streets of midtown Manhattan. And Times Square's omnipotent neon billboards and marquee lights transformed the dark evening into a visual landscape. *The great anonymous bodyguard.*

When she reached her office building, she looked around. She didn't know why she did that—just an instinct. Maybe since she was herself engaged in a clandestine operation, she was a bit jumpy. She smiled to herself. After nodding to the night security guard, she reached the fourteenth floor and walked to the wooden door bearing the large brass letters spelling out *Howard, Rolland & Stewart.* She punched the entrance code into the door's keypad and entered. She didn't hear the hum of the elevator as it was summoned back down to the lobby.

The floor was quiet except for two illuminated offices in the litigation department on the west side of the building. The only audible noise was the distant street sounds floating up from the concrete valleys between the buildings. Alan's office was on the southeast corner of the building with a view of the Winter Garden Theatre. She approached cautiously from the west side and noted that his office door was closed and darkness was perceptible beneath the door. Most partner offices had locking doors, but most rarely employed them, relying on the secured entrances to provide protection. Alan's door opened quietly and she slid inside.

Instead of illuminating the entire room with the ceiling light, she limited herself to the light provided by a small desk lamp. She sat in his chair and faced his computer. Fortunately, it was a desktop instead of a mobile laptop so it was available for inspection. Partners rarely found it necessary to carry a computer home the way associates did.

From inside his office, she could hear no sound except her own breathing and the airy whir of the computer boot-up procedure. The air around his desk still held the aroma of his cigar smoke. She wondered why the partnership let him get away with smoking illegally in the building. The building management was not the best, but it was curious that there'd been no complaints. A cigar butt lay in the gold embossed ashtray on his desk and she waved the palm of her hand over it, within an inch of its surface. She could feel heat still rising from its blackened end. *He must have just left. I hope he's not planning to come back.* Her palms began to sweat as she impatiently waited for the desktop icons to appear on the large flat-screen monitor.

Finally, she clicked on the email icon and waited, hoping she would not be prompted for a password before viewing his email inbox. Suddenly, a password prompt did appear but to her relief it had a series of XXXs already present in the response field, indicating that Alan had relied on his computer to "remember" his password. She hit "Enter" and Alan's inbox appeared, filling the screen with a list of thirty-three emails, most of which were received during the day on Friday. Only five or so were still unread so they must have been received in the period of time after he had left the office. She hurriedly studied the list, looking for any email announcement that might be related to Project Neon or Gerais Chevas. *Nothing.* She scrolled down through emails dated in arrears, but nothing looked relevant. Did she dare take the time to open some of these and read?

Suddenly, she heard a noise outside his office door. She froze for a moment and then on impulse reached over and turned off the desk lamp. She sat motionless in his leather office chair in the dark office and listened. She took slow measured breaths. The only light now came from the computer screen—she reminded herself that partners often left their computers on when they left the office so the blue-grayish glow shouldn't invite suspicion. She waited for several minutes until she was sure that all was quiet. She continued her search aided only by the incandescent light of the computer screen. The desk lamp's illumination would be too risky.

As she continued to read through the list of message titles, it suddenly occurred to her that the password may have *originated* with Alan. So if it had been communicated through email, it would be contained in

a message *from* Alan not *to* him. She clicked on the icon for *Sent* messages and a different list of message titles appeared. She scrolled down
a full screen before she saw it. A message drafted by Alan dated August
10th and entitled "Inner Circle."

She clicked on the message and a text window appeared on the screen.
There was only one string of characters in the file: "Z7Yb49BN." It looked
like it might be a password. It reminded her of the type of password that
was assigned by a system administrator at the initiation of a login. She
copied the characters on a piece of paper from her bag. She didn't want
to risk trying to access the file from Alan's computer so she slipped the
paper in her pocket and scanned the message titles again in Alan's outgoing mailbox. Another message sent by Alan in August caught her eye.

It was entitled "Fruition." She clicked on it, and it contained what
looked like a message drafted by Alan sent in response to a message
received by him that was attached at the bottom.

Alan's message read:

Will do. Adinaldo—present specifics during Monday TC.

The original message read:

Prepare the Docs. Arrange TC. Closing 9/20.

"TC" must mean "Telephone Conference," Evie guessed. The
exchange seemed to confirm arrangements for a telephone conference
to occur that next Monday with the probable closing for the deal on
September 20th. Not very informative. *Adinaldo . . .*

She had received a message from an Adinaldo *herself.* What she orig-
inally thought had been an errant email to her, now clearly linked to this
exchange of Alan's. She looked at the email address from which the original message had been sent: ARafael@gchqt.br. *The same address from
which she'd received that earlier email.* Presumably "ARafael" referred
to Adinaldo's username, so his full name must be Adinaldo Rafael. "GC"

must be Gerais Chevas so he was an insider—an employee of the firm's client of some rank.

The press release Evie had read indicated that Gerais Chevas was a Brazilian company, but she didn't know how many satellite offices were in existence. Whoever this Adinaldo Rafael was, it was likely that he was located in the Brazilian office to have a "br" domain address. The big mystery was the reference to "specifics." Evie retrieved the piece of paper from her pocket and made notes. *Did she dare try to print these messages? It would be immensely valuable to have a hard copy with Alan's user name . . .*

And then the unmistakable sound of footsteps caused her to drop her pencil. Luckily, it landed not on the hard desk, but noiselessly on the rug beneath the chair. She leaned down to retrieve it and stayed crouched behind the desk. The footsteps abruptly stopped. She looked up at the computer screen from her crouched position. The "Adinaldo" email message still showed prominently on the screen. She held her breath as the door opened.

She could feel the presence of another person standing at the doorway. The person seemed to be scanning the room deciding whether there was any reason to enter. Evie could smell some sort of aftershave that floated toward her. She knew the desk blocked her from view as long as the person stayed in the doorway. She held her breath again and remained motionless. A few unending moments passed. She couldn't see the doorway from her hiding position and so she waited.

The sound of footsteps again—this time they seemed to be turning in place and in the next second she welcomed the sound of the door closing. She waited until the footsteps proceeded down the hallway and faded into the distance before she moved, collecting her pencil and paper and depositing them in her bag. She clicked closed the open message on the screen and exited out of Alan's email. She shut down his computer and while she was waiting for a blank screen, she took a tissue from Alan's desk and lightly brushed over the keys on his keyboard and everything else in the vicinity that she suspected she had touched.

When she was satisfied that the office was returned to the state in which she'd found it, she stood behind the closed door listening for silence in the hallway. It was completely still now so she quickly opened the door and stepped through. She crept around the west side of the building to her office and noticed to her relief that she had not turned on her office light and that there were no obvious signs that she had been there recently. She grabbed her leather briefcase that she had left behind her door and walked quickly out of the reception area, feeling fairly certain that she had not been seen on the floor by the small number of people in the litigation department who still seemed to be working.

Once outside on the street, she felt enormous relief and almost succumbed to an urge to slip into a bar for a drink. Club Turquoise was not far to walk and her friend, David, had invited her to his performance, but a wave of exhaustion and post-adrenaline emptiness washed over her. She started for home.

As she made her way through the thickening pedestrian traffic, someone bumped into her hard and she fell to the sidewalk. She picked herself up, grabbed her bag and looked around, but couldn't identify the person with whom she'd clashed. She continued moving, but she had the haunting feeling that someone was following her. *You're being paranoid. There are hundreds of people around and they're all oblivious.* She walked on but couldn't shake the feeling of being stalked. She ducked into a Starbucks, turned around and watched out the front window. A man in a dark suit walked by and stopped. He looked toward the Starbucks door, but instead walked in an erratic manner over to one of the transparent front walls of the store and peered in.

Evie had backed away from the entrance and was standing behind a display of coffee accessories. She watched as the man seemed to search the interior of the coffee shop with a determined scowl on his face. This was definitely *not* the man she'd seen the night she went for Chinese food. He stood with his face to the glass for several minutes, studying the patrons of the coffee shop. She hid behind the display and continued to watch. Even though there were thirty or forty people in line, at the counter and seated at the tables, she suddenly felt very alone. *Who is this man? Is he following me? Could this . . . no . . . it couldn't have anything to do with Project Neon, could it? No! Of course not. Now I've really become paranoid.*

She stayed hidden until the man proceeded down Seventh Avenue. The coffee aromas were seductive and her mouth was dry, so, since she was already there, she decided to have a cup. Or perhaps it was fear, not thirst that kept her ensconced in the coffee-consumer crowd. She reached around in her bag, but couldn't locate her wallet. Concluding it was buried in the bottom, she found a twenty dollar bill tucked into an outside pocket and bought a small cappuccino. After a half hour of watching people come and go, she drained the last few drops from her Starbucks cup and grabbed her bag and briefcase. She cautiously walked out onto the street.

She waited for a large group of tourists that were approaching and fell in behind them. She followed them several blocks and then jumped in a taxi and headed for home. When her taxi pulled up in front of her building, she was relieved to see one of the nighttime doormen she recognized; after paying the fare, she rushed inside.

Once inside her apartment, she left the room dark and peered out the living room window facing Central Park West. Nothing but the usual street activity. She moved to the window in her bedroom that captured a partial view of 65th Street. A man in gray pants and a leather jacket seemed to be looking up at her building. She recoiled from the window, but then returned, confident that with the lights off, she could not be seen. The man seemed upset and was talking to himself. Or was he talking into some sort of electronic device? He seemed to adjust something on his ear. It could be just another strange street person, but he was dressed too well. His mouth seemed to form deliberate speech and his movements were controlled and sharp.

Evie's stomach dropped when she saw another man in a dark suit approach the man she was watching—it was the man who had followed her to Starbucks! He was easy to recognize because of his jerky bodily

movements that were in sharp contrast to the other man's. She wondered if she should call the police or the building concierge or maybe
even Joe. *No, that's ridiculous . . . What could Joe possibly do for me from
California?* He was probably not home now anyway. She couldn't be
absolutely sure that these two men were targeting her, but it seemed
extremely coincidental that a man she had noticed acting suspiciously
outside of Starbucks while she was inside, would just happen to appear
in front of her building less than thirty minutes later looking up toward
the residents' windows.

She watched, trying to decide what to do. The two men seemed to
agree on something and they both disappeared down Central Park West
in the direction of Times Square.

Evie retrieved a legal pad from a drawer and began to write, beginning with the overheard conversation over a week ago and ending with
her discoveries of this evening. Not knowing whether all these events
were connected or whether they had any meaning at all, it nevertheless
felt therapeutic to write everything down.

The process of remembering and writing also brought anger and
anxiety. She felt her body heat rise and opened the bedroom window.
This time when she looked out, there was only the usual street traffic.

When she finished, she tore off the pages from the pad and slid
them, along with the clipping from the magazine and the handwritten
note, into a file in her briefcase. On impulse she checked her front door
again to confirm that it was locked and then poured a glass of wine
and headed for the steamy comfort of the shower. She left the glass of
wine on the bathroom counter, dropped her clothing to the floor and
stepped behind the glass door. As she stood in the spray of hot water, she
remembered her discovery upon returning to her apartment last Saturday after grocery shopping. Her door had been unlocked. Had one of
those men been in her apartment? Could they have taken something or
left something?

As she toweled off, the buzzer sounded, indicating that the doorman
was trying to reach her.

"Yes?" she said into the intercom.

"There's a gentleman here who would like to speak to you. Says his name is Benjamin Myers."

"Who? I have no idea who that is. Did he say why he wants to see me?"

"No, just that it's important."

chapter

14

P lease ask him what he wants."

   She stood in her towel, listening to empty air and waiting for her doorman to do his job. After a few seconds, he said, "He has your wallet. Says he found it outside the building on the street corner."

Oh my God! No wonder I couldn't find it! Did I somehow manage to drop it?

   "Can you just . . . won't he just give it to you? I can't come to the door right now."

   "Okay, I've got it. He said he saw your identification badge, liked your picture and decided he wanted to meet you."

   "Well, please thank him for returning my wallet and . . ." *Should I have him check the contents?* If this man Myers had stolen anything, he wasn't going to admit to it and anything that was missing might have been taken before he found the wallet, so she abandoned the thought.

   "Now he's asking for a reward," said the doorman. "Since you won't meet him, he wants money."

"What happened to old-fashioned decency? No, there's no reward. Oh, okay, pull out a ten for him and send him away."

"Yes, maam. And I'll send your wallet right up with the porter."

"Thank you very much," she said. Although she recognized him, this was not a doorman she knew very well and she wasn't that impressed with his inquiry skills.

I've never in my life dropped my wallet out of my bag. How could I have ... and he said this Myers person found it outside THIS building, but I didn't have it when I was in Starbucks. She found her leather bag and examined it. No holes or openings. *Wait!* It suddenly occurred to her that when that person bumped into her on the sidewalk, someone could've stolen her wallet from her bag before she noticed. If that was a setup and that person was somehow connected to the men she saw on the street corner, its contents may have lead them to her building. It could've been one of the two men who dropped it on the corner. Should she call the police? What would she say? She didn't know anything for sure and she had her wallet back. *And,* she didn't want to make false accusations, but the whole situation was dubious.

She dressed quickly and answered the door, after confirming that it was the porter. He handed her the wallet through the crack above the chain and she tipped him. A hurried glance through the folds convinced her that the contents were intact and she returned it to her bag.

Now that her adrenaline was pumping again, her next objective was to log on to the firm's network and plug the character string she found in Alan's email into the password field of the third and fourth Project Neon files. If that string of characters was a valid password for one or both of those files, it might not be valid for too long.

She connected her laptop modem to the telephone jack in the kitchen and booted, but some problem with the telephone line prevented the modem from connecting. The firm's reluctance to go wireless sometimes plagued its associates. After a few failed attempts to connect, she left the computer and lights on in the kitchen and collapsed into bed.

The telephone rang, interrupting her descent into sleep, but when she picked up the receiver there was nothing but a dial tone. Finally, sometime after two o'clock A.M., sleep came.

When she sat up in bed Saturday morning, the memories from the night before rushed over her. She thought about the two men and walked to the window from which she had watched them. The street was starting to fill with parents and children and errand boys and delivery people. No one was pausing in the street. No one was looking up at her building.

After a quick breakfast and a flurry of unpacking, she settled down at her kitchen table with her laptop and rebooted the modem. While it was attempting to connect, she changed into a pair of old blue jeans and a snowy-white sleeveless t-shirt. When she returned to the kitchen, she saw the same error message that indicated that there was still a telephone line problem. She would go to the office. A knock on the door made her jump. She walked over to the door and asked, "Who's there?"

"It's Ralph, Love," came the answer.

"Oh, Ralph. Just a minute." She unlatched the lock and opened the door. When she saw him, she rushed toward him and threw her arms around his neck. He hugged her back and then gently dissolved the embrace with a concerned look on his face.

"Is something wrong? Are you okay?"

"Yes. I'm fine. I'm just glad to see you."

Ralph didn't look convinced, but he dropped his inquiry. "You look great," he said. "I hope that means you tallied some extra sleep."

"Yes. I did. Quantity if not quality. Everything okay in London?"

"Brilliant. Family crisis averted."

She admired Ralph. He was freshly scrubbed and his hair was gelled back, as was his preference. He wore a pale green linen shirt and a pair of brown crepe slacks, alligator belt and brown loafers.

"Want to go shopping?"

"I can't today, Ralph. I'm working."

"Okay, but you bloody well have to eat. Let's have lunch in that little Italian café we like on Madison. What is it?"

"Bartolli's."

"Yes!"

"Okay. I owe you a celebration anyway. But give me time to change clothes."

"You look lovely."

"Oh no, Ralph. I can't go out with you, dressed in these old jeans. You look too good. It'll just take me a minute."

"Okay, Love," Ralph selected a *New Yorker* magazine from a stack beside Evie's sofa and assumed a lounging position.

She stopped by the kitchen to try the modem connection once more. After a few seconds, the familiar message glowed on the screen. *I'll go to the office after lunch.* She shut down her computer, packed it in its carrying bag and slipped into the bedroom to get dressed.

Five minutes later, Evie appeared in the doorway in a pair of cotton tan slacks, a form-fitting navy jacket-style Ralph Lauren shirt and a pair of Bruno Magli sandals. She was supplementing the remaining cash in her wallet when the telephone rang. After picking up the receiver, she said "hello" several times, but was met with silence, then a series of clicks.

"Prank call?"

"Or wrong number." She hung up. "Similar thing happened last night," she said almost to herself, but shrugged it off.

The sun was high in the sky when they sat down at an outside table at Bartolli's and ordered chilled Caravella Limoncello Originale D'Italia, a citrusy liqueur. Evie ordered the asparagus ravioli special and Ralph ordered a penne with vodka sauce. Through her sunglasses, Evie watched the passersby over Ralph's shoulder as they talked. She had been conditioned by recent events to be watchful, although the only people she knew to watch out for were the Starbucks Man and his partner.

"You should consider meeting Nathan," Ralph was saying. "He asked about you again. Ya'know he *is* an Assistant U.S. Attorney and quite attractive."

"I can't see myself on a blind date."

"No, sweetheart, not *blind* . . . you met him last April. Remember that day we all met for drinks in SoHo?"

"Ummhmmm."

"Nathan was *there*, remember?"

"Yes, I do."

"Well, any interest?"

"I don't know, Ralph. Maybe. Hey, did you hear any more about that bribery investigation?"

He looked puzzled.

"You know," she looked around and whispered, "Senator Arbeson."

"Ahhh. Rumor is he eighty-sixed the evidence."

"What?"

Got rid of it somehow. They dropped the charges due to lack of evidence."

"I thought you said they caught him red-handed?"

"Well, the blighter has lots of mates. One of those buggers apparently helped him make the evidence *or witness* disappear."

Evie lost herself in her thoughts momentarily.

"You've got to occupy your mind with something besides work. We've got to get you out," said Ralph.

"I went out with a man I met on a plane recently."

"Oh brilliant! You didn't tell me. Who *is* he?"

"He's a technology executive for a French company—"

"Bloody Hell! Not another Frenchman! Didn't you get that French thing out of your system with Julien?"

"No, he's American. From San Francisco. Works out of the company's Los Angeles office."

"Are you going to see him again?"

"We've only been out once and I think it . . . I don't see it going much further."

"Why? I can see it in your eyes. You really fancy this bugger."

Evie blinked and continued, "He lives over twenty-five hundred miles from me. How could it possibly work?"

Ralph stared at her, frowning and shaking his head. "Give it a chance. Maybe there's a reason to have a go. Even long-distance. At least long enough to see if the relationship has legs."

"You know, I've done that long distance thing once already. It doesn't work."

"Across the Atlantic versus across the states."

"He *is* very appealing, but I don't know."

"You're just afraid of being hurt again."

"Absolutely right."

"Swallow that fear. C'mon. Straightaway, with your next bite of ravioli. As Elbert Hubbard said, the greatest mistake you can make in life is to be continually fearing you will make one."

"Who's Elbert Hubbard?"

"I have no idea, but he was a smart bugger. Don't you think, Love?"

"There's something to that, I have to admit," she smiled. "I *have* accepted a second date. We're going to a charity ball this Saturday."

"Brilliant! Wear red. It will make him crazy."

Evie smiled and gestured at the waitress for the check.

She arrived at her office, laptop in tow at around three o'clock P.M. After powering up, she typed the string of characters, from memory now, in response to the PRIVATE PASSWORD prompt for access to "Neon Three." To her chagrin, she received the message INCORRECT PASSWORD and the prompt re-appeared. She checked the case and content of the password. Then she repeated her attempt with "Neon Four." INCORRECT PASSWORD. *Was this ever the correct password to either of these files? If it was, who changed it and why?*

Evie abandoned sleep that night trying to fit the pieces of Project Neon into a neat package for presentation to Paul Wayford Monday morning. She spent hours thinking and scribbling, punctuated by late night wanderings for chamomile tea. The city was eerily quiet.

On Monday morning in her office, she was dialing Paul's extension before she had even taken a seat at her desk. She didn't leave a voice mail. After flipping through other client matters and answering some email, she noticed some standard traffic starting to flow on her floor so she grabbed her printout of the reps and warranties section of the Gerais Chevas agreement and headed upstairs to Paul's office. When she arrived at his secretary's desk, Barbara told her that Paul was on a conference call, but guessed that they would probably be taking a break soon. Evie decided to wait.

Barbara turned her attention back to her typing, and Evie sat in a chair adjacent to Paul's office door. She flipped through her scribbles from the weekend. Assuming the transaction described in the press release was the one under the firm's current stewardship, somebody within the firm was working on the $179 million sale of the statistical software division of a client called Gerais Chevas to another South American company called Romez Nuevo. The *"reps and warranties"* in the Purchase Agreement recruited a specific but unknown lawyer into a highly unusual performing role in the transaction that was crucial to the closing of the deal.

There was some aspect of the deal, most likely within the realm of that chosen lawyer's tasks, that was at least controversial, but potentially unethical or worse: *to promise to secure some type of project.* She could show Paul the contract language and suggest to him that the wording made the project suspect—what it was and whether the lawyer was to *obtain* it in some clandestine manner. The fact that these documents were under such restricted access didn't point toward an innocuous sort of law-yerly role. She could tell him that the files containing the documents for the deal were under restricted access on the system and two of them were protected by a second layer of security—password access only.

But, would that work to her advantage? These suspicions sounded speculative. Would this seem to Paul as if she was trying to invent some-thing controversial to divert attention from her own troubles arising from the Sangerson mess?

It seemed easy enough, given the power of Paul's position, for him to obtain the contents of the elusive Schedule B7. Viewing that document should provide some answers. Perhaps she could just raise questions to motivate Paul to investigate. She could point to the mysterious email from "Adinaldo" and relay her puzzlement over the documents. But how could she explain why she suspected that the unnamed lawyer's identity was hers? The overheard portions of Alan's conversation could not be proven or substantiated. The history of dialed telephone numbers on the conference room telephone had long since been replaced with more recent calls. Even the connection to Alan could not be definitely proven. The suspected closing date for the deal, September 20th, was pure conjecture and had come from surreptitious sleuthing in Alan's office. And if it was all a mistake, if Schedule B7 turned out to be benign, what would Paul think of her then?

She thought about her conversation with Jenna. *THE BROTHER-HOOD.* There was no way she could confide in Paul completely, especially given that he was still investigating the Sangerson matter. Her credibility was already on shaky ground and would likely remain under scrutiny.

Without solid evidence illuminating Alan's schemes she had little ammunition with which to fight. She had already implied that Alan set her up on Sangerson. *How would Paul react to accumulated accusations that Alan was setting her up? How would she explain her snooping around in files on a deal she claimed to have no part in?*

Suddenly the door to Paul's office opened and he walked out rapidly toward his secretary's cubicle. He hadn't yet noticed Evie. He seemed intent on communicating something.

"Barb, can you give a quick call to Alan and let him know that I won't be able to have lunch with him today? See if he can meet for a drink at my club at six thirty." He shuffled through a few items that were stacked in a tray on the wall of Barbara's cubicle. He turned and noticed Evie as she appeared to be about to walk off.

Lunch with Alan?! He was going to have lunch with Alan? In the eight years she had been with the firm, she had never known them to have lunch alone together. *Who initiated that?* Could this be Paul's planned opportunity to ask Alan further questions about Sangerson? Could she risk saying something to Paul that he might discuss with Alan? *Alan would then know I'm on the case.*

"Evie, did you need to see me?"

"Hmmm . . . Paul, I can see that this isn't a good time. I'll speak to you later. It's not urgent."

"Well," Paul looked at his watch. "I can take a couple of minutes. What's on your mind?"

"Ummm. Did you find out what happened with that Sangerson contract mix-up?"

Paul scratched his chin and turned to face her. "Alan was quite surprised that it went out to the client in that unfinished form, but suggested that maybe there had been a miscommunication. He defended you and took responsibility for the mishap."

"What does that mean? How did it go out from my email address?" *Easy to offer a meaningless defense.*

"He had no explanation as to how that happened, but he said he may not have made instructions clear. In any event, I smoothed things over with the client and I consider the matter closed."

"Well, that means he thinks I sent it out like that by mistake. Paul, I'm still concerned that my reputation has been—"

"Evie, don't worry about it. The client holds no ill will."

"Yes, I'm happy about that, but I want the partnership to know that I didn't—"

Paul looked at his watch. "I'm leaving tomorrow morning, but I'll be back sometime next week. Can we talk then?"

"Yes. Sure. That would be fine."

"Really," he said reading the concern in her face. "Don't worry."

She thought for a moment. Paul was going to be out until next week and she wouldn't be able to pursue these matters with Hanover until he recovered from his illness. Should she take advantage of the situation and spend a few days with Joe in California?

"Actually, Paul," she said, "I was thinking of taking a couple of days off early next week, but I'll be back in the office by Wednesday morning at the latest."

"Excellent. I know you've been working very hard. By the way, how did that negotiation go in Florida?"

"It was unusual, but I think Martini Investments was happy. The deal closed."

"Good for you. Thanks for stepping in. I know Jack will be pleased."

"Thanks, Paul. Talk to you next week." She offered a guarded smile and walked past him in the direction of her office. Steve Buniker's accusations in the Sangerson matter seemed to follow like the smell of an approaching fire. *Don't worry. Yeah, right.*

Well, telling Paul she was going to take a couple of days off seemed to insure that she would actually allow herself to do it. Maybe distance would provide a fresh perspective. Why not let Joe take her to California for a couple of days? Even if he turned out to be a passing presence in her life, at least he represented a respite from the entanglements of the firm. And, there might be some way to enlist his help with the technological barriers she faced. Her presence in the city would not exactly stop Alan's plan from progressing.

She perused her email and composed a message that she would be out of the office from Saturday through Wednesday, sending it to all the clients on whose matters she was currently working, to give them almost a week's notice. She sorted through the mail on her desk. The stack contained mostly State Bar notices of continuing legal education programs.

A voice message informed her that Joe would not be arriving in New York until Saturday for the charity ball, but would come by her apartment to pick her up at seven o'clock that evening.

∽

Elsewhere in the offices of Howard, Rolland & Stewart a cigar glowed in an ashtray. The telephone next to it buzzed and a secretary was told to put the call through.

"Alan Levenger."

"Alan, Dave Shilling, *Spellbound!* Magazine."

"What's the good word?"

"We're running a story on the model, Vi, and your name was given as her counsel."

"Yes, I represent a number of models."

"Are you also her significant other?"

"Absolutely not. I don't date my clients."

"No, just grope their wives."

"If you're referring to that photo you guys ran a while back, that was just a bit of harmless fun among friends. C'mon, man, her husband was right there."

"I remember the photo."

"What've you got?"

"I have a source who said that you have a lot of knowledge about Vi's—shall we say—'preferences.'"

"Well, I could say that about a lot of my clients. It doesn't necessarily mean what you're implying."

"And what am I implying?"

"I'll leave that to your readers to figure out."

"Is it true that you had a fight with her in a restaurant and ripped her blouse off?"

Alan chuckled.

"On the night of July 17th at Bacci. You were seen with a group of people—"

"No comment."

"We're running the story."

"I thought you said you had '*a*' source . . . as in ONE. Are you sure it's a credible one?"

"There were many people there that night. You didn't leave a good tip. People talk."

"Well, before you print anything, you'd better be damn sure you got good info. I'd love to put you guys out of business. Clean up the journalism in this city. I'll file a lawsuit before the ink's dry on your morning edition."

"So, your official response is 'no comment?'"

"No comment."

"Thank you, Mr. Levenger."

"Where the sun don't shine, asshole."

"Now, is that any way to talk to a reporter who's responsible for generating business for you?"

"I don't think you want to go there, but hey, you know what? I gotta lead for you. I know the identity of a woman who is having an affair with Senator Arbeson."

chapter
15

Moments after the doorman called to announce her visitor, Joe stood in Evie's apartment doorway in a custom-made tuxedo holding a sweating bottle of champagne, a lock of his wavy hair disobediently falling down over one eyebrow as if announcing he had been rushed in his efforts to arrive on time.

"Sorry I haven't called. I flew in this afternoon. Later than I planned." He nodded toward the bottle. "This is nicely chilled courtesy of Amelio on Ice," he said, dimples in full view. "I thought we'd have a private drink if you like."

"Joe, that's so . . . that's perfect. Please come in." She gestured toward the interior of her apartment.

Joe took a look around. Turkish area rugs covered much of the hardwood floors and an odd array of small oil paintings adorned the walls. There was a gold paisley sofa in the style of Queen Anne and an old tattered royal-blue velvet chair that was Victorian. A mahogany coffee table sat in front of the sofa.

"Nice place," said Joe walking toward the window. "Nice view."

"I could never afford such a view except for the largess of a very nice landlord," she said.

Joe handed the bottle to her and she disappeared behind the kitchen's swinging door.

She heard the door rotate open and twisted around to smile at Joe.

"I only have these old estate-sale flutes," she held up the mismatched Waterford knock-offs.

Joe stood in the opening, arms outstretched and hands grasping the casing on each side. After a moment, his eyes rested on Evie's back.

"Did I mention that you look absolutely amazing?"

Evie was wearing a fitted black crepe gown with a v-neck and draped back with only a pair of pearl earrings.

"Thank you." Evie looked briefly over her shoulder at him, smiled and pulled back the wire covering the mouth of the bottle. She started trying to pry the cork out, but felt Joe come up close behind her. He gently took the bottle out of her hands, took a step away from her and dislodged the cork, freeing a short spray of fizz in the direction of the sink. He poured the champagne and handed a glass to Evie.

"Shall we sit down in the other room?" she said accepting the glass.

"Yes," he said as he followed her into the living room, taking a seat next to her on the sofa. They toasted and sipped. "Interesting collection of furniture and art."

"A friend of mine calls my decorating style reminiscent of a renegade museum that's lost its funding."

"You seem to have a definite preference for things of the past." Joe stood and walked around the room sipping champagne. "Ever notice the artistry in common objects . . . like this?" he asked, picking up a tiny Dutch-style stone-carved windmill positioned on Evie's bookshelf. "I was looking at the design for a patent the other day and I was thinking. At what point does design produce art instead of just a utilitarian object? I mean . . . like those classic automobiles—Duesenbergs, Packards, Auburns . . ."

"Or even petroglyphs—communications between early Native Americans. One historian whose article I read insisted it was not politically correct to characterize them as art. As if calling a method of communication *creative* would somehow be . . . a bad thing."

Joe returned to sit beside Evie on the sofa. "I think you can find art in the most unlikely places," he said. "We tend to be too busy to notice."

"I really want to apologize for my abruptness the other night," she said suddenly.

"Not neces—"

"I want to explain. You were *right*. I do have a wariness where men are concerned. I'm sure I've turned people off with my uhh . . . whatever you want to call it . . . my *remote* attitude."

"Mmmm. I can imagine that such an attitude comes in handy at times," he said, taking a sip from his glass. She watched as he tipped the glass a bit too far. Champagne droplets glistened on his lapel.

"You've spilled a bit of champagne on your jacket," she said leaning toward him and dabbing at the moisture with a napkin. She smiled. "You may have spoiled your grand entrance."

"What's my punishment?"

"You don't want to know," she said and stood to open a window.

He glanced down at the lapel. "It took me years to actually tolerate wearing a tux," he said as he leaned against the back of the sofa.

"I'm the same way," she said from her position by the window. "Much more comfortable in jeans. Heels make me terribly clumsy." She was looking down at her ankle strap.

He rose from the sofa and stood next to her, turning toward the window.

"So where did you read about petroglyphs?" he asked.

"In a magazine at the doctor's office. I think it was *American Southwest* or something like that."

"Enlightened doctor."

"He's got a great collection of magazines," she said. "That's actually a terrible sign—means you can count on a long wait before he sees you."

He studied her. "So, Evie, have you considered my proposition?

"Spending a few days in California? Mmmm. Well, if I go, do I need to make a hotel reservation?"

"No. I've got three bedrooms in my house."

"Other than yours?"

"Including mine."

"And these extra bedrooms have single beds?"

"No, they have queen size beds, but you can select the one with a lock on the door if you like." He grinned.

"When would we leave?" She suppressed a smile.

"If you're not too tired, we could take a late flight tonight. Or if you prefer, we can fly out tomorrow."

"I have to be back in the office by Wednesday morning, so I would need to take a Tuesday return flight."

"Done."

The black car stopped in front of the Lexington Avenue entrance to the Waldorf Astoria. They walked together, Joe holding Evie's hand around his escorting arm. They walked up the stairs from Lexington Avenue to a branch of the lobby. Elegant stores lined the hallways . . . Cellini, Elliot Stevens Ltd., St. John, and ball gowns and tuxedos were abundant.

They walked around to the left and entered the elevator. On the third floor, they exited and followed the tuxedo trail toward the four-story Grand Ballroom, with its dramatic crystal chandeliers and spacious interior. There were elegant four-foot posters just inside the entrance, depicting the faces of women and children who had benefited from the efforts of Women and Children First. A silky looking banner swayed above the hostess desk announcing the Lollipop Lace Ball. A trio of designer-dressed women stood behind the wide desk accepting invitations and offering greetings.

Joe and Evie exchanged their invitation for a white linen envelope tied with lace ribbon. They nodded at the hostesses and joined the waves of people sliding toward the interior of the ballroom. The cacophony of voices in the ballroom resounded like an insect chorus on a summer evening. There were ice sculptures lining one wall and waiters weaving through the crowd carrying trays of hors d'oeuvres under their smiles. Joe placed his hand on Evie's lower back and gently held her as they slowly made their way through the clusters. Evie opened the envelope.

"We're at table twelve," she said, gazing out over the seventy-plus tables. The dueling perfume fragrances in the room served as a fitting backdrop to the ornament-laden table layouts. Each table was lavishly decorated with floating orchid flower arrangements illuminated by a wreath of small lavender candles at the base of each sculptured crystal bowl. The water in the bowl was tinted a pale lemon color. At each place setting was an enormous lavender-colored lollipop with lace ribbon matching the ribbon from the envelope.

He's very gallant to tolerate this for his sister. This is definitely not an event designed for male sensibilities. Joe began to guide her toward the table adorned with a yellow flag marked "12" when a beautiful blonde woman glided toward them, reached up and encircled Joe's neck with her arms. She completed her greeting with a peck on his mouth. Then she turned to Evie with a welcoming smile.

"Hello! Evie, it's very nice to meet you," greeted Ariel. "I'm Joe's sister."

Ariel had dressed for attention, it seemed. She had the same intense eyes as her brother, except that hers were a greenish color. Her makeup looked professionally done and the effect was stunning. Her thick, high-lighted blonde hair held perfectly still in a dramatic upsweep do. She was wearing a fire engine red gown with rhinestone straps that moved with a subtle sheen over satiny-looking shoulders. Her ruby and dia-mond earrings radiated the soft lights and her white satin gloves left only inches of arm exposed below the shoulder.

"Evie, is your first name Evelyn?"

"Yes."

"And you have a Central Park West address?"

"Yes."

"I thought so." Ariel turned to Joe. "Evie was sent her *own* invitation. I thought I recognized her name when you told me. She's one of our benefactors and in fact is one of the largest donors from among the category of single women under forty." Ariel turned back and smiled broadly at Evie, resting a gloved hand on her arm.

Joe looked at Evie, a mixture of questions and admiration on his face. "Evie, you amaze me. What other secrets are you keeping?"

"Oh, probably a few more."

Joe smiled and escorted the two women to their table.

"Evie," said Ariel. "Sit next to me. I'll tell you anything you want to know about Joseph." She laughed and kissed Joe on the cheek as she sat down at the table.

"I have *lots* of questions," said Evie as she took a seat next to Ariel.

"Did he tell you about his patent?"

"Yes, he did."

"Well, that's a perfect example of how resourceful he is. He's—"

"Okay, Ari, I'm not running for office," Joe interrupted.

Joe took a seat on the other side of Evie and sat back in the chair, obviously mindful of the futility of preventing the sisterly ambush. Evie glanced at Joe and returned her gaze to Ariel.

"What was he like as a child?" asked Evie.

"He was a bit *mischievous*. We used to hide in a woodshed in the backyard. We called it 'The Safehouse.'" She looked over at Joe and then back at Evie. "He fought with our dad a lot. Actually, we both did."

"Your father . . . mmm. Why was he so difficult?"

"Well, he had a number of bad habits. None bad enough to prevent him from functioning. He *did* keep a roof over our heads. When he slowed down a bit as he got older, I think Joe finally had some quality time with him on some trips they took together."

"And your mother?"

"She died in childbirth. Mine actually." She nodded at Evie anticipating Evie's thoughts. "I know. Hardly ever happens anymore. Anyway,

Joe and I sort of raised each other." Ariel's expression portrayed no sadness, only pride.

"And now you're raising your son."

"Oh, he told you about Bradley?"

"Yes, Joe is very fond of Bradley."

"Joe delivered him."

"*Really? He did?*"

"Yes."

"So . . . you were . . . unable to make it to the hospital?"

"Yes. My husband was out of the country, as usual. I was due around the middle of January. There was an enormous nor'easter on a Monday."

"How scary to be going into labor during a blizzard." Evie watched Ariel with obvious interest.

"I started having labor pains on that Monday night. Luckily Joe was in New York and he came out to Connecticut when I called. By the time he got there, my contractions were a minute apart and my water broke. He said the snow hadn't been completely cleared off the main roads and it had started snowing again pretty hard, so I called my doctor and told him I wanted to deliver at home. He stayed on the line and talked Joe through it. Joe kept me calm. He was incredible." Ariel beamed at Joe and returned her gaze to Evie.

Evie looked at Joe with approving eyes and smiled. "So . . . Joe, *your* secret life as a midwife. I want to hear more."

Joe laughed. "We were just lucky that Bradley was so cooperative making his entrance. There were no complications." He lifted the wine bottle and poured liquid into Ariel's and Evie's glasses. As he poured, he said in a low volume almost to himself, "I have to say though, it *was* thrilling to be the one to help Bradley take his first breath. *Humbling.*"

"So, Evie," said Ariel, "why are you so generous to my charity?"

"A little French girl I know. She has this rare hemoglobin deficiency called porphyria. If that wasn't bad enough, something happened between her and her uncle. Some kind of inappropriate behavior on his part. I never could prove it, but I know something happened. And I couldn't help her. Supporting this cause is my way of dealing with a situation over which I had no control."

Joe and Ariel looked at each other and nodded at Evie in understanding.

The awards presentation ensued and they were served salads, followed by a somewhat bland poached sea bass. After the presentation concluded, Ariel dutifully walked the room greeting guests, but returned to the table out of discernible fascination with her brother's new girlfriend. The woman on the other side of Joe offered him her asparagus and began to tell him about a trip she had taken recently to Turkey. Joe listened politely, with occasional glances back to confirm that Evie was still conversing with Ariel.

After some period of time, Joe turned away from the woman and watched Evie take a final bite. He leaned over to her and said in her ear, "Dance with me?"

Evie adopted a skeptical look, glanced at the orchestra and the empty dance floor and offered a weak smile. "You sure you want to do this?"

He helped her to her feet and led her out to a far corner of the floor. As they danced, they held each other, with the movement of one imprinting on the body of the other. They didn't stop dancing until the orchestra announced a break, and then they returned to their table, the electricity still surging between them. Joe pulled her chair out for her and then excused himself to find the men's room. Evie took her seat next to Ariel, who was deep in conversation with an Italian gentleman on her left.

After a few minutes had passed, a man approached their table and laid his hand on Evie's shoulder. She abruptly turned, and glanced up at the man's face.

"Hello, Evie. Mike Farraway. Remember me?"

"Oh, yes. How are you? I heard you're no longer with Collburn Regan. Is that true?" Evie said, rising to her feet and turning toward him.

"Yeah. Stan and I couldn't agree on a strategy for my division. We'd been clashing a long time. It was time for me to go. I'm now vice-president of June Banion & Krist Consulting."

Listening to Mike's words, Evie thought that she might have wrongly attributed Mike's firing to Alan. He'd boasted he was going to bring it about, but he might have just been using a situation he knew about in advance to intimidate her. There had been no proof, only her specula-tion. If she'd been mistaken on such a minor matter, might she also be wrong about Alan's other activities? Maybe she should step back and rethink this whole situation.

"Congratulations. I'm glad things worked out for you," she said, shaking his hand.

"I just wanted to say hello," he said, looking over as Joe approached.

"This is Joe Barton," Evie said, taking Joe's hand and smiling. "Joe, this is Mike Farraway, a former client."

"Maybe future client," said Mike. Evie smiled and nodded.

"Good to meet you," said Joe.

"Pleased to meet *you*, Joe." The two men shook hands and Mike left.

Ariel had heard the last of Evie's conversation with Mike and when they were all seated again, she said, "Joe told me you're a lawyer. What firm do you work for, Evie?"

"Howard, Rolland & Stewart."

"Oh my God," she scowled. "You must know or at least know *of* Alan Levenger."

"Yes," Evie said as if she had just discovered something distasteful in her mouth.

"Have you worked with him?"

"I've worked with him on a number of client matters."

Ariel frowned. "I hope he's not somebody you're too fond of. I would be careful of him. I saw him in Bacci several weeks ago and you won't believe what he did."

"Actually, I might surprise you." Evie sipped her water and braced herself for what she knew was not going to be a heroic tale.

Joe leaned closer to Evie to hear Ariel's story.

"This guy, Alan, was at a table with five or six other people obviously having a good ole time. The friend I was dining with said that she had once gone out with him, so we were sort of watching surreptitiously. Anyway, after about five rounds, several of them were getting a bit loud and obnoxious." Ariel looked around and raised her gloved hand to partially obscure her mouth as if she was afraid of being overheard.

"Apparently, this girl sitting across from Alan—who I think I recognized as one of those models from *Sports Illustrated*—anyway, she must've said something he didn't like, and he started screaming at her across the table. She seemed to be holding her own until he got up and walked around to her side of the table." Ariel paused and leaned forward, speaking more softly, "My girlfriend and I were blatantly watching at this point. We didn't care if anybody noticed. We were afraid he was going to hit her, but . . . and I couldn't believe this, he reached toward her and ripped her blouse completely off!"

Joe said nothing, but cocked an eyebrow at Evie, a playful frown on his face.

Evie shook her head and suddenly looked whipped, as if her association with Alan at the same firm somehow made her an accomplice.

Ariel continued the story as she removed the white glove from her dominant left hand, finger by finger. "Of course, Bacci's manager came over and escorted him out, but this girl just sat there stunned for several seconds before she realized she was topless. This silk blouse she had been wearing was now in tatters on the floor." Ariel shook her head. "I felt really bad for her. I'm sure she was trying to process what had just happened. Some of the people with her were laughing, some were yelling. Eventually, she just got up, muttered something, wrapped a friend's jacket around herself and left." Ariel fluttered her eyelashes and fanned herself with the liberated white glove. "It was unbelievable."

Evie shook her head slowly, closing her eyes to let the information sink in like a foul tasting medicine.

"Shocking. The public displays of affection some people engage in," Joe said leaning back in his chair grinning.

Evie turned to him shaking her head, and Ariel rolled her eyes. Both women laughed.

After a few seconds Evie asked, "Didn't anyone call the police?"

"The girl apparently refused to press charges. That's what someone at the table said."

"I will never understand Alan," said Evie. "That's not the first story like this I've heard about him."

The evening continued, and Joe was visibly pleased that Evie and Ariel seemed to like each other. The women exchanged promises to have lunch in Manhattan sometime soon. As the tables began to empty, Joe kissed his sister goodnight and took Evie's hand. Ariel said she and Bradley might be traveling to Los Angeles in the next few days to visit a friend and she would call Joe if their plans solidified.

Joe and Evie walked down the green-carpeted stairs onto Park Avenue and out into the night, hand-in-hand. At the curb he turned to her. "Shall we?"

Evie thought about the wisdom, or lack thereof, of taking time off while Alan was busy planning traps for her. Her body and mind screamed for relaxation. It occurred to her that clarity of mind might actually improve her ability to handle whatever might be ahead. She needed time away from the demands of the office to think.

"Let's go tonight," she said.

He smiled and squeezed her hand in agreement.

The black sedan door opened and Joe instructed the driver to return to Evie's apartment. Upon their arrival, he stayed in the car making some arrangements on a cell phone while Evie dashed inside to pack a bag. When she reappeared at the curb with a small suitcase in hand, his smile made her weak in the knees.

chapter

16

The sea breeze and the warm sun embraced her as she sat in the passenger seat of Joe's Mercedes convertible. The Pacific Coast Highway carried them on a succession of bell curves as the surf seemed to serenade them from a cordial distance. She looked over at Joe. He had one hand on the leather-wrapped wheel and one hand on the volume. A flamenco guitarist sent crisp rolling notes through the sound system. Her hair floated in slow, smooth choreography. Joe glanced over at her and winked.

"Nice to be on the open road, huh?"

She realized that she must be wearing her relaxation. "I've actually never ridden in a convertible before. I haven't owned a car at *all* since I moved back to New York."

"I want to introduce you to my favorite beach. From what you said, I don't think you've experienced how lovely a beach in California can be."

"I'm intrigued. You said this beach has very little traffic. Is it private?"

"No, but it's off the beaten path and slightly difficult to access."

Evie smiled. "And how did you find it?"

"Actually, it sort of found me. Kayaking a few miles north. I broke a paddle and the waves deposited me there."

"Do you believe in serendipity?"

"Well, I think it's more interesting to ask if coincidences happen for a purpose."

"Yes, well . . . do you think they do?

"Yes. Trick is . . . to recognize the purpose."

"So you think it was significant that we were seated next to each other on that New York flight?"

"Absolutely. We were supposed to meet."

"For what purpose?"

"Won't it be fun to find out?"

Evie smiled and watched the waves crash against the shore as they drove along the Pacific Coast Highway. Each series of waves was backlit by sun-filled accents that sent off cascades of luminosity.

"Yes. I think it will," she said.

She let her gaze settle on the rapidly changing vista as they crested each new hill, accented by the topography of the four-lane highway. Colors were softened by the ocean's moisture. The breeze felt feathery against her skin, like transparent cotton. The sun warmed without aggression. The acoustic guitar notes passed over her as if after entertaining her they had other engagements. There was easy theatre about the whole scene. It could not have been more perfectly orchestrated to set her mind to rest. She leaned back and closed her eyes as her hair continued to dance around on the headrest. She could feel Joe's gaze during the brief intervals his eyes left the road.

The time passed quickly; the hum of the car engine was soothing and comforting as she distanced herself from the other cars speeding by on the highway. She felt the car slow and turn onto an unpaved road and opened her eyes wide to a deserted sandy stretch that seemed to wind toward the ocean between some rocky shoreline hills. Joe was smiling at her, enjoying her reaction to the crowdless beach area. He jumped out of the car, grabbed a canvas bag from the trunk and walked around to Evie's side of the car. He opened her door and extended his hand to help her out. She grabbed her sun hat and her bag with one hand and took his hand with the other.

They walked single file through narrow cliff passages toward the stretch of open sandy beach. There were no other people in sight. Joe retrieved a blanket from the canvas bag and spread it on the sand twenty feet from the reach of the waves. Evie sat down and stretched out her legs in front of her. Her tennis skirt covered a tank bathing suit, but she felt shy about removing it. Joe took off his shirt and Topsiders. He reclined on the blanket next to Evie, his head resting against the bag, his eyes closed.

"This is unbelievable. A public beach completely empty on a Saturday. Joe, did you set this up?" She smiled, still gazing out at the water.

"Actually, this is the first time I've been here when it's been *completely* deserted. Usually there're a few people. I knew you were going to be good luck." Joe squinted up at her.

It was a recognizable feeling now, his eyes on her. Far from intrusive though, she felt his looks sought to give something to her rather than take something away. She finished arranging the deposits of sand through the blanket to create a smooth bed and turned to meet his gaze.

"So, Joseph, tell me. When was your last serious involvement?"

"*Involvement.* Hmmm . . . I'm always amused at the use of that word." He paused. "A relationship with a woman named Sandra just ended." Joe rolled onto his side facing her and propped himself on his right elbow, his eyes studying hers.

"May I ask why?" Evie took her first sustained look at his partially bare body. His broad shoulders were well-muscled, his chest was defined and his stomach muscles were toned, but he was not in exaggerated body-builder shape, like many California men she had seen. He had a strokable amount of hair on his chest and his skin was a golden bronze, but not darkly tanned. He wore dark green swim trunks with a faded sporting company logo on one of the legs.

"She probably has a different perspective, but . . . we let it go on too long."

Joe continued, "She's an engineer. Incredibly bright and twice as competitive." He paused. "She's a senior executive vice president at her company, Seismic Plans LTD in L.A., well respected in her industry and yet, she was jealous of my silly little patent." He grinned. "She seemed to enjoy finding technical weaknesses in it. She puzzled why I was able to make money from it."

He flexed his arm and shifted slightly as if trying to find a more comfortable position while continuing to lie on his side. "In the beginning, we argued about technical theories . . . industry strategy. Lately, we were fighting about everything."

Evie nodded in understanding and said, "You'd think she'd be happy about your success."

"Yeah . . . Y'know this patent is pretty basic stuff. I've met people who hold many more patents, who've originated sophisticated scientific breakthroughs and made ten times the money, who were less competitive. It was just a hang-up she had."

"Why did you stay with her?"

"I don't know. Yes I *do*. In all honesty I think it was because I knew our relationship would eventually end, so it was easy to let it go on. I know that sounds strange, but if you know someone is not right for you, you don't spend time asking yourself whether she might be. It was lazy passivity on my part."

"I know what you mean. Even if you understand something, I mean you can know what the right thing to do is and still not do it. Why do you think that is? Why do you think it's so difficult to do the right thing, so easy to do the wrong thing?"

"Maybe it depends on timing. Maybe people make the choice they are supposed to make for that particular situation. They don't see at the time that the choice they made may have actually been the right choice."

"Or maybe the lesson learned or the challenge faced in making that wrong choice makes it positive—a valuable overall experience."

"Remind me never to have a philosophical argument with you." Joe smiled and reached toward her face with his fingers, gently brushing the hair out of Evie's eyes.

"Are you always so tan?" she asked as she surveyed the expanse of his exposed skin.

"Let me put some sunscreen on you. I don't want you to burn," he responded abruptly as if her question reminded him of her vulnerability. He sat up and pulled out a bottle from his bag.

Evie paused and looked off in the distance for a moment. Then she stood and pulled off her t-shirt and skirt, revealing the black tank swimsuit she had put on in the LAX airport bathroom. The suit was modestly cut in front but hugged her well-rounded chest tightly and dipped down low from her shoulder blades revealing the gradual curvy smoothness of her back. It was French-cut at the legs leaving long outlined expanses of creamy skin at the tops of her thighs. She leaned down and rolled the discarded clothing tightly and deposited them in her bag. She sat again, her back to Joe, and reached behind to lift up her shiny brown hair off the back of her neck. With both hands she twisted the length of it into a bun and inserted a wooden pin at an angle. Over the bundled hair, she put on a straw hat that cast a shadow over her face.

She could hear Joe squeezing out the lotion and she could smell its aroma. Something like a coconut and—what was that—sort of a *spruce* smell. Unusual combination for a sunscreen, but very nice. It made her think it must be some kind of chemical-free product from a health food store—something that claimed to be organic and not tested on animals. She wondered about the potential for a relationship between a city-dependent, sunless, New York-workaholic attorney and an athletic, beach-critiquing, environmentally-aware scientist. She recoiled slightly at the cool lotion he massaged into her skin. Then she began to relax under his touch.

"Joe, did you know that people, on average, have about five million receptor cells on a membrane in the nasal cavities? These cells are responsible for the physiological process of smelling."

"No, I didn't know that," he said as he continued to caress her skin, spreading the suntan oil.

"Ever since I've been doing work for an aromatherapy company, I've been interested in the science of smell. Apparently, the more receptor cells a person has, the greater that person's sense of smell."

"Dogs have some fifty times man's ability to discern smells."

"Yes. For humans, there are only four basic tastes: sweet, sour, salty and bitter. Everything else is an odor communicated to the nose. We just attribute it to taste or flavor."

"Don't tell the restaurant industry."

She laughed. "It's interesting. There are often psychological connections between memories and specific smells."

"And do you classify men according to their smell?"

She turned around and glared at him with a playful frown.

"Evie, tell me why you're so wary of men." Joe moved his hands to her lower back and massaged in another palm-full of sunscreen. She was silent for several minutes. He stopped rubbing and froze in place inviting her to turn to him.

"I wish I understood *myself*." She shifted around to face him. He handed her the bottle of lotion and she continued its application on her legs and arms. Joe returned to his reclined position facing Evie and studied her face, supporting himself with his right elbow.

"At the risk of being melodramatic," she said, "I always seem to fall prey to men with hidden motives. Not always sex . . . I mean *other* motives. I never seem to realize what's happening until my reservoir of trust is depleted." She closed the cap on the bottle and placed it on the blanket.

"What type of motives? Free legal work?" Joe said as he took a bottle of water from his bag and unscrewed the lid.

"I know I must sound like a bleeding heart, but men are very creative, it seems, in the ways I can be used."

Joe looked at her, his eyes softening. "I'm sorry," he said. "That must've sounded insensitive." He offered her the bottle of water. "And you think I'm just another smelly guy out to take from you. Looking for a conquest . . . or a victim?"

After a slow breath and a drink from the water bottle, Evie handed it back to him and looked out toward the ocean as she spoke, "What makes you different?"

"I'll leave that for you to decide."

She extended her legs and submerged her toes in the warm sand and directed her eyes toward his. "Joe, what is this? I mean we live on opposite coasts. Long distance relationships are the least likely to survive."

"Who says? I've never lived by anybody else's rules," he said and then swallowed a few mouthfuls of water and looked at her. Then he replaced the lid and deposited the bottle under the blanket to keep it out of the sun.

"Have you ever had a long distance relationship before?" she asked.

"No. But I've never met anyone like you before." He held eye contact with her until she broke it. She turned her eyes toward the ocean and breathed in the salty smell. Joe watched her for a moment and then he stretched out again on the blanket, lying on his back with his arms crossed behind his head.

"What is it about me that you find so different?" she asked, maintaining her body position and glancing over at him intermittently.

"Your determination. Your intelligence. Your grace. Your intensity. Your sincerity. Your compassion. And your heart-stopping beauty." He turned his head and stared at her. "And I think also it's the way you make me feel. Should I go on?"

"I make you feel?" she asked.

"You bring out something in me—something *I like*. Maybe it's your hurt." Joe sat up and looked her directly in the eye. "I want to take it away."

Evie's eyes fell again on Joe's body and the sun illuminated all the rippled muscles. She studied his chest and stomach and noticed a small angled scar just below his ribcage. She wanted to touch it and she did. His eyes followed her hand.

"Joe, how did you get this scar?"

"Oh, just one of life's battles."

"You got that in a *fight?*"

"Yes."

"What were you fighting for?"

"I guess you could say I was fighting for principles."

"Did you win?"

"I'm still here."

"It must've been a pretty intense fight."

"Physical wounds are visible, but I don't think they have the effect on one's life that emotional ones do."

"I guess."

"Actually," he looked down again at the scar, which was barely visible on his tan skin, "that experience probably did make me more *stubborn* than I was before."

She smiled slightly and looked down at the sand where she was drawing delicate geometric figures with her finger. "Joe, what do you want from me?" The words sounded crude and accusatory and she was sorry she'd asked the question immediately after her mouth finished forming the sounds. She erased the sand art with a swipe of her palm.

"Evie, can I be totally honest with you?"

"Yes, please."

"When I first saw you, like any man, my first instinct was to want you sexually, but now I just *want* you. I just want you. In every way."

After a few moments, voices could be heard behind them. A group of teenagers were making their way through the sandy passageway toward the open unoccupied beach carrying surfboards, diving gear and coolers.

"Well, I guess our exclusivity ran out," she said, thankful for the well-timed distraction.

"Let's go get wet," he said as he stood and stretched.

chapter

17

Evie stood and dropped her hat. They walked hand in hand to the water's edge, and she watched Joe wade out a few feet and dive in. She stepped more carefully, the tender soles of her city feet navigating many new sensations. The water was brisk, but after a few moments, her body began to adjust to the temperature. Joe swam out a few yards and returned to encourage her. He grabbed her gently by the waist and held her steady as the foamy surf undulated around them. They walked out to shoulder depth. She felt herself succumb to the motion of the water and to him.

He held her suspended in the water and she felt serene, despite the murky ocean water of the Pacific, which obscured the view to the sandy bottom. In tandem she realized that she might be equally ready to accept the serenity that Joe's presence provided, despite the murkiness of *him*, and all the aspects of *him* that as yet were hidden from view.

After an hour-long swim, they jogged out of the surf and toweled off, laughing and gasping for breath. They gathered their things from the beach and quickly made their way back to the car. Joe pulled out a small cooler from the trunk and offered Evie a selection of juices and beer. She selected a Heineken and he opened it for her. He opened a John Adams for himself, shook out the blanket and then paused to watch her sip her beer.

"It's about a half hour drive to my house. Would you like to change out of that wet suit?"

"Yes, good idea." She refolded the clothing that she had been wearing when they had arrived at the airport, took a pair of tan cotton pants and a white linen camisole from her bag and walked to a building at the entrance that bore an announcement of the presence of a ladies room. When she emerged a few moments later, Joe was wearing a pair of slightly wrinkled linen pants, Topsiders and a lightweight faded blue jean shirt open at the neck. She deposited her wet clothes in a bag in his open trunk and took her seat in front. After closing the trunk, he slid behind the wheel.

"You can recline in that seat." He leaned across her and pressed a lever on the side of her seat, adjusting the position until she nodded approval. The midday sun warmed their damp hair. Evie took a deep breath of sea air and savored the post-swim exertion high.

They drove, listening to the flamenco guitarist play one romantic piece after another. A short distance from Joe's house, a few drops of rain began to fall and then a steady stream. Joe put the top up, but not before they had gotten fully wet again.

"I thought it *never rains* in California," she said laughing.

"Well, I guess not in the California of whoever it was that recorded that song."

They ran to the house and Joe unlocked the door. It was an A-frame split-level that sat on the edge of an ocean inlet. Inside the door, they were greeted by two Doberman Pinchers, who had apparently been anxiously awaiting Joe's arrival. Evie recoiled upon seeing the dogs and their exuberance.

"Aren't Dobermans dangerous? I thought they're known for violence. Without warning," she said, careful to stand behind Joe as she spoke.

"No. That's propaganda circulated by people who don't really under-stand the breed." He patted his chest and caught one of the Dobermans in mid-air as it leaped up to meet his gesture. "It's been reinforced by the perpetuation of that image in the media, but it's simply not true," he spoke as the dog covered his face with licks.

He scratched the dog's head with his free hand and then gently placed it back on the floor. "It's all in how you raise them." Joe turned and looked at Evie. She had backed against the door and was watching with wide eyes. He knelt down, glanced back at her frozen position and grinned. "C'mere, killer," he called to one of the dogs.

Evie glared at him and shook her head in mock disgust at his joke. Both dogs were focused on Joe, their tiny tail stubs wagging in unison. She walked over to touch one of the dog's heads. Once she moved closer, she realized that the dogs had not completely grown out of puppyhood. The dog she touched responded with an enthusiastic tongue kiss that covered her extended hand.

"What are their *real* names?" she asked.

"That one is Ajani, a male, and the other one, a female, is Ayoka," he was still smiling as he spoke.

"Are those Indian names?"

"African. Ajani means *'he who wins'* and Ayoka means *'one who causes joy.'*" Joe looked at Evie and watched her quizzically examine Ajani.

"They're very nice. *Very* nice." She petted Ajani. "And they smell so *good*." She sniffed Ajani's head and noticed a two-inch soft cotton object taped inside his ears that kept each ear erect. "What's that in his ears?"

Joe smiled and said, "Tampons."

She rolled her eyes. "No, really . . ."

"No joke. Tampons work really well for training their ears." Joe laughed and played with the taped ear. Evie looked more closely at the ear support and smiled in understanding.

"Hmmm. Who takes care of them when you're traveling?"

"My housekeeper comes by every day when I'm gone."

He stood and retrieved towels for them from a first-floor bathroom. He and Evie were still dripping from the rain shower as he lead her to an enclosed sunroom with a balcony overlooking the inlet. She began to apply the soft cotton towel to her arms and face. The dogs laid down across the doorway in silent observance. Joe rubbed his face with the towel and sat on a long wicker sofa and watched Evie towel off. She could feel his eyes staring at her again and out of a sudden plan of revenge for his teasing, she slid over to the wicker sofa and wrung out her wet hair over him so that a river of large water drops landed on his chest and face.

He leaped up and grabbed her by the wrists. Laughing, he wrestled her to the sofa, landing half on top of her, pinning her arms to the surface of the cushions. Her own laughter caused her to breathe hard. Still laughing, their faces were inches apart. He lowered himself slowly and allowed his mouth to cover hers.

The sensation of his mouth on hers was almost unbearable for her, overpowering like the first view of a two-hundred foot waterfall unexpectedly discovered while walking in the forest. *Stop . . . no please don't.* She let her instincts take over and her mouth kissed back. Their lips found contact again and again. She draped her arms around his neck and he pressed into her, their wet clothing squished between them. In what seemed like some distance away, a telephone began to ring. He ignored it, but reluctantly agreed to get up and answer it when she insisted. It had seemed perfectly timed. As much as she wanted him, she knew she was not ready.

He disappeared into the other room and Evie sat up on the sofa and looked out into the evening through the sunroom windows. An unknown euphoria. The sun was setting in a spectacular display of pastel reds and oranges, and the low-grade sparkle on the water was slipping into the framework of moonlight. Thoughts of Gerais Chevas were buried in the back of her mind beneath growing layers of relaxation. *And the fresh palate of images of Joe. His smell. His taste. His touch. The sensation of his body lying on top of hers.* And *no one knew where she was.* She could pretend for the moment that this was her reality.

She closed her eyes for a few moments and then stood and stretched and shook her head clear. She resumed towel-drying her long hair. While she tossed her damp hair she noticed a series of interesting carved masks hanging on the wall among framed photographs of wild animals, which she assumed were the result of Joe's work with a camera on African jaunts. She walked over to examine them more closely. She picked up a carved figurine with a look of sheer terror carved into its wooden face and was studying it when Joe re-entered the room.

"What's this?" Evie asked with curiosity in her voice, looking back at the direction of his footsteps.

"Just something I dug up in my backyard," he said, his dimples gracing his smiling face. Evie gave a look of resolve to his humor.

"You have a lot of African art." She walked back toward the windowed wall. "Did you collect it all while you were there?"

"Mostly. Some were gifts. Where were we?" He came over to where she was standing and placed a hand on the wall on each side of her, collecting her between his outstretched arms. She thought he was going to continue kissing her, but he stood there smiling at her, his eyes sparkling.

"I have some bad news," he said.

"What?"

"I just realized there's no food in the house."

"Oh, that's okay."

"I wasn't sure you'd come. Want to go out for dinner?"

"Actually, I really need a shower." She cupped her hands over his arms and gave him a quick kiss. "How about some takeout?"

"Okay," he said, walking back to the sofa for his towel. He finished rubbing his hair with the towel and draped it around his neck. "You like Mexican? I can drive down the coast to a great place that has organic vegetable burritos."

"Mmmm. That sounds great," she said softly. "Are you *sure* you don't mind if I don't go with you?"

"As long as you're here when I get back. I need to stop by a food market, too. It'll take an hour."

"Thanks, Joe."

Joe nodded at the two pups. "Are you comfortable with the dogs loose or should I crate them?"

"No, let them roam. They seem to've accepted me."

"They know quality when they see it."

chapter
18

After a hot shower Evie walked back out on the sunroom balcony in her towel. It was *so* quiet, as if the silent sanctuary of a distant ocean isle had been transported to the shore before her. She looked around quickly and confirmed to her satisfaction that the privacy of the balcony was complete. The closest neighboring house was a half-mile around the naturally curving cliff and there was a dense collection of palm trees and other leafy accumulations on each side of the bluff where Joe's property was located. She looked out over the Pacific. The balmy evening was sinking in around her. She felt lighthearted in defiance of the rumbling of unrest that lurked in her unconscious. She inhaled the oceanic perfume and looked up to find a silky moonlit sky ornamented by an array of star shapes.

A salty gust of wind erupted and displaced her towel. The folds of cotton fell around her feet, leaving her naked in the moonlight. She gasped but stood that way for several moments, in surprising tranquility, enjoying the sensation of the dry warm evening air on her skin. She wondered what an African night would feel like. She suddenly craved Joe's presence, his touch. It was very erotic to be standing nude on his balcony, where he had surely been soothed by the same dry, warm air. His essence was all around her. It would be so easy to succumb to her immense physical desire for him. Perhaps *too* easy. It just didn't happen this easily, this neatly. Not for her. In any event, she was pleasantly surprised at the expulsion, albeit temporary, of Project Neon from her conscious mind.

The telephone rang, severing her chain of thoughts and capturing her attention. There was an open kitchen window overlooking the sun-room balcony where she stood. The sound of the ring was clear and prominent, so she guessed the telephone was in the kitchen. Out of a sudden awareness of the existence of other people, she retrieved her towel, but her gaze turned back toward the ocean and she longed to drift back into that meditative state.

After three rings, she heard Joe's voice announce, *"Hello. Yeah, you're talking to a machine. After the beep, make it count."* There was a beep and silent slice of a second. Then Evie heard an alto female voice. *"Joe. Sandra. Oh Joseph. I've been thinking. Really honest, hard thinking. I'm . . . I've been a real bitch. I see now that I WAS jealous. I can't believe I let that come between us. Can I see you? I need to see you. I miss you. Call me. Please call me."*

Despite the sound of the soft washings of the rocks below, the message drifted out to Evie. *That must be the girlfriend Joe spoke about. I could have done without hearing that.* She wrapped the towel tightly around her, retreated to the bathroom and put on a pair of blue jeans and a t-shirt.

Maybe the workings of the answering machine or maybe the jolt of reality suddenly caused Evie to think about her own voice mail. In some kind of beach-inspired rebellion, she hadn't checked it since she'd left the office on Friday. Joe had encouraged her to avoid it. There were conflicting voices in her head that advocated checking it, not checking it. She finally decided to check. In the end it was always better to know.

Wasn't it? She walked back into the sunroom and turned toward the kitchen. She located the telephone mounted on the wall beside the open window and dialed.

> *You have* [beat] *three new messages. Message One* [beat]
> *left Friday six o'clock P.M.* [Adam speaking] *"Hey Evie.*
> *Adam. Glad to hear you're taking some well-deserved*
> *time off. We got a new draft from SerosaSoft. They came*
> *a long way toward meeting our concerns, but there are*
> *a few issues we should discuss. Call me when you get*
> *back, but don't rush. Not so much time pressure now. We*
> *should be able to wrap this up fairly quickly." End of mes-*
> *sage.* [beat] *Message Two* [beat] *left Saturday 10:26 A.M.*
> [in the weak voice of Hanover] *"Hello, Evie. I owe you a*
> *debt of thanks for your fine work in my absence. I'll try*
> *to see you when I come in this week. I'm on the mend and*
> *grateful to be alive. Thanks again for your help." End*
> *of message.* [beat] *Message Three* [beat] *left Saturday*
> *11:42 A.M.* [an unknown female voice with an accent]
> *"Eveleen, I'yave some information for you. Information*
> *about Project Neon. I need to see you. I call again."* [beat]
> *No more messages.*

She hung up the phone in a foggy state of mind. All the soothing sounds of the ocean, the peacefulness of the evening, the intimacy developing with Joe was sucked into a vacuum. She felt chilled and alone as the existence of Project Neon crashed back into her consciousness.

Did she recognize the voice? No, it was completely foreign to her and with an accent of some kind, possibly Latin but unclear. But the caller knew *her* name. Information about Project Neon. No specifics. Nothing in the message of substance. If this caller was part of the setup, it was clever in its brevity. Such a vague message could be interpreted as a common communication between lawyer and client. And there was a tone in the voice. A tone of familiarity, of frequency. *The woman sounded like she was calling someone she knew*—as if the tone of the message had been calculated to undercut Evie's claim that she'd had no involvement with Project Neon. For anyone hearing it, she wondered if the message would be read as incriminating or exculpatory. When she got back to her office, she would have to find that mini tape recorder and capture the message in a permanent form. Maybe Joe had one.

The message had been brief and included no names or contact information. And she was in the wrong place to receive any follow-up phone call. No matter what information was being offered, she would not be able to receive it. She looked at a clock on the wall. It was now 7:30 P.M. California time, 10:30 P.M. New York time. She briefly considered returning to New York immediately, but she couldn't bring herself to do it. *Not yet.* No matter what awaited her back home, she had to spend a bit more time with Joe. She'd promised to be here when he got back, and she wanted to be. Not only for the benefit of their budding relationship, time with Joe also presented an opportunity to try to solicit some help understanding the technological assault she was under. She would plan to leave tomorrow.

Walking around the house barefoot for a few minutes, trailed by her new Doberman friends, brought the anxiety down a fraction and she settled on a leather sofa in a paneled den to rest for a few minutes. The pups fell asleep on the floor next to her. Their presence now represented an enormous comfort to Evie, who only hours ago had considered them a danger.

She picked up an issue of *The Economist* and flipped pages. What was she really so tormented by? Was it the web Alan was weaving or the fact that he was weaving it? It *had* to be possible to convince the partners that she'd had nothing to do with the Gerais Chevas deal. No amount of mistaken recordkeeping should stand unchallenged. Her denials had not yet been fully tested, but even if Paul didn't believe her, Hanover would. But, how much of an impact would this smear campaign have?

How far would Alan go? The magazine fell open to a dog-eared page containing an article analyzing tribal conflicts in South Africa.

She began to read, but the next thing she would remember was being awakened by Joe, who was gently blotting the beads of perspiration from her brow with a handkerchief. She was disoriented for a moment.

"You were having a nightmare," he said.

"Oh. I don't remember. It was just all ethereal images and shadowy feelings of dread."

"Relax. Take a deep breath."

Evie breathed and blinked at him. "How long was I sleeping?"

"Not long. I was only gone about forty-five minutes."

She nodded.

"Hungry?"

She smiled. "Yes."

After a casual dinner in front of a fire, Evie followed Joe up the stairs to a bedroom with a queen-sized bed and a suite of furniture in a rustic Sante Fe style. It had its own bath. He deposited her small suitcase on top of the dresser and pulled back sheets that smelled of musk. She sat on the bed. Every part of her wanted to reach out and invite him to join her, but she resisted. He pulled a comforter out of a closet and laid it on the bed.

"It gets chilly here at night." He kissed her on the forehead and left the room, shutting the door behind him.

When she awoke the next morning, she could see the early morning light nestling in, but there was no sound except the subtle rhythmic waves as if charged with maintaining the intimacy of their ongoing weekend communion with the sea.

She looked at the clock and realized that Joe had let her sleep—it was now after nine o'clock in the morning. She could smell coffee and some kind of fruit-filled bread coming from downstairs. The morning sun was now aggressively warming the room. She energetically showered, straightened the bed and changed into a clean pair of jeans and a light blue pullover. Not sure how to tell him she was leaving, she descended the staircase slowly and found him typing on a laptop computer at the dining room table, a steaming cup of coffee to his right. He was wearing khaki colored shorts and a polo shirt and seemed to be deep in thought.

At the sound of her footsteps he looked up, a welcoming *"good morning"* in his face.

"Hey, Evie. How are you feeling?"

"Great. Leisure sleep is a rare luxury." She took a few more steps down the stairs. Ayoka waddled up to meet her and licked her shin. Evie smiled, patted the smooth head of her greeter and looked at Joe with an appraising gaze.

As she moved closer to him, she noticed that his hair was wet, he smelled freshly showered and his eyes glistened with the concentration of a man who was engrossed in his work.

"You look like you've been up awhile."

"Awhile," he said. "Would you like some coffee? There's this cranberry bread I bought last night. Or, we could run out for breakfast?"

"Just coffee for me, thanks." She looked over his shoulder at his laptop and noticed that there were no wires. "You're accessing your company's systems?"

"Yeah, we're all wireless."

"Don't you worry about security?"

"It's a relative concept."

"Law firms are starting to go wireless, but my firm hasn't come to terms with the vulnerability when we're transferring sensitive files. Our client file systems are still modem-only. Did you see where I left my briefcase? I need to check email."

"Now, why would you want to do that?" he said as he stood and faced her with a broad dimpled smile. He moved close for a kiss and she willingly received it. "It's on the table in the den." She draped her arms around his neck and they kept kissing. He broke away gently and disappeared into the kitchen. She retrieved her briefcase from the den and pulled out her BlackBerry, but she laid it on the table when Joe returned seconds later with a cup of coffee for her.

The coffee was presented, bacheloresque manner, in a black mug with a mismatched ill-fitting saucer underneath. A look of amusement on her face, she sat down at the table across from where he had been working and looked over at the spread of diagrams and documents circling his small laptop. He noticed her gaze.

"Just monitoring a new project we're working on," he said. "It's body-scanning technology. A database of thousands of stored images, identifying a specific person." He smoothed back a lock of wet hair that fell on his forehead.

"The database of images can then be used to create digital simulations of that person's movement. You've probably seen it used in media to create special effects."

"Oh, yes. I think I have. Did your company originate *that?*"

Joe sat down and started to organize the frenzied spread of hard copy. The edges of the paper clicked against the tabletop as he stood them in a vertical stack to align them.

"No. But we're working on variations. Artificial intelligence applications. For example, so a digital image can interact like a real person." Joe took a sip of his coffee. "Well, *almost,*" he continued. "The range of conversation for the electronic 'person' will be limited by the stored responses in the database file."

Hmmm, she thought. *What Alan could do to me if he had access to this technology with a database of my images.* "Does your company have any patents on this technology?" she asked.

"No. There are dozens of companies working on similar projects." Joe looked up from the pile of paper and his face seemed to animate when allowed to fully focus on her.

"Joe, Sandra called last night. She left a message for you. I didn't mean to eavesdrop, but I was on the sunroom balcony and—"

"It's okay. I would have played it for you, if you'd asked."

"You would?"

"Evie, I'm a pretty transparent guy. Do you believe that?"

"I want to."

"I have no feeling left for Sandra. I'll return her call, but it's over."

"Joe, I have to leave. I need to get back to New York."

"Evie, I promise. It's over."

"No, not because of Sandra," she said. "I listened to my voicemail. There was a message that was very disturbing."

"Did it cause that bad dream you were having?"

Evie sipped her coffee and tried to decide how much to confide in Joe. Maybe she could trust him. The telephone message from Sandra had supported Joe's recounting as if on cue.

Joe seemed to be reading her thoughts. "You can trust me, Evie. Is something bothering you? Are you worried about something?"

"I don't know if I should tell you. It's complicated. And actually, it's *confidential*. It involves client information, so I really *can't* tell you."

"Maybe I can help." He sipped his coffee. "If you tell me without revealing the identity of the client, you haven't really broken a confidence, have you?"

She regarded him on this second day in his house. He *was* very open.

"Okay." She sat forward, propping her elbows on the table. "Do you remember that password-protected client file I asked for your help with?"

He put down his coffee mug and nodded. His eyes targeted hers, his brow registering dedicated attention.

"I was trying to access a couple of files that contain documents on a specific deal someone in my firm has apparently been working on. It's a deal that places very unusual obligations on the seller's attorney, and we apparently represent the seller. There's some question in my mind as to whether these obligations are *legal*."

Joe shifted back in his seat, but remained attentive.

"I found out they existed and I had reason to suspect that there was something fishy about them, so I had to try to access them."

Joe's brow furrowed, but he sat silently.

"Okay. Let me back up," she said. "There've been a number of coincidental mishappenings with clients lately that have implicated me. My reputation in the firm is on the line. And, specifically on *this* deal, I've overheard things. Found things. An email was sent to me by someone who I think is involved. And this voice mail I just got—it's from a woman who says matter of factly that she has information for me related to the deal, as if I'm the point person. I'm *not.* These things taken together seem to be creating a picture that I'm the one who put this deal together, or is at least running it. Negotiating it. Drafting the documents. In short, I think someone is setting me up as a scapegoat on a deal that could have an illegal element to it and that someone is undermining my reputation with the firm to make me vulnerable."

"Hmmm. Can you be any more specific? What happened initially to make you suspicious?"

"It's a Brazilian deal. I overheard a conversation late at night over a conference room phone with snippets of a Latin-sounding language. Could have been Portuguese. My name was mentioned and there was something being said about a 'paper trail' and about somebody acting alone who 'won't be a problem.'"

"Do you know who was speaking?"

"At the time, I didn't clearly identify who it was, but now I think I know."

"You said *things.* What else did you discover that made you suspicious?"

"My name was added to an access list for this client's electronic files. In my firm, if a series of documents is restricted, it's a sensitive matter. It's highly unusual for someone to be included on an access list who has nothing to do with a deal. That access allowed me to read the main contract. It's a sale of a business unit. The file that contains the specific obligations I'm concerned about is still protected by a password I don't have, but I'm betting this file houses a key schedule. During the conversation I overheard, the person mentioned a schedule and that it would 'show the deal take shape.' As I said, I received an email from someone in the client company telling me to proceed with the deal, a Brazilian man whose name also appeared in an email sent by . . . by the *person* I overheard talking. It seemed to be suggesting a closing date for the deal."

"How did you get a look into this person's email?"

"I snooped around in the person's office." She watched Joe's eyebrows rise.

She continued, "Okay, I know this sounds crazy. You must think I'm a nut case, but there's more. There was this erroneous expense report filed under my name that had a list of Brazilian telephone calls attached. I never made any of those calls and I've never talked to any of those people. And, *this person* has been sending documents and email from my user name. I was working on another client matter with him and he sent out the wrong document from my email to make me look bad with the client and to get me in trouble with the partnership."

"Him? Is this—this isn't that guy. What's his name? Alan something? That guy with the penchant for undressing women in public?"

Evie let out a long sigh. Then she nodded slowly.

"So, this guy, Alan, has been stepping all over you politically, hijacking your user name and generally being an asshole. *Now* I understand why you didn't want to talk about him. But Evie, is there any way you could be mistaken about some of this? I mean, this guy is obviously not a stand up guy, but are you sure he's setting up something illegal?"

"No, I'm not sure of *anything*. That's the problem. It's possible that the deal is completely benign—some sort of perfectly legal role for the attorney to play. But, it smells. It's secretive. I have had no part in it but my name seems to be all over it. I *know* he sent out documents from my email address so he must've logged on as me. He must have gotten my system password somehow and I think he's created an electronic trail that leads to me. If I were to be assigned this deal legitimately, it would have . . . I can't imagine a deal to've proceeded this far that I was *supposed* to be involved with that I know nothing about. By the way, after I overheard that phone conversation, Alan came into my office and had the perfect opportunity to tell me about it. If I had been picked to work on it, it just seems strange he wouldn't at least mention it, since he'd just talked about it on the phone in association with my name. He said nothing about it and acted like we were the best of friends. We're not. *This* was *after* we'd had an argument earlier in the day over another client matter."

Joe rose with a set jaw and went to the kitchen to retrieve a fresh pot of coffee. When he returned, there was a look of contemplative consternation on his face. They moved to the sofa in the den and sat facing each other. Joe draped his arm behind her on the leather in a protective gesture.

"So, the client incidents you said have been happening. All with Alan?"

"Yes, mostly. His presence has been everywhere lately. Do you remember that former client of mine we ran into at the ball? Alan bragged to me in advance that he was going to get that man fired from his job. I don't know if Alan actually had anything to do with his termination or not, but it was disconcerting, to say the least."

"Why would this jerk want to target you, Evie? I believe you, but what—did you cross him somehow?"

"No, not exactly."

"He hasn't come on to you, has he?"

Evie bit her lip, paused, sipped her coffee and took a deep breath.

"He kissed me." She watched Joe and saw the anger rise, but thought she'd better get the whole story out.

"We were meeting with a client in Chicago. We walked back to the hotel together like any two colleagues would, but he followed me up to the door of my room and tried to push his way in. After he kissed me, I slapped him and threatened to call the managing partner, but he apologized. Said he got carried away with the success we were having with the client. He swore it was just an impulse and that it would never happen again. I didn't know him that well at the time and in a moment of stupidity, I agreed not to report it. I've regretted it ever since—for *many* reasons, not the least of which is that he might do it to someone else."

Joe's eyes flashed with a contained rage. After a few moments, he spoke.

"Evie, have you talked to the other partners about any of this? It's not too late to report the sexual harassment. It also provides a foundation for your distrust of this guy and validates your motive for investigating. And it adds another dimension to everything you've told me about this secretive deal."

"No, not yet. I was going to. Even without tangible proof, I was about to tell the partner who's managing the firm at present. Right before I left town, I found out he was scheduling a private drink with Alan, something I never heard of him doing before. I don't know what their relationship has become. I was afraid even if he lent a sympathetic ear to me, he might say something to Alan that would tip him off, let Alan know I'm investigating. I don't think he knows I am. That's why I've been able to discover what I *have*. And snoop in his office. I can't let him find out what I know or he'll really bury the evidence, or spin things around so I look crazy. He's already succeeded in damaging my credibility."

Joe listened intently. He rose from the sofa, walked to a window and stood staring out into the morning sun for several minutes. He took a breath and turned to face Evie, a serious expression on his face. The Doberman pups had sensed his unrest and had wandered over to stand at his feet, looking up at him expectantly. Evie was surprised to see that he declined to greet or even acknowledge them as he had each time they'd approached before.

"This guy, Alan, has a serious problem with the way he sees himself," Joe began at a low volume. "He has some kind of personality disorder. You've *got* to get away from him." With one hand, Joe leaned against the wall, with the other he kneaded his wavy hair. "Does it mean that much to you to stay with this firm? With your expertise, you know you could—"

"Joe, I can't leave like *this*. I can't let him just dispose of me because I wouldn't—I mean . . . In a way that's why he's doing it. *Because he can.* You have to understand that."

He walked over, squatted down in front of her and looked at her in a concerned manner she hadn't seen before. "I do understand. And I *respect* you. I'll respect how you decide to handle this, but I can tell you it will be very difficult for me to stand by and watch this guy at work." He took one of Evie's hands in his. "I have strong feelings for you, Evie. There are going to be strong male instincts here. You'll have to tell me if you want me to act on them."

"*Yes*. Please. Joe, I want your help. I mean—it's not going to solve anything to . . . Well, confrontations won't accomplish anything, but I *do* have to think this through. I need you to help me think this through. There's got to be a way to play this, prove my suspicions. I need you as a sounding board. I need your strength. I also need your guidance."

"You've got it. You've got me." Joe kissed the palm of her hand and continued to plant tiny rhythmic kisses there for a few moments while deep in thought. His eyes stared beyond her at nothing in particular. "Evie, you have to tell me the name of the client," he said suddenly. "Forget about confidentiality. If Alan is setting you up in the way you suspect, it's likely that someone from that client has to be involved in the planning. Maybe even this guy who's emailing you. You know there are exceptions to client confidentiality. This is self preservation."

"Not according to the Bar Association," she answered.

"The New York Bar must recognize exceptions like California. You know. If a client is involved in a crime or fraud and is using the attorney as a facilitator."

"I don't have any proof that that's the case."

"You suspect that you're being singled out to play some sort of role in something shady. An unconventional role for the attorney to assume. You know in your gut that the situation is not benevolent toward you."

"Okay," she said after a moment. "But just between us."

She searched for commitment in his eyes and continued despite not definitively finding it. *There was momentum now. She wanted so badly to trust him.* "It's a South American company called Gerais Chevas."

"Think about hiring a private investigator." Joe sat on the edge of the coffee table still facing her. "If you like, I can take care of it." Joe watched her eyes, which widened and stared. "Just to take a closer look at what he's up to. I know a very good one who's experienced at working corporate espionage angles. And he's *invisible.*"

"*Joe!*" She focused abruptly on the suggestion he was making. "Is he legal? Does he stay within the law?"

Joe smiled. "Yes. He's licensed and he *does* observe the law," he laughed, "to any degree he's asked."

"*Joooooooeee!*"

"Not to worry. I've only engaged his services from a *defensive* posture. Never as part of an offensive strategy."

She suppressed a smile and shook her head. "I don't know. Let me think about it."

"Unless—unless, you'd rather consult with someone on the outside. Do you have colleagues who litigate this type of case?"

"No, I can't think of anyone. Y'know, I haven't given the partnership a chance yet. I was waiting to find something more concrete. And, I need to see the contents of that secret document to evaluate the legalities. I'm not even sure Paul—he's the current managing partner—I'm not sure he believes me about that one matter I told you about—the one Alan manipulated. I need some tangible proof to have any chance of being believed." She looked off into the distance and blinked away some of her reluctance. "Okay. Maybe some aggressive investigation *is* what I need, but let me think about it."

"Are you working on any other client matters with this asshole?"

"Yes, but I don't think any of the others are controversial."

"Can you pass them off to other associates?"

"Not without committing career suicide."

"Well, maybe that's the conversation you need to have with the managing partner. Tell him about the harassment and give him some pretext—tell him that lately you're feeling uncomfortable working with Alan. He'll have to protect you or put the firm at risk."

"That's a good idea, but what if Alan gets word that I spilled the story about Chicago?"

"If he's setting you up for something illegal, you need the partnership to be aware of the bad blood between you. You need their eyes focused on this guy if you're planning to continue to walk the halls of this office."

"Okay. You're right."

"Good. And stay away from him."

She felt a rush of emotion and wanted to throw her arms around his neck, but she watched him think instead. His willingness to help was a welcome comfort. She could definitely find solace leaning on his strong shoulder.

He stood up quickly and walked to the door and opened it. The two black and gold canines rambled outside wagging their stubby tails, having concluded that the crisis was over. He leaned down and rubbed behind each set of ears. He was still visibly preoccupied, but the dogs didn't seem to care. He closed the door and stood motionless. He looked at her and there was an unmistakable sense of resolve on his face now, as if he had definitely decided that he would take a place on the front lines of this battle.

"I've got an idea," he said suddenly. "Let's send this asshole an email."

chapter 19

W hat kind of email? Do you mean let him know I suspect him?"

"Not from you, from me. From a hotmail account I have. Email address 'goliath.'" Joe winked at her.

"Will he suspect *me?*" she asked.

"Shouldn't. It's an account my secretary set up for me for remote communications, when our server's down or unreachable." He smiled. "No way to connect it to you."

"Goliath?"

"You think she was trying to tell me something?"

Evie grinned, beginning to enjoy their collaboration in spite of the coiled spiral of fear in her chest. She laughed, releasing some of the tightness in her throat.

"He won't know who sent it. Even if he finds out whose account it is, he won't recognize my name."

"Oh-*kay*. But what would it say?" She shifted on the sofa.

Joe walked back to the dining room table where his laptop sat idle and Evie stood and followed. He logged onto his hotmail account and began typing an email message:

> *I know what you're doing. I'm watching and I don't like what I see. You will rethink your short-term plans or there will be consequences that YOU won't like.*

Evie watched him compose the message. After he had entered the text, he typed in a series of keystrokes she couldn't follow, but she *did* recognize the familiar icon that meant "attachment."

"What's this guy's email address?" Joe asked.

"It's *alevenger@hr&s.com.*"

Joe typed the address on the line for receiving party and hit SEND.

"Nice and vague," she said. "Did you *attach* something to the message?"

"Yes. It's called a 'sniffer.' A handy little software script that will gather some information for us." He turned his chair away from the computer and pulled Evie into his lap. "It will surreptitiously track his incoming and outgoing mail and automatically send me copies of any that include a reference to Gerais Chevas."

"Joe, that's illegal surveillance! It's like . . . *email wiretapping!*"

"Don't worry, Eves. It'll only level the playing field. He *had* to have used some sort of Trojan horse or other clandestine software to swipe your password. And he's apparently practiced at impersonating you online and sending email with your name on it. *He's* committing a kind of identity theft—using your identity for some nefarious purpose. I'm just giving you a little electronic self-help."

She relaxed slightly in his lap. "And he won't know? He won't notice anything?"

"No," he said and pulled her toward him and kissed her neck.

"What about our firm's network. Won't the firewall block it?"

"I'd be surprised if your firm's firewall is sophisticated enough to catch this one."

"What do you think he'll do when he gets that message?" she asked, leaning against him and enjoying the comfort of it.

"Probably nothing. But at least it'll make him think." He sat upright. "Did you check your email?"

"Instead of using my BlackBerry, may I dial in on my laptop from your telephone line?"

"Sure."

She retrieved it from her luggage and handed it to Joe who set it up and connected the modem to a phone jack. She logged in, wandered through her new emails and replied to a few.

He gathered the dishes and disappeared into the kitchen.

One of the messages asked her to re-send a message she had sent a week or so back so she clicked on her history of "Sent" messages and gazed down the list, looking for the one requested. Her attention was diverted when she noticed an unknown message in the list posted from her email address dated last week, addressed to what looked like a group of pre-defined email addresses. Some of the user names had Brazilian extensions. The message was entitled "Neon Only." She clicked on the message and the contents appeared. The message read:

pw: Ninuccia

The back of her neck began to tingle, and her hands trembled as her fingertips slid off the keys.

She jumped when Joe, who had approached her from behind, placed his hands on her shoulders. "Impatient clients?" he asked. He rubbed her shoulders for a moment and then pulled up a chair next to her. She was staring at the screen.

"What's wrong?" he asked.

"This is yet another message from my email address that I didn't write," she said. Joe's face registered understanding. "And Joe, Ninuccia was my mother's name!"

"So, he's changed one of the passwords to something irrefutably tied to you and communicated it to the group of people involved in the negotiation of this deal . . . whoever that is."

"Yes. He's reinforcing the notion that I'm leading this transaction. Each fragment is designed to work together . . . it's like he's creating a mosaic."

"But, he has to know that you're going to discover some of this."

"I know. I don't understand that either. I was thinking about that when I got that message from Adinaldo. If Alan directed that, too, why would he pick that moment to let me learn about the existence of this deal?" "Have you received any other communication from this Adinaldo?"

"No. And I sent him a reply telling him it was mis-delivered to me. You'd think if it was supposed to come to me, he would've resent it."

"Adinaldo could've inadvertently undermined the covert operation."

A shiver went through her body with the additional puzzle piece and its weight.

"Let's look behind the scenes and see if we can capture the identity of the *real* author of this password message."

She watched as he attempted to communicate with the firm's system level—the backstage of the user interface. He typed a series of commands on the keyboard and began speaking simultaneously.

"Mmmm," he said. "Not getting very far. I can't break through to the underbelly. But let's forward this to my email so we can at least print it out."

"Oh good. Joe, that reminds me—do you know where I can get a tape recorder? I want to record that woman's voice mail message over the telephone receiver. At least then I'll have two pieces of tangible evidence that someone is trying to involve me in this deal, although neither of them make me look innocent. I can then go to the partnership and at least tell them I don't know anything about this transaction and I don't understand how my name is getting dragged into it."

"I've got one. I'll find it for you, but first let's try this new password to see if we can get access to those two files." Joe stood and let Evie sit in front of the computer to pull up the list of Neon files.

"You know Joe, maybe Alan *wants* me to find out about this transaction. This email's making me some kind of involuntary coordinator. Maybe he's inviting me to look at these files. I mean, when you think about it, that actually *furthers* his plan, doesn't it? The more I *know* about the transaction, the less credible my denial of involvement with it."

"Don't worry about that. No right-thinking person would fail to try to discover the details of a deal with their name all over it. Is there anything else in email form or in your voicemail that we could preserve for you?"

"There was that erroneous expense report I mentioned," she said as she entered the client number for Gerais Chevas and retrieved the familiar list of files.

"I was in Dallas in July meeting with a client," she continued. "I stayed at the Euphorion Hotel, but a false hotel receipt from the *Colonial Court Hotel* somehow got attached to my expense report. It included that list of calls to and from Brazil—more of Alan's paper trail."

"Did you call the hotel?"

"My secretary did. They claimed to have had an Evelyn Sullivan registered for the dates I was in Dallas, but I wasn't at that hotel."

"Someone must've registered as you, and someone stayed in the room and made those telephone calls."

"I wonder if there's any chance that someone there might remember what she looked like," said Evie.

"It might be interesting to know how she paid, too," said Joe. "Still have that hotel receipt?"

"It's on my desk back at the office."

"Fax it to me when you get back. I'll get my guy to check into it."

"Okay, Joe, but tell him to be very discrete."

Evie highlighted "Neon Three" and double clicked. The password query screen appeared, she typed in *N-i-n-u-c-c-i-a* and hit ENTER.

Evie and Joe stared at the laptop screen. The contents of "Neon Three" filled the screen.

"It's the payment schedule. Looks typical. It shows a pretty standard set of payments and securities transfers, and the purchaser's timing obligations."

They both read silently for a moment and then Evie spoke.

"Joe, look at this." She pointed to an entry labeled *Commission* with a corresponding amount of $25 million.

"Let's scroll down," said Joe and Evie obliged. "There doesn't seem to be any further detail on that commission, explaining who receives it and for what."

"I don't see anything either."

"It's not unusual to pay an agent or broker a fee for putting a deal together, but that's an awfully nice chunk of change."

"Yes and if there *was* such an agent or broker, he would have his *own* contract with the purchaser or seller, whoever hired him. Or *her.* That person wouldn't be a party to *this* agreement."

"Yeah, I've never seen such a thing. Parapier never pays brokers for deals. We find our own."

"Oh my God. Could this commission be payment to the *attorney?*" she said almost to herself. Then she turned back to Joe to explain.

"Joe, the reps and warranties in the main purchase agreement include this obligation of the seller to get its attorney to become a party to the deal. The language says that the attorney will be 'securing' some project, *Project Neon,* and that delivery of a sub-agreement will be evidence that this project has been secured. There's no explanation as to what Project Neon is and what the word 'secured' really means in context."

"So, presumably, the type of project and perhaps the details of the attorney's obligations are spelled out in one of these files?"

"That's what I think. The language referred to a Schedule B7."

"Well, let's take a look at the last file. Try the same password."

Evie brought up the password query screen for Neon Four and her mother's name again yielded the contents of the file. Just as suspected, it was a series of Schedules, Schedules A1 through A8 and Schedules B1 through B7, describing parts of the business unit being sold and the transfer details. On page twelve, there was a heading for Schedule B7, but it had nothing under it but the letters "TBD."

"To be determined," said Evie. "You know, that's what I overheard Alan say. Something about a Schedule. And, something about showing the deal take shape."

"So, this Schedule is going to evolve into a noose."

They both read silently again for a few minutes, then Evie spoke. "I don't see anything unusual in any of these. Schedule B7's the only one with contents that are still to be determined."

"So either Schedule B7 is not negotiated fully yet or someone has purposely left it out of this file for now."

"I guess I have to keep digging," said Evie. "At least I can point to this lack of detail regarding the commission as a reason for my suspicions when I talk to the partners. What could that commission be for and to whom would it be paid?"

"If it is to be paid to the attorney, it definitely raises legality questions. So, what would bind the attorney to secure this Project Neon?"

"The attorney's signature on the sub-agreement, which is to be delivered to Romez Nuevo at closing."

"So, the delivery of this signed sub-agreement binds the attorney to do something, presumably in exchange for $25 million."

"That's my theory so far. It just goes to show how ambiguous language can be and why attorneys spend so much time trying to clarify their references."

"In this case, I'd say the attorneys failed."

"I agree, although I think it's ambiguous on purpose—to make it difficult to pinpoint the exact nature of what's being guaranteed here."

"Okay. Then, do we think this Alan character is capable of forging your signature on that contract at closing?"

"I think he's capable of anything. Can we print these somehow? I've already printed out Neon One and Two, the purchase agreement itself and the term sheet, but this definitely raises more of a red flag."

He stood to retrieve his printer, but she stopped him.

"Oh, wait," she said after hitting the print command. "That's the same thing that happened to me before. The system wouldn't let me print."

Joe looked at the error message on the screen, took Evie's place at the keyboard and began typing. He performed a series of technical maneuvers and then clicked on the print icon on the tool bar and the same error message appeared: ACCESS REQUEST NOT PERMITTED.

"Okay, let's try to save an electronic copy." He issued the series of commands to save a copy of the file onto a diskette in his "a" drive. An error message THIS FILE IS READ ONLY—COPY PROTECTED appeared on the screen. Evie watched him type a series of system level instructions, but he was still unable to capture the file image from the network.

"We can see this file's contents, but it was created with access parameters that prevent certain actions, depending on the user. He probably has multiple groups of users set up. Some having permission to edit or do anything they want to the file, others having only the ability to read it. Your username isn't permitted very broad access rights." He minimized that screen and typed in another series of commands.

"Okay, I'll just take notes." Joe maximized the opened file's screen again, she sat down beside him and began writing on a pad of paper.

"Evie, that actually supports your position, doesn't it? If you were running this deal, you'd certainly have complete control over the documents, wouldn't you?"

"Yes, but Alan seems to change the access parameters almost daily. When I formally make my suspicions known to the partners, he may have changed it so I'm the *only* one to have *full* access. My username was only added to the 'read-only' access list recently."

Joe's telephone rang, breaking their concentration. He walked to the kitchen to answer it, leaving Evie taking detailed notes. When he returned, he said that it was Ariel who called. She and Bradley had in fact arrived in town and wanted to meet up with Joe and Evie at Sciori's for dinner.

Evie nodded in agreement as she continued to write.

"I can do some checking tomorrow to see if I can get another software tool that might be able to bypass some of this security."

"I *know* what you must be thinking," she said. "This is kind of an odd situation. On one hand wanting to gather as much information as possible, and on the other hand wanting to remain as distant from it as possible."

"Let's see what we turn up from my sniffer script. And, for the next few hours at least, let's put this whole thing out of our minds," he said as he gently raised her hands to his mouth and kissed them.

"You think I'm unnecessarily obsessing over this, don't you?" She gently withdrew her hands and looked at him like a scolded child.

"No. *No.* Absolutely not. In fact, I think you have to be very thoughtful and calculating about any contact you have with this guy. I just want to get your mind off of it for a bit. We'll keep fighting the good fight."

She took a deep breath and let him hug her.

"Joe, it's ironic," she said, the words spilling down his back as he held her in a protective embrace. "I've spent so many hours protecting the reputations of artists through carefully constructed legal arguments. Now I find that my *own* reputation is completely vulnerable to destruction at the whim of a renegade partner."

At eight o'clock P.M. that evening, they walked into Sciori's and were taken to a small private table in the corner, where Ariel sat rolling a stroller back and forth.

"One advantage of bringing a toddler," she said. "They always find an out-of-the-way place for you, which I prefer."

Evie and Joe nodded. "This is perfect," they said almost in unison.

"Is he asleep?" Joe asked.

"Yes, for the moment."

Ariel kissed each of them and they all took their seats.

"Ariel, you really look great," said Evie.

"The Spa at The Peninsula Hotel," said Ariel. "One of the few remaining perks to having been married to Max."

"How long have you been divorced?"

"Not long enough. Not to knock marriage or anything. I fell in love with a wealthy wasp, and I became another one of his possessions. But, of course, he gave me Bradley." She looked down at her Baume et Mercier 18K gold watch. "And he did spoil me a little." She laughed.

"Have you ever been married?" Ariel asked Evie.

"No, I haven't."

The waiter appeared and passed out mineral water and menus. He recited the specials and promised to return in a few minutes. A few seconds of silence followed.

"I should probably change the subject." Ariel chuckled. "You know, Joseph, I don't know how you stand living in L.A., all this sunshine and plastic surgery."

"Manhattan certainly has its drawbacks," said Evie.

"I still spend half my time at a pied a' terre on the Upper West Side that I got as part of the settlement," said Ariel. "Manhattan is the definitive city."

"So, you got the house in Connecticut and the apartment in New York," said Evie.

"Yes," said Ariel. "And he got his estate near Zurich, the flat in London, an island house in the Caribbean and a small apartment we bought in Madrid. He travels around Europe constantly and I didn't want the headache of maintaining those properties. *And*, I thought if I didn't challenge him on the property, he wouldn't challenge me for custody."

Evie nodded as Ariel turned to her brother and said, "Joe, your colleague, Francois, tells me you work too much."

"You can't believe a word he says."

"Are you bringing that ancient French company toward the twenty-first century or what?"

"With lightning speed. We'll soon leave Bill Gates in the dust." He laughed. "I've learned two very important lessons working with the French: *one,* to always have a case of wine standing by for budget approval meetings, and *two,* to use the great French art of expressing dissent." Joe demonstrated with a scowl and Gallic shoulder shrug. "Mais non! C'est ennuyant!"

"You could be useful at the next meeting of the United Nations." Evie winked at Joe.

"Are we still boycotting?" asked Joe, as he flipped through the wine list.

"No, the French still produce the best," said Ariel.

"I agree," said Evie.

The waiter approached and accepted Joe's request for a Chablis.

Everyone took a drink of water and opened their menus. Ariel offered around a platter of hors d'euvres she'd ordered. Then she turned to Evie. "Joe's work amazes me. I'm still writing on a paper calendar and can't get used to Joe typing away on his laptop with no wires attached. Has your firm gone wireless?"

"No, not fully."

"Do you think law firms take full advantage of technology?" continued Ariel. "How well does your firm use technology?"

"Sometimes, I think *too* well. Some of the partners are more aggressive with their use of technology than others." Evie glanced sideways at Joe. "I was once involved in a negotiation in a conference room full of attorneys seated around a long table. Every single one of us had a laptop and while the negotiations were going on, we were emailing contract language to each other."

Ariel's eyes widened.

"Each of us was typing away, sending and reading emails while we were engaged in discussions across the table." Evie took a sip of her cocktail. "One guy was even talking in a low voice over his cell phone in the corner of the room. As the meetings continued over the course of several days, they added a digital screen at one end of the room. We started receiving messages from other meetings taking place at the same time on a split screen with the stock market readings streaming across on the other half of the screen."

"That sounds like some serious multi-tasking," said Ariel.

"It was technology run amuck, and I have to say it interfered with our ability to isolate issues that needed to be discussed. Maybe sometimes you can have too much information."

Evie and Joe exchanged glances.

The waiter reappeared, took their dinner orders and collected the menus.

"Speaking of too much information, Evie, I just saw Alan Levenger's name mentioned on *Page Six* in the *New York Post*."

"Really?"

"Yes, he was at some party in the Hamptons and got in a fight with somebody over a woman. There was also a bit of gossip about your firm. It was in the '*We hear . . .*' section. It said that rumor has it that someone at your firm is about to be fired. I wonder if it's Alan?"

Evie shifted in her seat and felt a cold sweat break out on her forehead. Joe took her hand under the table and gave it a reassuring squeeze.

"I have no idea," she said.

chapter

20

E vie took a long sip of her water and said to Ariel, "Joe was telling me about some of his experiences in Africa. I want to hear more." She turned to Joe.

"Tell her about the time you saved Dad," said Ariel.

Joe was leaning back in his seat and sipped a glass of water. "Are you sure you want me to—"

"Yes," said Evie.

"Okay, but I think that was a joint effort. Dad and I were kind of dependent on a higher presence on that one."

"Thank God you were there with him," said Ariel.

"Dad and I were on the Selous Game Preserve in Tanzania. We had hiked away from our jeep a few kilometers to 'read the morning paper.'" He smiled and explained. "There's a fresh Braille to be read every morning in the ash-rich soil in that area. It captures the impressions of whatever feet, paws and hoofs have passed during the night. Some call it *'reading the morning paper'* to inspect the soil and draw conclusions about the night's traffic."

The women looked at each other and smiled. Then they turned their attention back to Joe.

An artfully arranged platter of lobster and crab was placed before them and they each took a portion. The wine was poured. Joe sipped, nodded to the waiter and continued.

"While we were hiking, we came upon a herd of Cape Buffalo." Joe looked over at Ariel and then winked at Evie. Ariel was grinning like a child listening to a father's bedtime stories that had been recited many times, but never often enough.

"Contrary to popular perception, Cape Buffalo can be more dangerous than lions or crocodiles. A charging herd of them is undeterable and relentless, as opposed to elephants that will often stop charging if challenged. We were watching a large bull that was visibly wounded—initially I thought by an encounter with a predator. But anyway, he saw us and decided to rush us. And his herd followed. Running like mad for a few minutes, we dove under a canopy of brush bordered by Baobab trees."

"Don't be modest, Joseph." Ariel took a bite and looked at Evie. "Dad was as drunk as a sailor. If Joe hadn't thrown him under the brush, he would've been trampled."

Evie looked over at Joe and smiled, a profusion of admiration in her gaze.

"Baobab trees. Are those the trees that look flat on top?" asked Evie.

"No, those are Acacia trees. Anyway, there's nothing in the world like a herd of buffalo thundering past just fifteen feet from where you're hugging the earth. It sounded like a locomotive and the ground shook like an earthquake." He took a bite of angel hair pasta and sipped his wine. "We found out from a ranger that a poacher had injured that bull the day before, so I guess there was this inherent fear of humans that caused the charge."

"Oh my *God*," said Evie, still sipping her wine. "Joe, the world needs more men like you."

"Speaking of Dad," said Ariel looking at Joe, "I think he's back on that sleeping pill, Bylinion."

She turned to Evie. "Our father has an addictive personality. His latest vice is a particular sleeping pill and he's found a doctor who's willing to keep writing prescriptions."

"I'm going to have to sit down with that doctor," said Joe. "He may not understand what type of person he's treating."

"So your dad has trouble sleeping?"

"He's always been an insomniac."

"I sometimes have trouble sleeping myself," said Evie, "and even when I do sleep, I often have nightmares about trying to complete something for a client."

"You know, Evie," said Ariel. "I can't imagine you working with Alan Levenger."

"Sometimes, I can't either."

Just then they all looked toward the stroller as Bradley began to fuss.

"Can I try?" asked Evie.

Ariel nodded.

Evie walked around to the front of the stroller.

"Hello, Bradley," she said to him.

"Hewo," answered Bradley.

Evie picked up a stuffed giraffe that was laying next to him in the stroller. Bradley smiled with the enthusiasm that comes with the introduction of a playmate. Joe stood and watched with a bemused grin. Bradley took the giraffe and began pulling on its tail. Evie relinquished control of the stuffed animal and sat down again. Bradley drifted off to sleep again clutching the giraffe.

"Have you thought about switching firms?" asked Ariel.

"Yes, but I can't."

"Why such loyalty? Are you up for partner?"

"No, it's not that."

"Ari, don't push," said Joe.

"I'm sorry, I tend to be a bit nosy."

"It's okay." Evie took a reconnaissance look around. "I need to stay around to save my reputation."

"Some kind of career politics?"

"There's some evidence that I'm being set up."

"Set up? Mmm. What do you mean?" asked Ariel.

"I can't go into it."

"You can trust her," said Joe.

"Okay, there's this deal that has my name all over it that I've had nothing to do with. After some digging, I've discovered that there are some questionable elements to it. Reputation-destroying at best, illegal at worst."

"Someone at the firm is doing a deal using your identity?"

"Yes. I know it sounds crazy. You were talking about the benefits of technology, well, it can be used in very destructive ways, too."

"What are you going to do?"

"I just want to find out the extent of the damage and convince the partners that I had nothing to do with it. I can't do anything until I restore my reputation."

"I can understand that," said Ariel. "Do you know who's doing it?"

"Basically, a partner whose advances I rejected seems to be using his position of power to undermine my credibility in the firm so he can use me as a scapegoat."

"Oh my God. That's worse than physical abuse. Just the type of experience that brings out the feminist in me. Is he well-respected?"

"I didn't think so, but he seems to have better access to the lead partners in the firm than I would have thought. And, it seems that he is surprisingly close to a senator."

"A U.S. Senator?"

"Yes, I'm afraid so."

"So fucking typical. Excuse my French. They all—I hate it when they protect each other like a bunch of self-centered juveniles. *Wait . . .* it's *not . . .* it's not that jerk Alan Levenger, is it?" Ariel frowned.

"It's probably better if I don't say any more."

"It *is,* isn't it! I can't believe a prick like that has a direct line to the United States Congress. Okay, well, *yes, I can.* Evie. It is him, isn't it? You poor thing," Ariel said as she checked to make sure Bradley was still sleeping and had not heard her outburst. He was stirring again so she stood for a moment and rocked the stroller until a sleepy sigh was heard.

"I have to go back tomorrow instead of waiting for Tuesday," Evie whispered to Joe during Ariel's brief absence from the table.

"I know. As luck would have it, I'll be in New York again later this week. More battles with the French," he whispered back.

"Will you call me when you get in?"

"I will."

Ariel sat back down and turned to Evie. "Is there anything I could do?"

"Nothing really, except, Ariel, please no further than this table, okay?" She looked over at Joe, who was nodding to Ariel.

"Of course," said Ariel. She thought a moment and said, "Evie, aren't there whistleblower laws that protect people like you?"

"I wish that were the case. From what I know so far, this isn't a wrong against the government and there isn't any threat to public safety. And the whistleblower laws don't apply to the pursuit of a personal vendetta that hasn't resulted in any quantifiable career damage."

"Well, isn't there someone outside the firm you can confide in?"

"Well, I'm evaluating my options." Evie paused and emptied her wine glass. Even with the vague references she felt like she had said too much. She swallowed and said, "Have you ever felt that your fate is out of your control?" She looked at Joe who draped his arm across the back of Evie's chair.

"Yeah," said Ariel. "When I was standing before the judge in my divorce hearing."

"And see? That turned out perfectly," said Joe nodding toward Bradley's stroller.

"Well, if you need them, I've got close friends in the media. The power of the press can be very effective when you're feeling powerless."

chapter
21

An uneventful flight the next morning and Evie was in the office by two thirty in the afternoon. She walked to Hanover's office still without a clear, cohesive story to tell. She wasn't sure he was in the office, but he was definitely the partner she wanted to confide in. As she approached Liza, Hanover's secretary, she was stunned to see Alan standing over the reception counter engaged in what appeared to be an animated storytelling. Liza was laughing and gesturing, and began her own counter-story. As Evie approached, she heard the final fragment of Liza's anecdote.

"... and I asked her what she wanted to be when she grew up. That little Miss Thing didn't miss a beat. '*A V.I.P.,*' she said!" Alan laughed as if Liza had paid for it in advance. As he threw his head for effect, he noticed Evie approaching. Liza turned and smiled a greeting.

"Evie," Alan said her name as if it tasted good. "The traveling associate has returned. Now that you're back, you'll be available for new matters?"

Evie had abandoned thoughts of fleeing and succumbed to the
social undertow pulling her toward Liza's desk, but she felt a surge
in her blood pressure and her limbs felt stiff and heavy. She tried to
keep an even tone in her voice while the words stumbled over her dry
tongue. "I don't know. I will have to check my availability and get back
to you."

Evie directed her attention to Liza. "Is Hanover in today?" Evie's
eyes darted quickly toward Alan and then she added, "I wanted to give
him an update on that client meeting in Florida."

"He was in for a few minutes this morning, but left for some tests,"
Liza said. "He hasn't been that cooperative and the doctors are getting
more forceful in their orders." Liza turned back to Alan. "Did *you* have
a chance to see him this morning, Alan?"

"Nope. No luck. But I know you will direct him to me the minute he
calls in, right?" Alan flashed an electric smile at Liza and then turned it
toward Evie, as he swaggered off with the air of a man who is confident
of his own charisma, convinced that he had succeeded in leaving the
two women wanting more of his company.

Evie felt perspiration form all over her body. For a brief moment,
she wondered if she should follow him and simply ask him about Gerais
Chevas and Sangerson. But the recent exchange in his office had taught
her that confrontations with Alan were pointless. He would either act
innocent and deflect blame or play some sort of word game about the
conversations that had occurred between them. Pinning him down
would be like trying to stick something to a slippery metal surface. He
was not going to offer some sort of admission, and after she'd confronted
him, he would know she was investigating. Her only advantage would
have evaporated. She asked Liza to let her know the next time Hanover
would be spending any time in the office, emphasizing the importance
of a brief conversation with him.

As Evie sat at her desk and thought about what to do next, she
unconsciously rifled through papers lying askew on her desk. She pictured a meeting with Hanover with a partnership committee present,

a he-said-she-said with Alan putting her on trial. She could hear him when asked about Sangerson: *"She misunderstood the instructions and drew erroneous conclusions instead of clarifying, and now she's back-pedaling since she was caught giving a client sloppy service. Accusations like the ones she's making flow from a paranoid, overly-suspicious mind and are designed to deflect blame from her own shortcomings."*

What evidence could she pursue that would be clearly exculpa tory? She began thinking about sending an email message to the sole Geraio Chevas contact she knew—the holder of the "Adinaldo" email account. The voice in her head abruptly said *no*—to write to Adinaldo would be a premature announcement of *"checkmate,"* no matter what she wrote. If she received a reply, it would not be easy to determine the authenticity and accuracy of the response, nor could she ascertain this person's motivations or loyalties. She answered emails from Adam Peyton and a client who was asking about legal attribution for joint works of art.

Liza called to inform her that Hanover should be back in the office the following Monday and she had added Evie to his calendar. Monday seemed a long way off. Could Evie wait that long to inform the partnership about her findings? There would be no time to think about it. She looked up to see Paul standing in her doorway.

"Evie, do you have a minute?"

"Yes, of course. Come in."

Paul walked in without looking back at Helen who was watching his entrance from her desk. The door shut behind him and he sat wordlessly for a few weighty seconds in the chair facing Evie's desk.

"Evie, I've always been very fond of you," he began, his eyes darting about. "Hanover hand-picked you and you've proven to have many good qualities over the years you've been with the firm."

Evie offered a guarded half-smile and studied Paul's face. She felt a growing queasiness in her stomach. She could sense that Paul was here to deliver some type of reprimand. *Or perhaps worse.* Had Alan *already succeeded* in convincing the partnership to fire her?

"I've never personally known you to neglect a client or mismanage a client matter," he continued. "I have unfortunately received several complaints lately that you've done just that."

Evie started to say something, but silenced herself.

"—Now, I'm sure that these claims are not without valid defenses, but I wanted to just let you know where you stood because, as you know, preliminary discussions are underway on who will be up for partnership this year."

"I assume one of the complainants is Steve Buniker because of Sangerson."

"Yes."

"Who are the others? Was Alan among them by any chance?"

"I discussed that Sangerson matter with Alan. As I said before, he actually *defended* you—said there must've been some misunderstanding. But, he said he *had* encountered a few problems with you lately on other matters. Missed deadlines. Sloppy work. Lack of preparation for conference calls."

"Hmmmm. I see."

"Tom Margolis said he had to discount our bill for work you did for a client of his. The client complained about the number of hours you spent working on—"

"Wait a minute! That was because that client kept changing things. They re-wrote the terms of their deal at least ten times. I kept updating the agreement to reflect their changes—"

"And there were client complaints."

Evie stared solemnly.

"Who?"

"Frank Mueller of VelloPro said you were weeks late on a memo."

"That's because Alan let it sit on his desk for weeks after I gave it to him. That delay was not my fault even though Alan made it appear that way when we were on a conference call with Frank."

"Jerry Habee from Neully said your work on a trademark issue cost them because the launch of a product was delayed."

"That was unavoidable. There was a strong likelihood of confusion with other marks and I simply gave them responsible legal guidance. Paul, you know very well that sometimes our best advice is not what the client wants to hear."

"And there was a complaint from Roma Sori."

"What?! *Adam* complained?"

"He said there was a breach of confidentiality. He said that the *New York Technologist* called him about his deal with SerosaSoft. That's your deal, isn't it?" Evie nodded.

Paul continued, "They wanted comments. He couldn't understand how they knew about the deal. He said that they claimed a firm source."

"That's impossible! I haven't talked to the press!" Evie raised her voice, but decided a change in volume was a mistake and softened it again. "How could you *think* I . . . I didn't—"

"Wait, Evie, it's our policy to investigate these things. We will investigate further. You deserve that."

"Thank you."

She stared and tried to control her rapid breathing.

"Well, anyway, I couldn't avoid informing you about these reports. Regardless of any personal view I may have, these statements are part of the record that will be evaluated at the appropriate time. Within the context of your overall record, of course. But consider this. You now have the opportunity that many are not afforded. You have the chance to improve your performance before official partnership discussions ensue. Now. If I remember correctly, you wanted to speak to me about something."

She felt a hot flash of rage and she felt her body bristle with a second wave of perspiration. She tried to breathe normally. She had never before received negative feedback about her performance. *Especially untrue and unfair feedback.*

"Okay, Paul. May I say something now?"

"Yes, of course."

"I've invested a lot in this firm. I joined the ranks of your associates with an attitude of loyalty and dedication. No associate has worked harder than I have to establish a reputation for quality service and client satisfaction."

Paul nodded.

Evie continued, "You know well my explanation on Sangerson, but I have to tell you what I think is going on here."

"What do you mean, Evie?"

Evie shifted in her seat. She was still trying to decide how much information to share with Paul. Her instincts were telling her to reveal what she could prove, but that wasn't much. She took a deep breath. "I think Sangerson is only a part of a plan to discredit me. To tarnish my reputation in the eyes of the partners, so that I can be made a scapegoat for something bigger. *I think Alan is setting me up."* The words came out finally.

"Evie, I realize you may be feeling a bit upset, but let's not make rash accusations. That's quite an extreme statement."

"I realize that."

"I think you need to take a breath and listen to yourself. As I said, Alan spoke out in your defense, and these are the impressions of *several* partners. And *clients.* Alan could not have manipulated the clients' complaints."

"I would not make such an allegation unless I believed it to be true."

"Evie, please. You should *not* take this personally. You have to just move on and do the work I know you're capable of doing." He shook his head slowly and sighed. "No one is out to get you."

"Paul, in each of those situations you described, Alan was involved or had influence, except Roma Sori. I don't know what happened there, but don't you think the others are a bit coincidental?"

"Tom Margolis was not—"

"Look, Paul, I know this must sound paranoid." She leaned forward over her desk, but felt as if she was leaning over a great precipice. "I mean it, this is going to be difficult to explain, because I don't have the complete story yet, but I see that I have no choice. There's something more going on here than what you've described. And you're in a position to protect the interests of the firm should they need protecting."

"Okay, I'm listening." Paul fixed his gaze and held no particular expression.

"I found some language in an agreement for the sale of a business that I thought was disturbing." She pulled the printed reps and warranties section of the Gerais Chevas master agreement from a file folder on her desk, handed it to Paul and paused to let him read. After a few seconds, she continued.

"I was troubled by the language that binds the attorney to fulfill certain obligations, even though this particular document doesn't spell out what those obligations are."

Evie paused and tried to read Paul's thoughts, but he was stone-faced. He glanced up from the document. "This Schedule B7 . . . Do you know what obligations the attorney is taking on? What this Project Neon consists of?"

"No. There's another file that contains the schedules and that particular one is blank at present. It was protected by passwords and I was only recently able to read the contents of the file."

"I'm not familiar with this transaction. So you're not assigned to work on this deal?"

"No. I had never heard of this client, Gerais Chevas, before."

"I'm curious. How did you happen to be looking into these files? Were you looking for some sample documents?" He raised his hand to his face and leaned his chin on an arched fist. His eyebrows dipped and froze, as if he was assessing a series of nonsequiturs. He didn't wait for her to answer. "Why would you seek out documents on a client matter that is secured by passwords you say you didn't have?"

"Well, I received an email from someone at the Brazilian offices of Gerais Chevas who seemed to be under the impression that I'm the one running the deal. And, there was a hotel bill attached to one of my expense reports that showed Brazilian telephone calls to and from a hotel room at the Colonial Court. But I never stayed there, and I never made or received any calls to Brazil. And, I received a voice mail from a woman who says she has information for me about the deal."

Evie paused and Paul must have decided that it was time for him to summarize. "So, you're saying that someone is using you as a front-person on a client matter without your knowledge?"

"Yes. That's exactly what I'm saying. And I'm saying it's Alan."

"But why in the world would Alan assign you a matter without your knowledge? He would want to involve you, transfer responsibility for the deal. What advantage would there be for him to keep you in the dark?"

"Because he didn't *assign* the matter to me. Instead, he's using me, my *identity,* as the deal's leader, but *he's* running it. Or at least he knows who *is.*"

"Why in the world would he do such a thing? Evie, this is a little hard to believe. You still want us to believe that he sent emails and documents from your email account to Sangerson. I'm having a hard time with these accusations. What could've prompted a partner to use the identity of an associate in such a way?"

"I'll tell you why. There's some aspect of the attorney's obligations in this deal that are unusual, maybe unethical, and possibly even illegal."

"That's a very serious accusation, Evie. What makes you think so?"

"Well, how common is it for an attorney to assume performance obligations in the transfer of ownership of a business?"

"There are certain tasks an attorney may be asked to perform."

"Yes, okay. Maybe serving as an escrow agent or communication clearing house, or to offer a legal opinion, but those kind of obligations wouldn't be hidden in a password-protected schedule."

"As I said, if it's password-protected and you have nothing to do with it, how did you happen to be able to access the file? How did you get the password?"

"It was in an email in my—" Evie paused. Should she tell Paul that an email sent from *her* email account contained the valid password and *that it was her mother's name?* How would he believe she had nothing to do with that?

"I've been doing some investigating because of that email and expense report . . . and, because I overheard a conversation." Evie knew she'd better get directly to the point as she was starting to make herself sound irredeemably paranoid.

"I was in the kitchen a week ago on Wednesday night." Evie shifted her eyes briefly in the direction of the kitchen. "Next to Conference Room C. I inadvertently overheard certain portions of a conversation that was taking place in there, over the speakerphone. Someone, I know it was Alan, was speaking Portuguese or Spanish mixed in with the English. Later, I concluded that it might have something to do with this Brazilian transaction. I was able to hear and understand a few of the words spoken and the voice of the person in the room was familiar."

She paused and took a deep breath. "Paul, *Alan mentioned my name.* That's what got my attention. I wouldn't have listened otherwise. And then he was saying that there wouldn't be a problem. There was some reference to a 'Schedule.' I'm guessing he was talking about Schedule B7. He said something about a paper trail . . . and something about acting alone."

"It's impossible to know the full context of a conversation from interpreting brief overheard portions. Frankly, I'm surprised that you thought it appropriate to listen in on a partner's conversation without making yourself known."

"But Paul, you're not looking at the big picture. If you take all of this information together, doesn't it seem a little strange? I have not been assigned to this deal, and yet I'm getting emails that indicate I'm in charge. Why would I make such accusations if I wasn't really confident in my suspicions?"

"As I said, you may be grossly mistaken about what you overheard. You're speculating based on a very few words. Evie, it's not unusual for an associate to be assigned to work on one part of a deal and left out of other parts, or included as backup on a large deal that may have multiple associate team members who serve interchangeably as time allows."

"But that's the point. I was never assigned to work on *any* aspect of this deal."

"Not yet. Perhaps this is simply a misunderstanding. I think you're overreacting to what may be a failure to communicate. Alan may have plans to involve you on some aspect of this deal and has simply not explained it to you yet."

"That was *my* first thought as well, but that's not all." Evie paused to watch Paul's reaction.

Paul's expression remained unchanged but seemed to intensify slightly and he flushed as if someone turned up his body temperature a few degrees.

"That same password allows access to the payment schedule for this deal. There's a mysterious commission in the amount of $25 million."

"Schedules, especially payment schedules, are often fleshed out during the negotiations and finalized at closing. Evie, you know that. When is this deal supposed to close?"

"September 20th, I think."

"Well, you are remarkably well-informed for someone who's not assigned. Is this about not *wanting* to be assigned? Are you resisting working for Alan because of the recent miscommunications between the two of you?"

There's nothing else she *could* do at this point, but tell him about the harassment. Her palms were sweating, as she knew Paul was not predisposed to believe her and she had *no* evidence to support *those* allegations. And, the passage of time would work against her. She knew she was walking toward the figurative edge of the cliff, but she took measured air into her lungs.

Paul's brow wrinkled with concern and curiosity. But there was a distance there. His attitude seemed to be taking shape in a fog of skepticism and disbelief. *Maybe I should wait for Hanover to reveal what happened in Chicago.*

Before she could open her mouth, he spoke again.

"How do you know it was Alan in that conference room? Did you see him?"

"No. I didn't, I smelled cigar smoke. Whoever was in there was smoking and he's the only one around here who ignores the smoking laws. And he came into my office a short time afterward. It was late. There weren't many other people around."

"Evie, that's not much to go on. Did he say anything about that client to you that night or at a later date?"

"No."

"Did he make any reference to that conversation that you overheard?"

"No. I don't know if he knew I was in the kitchen."

"Has he ever mentioned this deal to you?"

"No."

"Well, what did he say when he came into your office that night?"

"He just made small talk. Nothing of any consequence."

Paul said nothing.

"And the next day, when I tried to bring up the Gerais Chevas files from the electronic library, I was denied access because apparently my name was not on the security list. But then several days later, it *was*—I was allowed to bring up some of the files. So someone decided I needed to be in the group cleared for access."

"As I said, associates are assigned and de-assigned frequently. As you know, it's sometimes necessary to cc the entire group of attorneys who've been exposed to a deal to keep resources up to date. So then, if someone becomes dedicated to another matter, backup resources are ready to step in."

"But, Paul, isn't it unusual for a New York law firm to be counsel on a deal between two *Brazilian* companies?"

"Well, not necessarily. There could be necessary divestitures in the United States or other interests that require U.S. involvement. For example, there may be antitrust concerns if there's potential anti-competitive impact in U.S. markets. Do you know if there are U.S. interests?" He sniffed and leaned back in his chair. "How do you know that a South American law firm is not acting as co-counsel or primary counsel?"

"Well, if I was running the deal, as Alan is leading people to believe I am, wouldn't I know the answers to those questions? I don't."

"I'm not convinced that there's anything sinister going on here. Evie, I have great respect for you, but you said that it was late at night when you overheard this conversation. And, it was being conducted in part in another language. It's often difficult to accurately capture a conversation when the person speaking is in the *same* room and is speaking *English*. It sounds to me like Alan went out of his way to be very friendly to you when he saw that you were still in the office that night. You were both tired. Isn't it possible that he would have chosen to speak to you about this assignment when each of you was more fresh?"

"Yes. That's possible, but he didn't. He *hasn't*."

"Okay, not yet, but were you *ever* involved with this client? Sitting in on a meeting or even just participating in discussions about a possible deal?"

"No, I had never heard of them before I got dragged into this correspondence."

"*I'm* included in the correspondence on many deals on which I have no direct involvement."

Evie felt it unnecessary to point out to Paul that as part of the executive group of partners, he would of course be receiving cc's on most of the firm business. She decided to stick to the questions posed.

"The answer to your question is no." She repeated her denial for emphasis. "I've never billed any time to this deal or *any* deal for this client. I don't even think I had ever heard the client name before. Mmmm, Paul, what about that expense report receipt? Don't you think it's odd that two different hotels would have an Evelyn Sullivan registered for the same period of time? I've never stayed at the Colonial Court Hotel, by the way. Shouldn't that raise some questions?"

"I'll grant you that—that does seem strange. Get me a copy of that receipt and your verified time records for that period. I'll need the receipt from the hotel where you say you *did* stay. We'll get to the bottom of this. It will be easy enough to ask Alan about the origins of this transaction and any commissions involved."

"Okay."

"From now on, let's keep this matter between us until I have an understanding of what we're dealing with. In case there's something that might subject the firm to, uhhh, *criticism.* I will definitely look into this."

"Okay, but I *do* plan to talk to Hanover, too."

"I will fill him in myself."

"Thank you Paul."

He nodded, watched her for a moment and stood to leave. He paused, studying her face for another moment. Then he turned abruptly and left.

This whole process was starting to feel to Evie like she was traveling across country on foot. She closed her office door, sat in her chair and tried to assimilate what had just transpired. She thought she had done the right thing, but the conversation with Paul had left her feeling exhausted, uneasy and more confused than comforted.

She dialed Joe's office and his secretary put her right through.

"Eves," he greeted her. "Everything okay?"

"I just had a conversation with Paul and it didn't go very well."

"I'm sorry. Tell me about it."

"He came to me, I didn't have to go to him. He came in here enumerating all the ways I've been screwing up. Alan's responsible for every one of them in some way, except one, which I know has to be a mistake. But, I read it that I'm effectively on probation. Paul tried to make it sound as if he was giving me some inside information so that I could straighten up and still have a shot a partnership, but it really sounded like I've already been tried and convicted."

"Did you tell him about Project Neon and everything you've discovered?"

"I tried, but since my name is all over it and I've got access to the files, he just concluded that I'm on the team of associates and somehow there's been another miscommunication. Lots of miscommunication lately. He wasn't disturbed at that $25 million commission because it is an interim document that hasn't been fleshed out. And, of course, since he can't see the contents of Schedule B7 right in front of him, he's not overly concerned about that either. He did say he would check into the matter, ask Alan some questions and try to figure out how that faulty receipt got attached to my expense report, but he clearly didn't seem to believe me. I should have waited until I found something more concrete—I let those allegations against me cloud my judgment."

"It's natural to want to defend yourself. I'm surprised he wasn't suspicious of that commission. It could be a payoff of some kind, or a bribe."

"Actually, I don't think he believed that I wasn't assigned to the deal. He seemed to suggest that it was just about my disinterest in working with Alan."

"Did you tell him why you don't want to work with Alan?"

"No, since the conversation was going so badly, I decided to wait for Hanover. He's supposed to be in next Monday."

"Do you think it's possible that Paul was trying to minimize his reaction so as not to alarm you? Maybe he was shocked at what you were saying, but he's saving his real reaction for his fellow partners."

"I guess it's possible, but there was a bit of sarcasm. Because so much of my story is speculation and I knew the closing date of the deal and I'm on the access list for the files; he seemed to be almost amused at my denials. That's just what I was worried about. He apparently thinks I'm trying to throw mud at one of Alan's deals because we argued. And, I think because he started our conversation with a longwinded reprimand, it was as if nothing I could say could be taken independently."

"Not so easy to trust an authority who discounts your input."

No, it's not. Reaching out to Paul seemed like calling for help from a motionless elevator car stuck in an empty shaft. She had no control over what he would do next.

"You know, Joe, I just realized something. Since I didn't tell him about Chicago, he must think that *I'm* the one who's revenge hungry. Maybe, because I was blamed for Sangerson and because of all these new allegations against me, Paul sees *me* as someone trying to set up *Alan.*"

"Exactly what Alan wants."

chapter
22

As she was talking to Joe, Helen walked in and handed her a copy of her latest billing records for review. Joe had to put her on hold for a minute so she quickly flipped through the printout.

After a few minutes, he was speaking to her again.

"Eves, I'm looking to see if our sniffer has turned up anything."

"Joe, you're not going to believe this, but I'm looking at my time records. I email my time to accounting every month and they produce a report tracked by client. Gerais Chevas is on here. It says I billed fourteen hours to them in July."

"How could that be? Has Alan got control over the accounting records as well?"

"I'm starting to believe the whole firm is conspiring against me."

"Have you reported the error?"

"Not yet, I just got the printout. Oh, this is great. I just told Paul I didn't bill time to this client. He's going to see this."

"But it's an erroneous report."

"I know, but how do I prove it? Again, I'll be on the defensive."

"You can prove where you were and what you were doing during that time."

"I'm sure I can come up with something, but unless I was meeting a client on that date, I won't have absolute proof I wasn't working on Gerais Chevas while I was in the office, especially with my name on the *Hit History* of those files. Electronic records can be challenged, but I think they're presumed correct. That's why Paul's been so resistant to my claims."

"So, Alan is fairly adept at computer hijackery. I'm going to send him another email. If he opens it, it will install a spyware package."

"Joe, I don't know if I'm comfortable with that."

"The only way we may be able to prove his identity theft is to track his electronic movements. It just records keystrokes."

"There are legions of attorneys ready to argue that it's illegal to invade someone's privacy like that."

"Maybe for the government to do it, but not a private citizen, right counselor? At least not according to today's Internet etiquette. Information gathering's still fair game. We're not stealing *his* identity or defrauding him in any way."

"Well, let me exhaust my overt resources first. I still haven't talked to Hanover."

"Can you get in touch with Hanover before next Monday?"

"I'll obviously have to try. Did you come up with anything in Alan's email?"

Evie could hear him typing on his keyboard. "Here's something. A confirmation in response to an email from an Adinaldo Rafael. Some sort of meeting is going to take place. This Adinaldo is apparently going to participate by conference phone. There's a reference to a U.S. Senator."

"A *senator* . . . Is it Senator Arbeson by any chance?"

"It doesn't mention the Senator by name, just refers to him as 'that U.S. Senator.' It says that they need to address the *'gov proj profile.'* It's cryptic, but I get the feeling that some government contract work is part of the appeal of this business unit being sold by Gerais Chevas. If it's just been awarded a government contract, that fact would certainly make it more marketable." He paused and continued to type.

"How could I find that out?"

"Well, once a competitive bidding process had ended, the winner is announced publicly."

"How would I—"

"I'll do some checking."

"Oh my God! I wonder if Senator Arbeson . . . I heard he was being investigated on a bribery charge."

"Wouldn't your firm—"

"No. Not something my firm is involved with. I heard a rumor from a friend. Anyway, the thought occurred to me that he could somehow be involved with this Gerais Chevas deal. He's tight with Alan, he's married to a South-American, he's fluent in some Latin-sounding language and he has been notably active encouraging joint business ventures between New York and South American entities."

"It does raise questions now, doesn't it?"

"I would love to listen in on that conference call. Does it mention an AT&T conference call number or any other specifics?"

"No, not in this email, but there may be others to come."

"Print that out for me, okay?"

"Absolutely. Do you want me to mail it or bring it with me?"

"Bring it when you come. Have you talked to your private investigator friend?"

"No, but I've left messages for him," said Joe. "Should hear something soon."

"I need to find out more about this woman who called me. Is there any way to track her down?"

"Not much to go on, but I'll talk to him about it. She hasn't called back?"

"No. Joe, oh Joe, I'm looking at the reps and warranty language again and something just hit me."

"What?"

"It says that the main agreement won't be binding on the purchaser until the signature of the seller's lawyer is *electronically* affixed."

"Ahhh. So an easy way for Alan to forge your signature."

"I guess this means that an electronic signature will be sufficient to force the purchaser to go through with the deal," she paused. "And force the attorney to do whatever has to be done to *secure* Project Neon."

"Does it say what form the digital signature will take? Digitized handwritten signature or some kind of private key regime like was on that password-protected file?"

"No, it just says the signature will be electronically affixed."

"So, Alan doesn't need you to be physically present to close the deal. He can attach your electronic signature and presumably, you'd be committed to perform."

"Yes, it seems like that's the plan."

"Do you have a digitized version of your handwritten signature stored on your computer or on the firm's system anywhere?"

"Not that I can remember, but then I've signed hundreds of documents by hand while I've been at the firm."

"Yes, a written signature could easily be digitized without your knowledge. Listen, Eves, are you okay? I've got to go to a meeting, but we'll stay on his trail, okay?"

"Yes, yes. Joe, I'm fine. Thanks for everything."

"I'll be there in a couple of days. Not sure exactly when yet."

"Okay, until then."

She hung up and weighed her options. She dialed Liza's extension and was given Hanover's cell phone number. Evie had always been able to adequately communicate with Hanover using his regular extension and voice mail, but this situation would require immediate contact.

Hanover answered on the second ring.

"Jack, may I speak with you for a few minutes? It's very important."

"Evie, absolutely. What's up?"

"I didn't really want to go into this over the telephone, but I don't think this can wait."

She relayed the details of her conversation with Paul. Hanover listened without interrupting, then he spoke.

"Evie, I have been informed of these petty allegations that've been tossed around about you. In offer of apology, I didn't intend for you to be troubled with any of this. I'm not at all convinced they happened as reported."

"Thank you, Jack. I was hoping you'd give me the benefit of the doubt."

"Due consideration will be afforded."

"I can't understand how that happened with Sangerson, unless someone specifically hijacked my email account and sent out that document in its raw form. I specifically emailed my revised version to Alan that evening before I left the office, as he had requested. Short of some sort of virus in my email, I can't imagine how that document mix-up occurred. As for Roma Sori, I've got a call into Adam. I want to find out how his SerosaSoft deal was leaked to the *New York Technologist*—"

"You can stop there. I didn't find anything in those complaints to work up a sweat over. And, I'm sure there's some explanation for that leak. I don't have the details on that, but I'm going to find out."

"Thank you, Jack."

"Okay, now let's talk about this Gerais Chevas deal."

"Yes, I'm completely baffled by the inclusion of my name in the file access lists, the correspondence. I've—"

"I can't imagine you denying involvement in something untruthfully. You've laid out very clearly your concerns about the details of this deal. I appreciate you bringing this matter to my attention. I will speak to Paul and Alan and we'll get to the bottom of this. Should be easy enough."

"Okay, Jack. Here's the part I didn't tell Paul. I haven't told any partner."

"Evie, hang on a minute, I'm going to have to call you back on a land line."

The connection was lost, but within minutes, Hanover was put through to her desk.

"Sorry, Evie, my cell went dead."

"No problem. Jack, again, I know the telephone is not the best way to communicate this, but I can see this thing escalating rapidly now and I've got to get everything out on the table."

Hanover remained silent, but she could hear a formidable white noise in the background, as if he was standing in a train station or other large, echo-filled enclosure.

"Jack, Alan made a pass at me on a client trip last year and I failed to report it. It was that Simmons pitch we did together in Chicago—"

"Evie, you'll have to speak up. There's an enthusiastic salesman on the next phone."

"Okay, Jack." Evie spoke louder and despite her closed office door she looked around as she spoke as if she was shouting her most embarrassing moment to everyone she'd ever known.

"That Simmons pitch in Chicago, do you remember that? Alan and I did a joint presentation. It included my overview of our IP practice."

"Yes, yes, I remember."

"Alan followed me back to my hotel room afterward, kissed me and tried to push his way into my room."

"Mmmm, I see."

"And, after I threatened to call you, he made a good case at the time for why I shouldn't report it. He apologized and said he'd gotten wrapped up in the excitement of our success with the client. I wanted to be a team player and not overreact so I agreed not to report it, but I know now that was a mistake. And, I feel like that promise has been overridden by these recent events and what I believe is Alan's current agenda."

"Yes, I can understand that. Well, this does thicken the plot, so to speak."

"I hope I can be completely honest with you, Jack."

"Yes, please do."

"I really feel that Alan decided then and there that I would be a convenient scapegoat. I don't know what this Gerais Chevas transaction is all about, but to the extent that it *does* turn out to be controversial, I feel that Alan is arranging to be able to point the finger at me."

"It is a deal of some size, I understand. I will definitely become more familiar with the specifics. Evie, an ethics committee meeting will be convened as soon as possible. The partnership has duly noted your sexual harassment complaint and will initiate a discrete investigation into the matter immediately."

"Thank you, Jack. I assume you will have to question Alan about it directly."

"Yes, of course."

"I'm not sure what series of events that will put in motion."

"He will be instructed not to have any contact with you while this investigation is ongoing. Any matters you are currently assigned under Alan will be redirected, including Gerais Chevas."

"By the way, Jack. The billing report I just received shows that I billed fourteen hours to Gerais Chevas last month. Either it's a mistake or it's a manipulation. It's wrong."

"I'll take care of it."

"Thank you so much Jack. I knew I could trust you."

Evie hung up the receiver, took a deep breath and stood to walk to the kitchen for a cup of coffee. She opened her office door expecting to see Helen, but stared into the face of Alan Levenger.

chapter
23

U hh. Excuse me," said Evie. "I was just going to get a cup of coffee."
A look beyond Alan revealed that Helen was not at her desk.

Evie hoped that she was not wearing her thoughts on her face. There was nothing to talk about now with Alan. No reason to even share a hallway.

"Evie, I need to talk to you."

"Alan, I'm on a tight deadline, can we talk later?" She silently hoped there wouldn't be a "later" once Hanover informed him to stay away from her.

"It's very important." Had Alan been listening outside her door? Or maybe he sensed that the momentum was now no longer all his.

Unable to refuse to speak to him on any pretext, she sat down hard in her office chair and took a few breaths before she looked up to meet his gaze.

Insincerity oozed from his expression. Evie opened a drawer and her hand made a blind attempt to locate the mini tape recorder, as her eyes focused forward. Alan walked into her office and bypassed the visitor chairs, seemingly studying the framed diplomas on her walls and the books and small photographs standing on shelves. As he neared her side of the desk, she pulled out her hand from the drawer and closed it.

He stopped himself just before reaching her chair and turned on his heel. With his back to her he asked, "Do you have a hotmail account, Ms. Sullivan?"

"A what?" Her face showed no recognition, but her mind focused on Joe's "goliath" email message.

"A hotmail account. An account to and from which one sends electronic email."

"No. I don't." She kept her eyes on his back.

"It can be quite handy for sending anonymous email."

"That's interesting, but Alan I really have to get back to work here."

"There's just one problem with it, though. The identity of the sender can be ascertained in any number of ways."

"Alan, is this leading somewhere?"

"Just a reminder, professionally speaking, to be very careful with the confidentiality of the firm's clients. You need to consider the consequences and the damage that could be caused, not just to you and the firm, but to outside persons and entities. Actions may have unintended outcomes." He turned to face her as he spoke and stared.

"What does that mean?" She stared back at him.

"It's just important to remember that the actions you take have consequences, that's all. And they may have an impact that you didn't anticipate." He stood looking at her for a moment, then turned and left.

Evie suddenly felt like taking a shower—as if a foul-smelling unidentified substance had just been flung at her and was now dripping off of her in slow motion. A second stirring of the contents of her drawer uncovered a box containing the elusive tape recorder. She slid in a fresh tape and deposited it in her briefcase poised in the ready. A persistent flashing on her telephone told her Helen must still be away from her desk so she picked up the receiver and punched the illuminated line.

"Hello?"

"Is this *Eveleen* Sullivan?"

"Yes. Who is this?"

"I'm weeth a company called Romez Nuevo. You are familiar weeth it, yes?"

"Well, I am aware of a deal being negotiated between your company and Gerais Chevas. How did you get my name?"

"You are d'attorney for d'seller?"

"Uhhh . . . well, I believe my firm represents the seller, Gerais Chevas."

"You are dee one negotiateen' d'deal, yes? Huh-you know . . . Project Neon?"

"No. But, since you work for Romez Nuevo, I'm afraid I can't talk to you. It would be unethical."

"I t'ink you *need* to talk to me."

"Your company is represented by counsel. If you have information for Gerais Chevas, you should speak to your attorney who will then present the information to someone in our firm. I'm afraid I will have to end this conversation—"

"No . . . huh—you don't understand. I 'yave information for *you*."

"Me?"

"Yes."

"What kind of information? Why . . . *wait*, did you leave me a voice mail message before?"

"Yes. I am been trying to tell you." Evie was growing accustomed to the accent, but she couldn't quite place the nationality of the speaker. She grabbed the tape recorder, put the caller on speaker and hit PLAY.

"Tell me what?"

"I am on speaker phone?"

"Yes."

"Please, take me off."

Evie picked up the receiver and tried to position the tape recorder near enough to pick up the conversation. "Okay, you're off."

"You'ave problem."

"Uhhh. Huh? How do you—"

"If d'is deal closes, I lose everyt'ing."

"You mean the one involving Project Neon?"

"Yeah." The woman coughed and continued, "I not say somet'ing more over d'telephone. You can meet me, yes?"

"Meet you where? Are you calling from New York City?"

"Yes. Huh-hyou know Mangia on Fi'ty-Seven', yes?"

"Yes."

"Meet me d'ere tomorrow at eleven d'irty. Ho-kay?"

"How will I know how to—"

"Wait beside dee entrance on Fifty-Seven'. I will find you."

"But . . . *wait* . . . what do you look like?"

"I 'yave black 'air, and I wee-ll be wearing red dress."

The line went dead. Evie let the telephone receiver slide from her sweaty hand back into the cradle. Since Howard Rolland was representing Gerais Chevas in the negotiation with Romez Nuevo, she knew she could be disciplined by the Bar for meeting with a Romez Nuevo employee without its counsel present.

She left a vague message for Hanover on his voice mail asking him to call her on the matter they'd discussed earlier. Evie dialed Liza, but she didn't answer and Hanover's cell phone voice mail box was full. Other client work beckoned, so she handled the most urgent matters and gathered up the files she was working on with Alan to be redistributed.

Her thoughts wandered to the new information Joe had intercepted and how it fused with what she already knew. If Senator Arbeson was willing to play games with the IRS, what other legal compromises might he be willing to make? Could this entire $25 million commission be a bribe? Is it payment for channeling a government contract in a certain direction? Would this woman from Romez Nuevo be able to offer any relevant information?

Helen buzzed, interrupting her thoughts and announcing Adam Peyton.

"Adam, yes, I got your message about SerosaSoft and I've glanced through the revised agreement, but before we get into that I have to ask you something."

"Yes, of course. What is it?"

She struggled momentarily with how to word the next question. "I have to know something. Did you report to the firm that the *New York Technologist* contacted you about your SerosaSoft deal?"

"Yes, I did. I did complain. I didn't want that deal to become public knowledge."

"And did you have any information about who leaked the story?"

"The reporter told me that a man called him out of the blue. It was an anonymous 'well-placed source,' but then unfortunately, someone here confirmed the story so they went to print."

"A man. You said a man called the reporter?"

"Yes. Wait a minute. I hope no one suggested that *you* were the source. I specifically said that it *wasn't* you. I will call immediately and clear that up, if there's any confusion."

"No. Adam, no problem. You don't need to make any calls. I just needed to know. Roma Sori is very important to me. It matters to me that you know you can rely on my discretion."

"Of course! Evie, we have nothing but the highest regard for you."

"Thank you, Adam. I appreciate your candor."

"Absolutely. Okay, let's talk about these last few issues."

When Evie arrived at the office the next morning, there was a return voice mail from Hanover. He said he was boarding a plane to London, but had called an urgent meeting of the partnership's ethics committee, which had been conducted by conference call over the weekend. Alan had relayed a different story regarding the Chicago incident and the partnership was currently divided on whom to believe, but he said not to worry about it. He finished his message by saying that she should expect a visit from Paul, who would be providing additional detail. Nothing about her request for guidance on the proposed meeting with the female caller from Romez Nuevo. Had he not yet received that message? Maybe she would get another call from him from an airport somewhere.

At 10:20 she returned to her office after spending the morning at client meetings in Soho. No additional messages from Hanover and Helen had not heard from, or seen, Paul. *Of course Alan would deny the whole thing. What would they expect?*

She dialed Joe's number and was told he was out of the office. His cell offered voice mail. There wasn't time to track him down before she had to make a decision.

Still unsure whether to actually meet the Romez Nuevo woman, she decided to ask Jenna's opinion. Jenna was still traveling on client business, according to her voice mail greeting. Evie decided not to leave her a message. Should she meet with this woman without Hanover's knowledge? She dialed Paul and his secretary said he was unavailable, but did expect to meet with Evie the next morning if that worked for her. Evie agreed to a ten o'clock A.M. meeting and hung up. She would have to make a decision—the woman would be looking for her today at 11:30 and it was now a few minutes before eleven o'clock. Evie answered some email and shuffled through her inbox. She had to find out what this woman knew.

As she stood to leave, she was moist with sweat, and had a light-headed feeling that almost forced her to sit down again. She took a deep breath and steadied herself. Stretching her back, she extended her arms toward the ceiling as if she was trying to pull something out of herself. Despite the assurances from Hanover, she was in charge of her own delicate innocence. Alan was devoted to piloting this subterfuge, whatever it was, and had apparently managed to cause dissension among the partners. His poison was polluting what was left of her honorable reputation. If Alan had compromised the *firm's* integrity, this woman might have information crucial to their defense. *One good rationalization for the road.* Whatever she found out, she would report her findings directly to Hanover.

Before she closed the door to her office the telephone rang again. Helen placed the caller on hold and told Evie that it was a gentleman caller who would not identify himself. Evie slipped back into her office and picked up the receiver.

"You've been busy," said a deep male voice with an acidic resonance that created the auditory illusion that the voice was coming from inside the room.

"Who is this?" A smoldering silence followed. A chill shook her to the core. "Is anyone there? Who is this???"

"If you're smart, you will not keep the appointment you made for today."

"What? Who are you? How did you—"

The line went dead.

chapter
24

Joe threw down his overnight bag just inside the door and grabbed the telephone bearing the hotel logo on the nightstand. He dialed Evie's office number and sat on the bed, receiver to his ear counting the unanswered rings. This morning's attempts to reach her from the plane had been futile and his cell battery was now dead. Her cell phone must either be dead or turned off. He did not want to leave messages on her voice mail, preferring to speak to her directly. Maybe a quick trip by her office. He had to reach her.

He listened to the rings until he was again deposited into Evie's voice mail. This time, he left a message for Evie to call him at the Four Seasons, Room 3901, as soon as possible.

He took off his clothes, wrapped a towel around his waist and turned on the hot water in the shower. He was about to shave when the telephone rang. He jogged out of the bathroom and grabbed the receiver.

"Hello?"

"Hey Joey! How the hell's my favorite mama's boy?"

"Greg, is that you?" Joe sat on the bed and shifted the receiver to his other ear.

"Who the fuck do you think it is? *007?* Hey Joe, my man, what the hell are you doing back in New York?"

"Business. Hey, I've been trying to reach *you* for several days. What're you running from? Creditors or an angry wife?"

"I know, man. Sorry. Just got back from Germany and leaving for Japan tomorrow."

"Sounds like your skills have found a place in the global economy."

"Well, yeah. What can I say? I'm thorough."

"Have you got some time for me? I need a few inquiries and some background on a barrister."

"Wait. Not so *fast.* Right here. In my hand. I got this lovesick email from you. Pathetic romantic fool. Who is this chick with the incredible eyes you met in the air?"

"Forget that. Shred it, okay? I should've known better than to tell you about her. Okay, business. Seriously, Greg, I need your help."

"Okay, okay. How 'bout if I have Rich do some checking?"

"No, sorry. I'm going to ask you to handle this one yourself, okay? It's really important. The players are sensitive."

"Sure, man. Sure thing. Say, this doesn't have anything to do with this lady friend of yours does it?"

"Maybe."

"Is she a . . . ? Don't tell me. You want me to check out a *female* barrister, right?"

"No."

"Is she the one you want checked out?"

"No. It's—"

"You amaze me, man. You keep up with this dedicated-pursuit thing. There are so many women out there. You're a free man. Why limit yourself to one? You should taste all the flavors."

"Been there, done that, my friend. *You* should try focusing on that beautiful wife of yours for a change."

"Oh, you mean that pampered pigeon that spends all my money and complains because I don't make it fast enough? Huh! She has the credit cards, I have my freedom. No questions. That's the way we play it. Hell, I didn't even say anything when I started getting bills from her 'colon therapist' for some kind of green-tea detox powder. It seems she's become obsessed with her digestive system."

Joe laughed. "The modern American marriage."

"The less I see her the better."

"Epiphanies, my friend. I can't see mine enough."

"Oh jeez . . . you've got it bad. I don't wanna lose my supper here, so just map out the gig for me, will ya?"

"Sure. Usual discretion. As fast as you can. I emailed you some dates and details. See if you can find anyone at the Colonial Court Hotel in Dallas who ID'd the woman registering. I also emailed you some information about an anonymous phone call from a Brazilian woman. See if you have any ideas on how to find her. And, most important, see what you can dig up on a New York local—Alan Levenger. He's a partner at a law firm called Howard, Rolland & Stewart."

~

Evie walked along the Avenue of the Americas, barely aware of the minutes marching toward 11:30. Somebody did not want her to meet the mysterious female caller who apparently believed Evie was the attorney negotiating this Brazilian transaction. She could alter her route at any moment and forget about the woman expecting to meet her. There were hundreds of people populating the sidewalks in her immediate vicinity. An illusion of safety accompanied her as she walked, eyeing the faces she passed and weighing her options. Her mind sorted a series of thoughts.

It was possible that a number of people on *both* sides of this Gerais Chevas transaction believed she was running the deal. All communication on it could have been conducted exclusively by telephone and email. The use of her name and email account would have been enough. There would be no reason for those present at Project Neon meetings to suspect that a voice on speakerphone claiming to be Evie Sullivan was anyone other than her. And now she understood how easily her electronic signature could be affixed without her knowledge.

These possibilities agitated her raw nerves. If her suspicions proved valid, the theft of her identity could be almost complete. So who was this man with The Voice who told her to cancel her meeting? Something drove her forward despite her mushrooming fear. Maybe the woman from Romez Nuevo had some of the answers to her questions. The woman had said that she would lose everything if the deal closed, so she herself must also be vulnerable in some way. Could Evie trust her? Why had the woman selected *her* to contact?

It suddenly occurred to Evie that Alan might have mentioned that hotmail message when he was being questioned by the firm's ethics committee. He clearly suspected that the message had originated with her. She had told Hanover that she was putting everything out on the table. Should she have confessed her electronic sleuthing? No. She would not make Joe a known adversary to the firm, no matter what accusations flew.

She walked up to the 57th Street entrance of Mangia and glanced at her watch; she was right on time. She looked around. The sun was shining, and the street was crowded with the usual varieties of Manhattan foot traffic. She wondered if she was being tailed. She hadn't seen the man she had ditched at Starbucks since he hurried off from the street in front of her building. Could the Starbucks Man be the man with The Voice?

She let her eyes scan each direction. Tourists shuffled by, balancing cameras, shopping bags, fanny packs and maps. Business types wove quickly through the crowds with looks of impatience. Evie's eyes fell on each lone, dark-haired female moving in her direction until the non-red clothing they were wearing caused her to divert her attention. As each man passed, she gathered herself and measured the air for any indication that he might be the man with The Voice. No person she witnessed looked to be engaged in anything other than regular daily activity. She glanced through the windows into the Mangia café and saw a woman wearing a reddish dress, but she was blonde and speaking loudly with a southern accent. Evie turned her attention back to the street.

She looked at her watch again and sighed. Had she misunderstood the meeting place? No, she was certain the woman said Mangia on 57th Avenue. Well, 57th wasn't an avenue, but that didn't matter, unless . . . *unless* she'd been talking about someplace on *7th Avenue.* Maybe Evie had misunderstood the name of the café . . . and what she thought was "fifty" was part of the name of the café. The accent *did* present a challenge. Well, too late now. Evie waited a few more minutes and wondered what to do. There was no way to contact the woman and no easy way to find out who she was. She had said she was with Romez Nuevo. Could she find out if any of its employees were known to be currently in New York? Maybe Joe's PI could.

She looked again at her watch. She had now waited twenty minutes for the woman in the red dress. She decided that this meeting was not going to happen, at least not today. A siren broke her concentration and roared past where she stood. It turned onto the Avenue of the Americas and the siren faded.

Evie left her position by the door of Mangia, continuing to watch for any males of dubious appearance, and walked down 57th Street, still keeping an eye out for a dark-haired woman in a red dress. As she glanced down the Avenue of the Americas, she noticed the flashing lights of the ambulance that had passed her. It had stopped somewhere a few blocks away. She noticed a crowd gathering on the sidewalk near its parking place. Curiosity or fate caused her to walk toward the ambulance. When she got closer, she saw two police cars parked at the curb ahead of it.

She followed the rhythm of the sidewalk traffic and found herself adjacent to the gathering crowd. As people shifted and parted, she could see that there was the body of a woman lying on the sidewalk. There was a pool of blood next to the motionless head and she looked away quickly, wondering if the woman was still alive. She said a silent prayer for her. The paramedics were engaged in life-saving choreography, but they did not have optimistic faces. Something caused Evie to take another look.

She saw the paramedics place the woman on a gurney and noticed that she was dark-complected with black hair. Before a paramedic unfolded a sheet over the woman, Evie noticed she was wearing a *red dress*. Evie walked on with a queasy feeling in her stomach. *No, it couldn't be. Could it?*

No, this couldn't be *the* woman. Manhattan is a city of eight million people, with many more numbers of tourists and visitors, any number of whom are females wearing red dresses on any given day. What are the odds of a particular woman wearing a red dress, with dark hair, a few blocks from where they were supposed to meet . . . or, *prevented* from meeting? No, it *must* be a coincidence.

chapter

25

E vie! I've been trying to reach you. I've got to see you."

"Joe? You're in the city? I didn't know you were flying in today."

"Plans accelerated. Listen Eves, I need to talk to you, but it has to be in person. Can you meet me . . . uhh . . . meet me at the park. You remember where we paused on our walk that Friday night?"

"You mean when you talked to that hors—"

"Yeah. There. Can you meet me there? *Now?*"

"Uhh . . . sure . . . okay . . . yes, Joe, but why are you—"

"I just have to see you. I just can't wait to see you."

"Okay. I'll be there in fifteen minutes."

The air was sweet and citrus-crisp courtesy of a rainstorm that had lingered over the city the night before. Central Park was bustling with people lunching, exercising and otherwise managing to absorb the beautiful sunshine on this September day. After casually sweeping the area around her with his eyes, Joe rushed up to her. He wanted to be absolutely certain that they could talk privately.

"Hey Eves," he said encircling her with his arm and finding her moist mouth with his. He didn't let the kisses linger, but whispered into her ear, "I want to be sure you weren't followed, so let's walk a bit."

She looked at him wide-eyed but then took the cue and forced a casual carriage and expression, leaning into him as they walked arm in arm, in leisure harmony, albeit manufactured. He guided her to a vacant bench well within the park. There were joggers and bicyclists and the occasional pair of suited business people, and Joe was comfortable that they could freely talk, their voices masked by the surrounding park traffic noise and the currents of wind.

Evie read his unease. "Joe—what's going on? Why would you think I was followed? Did you find out something?"

"I'm afraid that there's a good possibility that some of our telephone conversations have been intercepted."

"A phone tap? You think my phone is bugged?"

"No, Eves, it's mine. My office phone. This has nothing to do with what you think. Parapier is involved in some classified government technology projects. It's routine. They monitor the telephone calls of the top executives."

"Why?"

"It's part of a security clearance. I should've anticipated . . . and I should have recognized the dial-tone interference and the background noise, but I didn't. The point is, I'm afraid they may have heard me tell you about the content of that email message I tracked . . . and, the *rest* of our conversation yesterday."

"The information about the Senator?" She thought for a moment. "Oh my God! And the possibility that he could be taking *bribes?!*"

Joe didn't answer immediately, watching a couple who seemed to be contemplating sharing their bench, but then moved on to a shadier spot.

"I know they sample randomly," he said, "but I don't know which conversations and what portions were collected. I'm hoping any recording made yesterday will be filed away in some government archive. But, if our words were intercepted and fell into the hands of an investigator, then it's possible that some of what we said could be misconstrued in any number of potentially incriminating ways."

"You mean, they might think one of our deals includes the bribing of a U.S. Senator?"

"Yeah, I'm afraid so. It may not be picked up because the screeners might not be focusing on anything unrelated to my project. But, it's possible it could land on the desk of someone who might want to do a little investigating."

"You mean the federal government may now want to investigate *me?*"

"The FBI specifically. If they did focus on anything, they would likely inquire openly with the firm. They wouldn't necessarily have enough information to target you directly. I can't remember if I even said your name over the phone."

"Not exactly. You called me Eves! But, would they have the direct dial number you were connected to?"

"I don't think so. It probably registered your firm's general number if caller identification was made. I doubt they track that for every call I make, though. And there'd be limits to the uses of any information they *did* manage to collect. You may know better than I do what the legal constraints are, but I don't think they can use the information from a Parapier surveillance to open a covert investigation into the activities of your firm without more of a concrete foundation. Your firm has an expectation of privacy in that telephone call that would have to be respected."

"Yes, I think that's correct, although they might consider it a sufficient basis to channel resources at us . . . to *start* looking into the firm's activities. Especially if political operatives on the left got hold of it and wanted to leverage the info to bring down a Republican senator. I wouldn't necessarily mind them investigating Alan, I have to say, but I certainly don't want them breathing down *my* neck. I can't even seem to get all the partners to believe me."

"What's happened since we last spoke? Did you speak to your managing partner?"

"Yes. It was a much more satisfying exchange of information. He believes me about Chicago, even though some number of the other partners are on the fence."

"I hope he'll keep Levenger away from you."

"He said he would while the investigation was underway, but phase one may have buried me deeper beneath Alan's mud."

Joe shifted over closer to Evie as a small Korean woman with a paper bag sat on the end of their bench and extracted a carton of yogurt and a spoon. Evie glanced at the woman and smiled. She looked at Joe questioningly, but their bench-mate seemed innocuous and completely unaware of their conversation, so they continued, although each became slightly more cryptic.

"I'm hoping the whole thing will ultimately be laid bare by the partnership. At least then we'll know if there's anything," she lowered her voice, ". . . illegal in this transaction. If there's not, all the better."

"You'll have to calculate your next move very carefully. If you don't get satisfaction from the partnership, you should think about contacting the feds. You'll be in a much better position if you *initiate* contact. If they undertake any sort of investigation on their own and your name comes up, you will be viewed as a potentially antagonistic target."

"I don't want that to happen before I build my file of evidence."

"I'm going to help you do that. My investigator is on the case and I emailed Levenger a little spyware."

"JOE!" The Korean woman looked at them, the spoon in her mouth. Evie sighed and darted her eyes, first at the woman and then at the random collection of people passing by. She turned her attention to Joe. She cocked an eyebrow at him and involuntarily clenched her jaw.

"I know, Eves. You weren't sure about that. Don't worry. I would be very surprised if your technical staff could detect this one. And, it's designed to gather information and then self destruct. It's not the kind that does any discernable damage or even makes its presence known."

"I'm not used to this sort of thing." She softened when he squeezed her against him. "I ran into Alan right after talking to Hanover. He mentioned that email message from your hotmail account. I'm afraid he might also mention it to Hanover. I was wondering if I should confess to Hanover that I've been sleuthing electronically."

"You *haven't*. I have. And there's no way those messages can be traced back to you."

"Okay. I'm going to wait and see what happens."

Joe shifted toward Evie blocking the view of the Korean woman who was now eating a banana.

"You know, Joe, it was interesting," she continued in a soft voice almost whispering into his ear. "Paul never asked me *why* . . . what motive Alan would have."

"Maybe he knows more than you think he does."

"Maybe. Yesterday, I got a second phone call from this woman who works for . . ." she glanced beyond Joe's shoulder at the Korean woman, ". . . this woman who works for the company that's the purchaser in this transaction. She repeated that she had information for me. Her English wasn't great, and she had a heavy accent, but she was insistent that she thinks I have a problem. She was supposed to meet me earlier today. We made an appointment to talk, but she didn't show."

"Eves, you have to be careful. This woman could be part of Levenger's plot."

"I know. But she was so adamant. She said she would lose everything if this transaction closes."

"Did she give a name or any information that could be used to track her down?"

"Only that she works for them, the purchaser, and that she was currently in New York."

"Not much. Maybe she'll call again."

Evie sat silently. *If she's still alive.*

"In the meantime, I want you to give some serious thought to involving an outside resource."

Evie thought about telling Joe that she saw a woman being taken away in an ambulance who matched the description of the woman she was supposed to meet, but something kept her from continuing. It just *couldn't* be the same woman.

Joe sat in silence with her a few minutes holding her close. Finally, the Korean woman stood and walked away.

"There's something else," he said in a serious tone. "Something important that I have to tell you."

"What?" asked Evie. She could sense that what Joe was about to say was not going to be pleasant. She took a breath and held it surreptitiously.

"You remember when I told you about Sandra?"

"Yes."

"Well, there's no easy way to say this. She's pregnant."

"What?! She's *what?* And she's sure it's yours?"

"That's what she's saying. She's having some tests—"

"So she doesn't know for *sure* yet if she actually is?"

"No, she says the home test was positive. She's at the doctor today. And she wants to find out if it's a viable pregnancy. She's had some health problems."

"Oh God." Evie closed her eyes and tried to control her breathing. She felt lightheaded and winded. She steadied herself and shook off the impact of the shock. After a moment and a deep breath she said, "So I assume she intends to have the baby. What does this mean for you?" She shifted her body so she could look him directly in the eye. She hadn't really recovered from the new information, and she found herself asking for another blow.

"It means I have to be there for her. Nothing more."

"Of course. I don't mean to sound unfeeling. *Of course* you have to be there for her. She needs you now."

There was a new unexpected emotion, a new layer of complexity in their evolving friendship. *Pain.* Her eyes stared into his. He might not ever be hers. It was possible that he belonged to an unborn child and some part of him would forever be linked to Sandra. He pulled her close again and held her, but she wasn't sure if she could allow herself to feel it. She fought back tears and gently pushed him away. This was it. This was what she dreaded. She thought back to their conversation at the California beach.

"If it's mine, well, I . . . Well, I guess I'll have to deliver another baby."

"Joe, it's no joking matter."

"I know. Sorry. Bad joke. I mean I'll have to accept the responsibility."

"Joe, yes, of course you will. It's an innocent child."

"I know. I know. There's no lack of emotion about this, Eves. I'm—"

"*I'm* sorry, Joe. I know this can't be easy for you. What can I do?"

He sat back and looked at her. He smiled that trademark dimple-laden smile. "You're amazing. With everything you're going through. Mmmmm. Can I kiss you?"

"No."

"Just tell me you know how important you are to me."

"You have become *somewhat* important . . . to *me*." She forced a weak smile.

"I'm not in love with Sandra."

"Joe, do you remember what I was saying about men—"

"Yes, I remember. And, God help me, I've done it to you again."

"No. No. What I was going to say was . . . that I'm impressed with you. You're standing up to your obligations. And you were upfront with me. I'm not disappointed with *you*. I'm disappointed with the circumstances."

"I understand." He leaned over to her and no one in the park even looked their direction as he kissed her.

Evie thought these kisses were sweeter somehow and more sublime than those in the past, possibly because he had confided in her, but more probably because of the possibility that there might be no more to follow.

He was something she might never have—a view to an oasis that had turned out to be a mirage. It was as if her ultimate openness to it, her submission, had been the invitation to take it all away.

When their lips parted, her eyes were directed downward.

"What's the rest of your day like?" he asked.

"I uhh . . . actually, I don't remember."

"Is there a chance you could pick up your laptop and disappear for the rest of the afternoon?"

"If I don't have any appointments, I could probably get away with that. I can take a few files home and work on them at home tonight. What are you suggesting?"

"I want to check on that spyware software back at my hotel room." He grabbed her hand, "Let's go do a little research."

"Wait," she said, pulling her hand back in a less than decisive manner. "Joe, if someone is watching me, I'd rather not let them see us walking into your hotel together."

"Worried about your reputation?" he grinned.

"No!" She gave him a stern look. "I just don't want to hand them any information. Let them wonder who I'm meeting at the hotel. I'll meet you there."

"Okay. Room 3901."

The crimson sun was starting toward the horizon. She watched him stand and walk away in the glow of the residual sunlight, the waves in his hair and the fabric of his dark suit catching swatches of light and casting a shadow in his wake. The voice in her head was saying that it would never be the same again. When he had walked some distance from her, he turned around and stopped and she watched him raise his hand in a departing wave. That vision of him would haunt her. She wondered if that gesture was foretelling a more permanent goodbye. Suddenly, she felt more sleepy than afraid, as if a sedative of sadness had permeated her bloodstream.

She waited a full ten minutes before allowing herself to move. She dialed Helen on her BlackBerry and was told that the afternoon was free of meetings. A quick check of her BlackBerry calendar confirmed that she would not be missed. Her voice mail contained a number of messages on several client matters, none of which required any immediate action.

When she finally walked through the lobby of the Four Seasons, she was feeling better, which she attributed to the brief sunbath she got while seated on the park bench. She was almost certain that she had not been followed, and, when Joe shut the hotel room door behind her, she felt confident that their privacy was absolute.

"So, Eves, how much do you know about this Senator Arbeson? You said you worked on his re-election campaign, right?

"Yes, to my discredit. I was moved by certain of his early campaign speeches. So when Alan, who was one of the campaign cochairmen, asked if I would help, I said I would. Of course, that was before I knew *Alan* very well either. I only saw the Senator in person a handful of times while I was working on the campaign. We dealt out the rhetoric consistent with the re-election objectives of an incumbent. I thought I was reading him properly, but then what do you ever really know *for certain* about a politician?"

Joe smiled.

"I've done some legal work for him since."

"So he turned out to be different. Was he one of the men in your life who disappointed you?"

"Yes, I guess he was. But I was never *personally* involved with him." She wondered whether or not she should tell Joe about the handwritten note questioning whether she'd had just such a personal relationship with the Senator. *Probably no point.* She continued, "I guess I'm just disappointed in retrospect that I spent so much time working on his campaign." Evie walked over to the bed and put down her bag and laptop computer.

"And you think Alan still has a close relationship with him?"

"Yes. The few times I was invited to so-called private functions, it was because I was there with Alan or on Alan's invitation. Also, I think he's been a client of the firm for some time."

Joe walked over to the desk and cleared off a space for Evie's laptop. He said almost to himself, "He's fairly senior and well-respected. I remember reading that he's thinking of running in the next Presidential primary. His voting record seems to be consistent with frontline Republicans for the most part."

"To think that Alan could someday have access to the most powerful man in the world."

Joe had booted up his laptop on the desk and called up a software program called Poirette. He typed in a series of commands that Evie couldn't follow, but then she watched as a systematic progression of pixels flashed on the screen. The electronic detective was accessing a remote site where any reports from the spyware would be stored.

Joe glanced over his shoulder at Evie. Then he stood up and twirled his chair around to face her in one swift move.

"So, what will happen now?" she said gesturing toward the glowing screen.

"It will give us a report, but it covers its tracks well. It may take a bit of time." He smiled.

"How long?"

"It depends."

"So, have you heard anything from your investigator?" she asked.

"Not yet. But, he's on the case."

"Will this guy *follow* Alan? Try to spy on him?"

"I've found it's better not to ask how he gets the information, but it has always proven to be reliable. And as far as I know, he's never been caught in the act."

"And you don't think Alan will be aware that he's being investigated?"

"No, Eves. I don't want you worrying about that."

"Okay."

She stood and walked over toward the computer screen, watching a flow of indecipherable text scroll northward.

Joe minimized the process on the screen and brought up an Internet browser. He began typing in commands and Evie came over and watched over his shoulder. He pulled up a government site where competitive bid results were posted. He scrolled through a recent list and conducted site searches for any reference to Gerais Chevas, GC Quadra or Quadra Numbers software and received successive NOT FOUND messages. He then looked through competitive bidding solicitations for which bids were still being collected. Nothing. Then he searched post-award status records. *Nothing.*

Evie sighed, gazing at the screen.

"It looks like GC Quadra hasn't recently won any U.S. government contracts," she said.

He continued to study the screen. "No award postings."

"GC Quadra has licensed their software to governments around the world. Why *not* the U.S.?" she asked.

"Statistical software. That's their expertise, right?

Joe continued to search other government and related sites. As he worked, he turned his head toward her slightly as he spoke.

"You know," he said, "government contracting can be a dirty business. Did you ever hear of Operation Ill Wind?"

"No, what's that?"

"It was the largest investigation of Pentagon fraud conducted between 1986 and 1990. A Pentagon official was caught . . . well, he was caught engaging in an illegal activity."

"Why am I not surprised?"

"Anyway, to avoid jail, he became an informant, and secretly recorded hundreds of conversations with weapons contractors. Something like ninety or more companies and individuals were convicted of felonies. Some big contractors like Unisys were either convicted or admitted wrongdoing."

Evie said nothing, but was listening as she watched him type.

He kept typing and continued, "I don't know the specifics of any one company's violations, but there were allegations of padding bids, inflated billings, trafficking in classified documents, and the *payment of bribes.*"

"Bribes?" She stood up, turned her head and stared out the window, as if the payment schedule from file Neon Three was floating outside in the air. The image disappeared. "Aren't there watchdog organizations that, well . . . watch?" she asked.

"Yes. And some of them have proven very effective. Some cases of fraud have actually been brought to light through their actions." He turned back to his computer and continued speaking.

"And government contracting is a very lucrative business. Some estimate that military spending alone exceeds four hundred billion dollars a year."

Evie began to walk around in the hotel room, partly to aid her thinking, partly due to nervous energy.

Joe suddenly looked up from his screen and turned toward Evie. Evie stopped walking and looked expectantly at him as he spoke, "I wonder if Senator Arbeson sits on the appropriations committee and is doing a sole-source deal under the table."

"What's a sole-source deal?" she asked.

"Sometimes a Federal agency decides to award a contract to a particular contractor, sort of side-stepping the Federal Regs that require such government projects to be offered on a *competitive* basis, or in other words, to the *lowest bidder.*"

"You mean *handing* a government project to Gerais Chevas?"

"Yes. Effectively, yes. And," he paused, "it's possible that *there's not even a real project.*"

"Oh my God! Are you suggesting blatant fraud? Could Senator Arbeson be involved in that?"

"Anybody's guess. I just think something more's at stake here for such a large commission."

"You mean like $25 million," she said. "I wonder who's in line for this."

Joe stood and walked over to the mini-bar and opened a beer.

Evie began pacing again and said, "I feel like we're searching for the proverbial needle-in-a-haystack."

"Speaking of searching, have you checked to see if any further detail has been added to any of those Schedules?"

"No, I haven't. Let's check."

She opened her laptop and Joe connected the cables and plugged a telephone line into her modem. Evie logged into her firm network, called up the fourth Project Neon file and entered the password. She scrolled down to page twelve and they stared at the screen. Under the heading, "SCHEDULE B7", text had been substituted for "TBD."

> *In my capacity as attorney for seller, Gerais Chevas, in the above entitled transaction, I _____ hereby agree to serve as escrow agent ("Agent") for the receipt and distribution of Software, as defined under the Purchase Agreement. Further details for said Agent roles shall be agreed between the parties.*

There were a few additional paragraphs describing the parameters that would govern the role of the escrow agent. It was all fairly standard legalese with no specific identities or logistics mentioned. There was blank space and at the bottom, there was a place for a signature, with nothing else on the page.

Evie spoke first.

"It's benign. There's nothing illegal in the role the attorney is asked to assume."

Out of curiosity, she tried editing the file and was allowed, so her access parameters to these files had been changed, presumably to prevent her from denying that she had created them.

"It doesn't seem to be a finished document," said Joe.

"Yes, and the players think I'm the one who's going to finish it! I wonder if the terms have been fully negotiated at this point, but not yet drafted into the language."

"That's entirely possible. Levenger may have figured out you're investigating. With the heat turned up on him, he might have just thrown this out there to cool things down. A red herring just to keep you from making an issue out of these files."

"Or this could just be a straightforward deal, perfectly legal. The role of escrow agent is fairly well understood. Standard. I can't believe it. I was sure there was going to be something unethical or illegal . . . but wait. There's still a $25 million payday for somebody."

Joe nodded at the screen and Evie brought up "Neon Three." The payment schedule remained unchanged with the commission glowing on the screen as if daring them to question its legality.

"Eves, there are still plenty of unanswered questions. For one thing, Alan hasn't owned up to drafting it."

"I don't know that yet. Maybe it is just a normal transaction and I've let my imagination run wild. I don't know what to think anymore."

"But, what about all these layers of security? A software escrow is not usually confidential. And, this woman who called you. She contacted you directly, clearly claimed that there was a problem, and set up a secret meeting to tell you about it. Doesn't sound so clearly above-board, does it?"

"No. I didn't tell you before, but I got this call before I left to meet her. A man's voice told me not to go through with the meeting."

"Eves, you've got to level with me. What else did he say?"

"That's it. He said I'd been busy, as if he knew I'd been investigating. He warned me not to meet her and hung up."

"Is that everything? Are you holding back anything else?"

"Only that I saw a woman being loaded into an ambulance a few blocks from the location of our planned meeting. She looked to be lifeless. And she matched the description of the woman who was supposed to meet me."

chapter
26

Will you talk to the feds? Eves, there's enough here for them to launch an investigation. I think it's time to tell them everything we know."

"But what do we know? *I mean with certainty.* We know that this deal has had an odd evolution, is more secretive than most and that someone has erroneously named me as its participant or even director. But this commission remains a mystery. I still don't have any hard evidence that it's a violation of the law and that it's Alan's handiwork, or that the Senator's involved. I can't prove I've been contacted by anyone for anything more sinister than the furtherance of the players' own personal agendas. Those emails you intercepted can't stand alone and we don't have clean hands as to their discovery. And now it appears under the new Schedule B7, that *Project Neon* is nothing more than a promise to act as an escrow agent."

"But you have to admit, the fact that it's so over-lawyered fans the flames of suspicion," said Joe. "I'm no attorney, but the drafting seems like a shell game. Just to establish an escrow agency? If that's all Project Neon ever was, why the secrecy and the code name? Why not just say so in the main agreement?"

"You're absolutely right. It is terrible drafting. But bad drafting and sloppy handling of a deal are not illegal. I've seen some terrible things patched together in the eleventh hour to get a deal closed," she shrugged. "And, I still can't prove Alan's pinning this on me. Why would an FBI agent believe my story if my own firm didn't? And I would be betraying the firm, and the firm's *client*."

"I don't see that the firm has done *you* many favors."

"Not yet, Joe. I want to dig a bit deeper—at least determine if there *is* a government contract involved somehow."

One of the government billboards was still blinking on Joe's laptop screen. He clicked on the icon at the bottom of the screen to maximize the window displaying the spyware's progress. The screen was suddenly flooded with a jumble of character strings showing Internet searches, keystrokes and emails Alan had typed on his computer. They both moved closer and scanned the list in silence. Joe spoke first this time.

"Eves, I should have warned you. This spyware program captures everything, backspaces, returns, *everything*. In order to be unobtrusive and invisible, it can't be a selective gatherer. It just captures everything and dumps it. We'll have to search through to find anything relevant."

"So, every keystroke Alan hits is on here?"

"Yes, but he has to be connected to the Internet for it to send back the data dump so it might be slightly out of sync with real-time."

"Wow." She let her eyes scan, looking for a collection of keystrokes invoking Gerais Chevas, Project Neon or anything that might be remotely related.

"I just sent the software to him today so, depending on how active he is building this transaction, it might take some time to capture something incriminating."

"It's quite voluminous," she said as Joe scrolled through screen after screen of typed phrases and keystroke responses.

"What's this?" asked Joe.

"*Bottom line. Five pop on Greta in Oct Cult. Approval on text and placement. In exchange for exclusive upon release of Death.*" Evie read an entry Joe was pointing to with his mouse. "Oh, that's probably an email he sent in a negotiation for mentions in the magazine, *Culture*. Publicity. Alan represents that actress Greta Bayless and she has a movie coming out during the Christmas season. I think it's called Death by Association. He's asking for her name to be mentioned five times in the October issue, with approval rights over the copy and where it appears in the magazine. In exchange, he's offering the magazine an exclusive interview with Greta after the movie comes out."

"Here's another interesting email," said Joe, reading from the screen, "*Meet you at ChicaLicious at 10p for fromage blanc island cheesecake and some PRIVATE cheesecake.* Sent to some 'chick' named 'fire&icewoman.'"

"I find it amazing that women respond to him, but some do."

"Look at this one: *$50 billion mkt. Wouldn't you like a piece? For a few months of shuffling bureaucratic paperwork and dancing the tango.*"

"I have no idea what that one's about," said Evie.

"This guy is a real class act," said Joe, scrolling down a page.

Evie smiled at her ally.

"Nothing must've happened with the deal today," she said.

"So, you're sure you don't want to alert the feds?"

"Yes, not quite yet. I want to see if I can get an audience with Hanover. In person. I need to find out what the partnership decided. How they're going to deal with Alan. I feel I owe them that. And, the truth is Joe, if Alan succeeds in tipping the partnership in his favor on Chicago, I will know I have very little chance of convincing them of my innocence on Project Neon."

Joe stood and walked to the window.

"Okay, Eves, we'll do it your way, but I want you to stay with me tonight. I won't be comfortable with you sleeping alone in that apartment."

"I have to go on as if everything is normal. They're apparently aware of what I'm doing. I have to proceed as if I don't realize I'm being watched. I *have* to sleep in my apartment." She stood up and looked in his direction. "But I *would* feel safer if you slept there, too."

"Done."

"Do you mind sleeping on my sofa?"

"No. Not a problem."

"How long will you be in town?"

"I'm here as long as I want to be. I'll work from New York. Normalcy. Just a slight variation."

Joe walked over to her from his stance at the window. He embraced her, but she pulled away slightly.

"Eves, what's wrong?"

"Things feel different."

"Sandra?"

"Joe, I can't deny I'm confused." She managed a half-smile. "I honestly don't know what it is I'm feeling."

"I understand. I know it complicates things, but I don't want to lose you."

"I can't possibly know how I'm going to feel when this baby is born."

"Let's wait and see."

She nodded and began disconnecting her laptop.

"Eves, I do need to make some telephone calls before I leave the hotel. Why don't you relax on the sofa, or better yet, why not take a hot bath? Five star bathroom. I won't be long."

"I'm going to go back to my apartment. You can just come over whenever you're finished, okay?"

"You've been threatened over the telephone and you think the person you were supposed to meet was murdered. There's no way to measure the risk you're taking walking around alone."

"You're coming right behind me. It's not dark yet. There are people everywhere. I'll go straight home."

Hours later, Evie was lying in bed listening to the faint sound of Joe's steady breathing as he slept on the sofa. It was comforting for him to be there, but she was now haunted by more than just Project Neon—what kind of relationship could she have with Joe if Sandra gave birth to his child?

~

Evie walked to her office the next morning, her deflated spirit slightly more buoyant.

She stuffed a file into her briefcase for a morning meeting with a non-Alan client, Cardinal Blue, as Helen appeared in her doorway.

"Helen, could you do a favor for me? Could you find out if Alan was in Dallas during the time I was? You know, the trip that resulted in that erroneous expense report."

"I can ask Beverly," answered Helen.

"Try to make it real casual . . . like part of everyday coffee-break chat. Put it in a general context. Say you were asked whether we had any Texas clients or if we had ever traveled that far south to represent a client. Something like that. Can you do that? Don't draw a lot of attention to the fact that you're asking and don't make it seem as if we are asking about Alan specifically. And keep all the details of this little conversation between us?"

"Yes, of course. Is everything okay?"

"Everything's fine, Helen, just checking on some things."

"I'll take care of it. Here's your mail from yesterday afternoon." Helen extended her hand full of envelopes of various sizes.

"Thanks, Helen." Evie took the stack and stuffed it into another pocket in her briefcase to look through in transit.

"Can I do anything else, Evie?" asked Helen with a concerned look on her face.

"That's all. Thanks for everything, Helen. I'd better go."

Evie arrived at Broadway and 44th Street and took the elevator up to the thirty-seventh floor. As she exited the elevator, she was surrounded by the cherry paneling and antique furniture of Bartlett, Warren and Ivy, a national firm headquartered in New York. Ramona and Diane, the software sales team from Cardinal Blue, stood up from their seats in the lobby, greeted her and briefed her on their planned presentation. The trio followed a Bartlett Warren attorney down a long corridor to a large glassed conference room adjacent to an open foyer. Dominating the room was a long mahogany conference table adorned with star-shaped telephonic speakers at each end. There were windows overlooking the Majestic Theatre and leather armchairs numbering twenty. They were offered coffee, orange juice and croissants and all participants clustered at one end of the large table, Evie and her clients on one side facing the open foyer, the Bartlett Warren lawyer and his clients on the other, facing the window.

As Evie listened to Ramona describe Cardinal Blue's proposal, she glanced up through the glass wall of the conference room into the foyer where busy lawyers hustled in each direction. One man stopped briefly and faced her direction. A chill shot up Evie's spine and she felt a jolt of fear. It was the same face she had seen peering through the glass window at Starbucks Friday night.

chapter
27

Her eyes fixated on him through the glass wall of the conference room. Even though he looked quickly away, she recognized the face that had been searching the interior of the coffee-house so intently that night. He had roundish eyes under heavy brows and his facial features were youthful yet stern, with high cheekbones and an angular jawline. And now, as he moved away in profile, she remembered watching the jerkiness of his bodily movements, first at Starbucks and later, on the corner outside her building as she studied him from her apartment window. Was this man an employee of Bartlett, Warren and Ivy or had he followed her into their offices? Was this man tracking her?

She leaned over and whispered to Diane that she had to make a quick trip to the ladies' room. Diane nodded and Evie rose from the conference table and walked out into the foyer. She casually glanced in each direction but the man was no longer visible, so she started down the corridor in the direction he'd walked. Her eyes pierced all hallways and open doors, but there was no evidence of him. After searching all areas she could without bringing suspicion on herself, she returned to the conference room and forced herself to concentrate for the duration of the meeting with Cardinal Blue, her head throbbing and her heart twisting in knots. She excused herself abruptly after the meeting and walked quickly back to her office, turning often to glance behind her back.

Breathing heavily, she dumped her briefcase onto a chair in her office and closed her door. She would have completely forgotten about her ten o'clock A.M. meeting with Paul except that Helen had left her a note taped to her telephone receiver. After splashing her face with water in the ladies room, she walked to Paul's office.

Paul stood, greeted her, then walked to the door of his office, told Beverly he did not want to be disturbed and closed his door. Evie detected a softness to his demeanor that was missing at their last meeting and wondered if it was born out of a belief in her version of the Chicago incident.

"Evie, Jack asked me to sit with you and go over a few things. I want to inform you that for the firm's record-keeping purposes, this conversation is being recorded. You may have a copy of the recording if you like."

"Okay."

"I've talked to a great many in the firm. Especially with what's happened in the last few days," he began in a routine tone of voice.

She nodded and looked directly at him.

"I want to reiterate that the firm owes you a tremendous amount of gratitude for your excellent work over the years. You have been described as a steady performer and a client favorite. The majority of the partnership had many positive things to say about you."

Evie didn't like the way his little speech had started, but remained quiet.

"Now I know there was an incident in Chicago last November. An unfortunate occurrence on a trip you took with Alan."

An unfortunate occurrence? Yes, RATHER unfortunate, she thought.

"You were apparently under the impression that Alan made a pass at you?"

"Well, I don't know what you mean by *'pass.'* He *kissed* me. I don't know if I would call that my *impression*."

"Yes, well, Alan was asked about that incident. He said that after a successful client presentation, the two of you had dinner together and, by the way, he fully admits it was a mistake, he said that the two of you gave into a weak moment and kissed each other in the hallway of your hotel."

"I didn't . . . I can't believe he . . . Paul, I didn't . . . there was nothing *mutual* about it. He kissed *me!*"

"Well, perhaps it was a misunderstanding."

"Paul, there was no misunderstanding. No mistake. Alan grabbed me and kissed me. It took me completely by surprise. And then he tried to push his way into my hotel room."

"He did?" He raised his eyebrows and shifted in his seat. "Then why on earth didn't you report it?"

"Because I didn't have any proof. I wasn't sure the partners would take *my* word and then I would be branded a woman who makes such claims. Anyway, I *should* have reported it. It was a mistake not to."

"Frankly, I *have* been surprised by some of Alan's behavior in the past. I did not approve of him taking you to any of those campaign events. It did not serve the firm well for the two of you to be socializing as a couple in that manner."

"We were *not* a couple. We were not . . . I just attended a few campaign-related celebrations because I worked on Senator Arbeson's campaign. We were just two colleagues from the same firm attending a public celebration. So, was that . . . ? Did the partners think that because I went to a few of the same events that Alan attended that I was somehow romantically involved with him?"

"Well, it did factor into the discussion when Alan claimed the incident in Chicago was a mutual lapse in judgment. You did apparently go to at least one event *with* Alan. He said you arrived with him."

"That Chicago incident happened just this last November. My meager involvement in Senator Arbeson's campaign was several years ago. I would've never agreed to go anywhere with Alan after he assaulted me. I have avoided any situation that would cause me to be alone with him. Except, of course, here in the office when I had no choice but to be in his presence for work-related discussions."

"Well, I'm afraid that even the female partners had difficulty with the knowledge that you've continued to work with Alan, in isolation at times, if you were afraid of another personal encounter."

"Alan begged me in Chicago not to report the incident. He promised it would never happen again. I wasn't really *afraid* of him. I thought I'd be a team player and let it go. I realize now that it was a mistake, but I've insisted on professional behavior since that time."

"Well, Evie, Alan said that you made some comment to him recently about . . . Well, this is not easy to discuss . . . something about not wearing underwear?"

Evie flashed hot with rage and swallowed hard.

"Paul, that was a stupid response on my part after Alan asked me what color underwear I was wearing. He's the one who brought it up. It was after that presentation I gave to the partners that day at your request. He stopped me on the way out of the conference room and said instead of listening, he was preoccupied with guessing the color of my underwear or something like that. I reacted stupidly out of disgust, but I never initiated any conversation or contact with him after that and I've tried to conduct myself with absolute professionalism."

"Well, as Jack may have told you, the partners were split on which version of the Chicago story was the more likely to have happened, but the partnership has agreed to give you the benefit of the doubt. The consensus was to presume some type of harassment occurred. However, without direct proof we cannot seek further redress against Alan. It's certainly not enough to ask for his resignation. He's an equity partner."

"Hmmm," said Evie. She knew at that moment her career with Howard, Rolland & Stewart was effectively over one way or another, voluntarily or otherwise.

"We would like to avoid any unpleasantness and we realize that it will be up to you as to whether you feel comfortable remaining employed with this firm, given that Alan is, and will remain, a member of the partnership. In any event, we are prepared to offer you, in terms of a settlement of any potential claim, an amount of $1.5 million. You will of course sign an agreement foregoing all potential claims against the firm and any member of the partnership, and you may continue your employment with the firm if you so choose."

Evie was frozen in place in the chair. Anger and frustration held her motionless and empty. A wave of exhaustion washed over her. *I don't want your hush money,* she thought.

Paul leaned forward and placed his elbows on the edge of his desk, supporting his chin on his clasped hands. He spoke more softly now, with a hint of fatherly reproach. "If you stay, you will be treated no differently than you would have been otherwise. As I said in our prior conversation, you've been a consistent performer in prior years, but lately, well, lately it seems that you've had difficulty concentrating on your work. And you may have made certain choices that are inconsistent with the tenor of this firm." She couldn't help but think she heard something else in his voice . . . something . . . it was as if he was trying to convince himself of what he was saying.

"Can you be more specific?"

"Well, in addition to the incidents I described to you in our prior conversation, you have apparently been somewhat pre-occupied lately with some personal agenda."

"Are you talking about my reports to you concerning Gerais Chevas?"

"Yes, in part. Listen, Evie. I don't see the point in detailing grievances. Why don't we focus on the core issues."

"Okay." *This should be interesting.*

"Evie, Alan suggested that the misunderstanding between the two of you may have caused you to pursue some sort of vendetta against him."

"What are you referring to?" *So we're not detailing grievances?*

"You're understandably upset about these negative performance reviews. The incident in Chicago must've been difficult for you. You have to admit that there's ample motive to want to discredit him."

"Discredit him! But I haven't done *anything* to undermine *him*. The Gerais Chevas deal I was telling you about has nothing to do with what happened in Chicago . . . at least from *my* perspective. I've been trying to alert you about an active deal that contains some problematic terms. Ones that could potentially put the firm in jeopardy."

"Evie, I looked at this Schedule B7. It looked fairly straightforward. There was nothing in the description of the attorney's role that I found to be improper. Alan did say that Gerais Chevas was a client he brought to the firm, through some of his South American contacts. That said, he had no familiarity with the specifics of this deal to sell its GC Quadra business unit. He said that you were assigned the deal and that you were running with it. Incidentally, he said Gerais Chevas was quite complimentary about your stewardship on the deal."

"With all due respect, no one has ever informed me that I was assigned this deal! I've never been introduced, assigned or billed any time to that client. I only know about it because I've sought out information on my own time. I was concerned about what I'd overheard and some of the specifics that came to my attention. Specifics I certainly didn't negotiate. That expense report I told you about—it's wrong. I never made or received those telephone calls to anyone in Brazil and I have never been present for any meeting on this transaction."

"You did bill time to them last month. Fourteen hours. And the access lists for all these password-protected files include your name. Alan showed me a handful of emails from your email address on the matter. He said he was carbon-copied, but hadn't yet paid much attention since the deal was not finalized yet. He said you were negotiating it quite nicely on your own."

"He's lying. What can I tell you? He manipulated the electronic files and communication. I didn't include them on my time report and I didn't send any emails. He's lying just like he's lying about Chicago. Wait a minute. What did Hanover say about all of this?"

"Jack is back in the hospital with complications." *Oh,* she thought. *He probably didn't have a chance to look into any of this himself as he promised he would. The expense report . . . and the billing records . . .*

"He's fully supportive of you," Paul continued, "but cannot make sense of the he-said she-said over this Gerais Chevas matter. It's unconscionable that this firm has a runaway deal with no one at the helm and the client confused over who their attorney is."

"As I told you before, Alan's plan is to discredit *me!* He made all of you question my competency so when I denied involvement with Gerais Chevas, I wouldn't be believed. He's using me as a scapegoat for a . . ." Evie lost her thought. She was running out of energy to defend herself and she knew word choice was of particular importance. It was clear that Paul was one of the fence-sitters at best. How could she convince him?

"Paul, let's call the client."

"What?"

"Did someone call the client and ask them who they've been dealing with? There's this guy, Adinaldo, who sent me an email, but I've never talked to him or anyone else from Gerais Chevas."

"Yes, actually Evie, we did speak to Adinaldo. He said you've been negotiating the deal for them by telephone and by email." *That's apparently what he told Helen, too.*

"I swear I've *never* talked to any of them. Don't you think that's strange that he's never met me in person? I've never been to Brazil and they've never been here to meet with me?"

"Not really. You know we've conducted many deals remotely, especially when the client wants to keep costs down. In this case, they specifically requested that Alan limit the time *he* billed to the matter because of the expense."

"I can prove I've spent all my billable time elsewhere. I have a document that I put together showing all the time I spent working on other client matters."

"Okay, send it to me and I'll look at it. I don't understand why they'd say they've been working with you if they hadn't. So, you're telling me someone has been impersonating you?"

"I don't know. I guess that's what's going on. All I know is that someone has hijacked my email address, sent emails, charged me with making telephone calls to Brazil and created files that I've had nothing to do with negotiating."

"I've never in thirty years of practice heard of anything like this."

"Paul, I can't explain, because I don't know what's going on either. All I know is that because my identity has been stolen for this deal, I can't imagine that it's a legal, boilerplate sort of transaction . . ." Evie suddenly stopped talking.

"Evie, are you okay?" asked Paul.

It occurred to her that the email Joe intercepted, with the reference to a conference call about a government project, proved that Alan *was* familiar with the details of this deal. She could catch him in a lie, but to do it she'd have to explain how she intercepted the email. And that seemed certain to deepen the hole she'd already dug for herself.

"I'm just suddenly exhausted," she said.

Paul leaned back again in his chair. "All the more reason that what I'm about to propose is necessary. I was thinking and the partners agreed . . . that maybe you should take a brief leave of absence. Just to think things over and evaluate your options. Fully paid, of course, in addition to the settlement amount."

Well, that's that, she thought. *I'm done protecting the firm.* "Okay," she said. "I understand. I understand that maybe I should take some time—"

"Evie, I'm not asking you to resign, you understand. I think you're just suffering from the effects of stress. I know you have been working extremely long hours for quite some time."

"Yes. Okay. I uhh . . . maybe I *do* need some time."

"Of course, since Gerais Chevas is Alan's client, he'll be looking into the specifics of this deal in your absence. He'll take care of any required action to satisfy the client." *Yeah, I'll bet he will.*

Paul shifted again and crossed his legs. "So, do we have an agreement on the settlement?"

"May I have some time to think about it?"

"Yes, of course."

"And I *would* like a copy of this taped conversation, please."

"Yes, of course. And, please keep your laptop and come and go freely. Just take some time off."

"Do I need to contact my clients about my absence?"

"No, not necessary. Can you just make a list of the clients you're working for and the matters that are currently open and leave it with Barbara? We'll just say that you're taking some personal time, which is actually quite accurate, yes? We can get other associates to cover for you."

"Yes. Okay."

"Okay. Thank you, Evie. By the way, please consider me a friend. If you want to talk, just give me a call. Why don't we see how we're doing in two weeks?"

"Yes. Thank you." *Yeah, thanks, friend.*

Paul reached down and flipped a switch turning off the recording device. He smiled, stood and offered his hand to Evie. She shook his hand briefly, nodded and left.

Evie returned to her office absolutely numb and was thankful Helen was not there. She didn't know what she would say. After powering up her laptop, she found the document she had created, detailing her workflow over the summer months and the clients she had served. She emailed it to Paul with a final bid to be believed.

The light on her telephone promised voice mails waiting so she picked up the receiver to retrieve them. The only one she cared about was from Joe. He said his plans had changed, that Ariel had called with a desperate plea for him to baby-sit for the evening. His message asked

Evie to go to Connecticut with him, if she didn't have any other plans. He didn't want her to be alone in the apartment and offered to spend the night again on her sofa. She dialed his hotel room, but there was no answer.

She didn't actually feel like organizing her files for re-assignment, but she forced herself, and began by cleaning out her briefcase. While she worked she dialed Joe's cell phone number. He answered on the second ring.

"Joe, it's Evie."

"Eves, are you okay?"

"Yes, but round two with Paul was more frustrating than the first."

"Did his investigation turn up anything?"

"I guess so, but everything he finds seems to bolster Alan's credibility and put mine into question. He thinks I'm pursuing some sort of vendetta against Alan, perhaps because of the negative performance reviews or a failed romance between us."

"He thinks you were involved with Alan?"

"Alan laid it on pretty thick, it seems. Pointed to the campaign functions we both attended, made it sound like his assault on me in Chicago was a mutual little fling. He even told them about a stupid thing I said to him out of anger and made it sound like I was trying to seduce him."

"Here's where it's difficult for me to just sit by and—"

"I *know*. I'm sorry. I considered not telling you, but I need your advice. Alan told them Gerais Chevas *was* his client, but that I was assigned this deal and he knows nothing about it, that whole 'acted alone' bit. I wanted to tell them about that email you intercepted, but how could I explain how I got it?"

"So they're really buying this crap. And, for the record, I'm glad you told me. Just because it's hard to hear doesn't mean I don't want to know."

"Oh, Joe, I can't believe this is happening."

"They didn't look into that expense report or the faulty time records?"

"Just like I predicted, Alan used his extensive electronic 'paper trail' to incriminate me and even had this guy, Adinaldo, verify that I'm the one who's running the deal and making all those calls, negotiating the terms and interacting with the Gerais Chevas insiders. They seem to be willing to take Alan's version of the records on their face, while looking at mine with suspicion."

"Unbelievable. And they just wrote off his attack on you in Chicago as a mutual indiscretion?"

"Paul said the partnership was split on who to believe, but they were willing to give me the benefit of the doubt, probably because they can't afford not to. He offered me one and a half million to forget the whole thing, but if I stay with the firm, I'd have to keep working with Alan."

"Not a very satisfying outcome."

"I don't know if I really want them to fire him, I just want to be believed. And, I'm just not getting anywhere with the partnership. And, I'm now officially on a leave of absence."

"So they can clean up this mess."

"I don't have high hopes."

"You can't be responsible for the final outcome of this deal if you're on leave. And the role you were being forced to play will have to be played by someone else, voluntarily or involuntarily."

"I was thinking about that, but my absence also prevents me from defending myself. Who knows what else Alan has planned or where else he's planted my name?"

"I think you should hire your own lawyer. Let someone scare the hell out of them."

"I think you're right. I don't have any other choice if they're not going to believe me. Joe, I really need you right now."

"I'm here for you. Want to go to Connecticut?"

Evie began flipping through the unopened mail in the briefcase pocket while she continued talking.

"I'm going to see if I can track down an old friend who does white collar defense," she said. "I think I'd better stay in the city in case he's available to meet, but may I see you later?"

"Sure. Until then, you know where I'll be."

"Okay. Talk to you later."

They hung up as Evie's eyes fell on a letter that was in an abnormally-sized envelope. It was an international envelope, slightly larger than the U.S. standard business envelope. It was postmarked a week ago from a New York post office, but there was no return address. She tore it open and took a breath.

chapter

28

Inside the envelope was an article in Portuguese from a Brazilian newspaper, *Folha de Sao Paulo.* In the margin of the newspaper clipping were scrawled the tiny words "In case we are not able to meet, E. Adelio." *This must be from the woman from Romez Nuevo,* she thought. Ms. Adelio apparently knew there was someone trying to prevent their meeting. Who could translate this? Maybe Joe had someone.

For a brief moment, she thought about walking back to Paul's office with this new piece of evidence, but without a translation, it was an unknown. There was no way to know whether it helped or hurt her claims. And, it offered up yet another person who thought she was running this deal. Not a conclusion she wanted to reinforce. She no longer cared as much about protecting the firm as she did about proving her own innocence and protecting herself. Evie put the article back in the envelope and returned it to her briefcase. She found the file she had been keeping on Gerais Chevas and added that to the same pocket.

She dialed her friend Huda to see if she was available to meet for lunch and they made a plan. A lunch with a trusted friend, who had no connection to the firm, was just what she needed.

She picked up the telephone again, hesitated for a few seconds, put down the receiver and grabbed her BlackBerry instead. She dialed and a secretary put her through.

"Michael Scott."

"Michael, hi. Thanks for taking my call."

"It's been a while. Still single?"

"Yes, still holding up my end of the statistic."

"Evie, are you okay? You sound a bit stressed."

"I'm fine. Actually . . . I'm *not* fine. I want to hire you to represent me."

"*Represent* you. Are you being investigated for some sort of crime?"

"You've done federal work, right?"

"Yes. Federal *and* state. White-collar crime, related civil litigation. Evie, what has happened? What's this about?"

"I'm being framed by a partner in my firm."

"You're kidding."

"No. Michael, I'm absolutely serious. Will you represent me?"

"Of course. Where are you?"

"In my office."

"At your firm?" he asked in astonishment. "Well, that's where I'd be if I were being framed by a partner."

"Seriously, Michael. This is very complicated. It involves an international acquisition that's being attributed to me even though I've had nothing to do with it. The partner who's running it may be involved in something which is possibly illegal. And . . . there's a U.S. Senator . . . *Wait,* I really should wait and explain this in person."

"You *are* edgy. A senator? I just settled a case. I've got a bit of time tonight."

"Where can we meet?" she asked.

"How about my office downtown . . . seven o'clock?"

"Can you make it any earlier?"

"Let's see, well how about this. Call me back this afternoon and in the meantime, I'll see if I can change my schedule around."

"Okay, thanks."

She hung up and looked around her office. *I'll finish organizing everything when I get back from lunch, if they're lucky.*

Once Evie had deposited herself at the sushi bar at Sushisay on East 51st Street to wait for Huda, she consciously dismissed the adrenaline that had supercharged the last hour. She felt herself relax as the first cup of sake did its work, but was abruptly distracted by a smell . . . *what was that?* It was a cheap man's cologne that'd been applied liberally.

She looked around and saw a black-haired, olive-skinned man with a strong mustache two seats away at the bar. He was wearing a navy pinstripe suit and starched shirt open at the collar, his tie pulled out of formation as if announcing that he had given up on the day.

"Are you dining alone? he asked, once he caught her eye.

"No." She thought her voice contained a measure of haughtiness, but she couldn't help it. The sensory assault was formidable and she was wary of any strange man, after the threatening phone calls and mysterious strangers trailing her around the city.

"You like sushi?" He didn't wait for an answer and gestured toward the cold fish fillets lying in the path of the sushi chef. "I *only* eat fish raw so I can see what I'm eating. I was once a regular at this five-star seafood restaurant that listed every type of fish imaginable on the menu. But I swear, no matter what type of fish you ordered, when presented at the table, it turned out to be the same piece of fish every time." He smiled at her.

She gave him a half-smile to be polite and glanced around the room searching for Huda. Her eyes fell on another hairy man who seemed to be watching her. This one was seated at a table facing her direction. He had a plate of sashimi in front of him, but he was not eating. She kept her eyes moving around the room, but in the brief glance in his direction she had noted his navy blazer and striped tie that seemed incongruous with his unruly curly hair and several day's growth of beard. She turned back toward the bar.

"Can I offer you another pitcher of sake?" asked the Mustache Man.

"Thank you, but I'm happy with this one."

"Did you know that the bride and groom in Japanese weddings drink sake to symbolize the unity between them?"

He was leaning toward her and shifting his body to slide over on the stool closer to her when she said, "Excuse me, please," and walked out to the sidewalk. She dialed Huda' cell phone and Huda told her she was five minutes away. Evie walked back through the door, but approached the hostess and asked to be seated immediately. The young woman gave Evie a sympathetic nod, retrieved Evie's pitcher of sake and led her to a table by the window.

After Evie had taken a seat and picked up the menu left by the hostess, the Bearded Man stood and approached her table. He smiled at her. *Wonderful,* she thought. *Another one.* She turned her attention to the menu, hoping he would take the hint.

"May I speak with you a moment?" he said in a baritone voice at low volume.

"I'm sorry. I don't—"

"I'm Daniel Weber, Special Agent with the Federal Bureau of Investigation." He extended his hand to shake hers, but she just stared.

Her heart skipped a beat. She looked around on impulse and saw that no one was really paying attention to what was going on at her table. The Mustache Man had begun chatting up an overly-tanned blonde woman at the sushi bar. Evie looked back at the man standing over her, took a breath and said, "Could I see some ID?"

He had opened a leather wallet while she spoke and she looked down at it as she finished asking the question. She studied the photo ID that read "FBI" in large block letters and "SPECIAL AGENT" in smaller letters, but wondered about the futility of her examination; it would be highly unlikely for her to be able to recognize a fake one. The photograph looked authentic and it definitely resembled the man standing before her. There was a gold badge imprinted with the FBI's insignia. She nodded to him and he sat down opposite her.

"Miss Sullivan," he began. She wondered how he knew her name, but then considered that thought silly. *Well, he must be who he says he is. Joe predicted this. I guess that telephone call with Joe WAS intercepted. Okay, here we go.*

"We are in the process of looking into some activities of your law firm. Would you be willing to answer some questions for me?"

"I'm sorry. I can't discuss any internal firm business with you." *He knows I'm a practicing lawyer. Why would he think I'd let myself be questioned by federal law enforcement without MY attorney present?*

"Well, it's really one particular matter that I would like to talk to you about."

"What would that be?"

"Do you represent a South American company called Romez Nuevo?"

"No."

"Do you or does your firm have *any* South American clients?"

"We don't discuss client relationships. Who we represent is confidential."

"But you *do* discuss these client relationships over the telephone with a man named Joseph Barton, do you not?"

"What are you talking about?"

"You do *know* a Joseph Barton, an American executive with the French company Parapier?"

"Yes, but he's not a client and he has nothing to do with the activities of my firm."

"Yes, we are familiar with Joseph Barton. We've had a file on him for some time."

The FBI has a file on Joe? Evie concentrated on holding an expression of polite detachment. Until she met with Michael and decided on a plan of action, she wouldn't risk handing out any information to the

FBI. If she was going to become the target of the investigation, the less she said the better.

"Miss Sullivan, we've been interested to notice your name more than once in recent reports generated by colleagues of mine. Is there something you're involved in that you'd like to unburden yourself about?"

"I'm afraid I don't know what you're talking about. If you don't mind, I'm waiting for a friend—"

"Yes, and were you waiting for a friend yesterday about this time?"

"What?"

"A woman was murdered yesterday on the Avenue of the Americas not far from your office." *She WAS murdered! That was her!*

"So. Why are you telling me this? What . . . do you think I had something to do with—"

"She had a note in her pocket with your name written on it."

Evie's mind raced. She tried to gauge how much trouble she could be in. How thoroughly the circumstances incriminated her. *How much does this agent know? Should I confide in him? What if he doesn't believe me? If I say the wrong thing, I could be handing them evidence against me. If I start spilling what I know and he DOES believe me, I could become an unwilling informant against the firm. And if he DOESN'T believe I'm not involved, a case assembled against me could become impossible to refute. Is this the point of no return? I need Michael's advice.*

"What did the note say?" she asked.

He ignored her question. "Do you have any idea why this woman would have your name written on a piece of paper she was carrying in her pocket when someone murdered her?"

Evie stared at him wondering how to avoid answering these questions without raising his suspicions. The fact was, *she didn't have the answers.*

"Did you have a plan to meet with a Latin woman yesterday?" he asked.

How do I answer that? I can't lie to the FBI. "Yes, I did," she said finally. "This woman, with what sounded like a Latin accent, called me at my office and asked me to meet her, but she never showed up. And I . . . I don't even know her name." *Not a complete lie,* she thought. *I don't know her name with certainty.*

"What did she want to meet with you about?"

"I don't know."

"So you're saying that you agreed to meet someone unknown to you, not knowing what she wanted to discuss or why she wanted to meet with you?"

Yes, that does sound unbelievable doesn't it. "Yes, that's . . . I *did* know that she wanted to talk to me about a matter that I was aware of. She said she had information for me. She hung up before I could ask her name or find out anything more."

"What matter was that?"

"That's confidential."

"Did you know that she was an employee of Romez Nuevo?"

"Yes. She *did* tell me that much."

"What else did she tell you that may have slipped your mind?" There was no mistaking his skepticism.

"Nothing. She was very brief. She said she didn't want to go into it over the telephone and told me where to meet her."

"Where was that?"

"I was supposed to meet her at Mangia on 57th Street."

"At what time?"

"She said eleven thirty."

"And you waited for her there?"

"Yes, but as I said, she never showed up."

"Did she say *anything* about why she wanted to talk to you . . . anything that's *not* confidential?"

Evie feigned the look of someone trying to remember elusive details and remained silent. How could she tell him that she thought the woman had information about a trap being set for her? She knew she didn't want to explain her suspicions about Project Neon to this federal agent with all signs pointing to her as the dealmaker. There was still too much incriminating evidence around that she couldn't refute.

"Miss Sullivan, I know you're an intelligent woman. You should seriously consider cooperating with the FBI. You may find that if you cooperate, you are less likely to become a target of the investigation yourself."

"I'm happy to cooperate with the FBI within the boundaries of confidentiality. As a licensed attorney, it's my duty to keep certain matters confidential. If you have a subpoena, my legal duty changes. But, until then . . ."

"Yes, ma'am." He pulled out a small notepad and began making notes. "Are you being blackmailed, Miss Sullivan?"

"What? No. Not that I know of." *Not that I know of. Setup yes, blackmailed no.*

"Do you own a gun?"

"No. I don't own a gun." She looked up to see Huda walking toward the table with a quizzical look on her face when she noticed the man speaking to Evie.

"Huda! Hello." Evie smiled at her friend in grateful greeting and tossed a look at Daniel Weber that seemed to say, '*Do I introduce you?*'

He saved her the trouble, extending his hand to shake Huda's. "Hello. I'm Daniel Weber with the Federal Bureau of Investigation."

"Hello," said Huda, looking back and forth between Evie and the agent not knowing what to say.

"Well," he said. "Thank you, Miss Sullivan, for taking the time to speak with me. Here's my card if you think of anything else you'd like to tell me," he said as he stood and offered a government-issue business card. "We'll be in touch."

"You're welcome," said Evie, taking the card. She shook his hand and watched as he nodded at each of the women and walked out of the restaurant.

"What the hell was that all about?" asked Huda, sitting down across from Evie and placing her hand on Evie's arm in a supportive gesture.

"He said the FBI is investigating something to do with my firm." *Don't get involved in this, my friend.*

"Oh my God. Really? Why are they talking to you?"

"I don't know exactly. They may be interviewing a bunch of different people from the firm."

"*Scary.* Are you worried?"

Yes. I am a bit. The FBI thinks I murdered a woman who was trying to blackmail me. "No. I'm not. And please, don't you be. I'm fine." Evie playacted the most relaxed smile she could manage. There was no use in telling Huda. There was nothing she could do to help. "Huda, thanks for agreeing to meet me. I really needed to see a friendly face."

"I can imagine . . . after a conversation with the FBI."

When Evie returned to her office, she decided to check for any updates to the Gerais Chevas documents. She was not surprised that the password remained unchanged—the successful password for both "Neon Three" and "Neon Four" were still her mother's name. "Neon Three" still showed a $25 million commission, but there were no details or explanations added as to its purpose or recipient. Schedule B7 in "Neon Four" was shockingly different:

> *In my capacity as attorney for seller, Gerais Chevas, in the above entitled transaction, I, Evelyn Sullivan, hereby guarantee the award of T-ASA Contract Number 56-8097-244221, and all associated Purchase Orders to the business unit of Gerais Chevas d/b/a GC Quadra, hereby known as DODAAC 639-001. This award is consistent with the DFARS concerning sole source awards in certain circumstances. See Sole Source Justification 23.459. In exchange for my agency, I shall receive a commission as set forth in the Payment Schedule to be paid upon*

Closing of the Master Purchase Agreement, as defined in said agreement.

SIGNED: _____

So, the final phase has begun, she thought. Alan had her guaranteeing that the business unit being sold was going to be awarded a government contract and had apparently enlisted Adinaldo to point to her as the negotiator! Just as Joe had predicted, there was a sole source award in the works. The tax game Senator Arbeson was playing was not his only sport. In his capacity as a member of the Appropriations Committee, he had apparently agreed to hand GC Quadra a government contract and she was being charged with delivering it. And she would receive a commission, it read—the only commission currently detailed in the Payment Schedule was the one for $25 million.

chapter
29

Even though she had expected it, to see her name inserted into the incriminating paragraph was horrifying, her identity a tool for someone to play with. She tried editing the document and was allowed to do so, but she left it intact so that the partners could see it. She was certain that if she deleted her name, Alan would simply add it again, anyway. She resisted the urge to copy the document to her laptop, creating the appearance that it had originated with her, but she did *print* a copy for her file.

As she worked, she pictured a smelly room somewhere with a group of Latin businessmen excited about the promise of a large revenue stream courtesy of the U.S. government, with someone's voice over the telephone claiming to be her and making lofty promises. Or maybe it had just been Alan on all those calls, and the illusion of her helmsmanship was just part of the conspiracy. She couldn't understand how the partnership could so easily accept her as the orchestrator. Perhaps the new Schedule B7 would tip the credibility scale in her direction. She dialed Paul's extension, but Barbara told her he was out at a meeting, so she sent another email to Paul asking him to look at the new Neon Four file.

After packing up her laptop, she made a half-hearted attempt to organize her client files to be redistributed and cleaned her office. At two o'clock P.M., she called Michael and he told her he was now free at 3:30. She used the remaining time to summarize ongoing client matters and after sending a final email to Paul, grabbed her briefcase and laptop and left the building. She took a quick look around as she slid into a taxi.

"Okay, I've got a pretty good idea of what we're dealing with," said Michael, holding Evie's copy of the latest Schedule B7 and pacing around his office. Evie had spent a half hour or so relaying the whole story and he'd listened intently.

She said in completion, "It's crystal clear now that I'm the scapegoat. It's certainly unethical for an attorney to act as an agent and counsel on the same deal. And I can't imagine on what *legal* basis an attorney could *guarantee* the award of a government contract." She coughed, took a sip of the water Michael had poured for her and resumed her thought.

"Ethically speaking, a commission payment this sizable could have been legitimate agency compensation, I guess, if the agent's role was pairing the buyer and seller in the transaction," she paused. "But for me to be acting as an agent to procure . . . No, not just procure, but *guarantee* that a government contract will be awarded to the company being sold—"

"And presumably in *advance* of the government contract being awarded."

"Yes! So it's not like a representation where an attorney would be declaring that a government project was already in the hopper . . . like when an attorney represents that a company has the right to a certain patent. In this case, the attorney is promising to *obtain* or use his or her influence to obtain something . . . and being paid to do it."

"A bribe. One would have to wonder about a company willing to purchase a business unit based on such a subterfuge. It's not as if there'd be a clear remedy if the attorney failed to deliver," Michael added as he walked around his desk and sat in a chair facing Evie.

"Well, apparently at least some of the buyer's management team was planning a mutiny." She pulled out the clipping from the Brazilian newspaper and handed it to Michael.

He glanced at it and said, "I've got a colleague here who should be able to translate this." He buzzed his secretary, asked her to make some copies of the article and pass one to the proposed translator.

"The Adelios will be a great source of information I would imagine," he said, "assuming they share Ms. Adelio's desire to stop the deal. Her death might make them more willing to talk than they might otherwise have been."

"Or *not*. Her murder may have been as much about silencing them as preventing me from receiving information. You'll know better than I, Michael, but there have to be any number of laws involved here. It depends on whether or not there's really a government project, whether this deal does follow the rules for sole source awards, where the money's really going. Who knows how Alan and his conspirators could be planning to divide up this commission?"

"We'll have to involve the FBI in order to get the discovery power we need. This guy, Alan, is on the take and perhaps our illustrious Senator is, too. At this point, we don't have enough in tangible form to nail this sonofabitch, but it exists on the firm's network . . . and possibly in the guy's office or apartment. With the FBI's subpoena power, we can go for electronic discovery. We'll want metadata—it will give us shadow information on emails he sent such as the original author, title, creation date, hidden email recipients. But, we'll have to hurry. Most email systems are purged every thirty days. Do you know how often your technical staff purges the email system?"

"No, I don't."

"We'll assume thirty. And maybe we'll put in a few inquiries with the Senator, although we have to tread lightly there until we have really strong proof. Senator Arbeson *IS* already under investigation for bribery. It's common knowledge among the guys I work out with. And who knows how vast his playing field is? On the criminal side, I can see possible RICO violations, conspiracy, maybe a Hobbs violation, fraud and, potentially, obstruction of justice, and possibly *murder* . . . if Alan can be tied to Miss Adelio. We don't know for sure yet, but the co-conspirator list might include our beloved Senator." Michael was standing and pacing again, tapping the rolled up sheet of paper against an open palm.

"Wait! Michael, you're going way to fast for me." Evie turned around in the chair and gripped the back of it with both hands. "I just want to keep *myself* alive and out of jail. I don't want to get that aggressive with Alan or the firm. And, anyway, Alan seems to play with the wording on these files almost daily. What's to keep him from changing them again and making it look like I'm making things up?"

"Evie, you're going to have to change your thinking from a business lawyer to a litigator."

"With all due respect, counselor, I think the client dictates the course of action. I don't know how I feel about suing, but I desperately want to solidify a defense and clear my name."

"You'll *have* to sue to let them know you're serious—sexual harassment and assault to get things going. By the way, this $1.5 million offer is bullshit. These cases often settle for five times that."

Evie frowned.

Michael continued, "Yes, the evolution of these files makes it difficult to file a claim without tangible copies. That's why we need the FBI's subpoena power."

"What about my conversation with that Agent Weber? Did I say anything to incriminate myself?"

"We definitely need to set up a meeting with the feds ASAP. I don't think *they* really think you had anything to do with this Adelio woman's murder, but we've got to get them working with us. We'll just say you were under duress at your firm and not ready to talk when Weber approached you. I'm going to arrange something. We'll see about getting you some protection, too, since we don't know who's sending this guy who's tracking you and issuing warnings over the phone."

"Okay. I'm ready to talk to them, but I want to try to avoid taking the firm down. There are several people there I really care about, Jack Hanover being one of them."

"You've got to forget about the firm. They're big boys and girls. They can take care of themselves. Think about yourself now."

"Okay. Okay. Michael, *okay*. But what about this ongoing runaway transaction? I assume it's going to keep moving toward a closing, and now I have no control over what happens with it. I'm officially on leave."

"Well, to a certain extent that works to our advantage as long as you don't toy with any of the documents. Alan's now responsible for the deal and anything new that appears would be his responsibility."

"But they officially let me keep my laptop and retain access to my office so they could *claim* I was still tinkering with the documents, in theory. He put my electronic seal of approval on these changes that showed up today. He's faked so much communication already."

"Well, at least some part of the record now reflects that you're off the responsibility list as of today. You need to stay off the firm's network from now on. Dates will be crucial. We'll be able to compare the date that tape was made against the electronic record of when the changes were saved to this file. The date of your conversation is captured nicely for us on that recording waiting for you in Paul's office. You need to follow through and get your copy of that tape. You'll have to go to the office and pick it up. We don't want them to know you've hired your own lawyer just yet. We'll need that recording before we file suit."

"Okay."

She dialed her office and left a message for Helen to retrieve the tape copy for her and have it messengered to her apartment.

"After we speak to the FBI," Michael continued, "I want to arrange a meeting with your firm. I assume Paul will be the managing partner while Jack Hanover is recuperating. I want Alan there, too. He might lose control and say something really juicy we can use. In the meantime, it will be interesting to see if you get any reaction from Paul in response to those emails you sent earlier."

Evie smiled. "Okay, but I'm not sure they'll let Alan attend. Oh, something else. I think Joe's spyware might turn up some good material. Can we use it?"

"We can definitely use it in our negotiations. Don't worry about admissibility in court right now."

"What about Joe's PI? He's doing some checking, too."

"Great. I think you should put me in direct contact with the guy."

"I don't know him, but I'll introduce you to Joe."

"Fine. Okay, Evie, I'm going to get started with a strategy. Clear your schedule for a meeting with the feds. We'll offer a cooperative effort with concentric goals. If we have something to offer the FBI on those criminal matters, it will keep you on the right side of their investigation and could yield something for our civil action. If we can't find an actual or constructive fraud angle for you, our strongest claim will be a combination of state law tort claims and claims brought under the discrimination and federal anti retaliation laws. We can make a case that those reprimands and performance reports were a quid pro quo because you rebuked his advances and, recently, because you were looking into his dirty deal."

"Well, a couple of those partner complaints are partly true, just blown way out of proportion. The rest I know were manufactured by Alan."

"That will be our argument, and we'll get some backup from discovery."

Someone knocked on Michael's door and a dark complected woman entered, introducing herself as an international associate in Michael's firm.

"Here you go." The woman handed a piece of paper to Michael.

"Thanks, Maria," he said and watched her leave.

Michael shook the paper at Evie, smiled, looked down and read it aloud:

Friday, September 3, 2004—A new turf battle has begun in the ongoing war among the principals of a once-admired PHC, Romez Nuevo. Owned jointly by the Adelio family and our own international frontiersman, Gustavo Oneda, the privately-held partnership, based in Argentina, boasted an impressive 52 consecutive quarters with expanding net revenue, until Oneda convinced the senior Adelio to grant him control in executing a series of business strategies designed to make Romez Nuevo a global player. In a surprising move, Oneda abandoned the jointly-conceived plan and has implemented an aggressive acquisition agenda, heavy on outlay and vague on integration detail, our sources tell us. The imperialistic plan is said by some to be merely an effort to achieve a superior number of operating units to Hidega Enterprises, helmed by Abel Caldas, a longtime nemesis of Oneda. "He is engaging in business terrorism," said the senior Adelio of Oneda, who is considering legal options to regain control of the company his family founded decades ago. Our sources tell us that the Adelios are afraid their company will not be able to survive under the burden of the new organizational structure.

"Well," said Evie after Michael looked up, "the Adelio woman said to me that she would lose everything if the Gerais Chevas deal closed. I guess their family fortune is tied up in the company and this partner of theirs is gambling with it."

"And paying $25 million for the privilege, apparently."

"Interesting that she would come to me to stop the deal. She must've known there was something wrong with the way it was being negotiated, and she must've believed I was *not* in on it."

"Probably part of the reason she's dead. The illusion of your culpability was in danger of being shattered."

"Would you approach the Adelios for information while they're grieving over the loss of their family member?"

"I'll have to consider the options. When we get the feds involved, they're likely to call in Interpol. They'll have their own ways of gathering information."

Michael placed the paper on his desk and began walking around his office as he continued to speak.

"Anyway, getting back to our short-term strategy, we'll be seeking details on their investigation."

"And the leave of absence. It wasn't my idea."

"Yes. If we can prove our case on sexual harassment, it was Alan who should've been put on leave. I'm glad we'll have on tape that Paul suspects Alan and has questioned his judgment in the past. Retaliation could be a strong case, maybe even constructive retaliatory discharge. That incident in Chicago and those more recent incidents you told me about could support a hostile work environment claim. There's also a basis for defamation claims here; we can toy with intentional infliction of emotional distress, appropriation of name and maybe even false light. I'll have to do some more research, but depending on where the trail leads, there may be a whistleblower claim, forgery . . . and I don't know what else."

Evie nodded, crossed her legs and tapped her pen. "Just don't do anything without checking with me first, okay? And I want to have ample time to review and discuss any complaint you plan to file."

"Doctors make the worst patients, and lawyers make the worst clients."

Evie nodded, grinning with a sense of relief. She had an aggressive advocate in addition to her technologist and his private investigator.

Michael continued, "I don't think we have enough yet to file or even set up a meeting with your colleagues at the firm, but with the enforcement arm of the FBI and your pledge of cooperation, we could gather enough to clear you and craft a nice civil claim on your behalf. Evie, you deserve it, given what they've put you through. I don't expect to go to trial, but we can shoot for a bit more than one and a half million."

Evie sat back and felt a bit more in control, but knew there was a long road ahead.

chapter

30

Whcn she was safely back inside her apartment, she looked at her answering machine before she even laid down her briefcase. It glowed with messages. She walked over and hit PLAY.

"Hey Eves . . . Missing you. Playing Indian Warriors with Bradley. You know . . . I could find a use for some of these Indian moves when I meet the other man in your life. Ari is out until eight or so. Call me if you need me. I can be in the city in forty-five minutes." Beep. There were several more messages that played, but she didn't hear them.

She dialed Ariel's number. The tidbits of the day floated in the air like pollutants. There was now time to reflect on the realities she faced.

Ring. Ring. Ring. Ring. Ring. She was shifting the receiver from her ear to hang up when she heard, *"Hewo?"* It was a tiny hello. A high-pitched, angelic voice.

"Hello, Bradley?" she said.

"Wes. Bwadley."

"*Bradley.* Hello! Remember me? Is your uncle there?"

"Unca Joe."

"Can I speak to Uncle Joe, honey?"

"Outside. Noise."

"A noise? What kind of noise?"

"Noise."

"Wait! Sweetheart, when Uncle Joe comes back . . . can you ask Uncle Joe to come to the phone?"

There was silence. Then the receiver dropped against what sounded like a table. There were many moments of electronic silence laced with white noise. After what seemed like five minutes, she heard the receiver move across the surface of its resting place.

"Hello?" said Joe.

"Joe! It's Evie."

"Eves? Are you okay?"

"Are *you* okay? Bradley said there was a noise outside."

"Yeah, I know. He imagines things. The therapist says the divorce has created an insecurity in him. I had to go check."

"I was worried about you."

"Everything here is fine. How's Eves?"

"Oh, Joe. I have to talk to you, but I don't know *w-h-e-r-e t-o s-t-a-r-t . . .*"

Suddenly, the buildup of recent events assaulted her in an unmanageable slap of emotional overload. She unexpectedly felt herself start to choke up and she fought back tears.

"Evie! What the hell happened? Are you home?"

"Yes, I'm home." She sniffed and regained control of her voice. "I'm fine. Really. I think things are just starting to get to me."

"Listen. Make sure your door's locked. Ari's home in a few minutes. When she gets back, I'm coming over."

"Joe. I'm sorry to worry you. I'm okay, really! Really I am, but can you? *Can* you come over?"

"Yes. As soon as Ari gets back. I'm just going to get Bradley to bed. And then I'll be there. Okay?"

"Okay."

Evie hung up. She felt a wave of sweet relief wash over her. She checked the front door again to make sure it was locked. Then she drew a hot bath and soaked. She almost fell asleep in the tub and lost track of time. The sound of the buzz of her intercom caused her to jump out of the tub and throw on her kimono. She told the doorman to let Joe in and scurried around looking for clothes to put on. The knock on the door prompted her to abandon the search. Joe would likely see her in worse states of disrepair before this situation resolved itself.

He smiled when she opened the door. After walking in and locking the door, he turned back to face her in a fluid movement, hugging her tightly against his body. When they parted, Evie regarded him. He looked ruggedly handsome with a two-day beard, his tanned skin and a denim shirt. Facial hair suddenly seemed very appealing. He wore beige linen drawstring pants and Topsiders. His wavy hair was slightly messy and his eyes sparkled; there was no mistaking that he was glad to see her.

"Hey, Eves. I was really concerned."

"I knew I worried you. I'm sorry."

"If anything happened to you . . ." He let a slow, tender kiss finish his thought.

She grabbed him again and for several minutes held tight to his neck.

"I've got some good news," he whispered into her ear after a few seconds.

She stepped back slightly, but let her fingers stay intertwined in the hair on the back of his head. "I could use some."

"I spoke to Sandra. She's *not* pregnant."

"Oh my God! That *is* good news! Is she okay?"

"Yes. She will be. Apparently, some drug she was taking caused her to miss her period . . . and I guess it somehow caused her to mis-read that initial pregnancy test." He paused and moved toward her sofa. "I'm so sorry to have put you through that."

"No, really. It's okay," she said as she followed him.

"Bad news today?"

"Schedule B7 now reads that I, personally, am guaranteeing that GC Quadra will be awarded, in the future, a government contract and that I will receive a commission for my trouble."

"So it's exactly what we suspected it was going to be. And it *is* a sole source," he said as he sat down on the sofa. "Yes, but who knows if the government project is real?" she asked as she headed toward the kitchen to get some drinks. "I'll be right back," she said as she disappeared into the kitchen, returning in seconds with a couple of open beers. She handed one to Joe and sat down next to him.

"This should cheer you up," he said. "I got a message from Greg."

"Greg?"

"My PI."

"Oooh. What? Did he find something?"

"Some interesting information," said Joe, pulling Evie into his lap. Joe's presence was so much more soothing than the soak in the tub had been.

"I should put something on," she said suddenly, looking down at her kimono.

"I wouldn't change a thing," he said after a sip of his beer. He grinned and she blushed. "Greg's been checking on Levenger," he continued. "The first thing he said to me was 'this guy's dirty'."

"How so?"

"Whatever else he's into, he apparently likes to set up those 'lazy-susan' deals. Do you know what that is?"

"No."

"Levenger arranges for a company to offer a sizable investment to another company that turns around and pays the money back as a bogus service fee for some non-existent service. One gets the backer bragging rights, the other gets phony revenue to report on its income statement."

"And he gets a cut off the top?"

"Yeah."

"So in a way, I guess Project Neon is the ultimate lazy-susan deal."

"Were you able to track down that attorney you mentioned?"

"Yes, Michael Scott." She gave Joe a brief synopsis of her meeting with Michael.

"I'll call him and give him Greg's contact information," said Joe, rubbing Evie's feet. "Apparently, Levenger's also been fighting the effects of some bad investments. Wrote off a lot of personal losses last year. His financial records could be telling the story of a desperate man."

"And if a man like Alan is desperate, look out," said Evie. "Did your man find anything else?"

"He turned up a copy of the ID presented by the woman who checked into the Colonial Court Hotel under the name Evelyn Sullivan."

"Oh, that's great! Michael can use that to prove it wasn't me making and receiving all those Brazilian calls!"

"Not a bad fake, Greg said."

"No one ever said Alan doesn't know what he's doing."

"I collected a few more interesting emails and Internet searches from Levenger's computer. He was trading tales with some geek about Back Orifice tools, which are Trojan horses that allow remote control of someone else's computer."

"Wow. That must be how he electronically impersonated me sending out Sangerson and all those Gerais Chevas emails."

"Likely. So did Michael convince you to go to the FBI?"

"Yes, but I have to back up a little bit. An agent confronted me today while I was waiting for my friend, Huda, at a sushi restaurant. He told me that my firm was being investigated. He mentioned you, so they must have intercepted that telephone call, as you predicted." Evie took a sip of her beer and leaned against Joe's body for warmth and comfort. "Joe, why would they have a file on you? Would that be the security clearance procedure?"

"Well, I had another experience with the FBI. The file they have relates to that earlier incident."

Evie repositioned her body so she could look into his face.

"Remember that scar you noticed on my stomach?" he continued.

"Yes."

"I was shot at Kennedy Airport."

"You were *shot*? With a gun? *When?*" she sat up and faced him.

"It's a bit complicated. Let me start at the beginning. On one of my trips to Kenya, I discovered some poaching going on. Ivory. Dead elephants. I tried to stop it. There was some violence."

"You caught them in the act?"

"Yeah. I disrupted one of their expeditions and chased them off, letting the elephants escape. A few of those guys decided to pay a visit to our camp."

"Was anyone killed?"

"No, but while I was having a physical dispute with one of them by the campfire, the other was in my tent going through my things. I found my plane ticket on the ground. I guess you could say I had aggravated the situation pretty well, because when I left the country the next day, they must have arranged for an ambush at Kennedy."

"Oh my God! What happened?"

"I got through customs and . . . one of the poachers . . . he apparently had a fence here. They were waiting for me when I came out of the airport. I guess they perceived me as a threat to their ivory smuggling operation. Turned out the FBI had been tracking these guys."

"So this guy shot you and ran off? And an ambulance came?"

"Something like that. But, I uhh, I killed him."

"You *killed* him?"

"Yes. I'm not especially proud of it. He shot me, but it wasn't that bad. Missed all the crucial organs. I chased him. He dropped his gun. I guess I had better aim than he did. And I was pissed off. I shot him in the back with his own gun. He didn't get up."

"Oh my God! Were you . . . did they charge you with a crime?"

"No. It was written off as self-defense. They were pretty glad that I'd helped break up the crime ring. I know. Technically, I went a bit far for a claim of self-defense. I was chasing that son-of-a-bitch, and I should have taken a less fatal shot."

"But he'd put a *bullet* in you! You had every right—there was no way for you to know if he had *another* weapon of some kind . . . he could have turned right around and finished the job. Retreat is still part of the commission of the crime, at least for some distance."

"Hmmm." He smiled. "You would've made a good defense attorney, had I needed one."

"And . . . then, what happened?"

"There was a lot of talking. The feds interviewed me the first time in the hospital. Several times after that. The news cameras came around a bit. I testified. They got the rest of them. At least the ones in the States. I guess they're still serving time."

"Oh my God! What an incredible story." Evie leaned back against the sofa. "Have you been back to Africa since?"

"No. That was the last trip. But, I've thought about going back. I'd just stay out of certain areas next time." His eyes softened as if he was reliving a pleasant memory from one of his safaris.

"Did they get the bullet out?" she said, her hand on his stomach.

He nodded.

"Do you have any lingering effects?"

"No, not really. A bit of soreness when the weather changes." He smiled. "So, an agent confronted you? I was hoping we would have some good luck, there. Sorry, Eves."

"He caught me totally off guard. I really kind of brushed him off—I guess I only committed *half* a felony." She smiled a half-smile of consternation. "I didn't really tell *lies* to the FBI, just withheld some information. Michael says he can clean it up. But, the interesting thing was that Weber, this agent, tells me that a woman was murdered a block from my office that day, a woman who had a slip of paper in her pocket with my name on it."

"So it *was* that woman who called to meet you, hmmm. So the FBI is interested and trying to quantify your involvement."

"Yes. I'm hopeful they'll forgive my stonewalling when they understand the whole story."

"Evie, you've got confirmation now that she *was murdered*. You've got to raise your level of self-protection now. There are people involved in this thing—people who apparently will kill."

"It's such a shame," said Evie. "She risked a lot and ultimately paid with her life."

"Well Eves, I'm sorry she became a murder victim, but I'm actually glad they prevented the meeting. She could've made *you* more of a target if she had succeeded. There's definitely a foul smell to this deal, but it sounds like the tide has turned. With the feds involved, there will be all kinds of ways to gather additional evidence."

"Yes, but I'm afraid that much of that evidence will have my name on it. My name's all over the correspondence and files for Gerais Chevas. There's nothing to prove it wasn't me billing time and writing emails."

"Do you have the translation of that Brazilian news article?"

Evie stood and retrieved the newspaper clipping, its translation and the envelope it was mailed in from the growing file in her briefcase. Joe studied the news article and examined the envelope, focusing on the markings. "It's international style with a New York postmark." He studied the copy of the translation for a moment. "So, as much as the Adelios don't want this deal, apparently this guy Oneda *does*."

"Do you think *he* could be behind the murder of Ms. Adelio?"

"You can never tell what the drive for power will do to a man."

"I don't know what Ms. Adelio was trying to tell me other than her family was opposed to the deal. Someone apparently needed to keep her from revealing what she knew."

"I'm staying here tonight. I'll sleep on the sofa," he said suddenly, placing the collection of paper on the coffee table.

"Can we just sit here for awhile? Will you hold me?"

"Of course, Eves. I'll hold you as long as you want."

She kissed him, and leaned back against his chest. He encircled her with his arms.

"I noticed that your clothes looked pretty clean despite having spent the evening with a two year old," she said. "Do you want me to wash them? They'll be dry by morning."

"No need. I dodged all the airborne food."

She laughed for the first time all day.

~

Evie got up first and cooked egg-white vegetable omelets, which she was placing on the table when Joe came in, dressed in his clothes from the night before.

"You're even hairier this morning," she said smiling.

"I'll shave at the hotel. I actually have a meeting today, so I have to look like an executive."

"You do? Do you need a place to have your meeting? I think I still have conference room privileges, I could arrange a room at the firm."

"Thanks, Eves, but my secretary set it up for one of the hotel's meeting rooms. Only five or so attending, I think. Two Frenchmen, two Americans and an Israeli. Should be very interesting."

"Hmmm. Sounds like you might *need* a beard for that one."

He smiled and looked down at the breakfast buffet. "Wow, five star service here."

"Would you like coffee, tea?" He nodded toward the coffee. She continued, "I think I forgot juice though, and I don't have any fresh oranges or grapefruit to squeeze."

"I guess I set a high standard for breakfast when you stayed with me." He laughed.

"I'm just trying to impress you with my domestic skills."

"It's working."

He walked up behind her and put his arms around her waist. She turned to him, gave him a kiss and turned back to grab the coffee pot.

"Eat your breakfast," she said as she poured coffee into two cups on the table. She offered him a napkin, and they both sat down, at perpendicular sides of the table, knees touching. The morning sun was bright and illuminated the tiny kitchen. They were lost in each other's eyes as they took a few sips of hot coffee.

"So Eves, what are your plans today?" He deposited a large bite of omelet into his mouth and washed it down with a swallow of coffee.

"I'm going to spend some time at the Association of the Bar of the City of New York. They have a great law library and I thought I'd try to do some research. These are areas of the law I know very little about."

"You know this wasn't thrown together on the fly. You've had Levenger plotting against you much longer than you think."

She stopped eating and took a deep breath, her eyes glazed and pensive. "I guess *I've* been wearing the spider for some time now without even knowing it, haven't I?"

"You know, Eves, we don't even know if this twenty-five million is the totality of it. There could be even more money being passed around that's not accounted for and other side deals that won't be reflected in any written agreement."

"One has to wonder, though. I mean, if I'm the one who concocted this scheme of fraud and deceit, why would I not suddenly just disappear with the money? What did he plan to do and say after this thing closes? Did he really think I would just go along with this?"

"Eves. That's what I'm afraid of. He might not stop at setting you up. I don't mean to scare you, but maybe he intends to *silence* you. So that you can't defend yourself . . . so that he can say that he discovered your sinister plot and tried to stop *you*. And you won't be around to say anything different."

"You meeeaaan . . . *kill* me?" She swallowed a bite of omelet with a gulp. 'Oh Joe, no. No. No he couldn't. I can't imagine even Alan going that far. Miss Adelio was a threat. She was trying to reveal something they didn't want revealed, and we don't know who killed her. It could've been someone connected to their business partner. I'm actually of some importance to Alan's scheme. At least until the deal closes, right? Otherwise, how could he claim I was the one to've closed it behind the firm's back?"

"I just want you to be very aware, stay off the streets as much as possible and check in with me."

"I will." She took a bite of omelet and stared off into space.

"I'd love to stop this deal," she said. "That would support my argument that I had nothing to do with setting it up."

"The last woman who tried to stop it is in refrigeration at the morgue. Let the feds take over. Promise me you'll stay in populated areas and you won't take any chances."

"Okay. So you're in New York for how long?"

"Fortunately, today I have this meeting that would've been held in New York anyway. I can shuffle things around next week. Then, we'll see."

"Who's going to take care of Ayoka and Ajani?"

He smiled. "A friend of mine agreed to stop by and get them. They're going to stay on his ranch for a few days."

"They will probably enjoy that."

"Eves, I'm reachable by cell all day. I want you to call me if you need me. Promise?"

"Joe?"

"Yes?"

"I love you."

He smiled and raised the last bite of his breakfast. "You know, you make a great omelet."

"So glad you like it."

chapter
31

She stopped by the firm later that morning just to see if there was any more mail containing handwritten accusations. To her relief, there was nothing. Once in her office, it was almost as if nothing had changed, none of the administrative staff reacted any differently to her, and she wondered if any announcement had been made.

Since she was there, she checked her messages. Adam. Roma Sori. It broke her heart not to be able to continue working for her favorite client. That SerosaSoft deal would definitely be active over the next two weeks. Despite the instructions from Paul, she dialed Adam's office. His secretary, Kim, answered and asked her to hold. Kim added that Adam wanted very much to talk to her. She waited.

"Evie! How are you? I've been very interested in the current events at your firm. I was sorry to hear about Hanover. How's he doing?"

"Adam, I'm actually not sure, but thanks for your concern."

"Well, I've heard rumblings this morning about changes to be made in your firm. And, well, let me get to the point. I would like very much for you to consider an in-house position."

"A job with Roma Sori?"

"Yes. As you know, our general counsel recently resigned and since then we've just been outsourcing all our legal work, relying on your firm for all our legal needs. Actually, we've been relying on *you* for the most part. You've been just an *enormous* asset to our company We think that you have exceptional talent and that you would be a great addition to our organization."

"I'm very flattered, Adam. And I appreciate your confidence in me, but I've never worked in-house, with responsibility for the full array of legal needs of a company such as Roma Sori. I will have to consider this very carefully—"

"Yes, of course. Let me just say that there would be several options for you to consider. If you wanted to serve Roma Sori as legal counsel, that would be welcome and you would still have a budget for outside legal support. If not, I would want to talk to you about other options. There could be other positions within the company you might find interesting, uhh . . . Evie, excuse me one minute." She could hear him speak to someone in his office.

Working for Roma Sori exclusively. Now, this is an interesting proposal.

Adam completed his local conversation and continued, "For example, and this is just a suggestion as you may have no interest in anything outside a pure legal role, but I'd like to talk to you about taking your career a completely different direction. I've been thinking about this for some time. There are some new Roma Sori product lines that need leadership. Perhaps you might consider heading up a division. I'm talking about an Executive Vice President position."

"Adam, I don't know what to say."

"Will you think about it? I mean I can't yet offer explicit details on the scope of the position, but you have demonstrated an unusual skill for marketing and the decision-making that goes with managing a product line. You're a quick study. And, whatever position you selected, your legal mind would be a valued internal asset."

"Adam, thank you for the offer. I'll give your proposal careful consideration."

"No rush, Evie. The reorganization I'm planning would take place over a six-to-eight month period."

"Adam. One more thing. I should tell you that for the next two weeks at least, you can reach me at my home number or on my cell."

"Taking a vacation?"

"No. Actually, a short leave of absence. So interestingly enough, your proposals are incredibly well-timed."

"Good! If you decide that either one of them is the least bit attractive, call me and we can put some flesh on the bone. Talk specifics."

"Okay, Adam. Thanks again. I'll be in touch."

Evie hung up and was about to dial another client when she looked up to see Jenna stick her head in.

"Jen. Hey, how are you?" Evie said hanging up the telephone receiver.

"It finally happened," quipped Jenna as she walked into the office. "I used a handicapped stall in the bathroom at the airport like I always do, but this time there was *actually a woman in a wheelchair* waiting when I got out."

Evie smiled. "I'm sure she didn't mind."

"Have a minute?"

"Yes. Of course," Evie said waving her over to sit down.

"I've been traveling nonstop. I just got back this morning from Philly. Is it true? Are you taking a leave?" She sat down frowning and looked down at Evie's desk as if the answer was there somewhere.

"Yes."

"Was it your idea?

"No."

"I can't fucking believe it. Hanover's laid up for a few days and the vultures are circling. All kinds of rumors about changes to the firm.

I think there's a merger in the works. Do you think you've lost your chance at partnership?"

"I think that's the reality, even though nothing was said. I guess it's up to you now, Jen. This round is all yours."

"Damn! I can't believe they're doing this to you. What a bunch of short-sighted pricks! Does this have to do with that Gerais Chevas deal?"

"I think so. I think it's that and bad performance reviews and the fact that I finally reported that Chicago incident. They want to be seen as indulging me with time to evaluate my options. They've left it up to me whether or not to stay, but I can't imagine ever being trusted by the rest of the partners if I ever did get an invitation to join."

"That sounds like retaliation for having reported a harassment."

"Well, I guess they see it as giving me a paid breather, but I know they're using it as a way to keep Alan from interacting with me until the temperatures cool. Anyway, it doesn't feel like a positive."

"What are you going to do?" asked Jenna as she sat down across from Evie.

"I don't know." Evie was not going to confide in Jenna about hiring a lawyer or any more of the Gerais Chevas details. While being somewhat self-protective, she knew that involving Jenna in the secrecy and imminent confrontation undoubtedly ahead, might interfere with her friend's own career objectives. There was nothing to gain and everything to lose.

Evie stood, walked around to the front of the desk and hugged Jenna.

"You're a good friend, Jen. I'll stay in touch."

Jenna hugged her back, frowned and made her promise to call when she made up her mind about her future.

After Jenna left, Evie sorted through new messages on her desk and there was a note in an envelope from Helen saying Beverly had confirmed Alan's presence in Dallas on the same dates Evie was there. *I'm glad I found this before someone else did,* she thought.

Before leaving, she docked her laptop and powered it up to see if Paul had responded to her email. Her eyes fell on her inbox, its messages filling the screen. Not only was there no new email from Paul, she noticed as she looked more closely that she'd not received a new email in several days. The date of the last new one was two days before her meeting with Paul. Could the cessation have anything to do with the partners' decision for her to take a leave? Paul had said she would still have office and computer privileges during the leave. She immediately suspected Alan and wondered how he could have unilaterally stopped her flow of email.

A few of the final ones in the inbox were unread, so she opened each of them. One was from a female trademark paralegal from within Finley Regent. It read that she was confused about the initiation of a trademark search for a list of product names, Neolactin, being the most recent. She'd written that there was no one in the paralegal departments of any of the divisions by the name of Beth Hoffman. Evie remembered that there had been a whole series of new drug names, for which trademark clearance had been requested by that same woman. Evie looked for the latest email she'd received bearing that name. She found it and opened it. It contained the internal firm client number for Finley Regent, 1270, which she remembered thinking was strange. Where could those inquiries have come from?

She forwarded both emails on to Paul with a question so someone could follow up, but then wondered if her ability to *send* emails had also been squashed. Maybe Paul had not received the email she'd sent with her time record and workflow attached. *Maybe that was by design.*

Her BlackBerry rang, and she recognized the number.

"Hello, Michael."

"Evie, can you be at my office at two? The Bureau is sending a couple of agents to meet with us."

"Yes, I'll be there. Michael, I just noticed that my ability to send email seems to have been discontinued."

"What are you doing logging onto the firm's network? I told you to stay off."

"Well, I was here and my computer was docked. I wanted to check to see if Paul had responded to that last email I sent."

"Oh. So, you don't have any new emails? Are you able to send?"

"I don't know. I didn't get an error message."

"Try sending me a test message and we'll bring it up when we meet with them."

"Did Joe call you?"

"Yes, I've got a call into his PI."

"Did he tell you what else he found?"

"No, we didn't talk directly, just exchanged messages."

"Okay, we'll talk when I get there. I'll see you a little before two."

Evie logged off the firm's network for what felt like the last time. She looked around her office and took a breath. This was probably it. There was sadness after eight years servicing clients in this tiny office. For what purpose had all those hours been expended? The pride and satisfaction of practicing her craft was to be left behind like the echo of a passing parade, bouncing off these walls in silence until the next fledgling attorney and wanna-be partner enthusiastically took up residence here.

She carried her briefcase out the front door of the building and hurried to the City Bar building on 44th Street to bury herself in research until her meeting with the FBI.

After some reading among the law treatises, she sat down at one of the library's computers that was connected to the Internet. A news site she frequented had links to other news organizations and she did some reading on current events, before clicking the link to a local New York site called *Press Time Gotham*. It was known as a political debate forum and was used routinely as a vehicle for campaigning politicians.

There was an icon with Senator Arbeson's photo attached, so she clicked it to see what he was currently releasing to the press. His campaign for re-election was in full swing, so the bullet points listed the series of stump speeches he was to make over the coming months. There was an icon inviting the viewing of video clips. Most of them were archived versions of televised interviews given by his various campaign lieutenants, of which Alan was one. She clicked the video choice bearing Alan's name and a small window appeared showing Alan, seated in a guest chair, opposite a news analyst. She turned the volume low so she wouldn't disturb the few other lawyers sitting at nearby tables.

". . . And so Mr. Levenger, you're saying, on behalf of Senator Arbeson, that the allegations of bribery are unfounded?"

"Yes. You know, last time I checked, our justice system entitles a person to the presumption of innocence until proven guilty. Senators Broewer and Mayor have made outrageous statements that are designed to convince the public that Senator Arbeson is guilty. There is no basis on which to make those statements. This is a political assault and battery. When the facts come out, and let me reiterate that the Senator has been more than cooperative in the investigation, it will be proven that Senator Arbeson is innocent of the charges that have been made against him. And I can tell you that I think the American people will agree that he has handled this incident with tremendous grace."

"What about the specific allegation that Senator Arbeson solicited a bribe to grant favors to a Mr. Wheeler, an industrialist from New York . . ."

"This is the worst kind of politics, Harvey. It's crystal clear that Senator Arbeson has become a target by the Democrats who want to steal his senate seat in the coming election. A smear campaign can always find a spokesman. And, Harvey, as you well know, when one dog starts to howl in Washington, well, they all chime in."

"So, Senator Arbeson has decided to run again?"

Alan leaned over the desk and put his hand on the host's arm, his smile a display of arrogance. She noticed the crows feet take form on the palate of freckle-spotted, tanned skin—an expression of canned charm she had seen close up.

"*Harvey,*" Alan said as if he was taking Harvey and the entire nation-wide-listening-audience into his confidence. "*Senator Arbeson is a great patriot who understands that he has a job to do. He will not be deterred by the jealous, leftist liberals. He will not disappoint the majority in this state who elected him to represent their interests, despite the superficial flesh wounds inflicted by an overzealous challenger and his henchmen.*"

"*Well, thank you for your comments, Mr. Levenger.*"

Evie closed the link, her hands sweaty. Just as Ralph had said, even prior to Project Neon, there *were* already allegations of bribery out there against the Senator. His campaign had not yet managed to establish those allegations as merely a political ploy. They were fighting the typical dirty campaign dogfight.

At 1:30 P.M., she headed downtown to Michael's office. While in the taxi, she checked in with Joe, who was just finishing his meeting and heading out for a lunch with his colleagues. He asked her to meet him at the bar in the Four Seasons hotel around six o'clock P.M. and reminded her to be *very careful.* She agreed and hung up just as the taxi pulled up in front of Michael's building.

In Michael's office, they sat down for a few minutes before the FBI agents arrived.

"It was difficult to know what to say to my clients," said Evie. "I spoke to two of them while I was briefly in my office."

"Perhaps they'll follow you to your next firm."

"Hmmm," she replied. "Did you receive the test email I sent you?"

"No, I didn't. They'll hear about that loss of email access."

"That spyware tool Joe sent Alan invisibly collects everything that Alan types and sends it to a remote website. He said one of Alan's email correspondence trails was a discussion about a Trojan horse that gives someone the ability to control somebody else's computer."

"Well, that would tend to prove the method by which he electronically impersonated you. And, maybe the way he's changed your email status."

"Yes, starting with the Sangerson deal. He sent that original version of that Zoomhelix contract out to get me in trouble and deleted my revised version off the firm's network. And, then he masqueraded as me to send out all those Gerais Chevas emails."

"If you can't receive email right now, who knows what he's continuing to plant in your inbox? All the more important to get the FBI working on this."

At two o'clock P.M., Michael escorted Evie to a conference room. Two FBI agents had been shown in and were waiting for them. Daniel Weber re-introduced himself and a second agent, Mark Harrison, stood and shook her hand.

Weber spoke first, "Ms. Sullivan, I want to apologize if I seemed a bit aggressive when we met yesterday. We've been investigating the murder of this Brazilian national, Emira Adelio, with Interpol and we had very little to go on. That's what I do in the face of resistance—I push. In your case, probably a bit too hard."

"No problem," said Evie.

Michael spoke up next. "Evie, the FBI has offered you an immunity deal related to Gerais Chevas. They're not targeting you. They're operating on the theory that you're an unwitting victim in this scheme and a very valuable source of information. They also see you as an *ongoing* source. In exchange for the immunity, they want your cooperation in the investigation, your willingness to testify, if necessary, and your commitment to help gather some additional information while still employed with the firm."

"You mean spy on my firm?" She looked at Michael, then at the two agents, then back at Michael.

"Well," said Agent Harrison, "our investigation will go forward with or without you. If you work with us, you will be immune from prosecution, even if we find something incriminating where you're concerned. You're not a suspect, you understand, it's just that you may have inadvertently committed a technical violation of law or become an accessory by certain actions or failures to act. You will have the comfort of knowing that you will not face criminal charges if any such evidence comes to light." Evie flashed on those surreptitious email intercepts and spyware dumps.

Weber added, "We will also provide an agent to shadow you, providing protection until the culmination of any involvement in the case."

Evie responded, "I'm not sure I still have enough standing in the firm to be of much assistance. I'm on a leave of absence, and I've been under reprimand for some negative performance reviews. I don't think I'm in the running for partner anymore, and even though I've been given the option to stay with the firm, under the circumstances, it wouldn't necessarily be on the same level of professional respect that I had a few weeks ago."

"We know about your sexual harassment claim. It may actually be a catalyst for realizing a greater degree of information," said Weber. 'They're going to be overly sensitive to your needs until that claim is settled."

"But I haven't made a claim, yet."

"You will be." Michael smiled broadly.

"What about immunity from state criminal prosecution?" Evie spoke to the agents, but then looked to Michael for an answer.

"Evie," said Michael, "we'll have to negotiate our own deal with state prosecutors, but the Bureau has agreed to support our efforts for state immunity as well. That's assuming you've done anything that the state would want to pursue. Chances are that even if any of your actions were unlawful, they would be interested in the big fish here . . . Alan Levenger and, of course, Senator Arbeson."

"What about attorney-client privilege? I'm not at liberty to discuss client information without the client's waiver of the privilege."

Weber spoke up, "There's been at least one murder. You've been threatened by telephone. When you're in physical danger, I think the privilege is obviated."

"I don't have the liberty to discuss Senator Arbeson's other matters since there's no way to know if they're related. They're still protected under the privilege. And, I'm not absolutely certain he's involved with this Gerais Chevas deal."

The two agents signaled acknowledgement with silent acquiescence and waited.

Evie looked at each agent squarely in the eye. She studied each of their faces, then looked back at Michael who was nodding at her. *Michael doesn't know how hard it is to betray Jack Hanover and the firm I've worked so hard for,* she thought.

But Project Neon was going to play itself out to closure and leave her name fermenting in its wake. There was just no way to avoid the fact that this mess would have to be cleaned up. It was not biodegradable.

"I'm ready to tell you everything I know," she said.

chapter
32

This is the real turning point, she thought as she sat down at a round cocktail table in the FiftySevenFiftySeven Bar at the Four Seasons hotel. The agent assigned to protect her sat at a table not far from her, sipping a water and lime. She positioned herself in the tan leather armchair facing the entry stairs, drinking a Vodka spritzer, feeling more vulnerable than she had ever remembered feeling in her life.

She looked across the room toward the bar and to the mirrored wall to her right. The room was more generously lit than the typical bar. A quartet of geometric-shaped chandeliers balanced overhead. As she ordered her second vodka spritzer, she felt her eyelids began to sag.

Then, at 6:20 P.M., just as the waiter deposited her second vodka spritzer on the table, she saw Joe. She actually saw his reflection first, in the mirrored wall, then she turned and he was walking toward her table, smiling. He was clean-shaven, his wavy hair was fittingly combed into place and he was wearing a tailored gray Italian-cut suit. Only his clothes indicated the time of day. The jacket was open, his black-and-gray-striped tie loosened, and his white shirt was showing the wrinkles brought on by a day of meetings. He carried a leather portfolio. He leaned over to kiss her before taking a seat.

He motioned at the waiter, who walked over in five-star cadence to take his order. Joe ordered a Macallan scotch whiskey. He looked at the empty Vodka glass from her first drink that the waiter was carrying away and glanced at the over-stuffed briefcase and laptop case sitting beside her.

"How did it go?"

"I'm now a government witness in the witness protection program." She nodded her head toward the agent, eating peanuts between sips of water. "And, I'm about to go to work to destroy my firm."

"Good. I know this is hard for you, but I want you to see your name cleared. Those partners don't deserve to have you working for them. And they certainly don't deserve to have you join their partnership." Joe stood and took off his jacket, revealing dark suspenders joined to the tops of his suit trousers. As he sat back down, the waiter placed the glass of scotch in front of him.

"I found out today that Alan was in Dallas the same time I was. I bet he was directing the woman who was impersonating me and I'm sure he was the one who made and received all those Brazilian calls. I don't have any proof of it, just secretary-to-secretary talk."

"Greg has a 'smoking gun' piece of evidence for you."

"Really? What?"

"On your harassment claim. The Chicago hotel . . . The Claremont . . . they have video cameras on every floor."

"You mean? They have a *video* of Alan kissing me?"

"Yes, and his less-than-gentlemanly push of you into your room."

"Oh my *God!* That's amazing! I didn't even think about that. I can't believe they would still *have* it. That was months ago."

"It seems they have this policy of filing away copies of video where it looks like there may be some possibility of foul play. Sometimes, of course, they're misinterpreting a situation, but they keep the copies until they feel certain that whatever was recorded is not going to be pertinent to some police investigation."

"That's . . . that makes my case. Concrete proof that Alan harassed me and that he's a liar! Michael's going to *love* that. And, it couldn't come at a better time. We're about to meet with Paul and Alan to discuss the settlement offer." Evie felt a wave of relief and calm that had nothing to do with the alcohol.

"This should go a long way toward clearing your name, Eves," Joe said as he pulled a videotape out of his portfolio and slid it into her briefcase. "The partners who doubted your story will have to eat a little crow and figure out what to do with Levenger. He's going to cost them some serious money if you sue."

"I don't really want their money, I just want to clear my name."

"Take the money. You've earned it. Do something for yourself you've always wanted."

"I'm not sure what I want, other than to prove I had nothing to do with arranging Project Neon."

"Well, this should destroy what little credibility Alan has left. I think your version of the story will carry much more weight than his."

"He's not going to fold that easily. He's had trouble keeping his hands off women before and he's always managed to convince the partners to look the other way. He'll draw a line between the incident between us and this deal he claims I'm running. I'm sure he's polished his speech about a renegade associate acting beyond the scope of her authority with the firm. The electronic paper trail is 'proving' that I 'acted alone,' just the way he planned."

"Diabolical. But, the question remains—how deep in the mud is Arbeson?"

"I don't think anything would surprise me now. Alan is apparently not content to lawyer. He wants to create business leverage, even if it's just illusory."

Joe sipped his scotch.

Evie continued, "GC Quadra's principal asset was apparently that statistical software package. I guess that's what gave Alan the idea that the promise of a U.S. government contract award to GC Quadra would cement the deal's appeal to Romez Nuevo."

"The feds will harvest some good material from Levenger's computer. Even as computer-savvy as he is, he probably doesn't realize how much of his computer activities remain etched on his hard disks. Even deleted and scrubbed disks can yield valuable evidence, given the right tools and a nice broadly-worded warrant. If it turns out that there's NOT a statistical-software defense contract in the pipeline, that information alone should go a long way toward securing a warrant."

The next morning Evie was in Michael's office by 9:30 A.M. He greeted her and they sat down in one of his firm's conference rooms to await the arrival of Paul Wayford and Alan Levenger. Evie's protection agent sat in Michael's office reading, standing by in case he was needed.

"Okay Evie, we want to apply some pressure, but we don't want to show our hand yet because the deal with the feds requires you to be able to continue your association with the firm. At least for a bit longer."

"How much are we going to reveal?"

"Well, for one thing, we're going to play dumb on Gerais Chevas. Try to get them to give us what they've discovered, if anything. We'll play a little settlement poker and see how cocky they are."

Michael poured some coffee for Evie and for himself and, wearing a sly grin, pulled out some old copies of the tabloid, *Spellbound!* from an envelope.

"Where did you find those?" Evie said, her eyes sparkling with amusement. She flipped open to the pages where photos of Alan and various women captured indiscreet moments—a dossier of bad behavior to set the mood for the discussions.

"Just something to have visible on the table." Michael chuckled. "Just want Alan to know I'm doing my research on his background."

Evie laughed and sipped her coffee as she pulled out copies of the emails she'd tried to send Paul. The timeline of her client work over the summer, she left on the table, but the Neolactin trademark message, she put back in her file deciding it would be a distraction. Michael saw the file and said, "Let's have my secretary make a few copies of all the stuff you've accumulated so we can get our background discovery work going here at my offices."

She handed the file to Michael who buzzed his secretary to come and get it, which she did in record time.

"Are we going to reveal that we have that video from the Claremont?" Evie asked.

"Not yet."

At ten minutes after ten o'clock A.M., the appointed time for their meeting, Paul Wayford and Alan Levenger appeared in the doorway of the conference room escorted by the receptionist. Michael stood and welcomed them in, showing them to two seats opposite Evie. Evie stood when they entered, but the temperature seemed to drop in the room as they approached the table so she took her seat again. After introducing himself and shaking Michael's hand, Alan was quiet and wore a controlled confident smirk.

Paul spoke first, "Evie, I'm surprised you've taken this step . . . to hire your own counsel. I thought we'd worked things out between us."

Evie started to speak, but Michael stepped in. "Evie has done what anybody worth their salt would do and that's get an independent opinion about her situation. She has every right to evaluate her options."

"Absolutely," answered Paul as he took a seat, "I'm not suggesting that she's done anything wrong or is not entitled to outside opinions, I just thought she would get back to me directly."

Evie glanced at Alan, but spoke to Paul, "Paul, I appreciate your settlement offer and your time today for this meeting. The fact is, I don't know much about this type of situation so I sought some outside advice. It doesn't mean I don't want to work things out with the firm."

As Evie finished speaking, she saw peripherally that Alan had noticed the copies of *Spellbound!* laying on the table. She thought she could see him bristle as a flash of anger passed over his features, but he quickly regained control and the confident smirk reappeared.

"Okay," said Paul, "what are your feelings about continuing your association with the firm?"

"I'm not finished thinking things through," said Evie.

Michael interjected, "Evie is considering your offer, but is concerned about a few matters."

Paul nodded, but Alan remained stoic.

"As an example, she has been checking her email as part of her efforts not to let any client issues drop while she's on leave. She noticed that she has not received any new email over the last few days. Is this intentional? Has the firm changed her access level to the network?"

"No, not that I'm aware of," said Paul.

"She'd like to know whether this is just a technical glitch or whether it amounts to some type of constructive termination." Evie looked over at Michael and let him continue uninterrupted.

"She would in fact like to keep coming in and using her office while on leave, if that's acceptable."

"Definitely, absolutely." Paul took the bait. He did not want to appear to have authorized or acquiesced to any sort of reduction in Evie's status. He looked at her. "Evie, please, as I said, use your office freely, your laptop, come and go as you please. Nothing has changed other than we've given you paid time off and relieved you of the pressure of meeting client deadlines for a couple of weeks while you think things over."

"Okay," said Michael. "I'm glad we have that straight. So you'll check and fix the technical problem with the email."

"Yes."

"Okay, next, Evie wants to know the status of your evaluation of these complaints against her. Apparently, Jack Hanover expressed a different opinion to her about their significance."

"By the way," interjected Evie, "how is Jack?"

"He's still recuperating in the hospital, showing steady improvement, but not able to lead the firm at present. I do speak with him almost every day and he has conferred with me on these matters. Now, before I continue, I need to get your agreement that what I'm about to discuss with you is not to leave this room."

Michael looked at Evie. They both nodded and held Paul's gaze.

"Howard, Rolland & Stewart is in merger discussions with Newly, Boyce, Tate and Wells. It is not public knowledge, of course, and we would not want it revealed that we are engaged in these discussions until we're ready to make a formal announcement."

Michael scribbled some notes on a pad as he nodded.

"Anyway, with Hanover's medical challenges and the merger discussions, it is a sensitive time for the firm. Perceptions in the marketplace are so important and, well, it goes without saying that a sexual harassment claim would be very damaging at this juncture." Alan swallowed perceptibly as Paul was speaking, but remained silent. Evie wondered if he had been instructed to keep his mouth shut.

"We understand the situation very well," said Michael, "and we certainly have no intention of gratuitously and unnecessarily causing the firm damage. Now, about those complaints against Evie?"

"We've looked into those and of the ones that we've been able to confirm, there's no real damage to any client relationship so those have been dropped. We still don't know what happened with Sangerson. The breach of confidentiality was not Evie's fault. A recent inquiry with Adam confirmed that Evie was not the source. Gooseneck-dot-com seems to be a similar situation to Gerais Chevas—Evie says she never worked on those matters, but some electronic data conflicts with that conclusion."

Evie spoke up, looking directly at Alan, "Alan, you said you'd fixed those records on Gooseneck. It was not me who worked on that deal either. You admitted to me that my name being listed on that matter was a mistake."

Alan stared, with glib expression painted on his face, his eyebrows stretching upward.

Paul looked at Alan, paused, took a deep breath and wiped his brow before speaking. "Let's assume Evie was not involved with Gooseneck. Let's just give her the benefit of the doubt."

Michael continued. "In the interest of shortening this meeting and avoiding a prolonged settlement negotiation, we're wondering if the one and a half million dollar number is the firm's final offer?"

Evie thought she saw Paul deliver a slight kick to Alan under the table. Alan registered no reaction and continued to stay silent.

Paul spoke again. "Well, what do you have in mind?"

"We haven't settled on a figure, but would very much like to hear the firm's final offer before providing any sort of definitive reaction."

"Alright. I will discuss this with Jack and the rest of the partnership. Of course, there would be certain conditions attached to any settlement arrangement. We would not admit any wrongdoing and the terms would remain confidential indefinitely, to name a few."

Evie felt a slight pang of regret knowing Jack would be facing this unpleasantness while trying to recover, but then again, this situation wasn't her doing.

"I'm sure we can work through all those terms," said Michael. "One other thing, though. Have you been able to determine who has been at the helm of this Gerais Chevas transaction?" said Michael, purposely avoiding eye contact with Alan.

"That has been a troubling situation," said Paul. He glanced at Alan and looked back to Evie and Michael, focusing on Evie. "One evaluating the correspondence and document drafting would have difficulty believing you were not involved, Evie."

"Since there's a technical glitch with my email, I assume you didn't receive the last messages I sent you. I sent you a timeline showing my client service over the summer months. Gerais Chevas has never been included on any time report I drafted." As Evie spoke she pushed the timeline copy across the table. "And, I alerted you to a change in one of the Gerais Chevas documents. Conveniently, after I left the office, Schedule B7 changed dramatically. You might want to take a look."

"Okay." Paul accepted the timeline document, gave Alan a look that was hard to read and turned his attention quickly back to Evie and Michael. "I'm also waiting to hear from a Mr. Tulio Tobias and a Mr. Pedro del Torro from Gerais Chevas on the breadth of contact within our firm. Some of the other players from Gerais Chevas have enumerated multiple contacts with Evie, including a man named Adinaldo Rafael. All were either over the telephone or by email, but Evie, you have to admit, this is very strange. Why would they lie about talking and interacting with you? What do they have to gain by pointing the finger at you as the person running this deal?"

"Well—" began Evie.

"Evie has stated repeatedly that she had nothing to do with initiating, arranging, negotiating, drafting or guiding the progress of, this Gerais Chevas deal," Michael replied. "Someone else must've participated in those discussions and correspondence, claiming to be Evie."

"Hard to believe."

"That's what happened. She is waiting to hear what you discover through your internal investigation."

"Fair enough. By the way, the closing for the deal has been delayed due to the unfortunate demise of one of the key people they were dealing with from Romez Nuevo."

Michael and Evie could sense each other shift slightly, but they held their forward gaze.

"The deal has apparently encountered a number of obstacles, but the negotiations have continued . . . beyond where they were when Evie's leave began." Paul leaned forward in his chair glancing down at Evie's timeline.

"Evie, please feel free to come back to your office. We will get to the bottom of this. You can check in with me, and I'll let you know of any developments I discover. In the meantime, I hope you are taking some time to rest."

Michael spoke. "So, you agree that whatever one chooses to believe regarding Evie's prior involvement, this Project Neon transaction is proceeding on a going forward basis, and she has absolutely nothing to do with its evolution."

"Yes, that much is certainly clear," said Paul. Alan sniffed and shifted in his seat.

Michael responded, "We will honor your confidence, of course, and expect Evie's email status to be restored. We will wait to hear the firm's revised settlement offer and when we do, perhaps we can have one more meeting to wrap things up?"

"Terrific," said Paul. He got up from his chair and shook Michael's hand first, then Evie's. "Evie, I hope you feel that the firm is being fair to you and sensitive to the situation. As I said before, I've never seen or heard of anything like this in thirty years of practicing law."

"I appreciate the firm's efforts on my behalf," said Evie.

Alan stood, told Michael it was a pleasure to have met him and followed Paul out the door. Michael walked out behind them, leaving Evie in the stale air remaining in the conference room.

After a number of minutes, Michael returned.

"Evie, it's going to be so easy to get a good settlement here." He smiled, pulling a cassette tape out of a mini recorder in his pocket and waving it in the air. "With their fear of bad publicity and that idiot they're partnered with, Levenger, they've got to be losing sleep over how much this is gonna cost. And, they haven't seen the visual evidence yet."

"I feel terrible about Jack Hanover. I feel like I'm contributing to the worsening of his heart condition."

"You have to remember. He had the power . . . no *has* the power, to send Alan packing. It's not as if he's at the mercy of the circumstances. He runs the place."

"I don't know how much control he has right now from a hospital bed."

"Plenty. Believe me. We'll let them come back with something and continue to collect any information we can."

"I wonder how much they know about that Adelio death. It didn't sound like they knew she was murdered."

"At least not openly within the firm."

chapter
33

This is getting to be a habit," said Joe, standing at the front door to
Evie's apartment, this time with a small hanging bag.

"I like it," said Evie. She hugged him before he could walk in
and put his bag down.

"You look relaxed. I hope it's because of me and not him," Joe said
pointing to the federal agent sitting in a chair in the foyer adjacent to the
elevator on Evie's floor.

"I'm so glad to see you. And, I'm feeling slightly more in control of
the situation with the firm. At least certain aspects of the situation are
not that scary anymore."

"Are you sure you want me to spend the night even though you've got
an armed guard out there?"

"Yes, I'm sure." She kissed him softly and took his garment bag to her
room to hang up.

"Michael was great today, but he's really angling for the big payoff."

"That's what you're paying him for."

"No, not really, but I guess if it turns out that I can't continue with the firm, I could use a bit of financial independence."

"You can do whatever you want. You don't have to practice law anymore."

"Well, funny you say that. I am considering some other options."

"No more firm?"

"Even if this all gets cleared up and my reputation is restored, I don't know if I can trust these people anymore, even Jack. I do have an affection for him. He's done a lot for my growth as a lawyer, but I don't know if I could ever be partners, legally bound with these people."

Joe followed Evie into her bedroom. She hung his garment bag in the closet and they walked to the kitchen to find something for dinner.

"It's not clear to me that these guys don't have the inside story on what Levenger's doing," said Joe. "They all may be in on the take. If so, they may have even rationalized their way around it, especially if they've engaged in questionable practices before."

"That's hard to imagine. I've never seen anything like this the entire time I've been with the firm."

"Take the insurance industry, for example. Some people have come out and said that the type of contingency agreements that Babcock & Sherwyn was investigated for have been common in the industry since the seventies. Corruption can be so ingrained that it's not viewed as corrupt anymore."

"Speaking of corrupt. Even though Paul encouraged me to continue to use my office, laptop and email while on leave, I haven't been able to receive any new email messages for several days. Paul said he thought it must be due to a technical glitch, but I think Alan did something. Possibly, to keep me from seeing emails that he's creating in my name."

"Well, let me see if I can tell what's going on." Joe took her laptop and she followed him to the kitchen where they set it up and Evie traversed the electronic course for logging on to her firm's network.

"They agreed to fix it this afternoon, but I guess the order hasn't gone through or technical support hasn't yet had the chance."

After a few minutes and a series of commands that Evie couldn't follow, Joe looked up from the screen and said, "It looks like your IP address has been manipulated through the firm's operating system."

"More of Alan's chess game, I guess."

~

Monday morning, Evie flipped on the light switch in her office one more time. Her office already had that abandoned feel to it, although she realized it was probably just her imagination. She'd been at her desk for less than two hours when her BlackBerry rang mocking the silence of her desk phone.

"Evie?"

"Yes, Michael."

"Paul called and said he's ready to provide the firm's revised offer. He's ready to deal and really wants to wrap this up for obvious reasons. Can you be here this afternoon? There'll be federal agents escorting you in a government car."

"Sure. This is so odd . . . being here in the offices while you're negotiating on my behalf with someone a floor away from me."

"I know it must be uncomfortable for you being there. If you could manage to get anything else tangible to throw the feds, that with Schedule B7 and all your statements would likely be enough for them to get a search warrant and take it from there."

"You know, it's interesting that Paul failed to follow up on that expense report. I couldn't have been at two hotels at the same time."

"I think they all know perfectly well what's going on, but they don't want to make any admissions to a potential adversary."

"Oh, so you think they're just waiting me out, assuming I'm going to want to leave the firm and they won't have to give me any answers."

"Yes, and then they'll figure out how to handle Alan without you around."

"Almost makes me want to stay."

"Are you serious?"

"I said *almost*. I was doing some reading at the bar library. Michael, what about the Foreign Corrupt Practices Act? Does it apply here?"

"That Act makes it illegal to bribe a foreign government official to get business under the jurisdiction of that official. It may apply to Gerais Chevas if its stock is listed on the NYSE, but again it's a law enforcement issue. It certainly won't apply to our civil action. Some of those other criminal acts have corresponding civil remedies that we will make good use of. There are some juicy crimes here, though."

"I really do want to get out of here and pave the way for the feds to clear my name."

"Try to find anything you can while they still think you're benevolent toward the firm. But, be careful."

"Okay. I'll try."

She plugged in her laptop and brought up her email inbox. There were a few new ones today, so something had been changed, but there was nothing of any substance from any client. She suspected Alan was still screening and manipulating, trying to create the impression that her status was restored, but keeping control over what she actually received. She brought up the now-familiar Neon files.

The payment schedule was a different document. No more $25 million commission, but many other details were filled in identifying components of the purchase price and schedule of payments. The commission field was now missing. Was it the subject of further negotiation? Was it going to increase? Or, was it now just an amount to be paid under the table while the documents remained silent about it. She tried to print, but her request was denied. Not surprising since she was now an adversary on their territory.

She opened Neon Four and scrolled down to Schedule B7. It was the same incriminating document she'd last seen and she already had a copy so she closed it. She needed to find a way to print that new payment schedule.

She no longer cared what trail she left behind and dialed the firm's technical support. One of the youngest and newest members of the team, Henry, answered. She explained that she needed to print a file on a deal she was assigned to, but her file access hadn't yet been broadened. Not exactly an untruth, given that Alan was claiming to have assigned her.

Henry promised to come to her office and help her out and he was there within five minutes. It was obvious that he had no knowledge of any change in her status within the firm. She looked around outside her office and fortunately, the hallway was empty. Despite all the assurances that she was still a member of the firm in good standing, she knew that if she was caught trying to get copies of these files, they would not be pleased. The investigation was supposed to be in Paul's hands now. She closed her office door and Henry sat down at her keyboard. He layered some commands and pulled up the file she identified.

"Can you set the print command so that it prints the firm ID, date and time at the top of the page? I want to keep track of the date of this version."

Henry looked up at her and nodded as he continued to type furiously. She was lucky it was Henry who was available to help. He was eager to please, being the new hire, and he would hopefully be kept too busy for this exchange to stand out in his mind if someone asked him about it. Henry issued a print command and the file showed up on the queue for the printer.

"Great!" she said. "*Henry,* is there any way to print the Hit History on a few files? I need to know all the people who've accessed them so I know who to ask if I have any questions."

"Yeah, hold on," he said typing at lightning speed. It was a sweet bonus that he was such a fast typist. She wanted to get her sleuthing done before anybody came in and discovered what she was doing. The seconds ticked by as Henry logged on to the network with his system password, which seemed to Evie something like a master pass-key. He had broad powers to explore the system and she thought about asking him to do more, but she decided against it. She didn't want to press her luck.

"Okay," said Henry. "You've got the Hit Histories for the files." He looked back at the screen. "Neon One, Two, Three and Four in the queue for the printer on this floor."

"Thanks so much!" said Evie as she headed out the door to grab the printouts. The Hit Histories had to show historical proof that Alan had manipulated these files! He couldn't possibly have logged in as her *every* time he'd accessed them. Even if it didn't prove definitely that he was the one who edited the documents into illegal territory, it certainly proved that he was familiar with the details of the transaction—a direct contradiction to his claims.

No one was around as she let the paper feeder drop the print jobs into her hands. As the last page fell onto the stack, she looked up to see Alan walking down the hall toward her. She knew he had been instructed not to speak to her, so she looked away and hugged the paper to her chest in what she thought was a nonchalant gesture.

"What are you printing?" he asked.

"Alan, you're violating Hanover's order not to speak to me. I just printed some personal emails so I can answer them from home." She thought it would be better to give him an explanation than to avoid talking at all.

He nodded and walked on down the hall. Despite his perpetual arrogance, he'd looked a bit tired, she thought.

After retreating to her now empty office and shutting the door, she looked at the copies. They were perfect—the printout of the payment schedule had captured the date, time on the top right corner and the firm name appeared in the upper left corner. The Hit Histories showed a list of names with dates and times under the name of the corresponding file. There were a number of other characters and firm identification numbers that she didn't understand, but hopefully, those identifying features would authenticate the documents and establish them as uniquely produced by the Howard Rolland's computer system.

She tucked them into her briefcase and took one last look around her office for any personal items she'd overlooked before. There was a bit of time before her FBI escort would be meeting her downstairs to accompany her to Michael's office, but she knew she needed to make a quick exit. There was no certainty that Alan wouldn't try to find out what she had *really* printed. She felt a sense of completion now and was really ready to leave, physically, psychologically and completely.

As she headed out the door, the telephone on her desk broke its silence. It was an outside caller with no caller ID so she decided to pick it up in case it was her FBI escort.

"Evelyn Sullivan," she said.

"You didn't listen to me." It was *that voice*. That same voice that had called her and demanded that she cancel her meeting with Emira Adelio from Romez Nuevo.

"What? Who is this?"

"You kept that appointment when I asked you not to. But you may have noticed, your friend never showed up."

"What do you want? Why are you calling me?"

"I think we've proven we're not afraid to spill blood."

Evie's mind raced. Her hands shaking, she almost dropped the receiver.

"Are you there?" the Voice asked.

"I'm here. Who are you working for?" Evie said into the receiver.

"Next time it might be the blood of someone you care about."

"Who are you working for?"

"You just keep your mind on staying quiet. You will not contact the police, the FBI or anyone else. You will keep to yourself or you will be sorry. Very sorry." Apparently, the Voice was not up on current events. *Fortunately.*

"What are you trying to accomplish?" she asked.

There was silence, as Evie looked around for a way to contact the FBI agent who was supposed to meet her on the street below. She grabbed her BlackBerry and dialed the number they'd given her. It rang twice and Agent Neeley answered just as her desk telephone clicked and the dial tone hummed.

She explained to the agent what had transpired.

"Are you okay?"

"Physically, yes."

"Do you want me to come up there?"

"No, I'm coming *down!* Right *now.* I just wanted to make sure you were here and tell you to expect me."

Evie hurried out of her office, down the hall, past reception and headed to the elevator. When the elevator doors closed, she realized she was sweating. Agent Neeley was among the people standing in the lobby when the doors opened with a chime. She saw him nod slightly, but said nothing to identify himself and stood beside the concierge's desk until the people completed their shuffle out of and into the elevator car.

When no one was looking, he motioned to Evie to walk out of the building and head to the right, and he followed. There was an unmarked, black car waiting with the back door open, which she assumed was an FBI vehicle and another agent she'd met was in the driver's seat. Evie got into the back and Agent Neeley appeared and took the seat next to her. The door closed and, at Evie's request, they headed to her apartment on Central Park West.

While seated in the back seat, Agent Neeley took down the details of her conversation with The Voice. After they had finished, she dialed Joe on her BlackBerry with shaky fingers.

"Joe, can I stay with you tonight?"

"Sure, Eves. I may have to go to California tomorrow morning, but I'll—"

"Joe, I just got another one of those calls. That man . . . that *voice* that threatened me."

"Where's the FBI?"

"I'm with two agents in an FBI car, but I don't want to stay in my apartment tonight."

"Are these agents you're familiar with? You've met them before in the company of the ones we know are legit?"

"Yes, yes, I have. Agent Weber introduced us the other day, but you're right. I should be suspicious of everybody."

"I'll cut my meetings short and go back to the hotel and make some arrangements. I'll cancel my trip back to California."

"I don't want to cause you any trouble."

"Eves, you're not making any sense. The woman I love is in distress. It's no trouble. Get to the Four Seasons."

The woman he loves . . .

"I have a meeting at Michael's office," she said. "Ironically, it's the meeting with Paul and Alan to try to resolve the situation with the firm."

"Let the Federal Agent keep a close distance, okay?"

"Before the meeting, I was going to stop by my apartment and get a few things, but I'll have the agent with me. I'll meet you at your hotel later, okay?"

"Yes, okay. Be careful. Don't take any chances. I'll come get you if you need me to."

"I wish I knew who this person was working for. I don't know who the enemy is."

"You've got to paint with a broad brush. Don't trust anyone, except Michael and the feds."

"I wonder if Hanover is in on this?"

"You have to assume he is."

Evie hung up and her skin felt clammy as she leaned back in the seat and tried to relax.

They arrived at her apartment building and the agent driving waited downstairs in front of the building. Agent Neeley followed her inside and opted for an investigative look around in the lobby while Evie took the elevator to her floor.

"Who set your knickers ablaze? Where in bloody hell are you going?" Ralph asked looking down at Evie's suitcase, as she raced past him in the hallway a half hour later.

"Ralph! Oh Ralph. I'm so sorry. I was in a hurry and I—"

"Well, I already worked out that one, sweetheart." He was just getting a good look at her face. "Evie! God, look at you! Your face is really pale. Even for *you*. Is everything okay?"

"Ralph, I uuhh." She took a moment to collect herself and looked him in the eye. "Ralph, I'm working through something. I can't talk about it. I just have to be out of my apartment for a few days."

"Does it have anything to do with the bloke with the bulge in his armpit who's been hanging out in the foyer?"

"Ralph, I can't tell you. It's for your own protection. You're the best." She hugged Ralph and gave him a peck on the cheek. "I have to go, but I'll be in touch."

"Okay, love. But, be careful. Let me know how to reach you, okay?"

"Okay." She forced a smile and walked to the elevator. Agent Neeley was inside, out of view, and she took a longer breath when she saw him. It was against instinct to distrust Ralph, but Joe was right. She didn't know who *could* be trusted. After all, Ralph *had* brought up Senator Arbeson's difficulties and questioned her about the work she was doing for him. And, why was he home in the middle of a workday anyway? He'd offered no explanation, but then, she hadn't asked. She chastised herself. Ralph couldn't possibly be involved, but could he have inadvertently been a source of information? Paranoia was setting in. Be suspicious of everyone, until proven wrong.

chapter
34

The mood was jovial as Paul, Alan, Michael and Evie sat down together for a second time in the conference room at Michael's offices. Her nerves now a bit less raw, Evie was nonetheless grateful to have Michael in control. As Michael and Paul exchanged cordialities, Evie wondered why Alan was allowed to attend these meetings while being forced to remain silent.

Michael brought the discussion to the topic of focus. "Gentlemen, we're pleased that you've returned so quickly. One would assume that your request for this meeting means that you've revised your settlement offer."

"Yes, we have." Paul turned to Evie. "Evie, we'd like to offer you in settlement, the amount of two million dollars, subject to a list of conditions to be agreed."

Evie said nothing and Michael let a second or two pass before he spoke. "Well, that's not much different than your original offer. Is that final?"

"Michael, I'm not sure what you mean by 'final,'" said Paul. "As in any such situation, nothing's final until the parties have nothing else to say to each other."

"With all due respect, Paul, I have to say we're disappointed. Do you have anything *else* to say to us?"

"I'll tell you what we have to say," Alan spoke finally. Paul raised his hand as if to stop Alan from speaking, but then seemed to change his mind and his hand gesture transformed into an invitation to speak.

"This Chicago incident Evie described didn't happen that way at all. She and I . . . well, she and I had a mutual night together and she knows it."

Okay, I was wrong, thought Evie. *I can still be surprised.*

"Oh, really? That's news to us. Evie denies ever having any sort of relations with you of any kind. She's never considered any type of relationship with you other than professional. She maintains that she was accosted by you in the hallway outside her hotel room. Kissed unexpectedly on the mouth, without invitation, and that you then attempted to push your way into her room by physical force. She was determined to report the incident until you expressed embarrassment and remorse and pleaded with her to forget the whole thing, promising it would never happen again."

"Pleaded? I've never *pleaded* with her for anything, except maybe decent client service. She and I had a nice, romantic dinner after a successful client pitch. I'll concede that she did a great job on the client pitch and we were both ecstatic—it was a big client. We won the representation and were admittedly a bit drunk and celebratory by the end of the evening. We walked back to the hotel together and kissed outside her room before she invited me in."

"Oh, really?"

"Yes. That's the way it happened. I know it doesn't support a sexual harassment claim, but unfortunately, that's it. Fortunately for you, the firm's in publicity-shy mode and is willing to pay you to fuck off."

"Alan, let's keep a professional tongue, shall we?" said Paul, raising his hand again—this time it was clearly designed to end Alan's contribution. Alan ignored the message and continued.

"I don't appreciate anyone trying to extort money from my pocket. I disagree with my fellow partners' approach so if I were you, I'd take the two million and retire to oblivion. Okay, Evie?"

"Evie is represented by counsel," said Michael. "I'm going to have to ask you to address me, will you please?"

The new chill in the room caused all the coffee to grow cold and Evie noticed Paul lean forward in his seat, placing his elbows on the table in a sort of gesture of intimacy. It was clear that his intent was to warm up the discussion again.

"We really don't want to get into a he-said she-said about what happened," he said in a neutral tone. "Let's remember, that there *is* no lawsuit. You've filed no claim."

"Would you like us to? The papers are ready to submit to the court clerk, we've only waited out of courtesy to you. The minute we file, everything's public."

"What amount did you have in mind?"

"We will settle for fifteen million and we're willing to consider confidentiality and no guilt clauses."

"Fifteen million!! Are you insane?" Alan spit out the words and sprayed saliva on the table with each hard consonant.

"That is quite a large amount of money for a firm of our size," added Paul in his soft voice. "Jack is personally willing to mortgage his home to provide the extra cash we need, but I'm afraid we won't have an easy time with that amount."

Evie felt the warm flash of guilt that she knew was intended. Michael sniffed and stayed silent when he saw Paul open his mouth to continue speaking.

"Evie has been a respected member of our senior associate membership. She was, and still is, in line for partnership, despite the incident in dispute. We didn't want to have to bring this up, but I see we have no choice, given that we can't settle your claim." Paul paused, looked at Alan and leaned back in his seat. "Evie, we recently received a written letter from a credible source that indicates you had a surreptitious relationship with Senator Arbeson."

"That's an outrageous lie!" This time, it was Evie who lost her composure, as her mind flashed on the clipped photo from *New York Magazine*. She was glad she'd included the clipping and handwritten note in the file that Michael had seen so he would not now be hearing this for the first time. "I've never even been alone in a room with him, except for one brief meeting that was called by Jack," she said. "And I didn't find out Jack wouldn't be attending until the last minute." *Oh my God! Is Hanover in on this effort to destroy me?* Her emotions churned with this new slanderous allegation.

"Who is the source?" asked Michael.

"In any event," said Paul, ignoring Michael's question and continuing in the same even tone, "the letter accuses you of using this alleged relationship with Senator Arbeson to attempt to set up the grant of a government contract to a subsidiary of Gerais Chevas," he paused. "Didn't you have some copies of *Spellbound!* here at our last meeting? There was a story in yesterday's issue making the same allegation."

"Probably had the same source," said Michael.

"Although we hadn't planned to do anything with the note or its contents," said Paul, "we'd be forced to use it if we're sued."

So they're apparently willing to sacrifice Senator Arbeson along with me. That must be some merger deal.

"Well, it seems painfully obvious who would have incentive to create such a libelous document and pass it to a reporter," said Michael tapping his pen on the table. "What a coincidence that the current Schedule B7, defining Project Neon, which Evie drew your attention to but had no role in drafting, says something similar. What relevance does it have to whether Evie was sexually harassed in Chicago, anyway?"

"It certainly shows a pattern of behavior, a willingness to form relationships in the workplace."

"Yes, okay. I guess if it were true, but it's nothing but manufactured libel designed to condemn my client."

"The letter says what it says. I'm not saying we necessarily take it at face value, but it certainly raises questions."

"Then why even mention it except to intimidate my client?" Michael's voice took on a slight edge.

Paul licked his lips. "We are just sorting through a situation thrust upon us, the same as you. In any event, the fact remains, Evie, that you never reported this incident in Chicago until it was expeditiously prudent for you to do so. If you were offended to the tune of fifteen million dollars, you would have reported the incident *despite* Alan's capitulation, as you describe it. And, as I reminded you before, you did admit to attending certain political events and celebrations relating to Senator Arbeson's campaign, some in the company of Alan. You were under no duress to do any of those things and apparently enjoyed yourself each time, agreeing to continue working on the Senator's re-election effort and raising no objection to working on Alan's legal matters in your capacity as an associate with Howard Rolland. It doesn't sound like you felt you'd been sexually harassed."

"Let me add, Miss Sullivan," said Alan, "if you persist in this insanity, we might have to consider filing an extortion claim against *you*. It's clear that you're just out to line your pockets at the firm's expense because you're angry at the performance review you received."

Evie, having regained control of her emotions, stayed silent, taking deep breaths and sipping a glass of ice water after having abandoned her coffee.

"If I may be so bold as to point out," said Michael, the edge in his voice becoming sharper still, "that it takes more than monetary demands to prove an extortion case."

"It takes a money demand that is grossly disproportionate to any conceivable injury," snapped Alan. "The courts in this state call that prima facie evidence of a breach of professional responsibility." Alan scowled at Michael as he spoke. "Your motivation is obviously for us to buy your silence. And, how about this? I received a nasty little anonymous email right after Evie and I had our first clash over her performance. The email threatened me if I didn't withdraw my complaints about her performance."

I wonder if that's the way he really interpreted that email Joe and I sent, thought Evie.

She looked at Michael, who didn't flinch. Everyone at the table except Paul knew that Alan was stretching the wording of that email to fit his current purpose.

"In addition to the Chicago incident, Evie has labored for some time in a hostile environment created by Mr. Levenger," continued Michael.

He let that statement sink in and then delivered his knock-out punch. "By the way, you may be interested to know that the Claremont Hotel routinely videotapes activity in its public hallways and keeps copies of incidents that they perceive to be potentially criminal. They kept the one recorded on Evie's floor the night of November 12th of 2004. They decided it looked sufficiently like an assault, so they kept a copy of the tape just in case the police made an inquiry."

Alan smirked and shifted in his seat. Paul looked like he'd been punched in the gut.

Michael continued, "The manager, who was quite willing to cooperate with us to authenticate the tape, said he never wanted to be in a situation where he had a dead female body and no videotape of activity on the dead woman's floor preceding her death. So, Mr. Levenger, it seems we have assault and battery to add to our list of claims against you."

Paul glared at Alan, and Michael continued, "There is also the matter of some gentleman who continues to call Evie and threaten her if she continues to investigate this Gerais Chevas matter. Whoever is responsible for doing this deal does not want Evie to keep looking into it."

The clock on the wall ticked by seconds adding up to almost two full minutes.

"You might also want to consider that we can make a case for retaliation, with this leave of absence you so conveniently conceived of to tidy up your little mess. Retaliation makes a sexual harassment claim so much more fragrant. Evie lost email, she lost access to her clients, and she's had to explain why she won't be able to continue to serve on deals for Roma Sori and others for whom she'd built strong, solid client relationships. She suffered the loss of her momentum, damage to her reputation and the inability to achieve partnership in this round of invitations. Her only misstep was to fail to report the incident *promptly*, but case law lends an understanding ear to such situations."

"I have to say, I'm dumbfounded," said Paul. "Okay, assuming what you've said is true, we have no choice but to settle. Evie, what damages do you have that add up to fifteen million dollars? Would you be willing to explain that to Jack Hanover?"

"We will settle for ten million, but not a penny less," Michael said as he stood and looked ready to end the meeting. "And, as Evie stands accused of wrongdoing in this Gerais Chevas matter, we will take that to mean that you still believe her to be the one running the deal and will act accordingly. Since you contend that she's the one who represents them, that means we will feel at liberty to contact Gerais Chevas executives ourselves and proceed with our own investigation."

Paul took the cue and stood, but Alan stayed seated glaring at Evie.

"Please extend us the courtesy of one final internal discussion among the partnership before you take any such action, as it would further damage the reputation of the firm."

"Okay, we will wait to hear from you until this time tomorrow afternoon. If we have not heard from you by then, your silence will be interpreted as permission for us to contact Gerais Chevas and Senator Arbeson, and make any inquiries we deem appropriate." Michael walked around the table and stood between Paul and Alan, in an effort to escort them from the room. After a few weighty seconds, Alan stood and followed Michael and Paul out.

"Well," Michael said appearing in the doorway. "I'm quite pleased with how that went."

"Can you believe this letter business?" asked Evie. "Credible source? Are they kidding?"

"I know. I'd be willing to bet that one would be laughed out of court. They're really desperate and I think we added to their desperation. And, I have it all on tape." He patted his chest pocket.

"And you haven't even told them about the fake ID presented by some woman checking into that Dallas hotel as me or what we know about Emira Adelio."

"We'll save that for trial if they persist in trying to saddle you with this Gerais Chevas mess of Alan's."

Evie followed Michael out of the conference room and back to his office. Agent Neeley was not there, but had promised to meet her downstairs when summoned.

"And I have some copies of the new payment schedule *and* a system level printout of who's been accessing these files," said Evie, pulling the documents out of her briefcase and handing them to Michael.

"Excellent! Okay, Evie, I think you can consider yourself having darkened the hallways of Howard Rolland for the last time. I'll turn these over to the feds and we'll declare your undercover work complete. Now, it's just a matter of letting the feds do their job. Are you going to take a room at a hotel?" he asked, noticing her suitcase in the floor beside his desk.

"I'm going to be at the Four Seasons with Joe," she said.

"Mmmm. This sounds serious."

"I hope so."

"Can I reach you on your cell?"

"Yes." She pulled it out and checked for power. "It's on." Then she returned it to its storage pocket.

Michael agreed to call her if he heard anything. They put in the request for Neeley to meet her downstairs and accompany her to the hotel. She thanked Michael, took her bags and left.

The unmarked FBI vehicle, a black Dodge Intrepid, was waiting for her in front of the building. A man emerged from the backseat, introduced himself as Agent Bowers, Agent Weber's partner, and said that Agent Neeley had been detained, but that he and Agent Fisher, seated in the driver's seat, would escort her to the Four Seasons. He flashed the now-familiar FBI badge with his photo and name and invited her into the backseat, while Agent Fisher got out of the car and loaded her suitcase into the trunk. She hesitated.

"May I see your FBI badge again?" she asked.

"Of course," said Agent Bowers, handing her his badge for inspection. It was in exactly the same format as the badge Agent Weber had shown her and the photograph matched Agent Bowers's appearance.

"If you'd like, we can call Agent Weber and he can confirm our identity," said Agent Bowers.

"Yes, if you don't mind, I'd like to do that."

Agent Bowers pulled out his cell phone and asked her, "Would you be more comfortable if you did the dialing?"

"No, that's okay, but I would like to compare the number you dial to the number he gave me."

"No problem." Agent Bowers smiled. *He must be used to nervous witnesses,* she thought, as she retrieved Agent Weber's card from the pocket of her briefcase.

He punched in each number as she read them off and he showed her the screen, displaying the full number, before connecting the call.

She nodded her approval so he took the phone back, punched something to initiate the communication, verified the connection and handed the phone to Evie. She took it and held it up to her ear.

"Weber," said a voice.

"Yes, Agent Weber," said Evie, "this is Evie Sullivan. I'm sorry to trouble you, but I just wanted to confirm that the men here to escort me are—"

"No problem," he said. "I understand your reluctance to trust men you've never met. I owe you an apology. I'm tied up and Neeley's been called away on a murder investigation so I asked my partner and a colleague, Agent Fisher, to escort you."

Evie listened to the quality and cadence of the man's voice. He sounded like her memory of Agent Weber when they met, so she thanked him and hung up, handing the telephone back to Agent Bowers with a smile. She slipped into the seat behind the driver's seat, exhausted.

She explained that she wanted to be taken to the Four Seasons and she watched Agent Fisher enter the FDR Drive. Agent Bowers, seated next to her, looked through a notepad. She was feeling relaxed now, the FBI would be launching a thorough criminal investigation and she would reclaim her reputation, if not her position, with Howard, Rolland & Stewart. Hopefully, this whole ordeal would soon be over and she could end this chapter in her life. She leaned back against the seat and closed her eyes, falling into a brief sleep, lulled by the hum of the engine and the routine traffic noise.

Suddenly, she felt herself lurch forward almost touching the back of the driver's seat. Their car had been bumped from behind while at full speed on the highway. She looked around with horror, grabbing the seat in front of her for stability.

"*What the . . . !*" exclaimed Agent Fisher. He grabbed the wheel tighter and looked intently into his rearview mirror. Agent Bowers leaped over the seat in an astonishing, fluid movement and, from the front seat, began offering his advice on defensive driving maneuvers. Each man kept looking into the rearview mirror repeatedly as they shared their attention between what was in front of them and what was behind.

Agent Fisher sped up and moved into another lane, shouting back at Evie to secure her seatbelt and hold on. The pursuing car mimicked the lane change and inserted itself behind them. Agent Fisher slowed down slightly, moving gradually toward the slow lane. Another bump, but this one was even sharper—a harder hit. There was no question that it was intentional. Evie's body shot forward again, straining against the seat belt that held her.

The sedan swerved and slid, skidding and squealing its tires, as the speed angled the body first right, then left, and back again like a

delinquent carnival ride. Through a heroic series of measured maneuvers, Agent Fisher managed to control the errant vehicle and ease it over
toward the rightmost lane.

After shouting for Evie to get down, Agent Fisher began loudly
reciting his rearview mirror observations, including the number of
men in the pursuing car, their descriptions, the license plate and make
of the vehicle and a chronicle of movement. As Evie crouched in the
seat, she guessed that they must be following FBI procedure and were
in the process of preserving information on a recording device hidden
in the car.

Evie peeked over the top of the front seat and saw Agent Bowers draw
his Glock 9mm pistol and point it out the passenger window, as Agent
Fisher turned the car onto a ramp and began exiting the highway. When
Evie felt the car slowing down and realized what they were doing, she
began yelling, "No! No! Don't stop! Keep driving! Please! Keep going!"
She was still stealing looks over the seat and watched Agent Bowers lean
out the window, his Glock in hand. He seemed poised to jump out of the
car and confront their pursuer.

Evie, stretched herself sideways across the back seat, but her seatbelt was still fastened so the range of her movement was limited. Faced
with a choice of freeing herself from the restraint or trying to locate her
cell phone, she chose first to reach down into her briefcase in search of
her BlackBerry. It had fallen out of its pocket during the car's extreme
zigzagging and her hand searched blindly for it in the other areas of the
case and in the floor of the backseat.

Agent Fisher had ignored her protestations and continued slowing
the vehicle, finally inching to a stop on the shoulder to the off-ramp.
Evie flipped the latch on her seatbelt, releasing it, and crouched on all
fours down on the floorboards. Her hand found her BlackBerry and she
began scrolling for Joe's number as she glanced upward over her shoulder. Men were shouting around her and car doors flew open.

She heard a man yell, *"Freeze, FBI!"* several times and for a moment
she was confused because the voice sounded far away. Had the agents

left her alone to confront their pursuer? She glanced down to see if her call had connected and for a fraction of a second, she puzzled over the phone's dark display screen. Flipping the phone over in her hand, a chill ran through her with the reality that the battery was gone. *When did that happen and who . . . ?*

In the same moment, she realized her BlackBerry's power source was missing, her peripheral vision caught Agent Bowers flying back over the seat toward her. Before she could gather her thoughts or say anything, he grabbed her under the arm, jerked her upward and pointed his Glock at her head, yelling in the direction of the back window, "Get the fuck away from the car or I'll waste her right here."

chapter
35

E vie winced with pain from the physical force, and whispered,
"You're not FBI," almost to herself. She looked out through the
rear window of the vehicle and saw Agent Neeley, with a ban-
dage on his head, and another man she didn't recognize. Both men
were standing in a shooting posture pointing their guns at the car
where a man, who she now knew was not an FBI agent, still held her
immobile.

A muffled shot rang out and she realized that this man had tilted
the gun's barrel, now fitted with what looked like a silencer, a few inches
backward and squeezed off a round just behind her head. The discharge
sounded like a muted dart whizzing through the air. There is no silence
more intense than the few seconds after a gunshot. Even a muffled one.

Only a second or two crept by in slow motion as Evie simultaneously pierced the silence with a scream, which ricocheted around inside
the automobile before reaching the agents' ears, and glanced down frantically searching for her BlackBerry. The sudden yank of her body had

knocked the device out of her hand and it was on the floor of the back-seat. In her panic, she'd forgotten it had no power.

At the sound of the shot, Agents Neeley and Flynn had backed away from Evie's vehicle and had taken positions behind their open car doors, waiting for another opportunity to make a move.

The man who had grabbed Evie, still held her by the upper arm, despite the downward turn of her head and he once more jerked her upward to get a better hold on her. The other man had been somewhere outside the car during the shot, but he slid back into the driver's seat and said, "Tire's losing air, Dennis. Musta hit something when we exited."

Dennis turned his face toward the front seat in an abrupt movement and cursed. They sat for a few seconds, nobody moving and then Dennis transferred his Glock to the hand he'd used to hold on to Evie, reached over with his free hand and pulled the handle on the back seat's door. He pushed it open with his foot. In the instant he let go of her, Evie lunged for the opposite door, reflexively clawing at it with both hands. It was futile she knew because Dennis was reaching for her again, but it was an automatic move to buy time.

"Okay!" he screamed, after yanking her back over to his side of the seat. "I'm really gonna kill her if you don't do what I say." He touched the warm silencer-covered barrel to her temple once again as he spoke, and his fingers dug into her arm, determined to maintain their control of her.

"Drop your weapons and move away from the car," Dennis barked at the agents, still visible in positions behind their doors.

"Give us the girl and we'll let you walk," Agent Neeley shouted back.

Dennis chambered another round and abruptly jerked Evie sideways, making her cry out in fear and pain. A few tears started to well up in her eyes and she held her breath. Agents Neeley and Flynn reacted by throwing up their hands.

"Don't hurt her," Neeley yelled. "Okay, we'll do what you ask."

Neeley and Flynn slowly began to move away from the car with their hands in the air.

"Throw your guns *DOWN!*" screamed Dennis.

The agents complied and continued their slow, backward steps away from the car. Just then, police sirens could be heard, increasing in volume as they neared the location.

"We've got to get out of here," bellowed Dennis at the man in the front seat. They each quickly heaved themselves out of the car, the driver pointing his gun at the FBI agents as Dennis pulled Evie out through the door.

"Don't forget to get her stuff," said Dennis. He half-dragged Evie along toward the *real* FBI vehicle, her muscles straining in the opposite direction to break free. When they reached their destination, Dennis shoved her into the back seat and re-aimed his gun, now pointing it at the unarmed FBI Agents.

Standing guard, ready to shoot if either FBI Agent made a move, the driver now lowered his gun, gathered Evie's possessions from the trunk and the floor of the back seat and deposited a bullet into a tire of the abandoned vehicle for good measure. He walked over and dumped his load into the getaway car. Then he walked around, closing its doors and headed to the driver's seat.

"Cover me," Dennis said, prompting the man, in tag-team fashion, to turn his attention and his gun back in the direction of the agents. Dennis pulled a bag from a pocket inside his jacket. He released his grip on Evie as he tore open the bag. She made another lunge outward to try and open this second car door, just as a hand holding a cloth, moist with some kind of chemical, covered her face. There was a wetness to the darkness and it had a distinctive odor that she didn't recognize. She felt some of the moisture enter her mouth and there was a slightly sweet taste that she pushed away with her tongue.

She fought violently with her arms while listening to the agents screaming at them from their positions ten feet or so from the car. For a moment, she successfully pushed away the arm and the malevolent cloth. In the next moment her nose, in a heightened state, documented a half-dozen smells . . . the idling engine, the body odor of her abductor, the smell of the chloroform-laden cloth and the musty smell of the interior of the FBI vehicle. She saw an iridescent array of color and the combination of the visuals and the smells overwhelmed her. That maelstrom of sensations was the last thing she remembered until she woke up in a semi-dark room with a raging headache.

It was a struggle to open her eyes. Even the tiniest amount of light caused a searing pain in her head, but she blinked and tried to move. A chill was followed by a wave of nausea. She put a hand to her face and there was heat coming off her skin. As if in a different reality, she could hear muffled Manhattan street noise—traffic, honking, laughing, yelling, footfalls, machinery and the vibration from the subway. She had no idea how long she had been unconscious, where she was or who had put her there.

She looked up at a series of darkened recessed light fixtures and tried to focus on the detail. For a few seconds, what she was seeing was as indecipherable as a torn and weathered billboard. Her mind processed the residual images that remained from before she'd lost consciousness. A man, a cloth over her face, some kind of chemical, the smells, a gun shot, the shuffle to change cars. She began to move slowly and realized that she was lying on a very large four-poster bed.

She moved each of her limbs and discovered that no part of her body was bound, but every part of her ached. Her eyes were instinctively drawn toward the only source of light coming into the room. It was a lone window with opaque or glazed glass near the ceiling. Light was seeping through the glass, but there was no ability to discern anything on the other side. She sat up and carefully stretched. What kind of drug or chemical had been on that cloth? She had never felt this bad that she could remember.

There was silence in the near; in the far there were still the sounds of her city—if she could just figure out how to get out there to it. She forced herself to stand, separating herself from the surface of the bed, using the headboard to steady herself. She walked toward the bedroom door and opened it. She was looking into a large room with high ceilings. It was ornately decorated and massively framed oil paintings covered the walls. If she'd paused and really focused on them, she would have recognized the artistry of Picasso, Renoir and Andy Warhol. She seemed to be in a large loft. She wondered if she was in SoHo.

She slid her aching body into the room in slow, silent increments. As she looked around, she wondered about her suitcase, briefcase and BlackBerry, but knew they were probably in the hands of Dennis or whoever hired him. Her head was spinning, aching. Her lungs suddenly felt as if they were being pressed into nothing. Her throat burned. Her eyes teared. Her stomach was knotted and twisted, and she wondered if what she was feeling could possibly be the after-effect of that chemical-soaked cloth.

The temperature in her body vaulted between hot and cold and she felt herself shake. No one was in the apartment that she could see or hear. She saw the front door and with labored steps, headed toward it, but fainted in the middle of the cavernous room, falling into a nightmarish sleep punctuated by sounds and fears and chills.

$\sim$

"Your girlfriend's all over the papers," said Ariel as she stood in the living room of Joe's suite at the Four Seasons. She threw down a stack of newspapers on the coffee table. "They're making her into a publicity torpedo aimed at Senator Arbeson's re-election campaign," she said. She spread out the periodicals and read out loud, "*Senator Arbeson's Marriage Jeopardized by Secret Mistress, Girlfriend of Senator Arbeson in Hiding, New York Law Firm Associate Disappearance Linked to Senator.*"

"Is it possible she could be in hiding of her own volition?"

"Ari, she was chloroformed and kidnapped. This impotent asshole, Agent Neeley, saw the whole thing."

"Joseph, you've got to get yourself under control. You said the man was knocked cold. Didn't he say that because they didn't kill her, she was being taken for some purpose and that after that purpose was fulfilled, she might be let go?"

"I think he was just saying that to try to mitigate my anger over his incompetence. What kind of ineptitude does it take to lose a government witness?"

"Wherever she is, if she has any idea what's going on in the press, wouldn't she want to lie low? Even if she has been let go, she might want to hide out until this blows over."

"She'd be in touch with me."

"What if there *was* something between her and the Senator? In the past, I mean. I wouldn't blame her if there was. He's a very sexy man. She may not have felt comfortable telling you about it, given the circumstances."

Joe stared at his sister with a scowl on his face.

"This issue of *Spellbound!* from September 12th has a detailed story about an alleged affair between an associate of Howard Rolland and the Senator. There's a re-print of a photograph from *New York Magazine* that shows Senator Arbeson with his arm around a woman who looks a lot like Evie."

"Ari, you're speaking about the woman I love. Evie is *not* the girl in that photograph. She did *not* have an affair with Senator Arbeson. I can't believe you're willing, along with the majority of the partners of her firm, to believe the worst about her."

"Joseph, I'm your sister, and I love you. I'm just trying to get you to think about this in an objective way, exploring all the possibilities. I really *do like* Evie. I've come to think of her as a friend, but are you sure she's told you everything? It's not that hard to imagine Senator Arbeson coming on to her. She's a beautiful girl."

"This is a case of mistaken identity. It's a *mistake*. Her identity has been stolen and manipulated, and now the press has joined in. I have a pretty good idea who set it up."

"Then why wouldn't her firm put out a statement refuting the implication?"

"I think that's obvious. They're staring down a multi-million dollar lawsuit. They gratuitously benefit from a seemingly independent assault on her reputation in the press."

"I'm sorry, Joseph. I'm not accusing Evie of anything, I just don't want to see you—"

"Ari, you know I love you, but you're a pain in the ass sometimes. I told you, she saw this coming. She said she thought Levenger was going to try to link her to the Senator as part of his scheme to smear her with this shit he's into."

"So, if that's what's going on here, it means that Alan is throwing darts at Senator Arbeson's campaign *himself.*"

"I don't think Levenger would hesitate to sell out anyone who threatened his objectives. I think his loyalty to the Senator is as illusory as his firm's resolve to find the truth."

"This is unbelievable. I knew Alan was bad news, but I had no idea what he was capable of."

"I'm headed back to Weber's office. You should take a car back to Connecticut, Ari, I'll call you if we find her."

~

"Mr. Levenger, there's someone here who's asked to see you."

"Who is it?" asked Alan into the speaker on his telephone.

"He says he's looking for representation. He's with a company called Para . . . Para-pee-yay. Yes, I think that's how you pronounce it. His name is Joe Barton.

"Uhhh. Okay, I can squeeze him in. Call Mary to come get him."

After a few minutes, Mary appeared at his office door, announcing his visitor and a tall, well-built man dressed in a navy suit with dark wavy hair, stood in Alan's doorway. Alan stood and gestured for him to take a seat in one of the chairs opposite his desk. Joe walked into the office and closed the door behind him, taking off his jacket and draping it over the back of a visitor chair.

"Joe, is it?" said Alan, eyebrows arched as he watched Joe make himself at home in his office.

"Joe Barton."

"Parapier? I've heard of your company. U.S. headquarters in L.A., right?"

Joe stayed silent for a moment as his eyes took in every detail—the location of windows, the configuration of the furniture and the weight and degree of fitness of the man he was staring at. He was calm, but his blood was hot.

Alan ignored Joe's silence and asked, "And you're looking for a New York lawyer?"

"Specifically, I'm looking for you."

"Me? Well, yes, I do have a reputation." Alan stretched back in his chair, placing his hands behind his head. "What kind of representation are we talking about? Have you got a legal problem or are you doing a deal?"

"Actually, I've been following a deal *you've* been doing."

"Really. Which deal's that?"

"Gerais Chevas."

Alan brought his arms around and gripped the armrests. He nodded slowly as he curled his lips in. A few seconds of silence passed as his knuckles went white and his salesmanship stare turned into a glare.

"Who are you?" Alan asked in an acidic tone.

"I told you who I am. I'm here because I want some information from you. If you give it to me, I'll consider walking out of here without making a scene. If you don't, I'll have to do some damage."

"Listen, asshole. I don't know who you think you are . . . Hey, did you send me an email from a hotmail account? Goliath or some such shit?"

"Yes."

"What are you, some kind of hacker or corporate spy?"

"No."

"Are you FBI?"

"Okay, listen carefully," said Joe. "Here's the question: *Where's Evie?*"

"Evie who?"

"Let's not play games, okay? I don't have a lot of time. Where is she?"

"I don't know what you're talking about, and I'm about to call security."

"I wouldn't do that if I were you."

"Get the hell out of my office," said Alan as he picked up the receiver.

In a split second, Joe was over the desk and his body slammed into Alan's, the leather chair spinning, tilting then toppling over. The force of Joe's movements caused an avalanche of objects from Alan's desk. As paper, files, an ashtray and other items scattered, Alan's body broke through one of the armrests, aided by the impact of Joe's full body weight, fueled by anger.

They crashed to the floor and Alan started swinging wildly into the air. Before they hit the ground, Joe's palms were cupped around Alan's throat, one of the heels of his hands on Alan's windpipe. Alan twisted his body in voluntary spasms like a beheaded snake, in an attempt to knock Joe off balance and force the release of the pressure. Joe squeezed tighter, the strength in his hands nourished by a profusion of rage.

Gasping for breath, Alan clawed at the fabric on the back of Joe's shirt, but was unable to shake off the pinch. He threw punch after punch at Joe's head and body, but couldn't make contact. A guttural gagging sound escaped through Alan's compressed vocal chords just as Joe released his grip.

"Okay, Levenger," said Joe. "No more games. You and I both know you ordered a kidnapping and had her taken somewhere. Are you ready to tell me what I want to know?"

"I . . . uhhh . . . haah . . . kahh . . . uhh . . . *fuck!*" coughed Alan. "You motherfucking choked me! *Get the fuck off me!*" Alan yelled as he squirmed and fought. He swung hard with his left hand and landed an awkward punch against Joe's ribcage, but his attacker didn't flinch. Alan's hand searched the floor and found a small brass figurine of a woman that had fallen and he slammed its base into the side of Joe's chest. Made of solid brass, the block of metal landed with a crack against

Joe's bulk. His positioning shifted and he groaned. Alan crashed the brass object into the same spot a second time causing Joe's body to jerk in the opposite direction, as he let out a low moan.

Alan arched his back and knocked Joe off balance, using the leverage from the floor to swing a third time with the figurine. It landed hard against Joe's shoulder, almost ejecting him from his perch, but Joe regained his strength, took the brass figurine from Alan's hand and flung it off to the side of the room. His right fist landed hard against Alan's left jaw. Alan yelped and cursed. As Joe began to rise from his position on Alan's chest, Alan attempted to knee him in the groin, but Joe shifted his body out of range and jabbed his elbow into Alan's stomach. Alan cried out and struggled for a breath, as Joe again hovered over him in dominance.

Just then a rapid knock was followed by a swift thrust of the door into the room and Steve Buniker stood in the opening. He yelled for Mary to call security and entered with purpose saying, "It's finally happened, buddy, you finally pinched the wrong ass." Alan strained to turn his head and issue a plea with his eyes as he flailed his arms.

Joe looked up at Steve as he approached.

"Just step away," he said through labored breathing. "This has nothing to do with you. It's between me and Levenger."

Steve stood for a moment seemingly trying to decide what to do. Physically, he was the smallest man in the room. Joe turned his attention back to Alan, still underneath him, and asked again, "Time's running out. Where did you take Evie?"

With those words and the recognition of the name, Steve stopped in his tracks and stood watching the two men on the floor.

Alan slapped at Joe's face, trying to poke at his eyes. Joe swung his right arm out to the left and backhanded Alan's head with his closed right fist. Alan groaned and cursed and spit, his body continuing its attempt to summon the strength to knock Joe over.

"I . . . don't . . . *know,*" he managed to sputter. "I . . . don't . . . know . . . where . . . she is."

Suddenly, two uniformed men rushed into the room and one of them said, "Okay, you're taking a one-way trip, mister," as they each grabbed one of Joe's arms and began lifting him off Alan, whose breathing immediately accelerated. Joe offered no resistance as the men pulled him into a standing position. Joe took a slow, painful deep breath and the two men escorted him out of the room.

"I'm pressing charges!" yelled Alan as they began walking. He was painfully pushing himself off the floor into a standing position, extending his limbs, dusting himself off, rubbing the side of his face and cursing in a low whisper.

"I'll look forward . . . to our next meeting," said Joe in a calm voice as he walked between the uniformed men out of the office and toward reception where two New York police officers had just appeared.

⁓

When Evie woke again, she was covered in a sticky sweat and moist clothes. She had won her fight with the fever, but her mind was swimming in pea soup. A wave of nausea prompted her to look for a bathroom. Her stomach churned and lurched, followed by a series of cramps. After finding a marble bathroom, she held tight to the sink as she swerved and swallowed. For a brief moment, she wished she were dead. She vomited into the toilet and collapsed onto the floor.

Five minutes or more went by as she let the marble floor cool her skin and steady her dizziness. She sat up suddenly, thinking she heard someone coming into the apartment, but after counting seconds, she was convinced it was just street noise. She stood slowly and splashed water in her face. It was reviving and cleansing.

She found the front door and turned the knob, expecting the resistance of a lock, but it opened. *I have to find a police officer, and get to the Four Seasons or Michael's office or the hospital . . .*

When she found her way to the street, the intensity of the sun gave her a moment's clarity, but flashes of overwhelming weakness continued to come in waves. The drug had disengaged her senses. She could feel her face flushing and her body heat rise again. A woman scowled at her as she walked passed. Somewhere in her state of awareness, she knew she must look a mess—sweaty, dirty face, messy hair, rumpled, stained clothes and irregular movements. *This must be how homeless people feel,* she thought.

She kept walking, looking for a police officer, or a friendly face who might help her find one. There was no restaurant within view that would have English-speaking staff and she did not have the stamina to do much explaining. Her head was spinning again and her mouth burned. She felt an overwhelming thirst and her stomach churned. She forced herself to focus her mind and she collected all her energy to make each step look as normal as possible. A few more minutes of walking and the faces that passed started merging into one another as if they were wet paint—one in blues, the next like the veined red of stained mahogany.

A man stopped and asked her if she was okay. She tried to form words with her mouth, but she couldn't talk and she couldn't swallow. Her voice didn't work and her motor control was dissipating. She didn't see the lamp post of the street light until it collided with her head and she fell in a heap on the sidewalk, right in front of the man. A few other curious New Yorkers clustered around, one frantically dialing 911 on her cell phone.

chapter
36

O kay," Michael was saying, "but what did you really accomplish
by that little stunt? Did you really expect this idiot to tell you
where she is?"

"No. I didn't. But it *did* feel good to pop him," said Joe, wincing as he
shifted in his chair.

"I bet." Michael shook his head, paced the room and frowned at his
newest client. "You know, you really should get yourself looked at. Did
you see a doctor yesterday?"

"No. There's nothing they can do for broken ribs. I'll live."

"So did Alan tell you anything?"

"I figured he'd deny everything, but that wasn't really why I was
there. I really went there to find out which office was his and get a look
around."

"Why?"

"So I could go back and do a little purging of files for him," Joe said
as he handed Michael a stack of papers clipped together with a black

368

binder clip. "After you sprung me yesterday, Greg and I made a little reconnaissance visit to the offices of Howard, Rolland & Stewart. Amazing how gullible the night shift is, especially after nine-eleven."

"Well, I can see your case is going to be a challenge," said Michael, taking the stack of paper and shuffling through the pages. "What's this?"

"Looks to me like a stack of purchased FDA approvals," said Joe.

"What does this have to do with Gerais Chevas and Project Neon?"

"Nothing. I went there looking for something more to tie him to that, but I found these. He's apparently leveraging his relationship with *another* U.S. Government insider."

Michael looked more closely at the first document. It was a letter on the official stationery of the Food and Drug Administration, granting an expedited approval for a drug called Hepaprex pursuant to CFR 56.105 of Title 21. It looked official and was signed by the chairman of an institutional review board. Michael flipped through the stack. There were thirty-seven letters in the stack, twenty-two of which were approvals, with handwritten notes in the margins of each copy, detailing the application's history, its date of origin, the number of interactions with the FDA and a series of dollar figures. The ones that weren't approvals were professional looking inquiries and responses, with approval looming on the horizon. On most of the letters, there were scribbles and doodles around the FDA logo, as if decorated during a telephone conversation.

"How do we know these are not legitimate approvals acquired through the proper procedure?" asked Michael.

"There are only something like *seventy* new drugs approved in a typical *calendar year* by the FDA, that have progressed legitimately through all the phases of testing. I would be very surprised if that many legitimately pass through a single attorney."

"These monetary amounts—the final number seems to be a percentage of this larger number. The larger number seems to be a multiple of some number of years times EPY? What do you think that is, estimated profit per year?"

"Yeah, that's what I think. I think that final number is the payoff for expediting the approval process. By rushing the drug to market years ahead of its natural introduction to the market, the profit is exponentially increased. I think Levenger's taking a piece of that action."

"I don't know much about how new drugs are approved. Why would a drug's approval be expedited?"

"I know a little bit about this," said Joe, "from some people I know who hold medical patents. It normally takes a drug manufacturer ten to fifteen years to navigate from the lab to the American patient. Drug approval is a pretty lengthy and very expensive process. There are pre-clinical trials, at least three phases of testing on humans, independent review, and hearings. If a drug has the potential to treat a particular type of patient, say one who's terminally ill, or if it's deemed to carry little or no risk, an institutional review board can use an expedited review process, which may be conducted by the chairman or senior members alone."

"Then, it could mean quite a bit of money to an unscrupulous manufacturer to bypass that whole process," said Michael.

"And it would be worth a nice little 'administrative fee' for the attorney streamlining the process and the IRB chairman making it happen," added Joe.

"I remember reading about a House Government Reform Committee criticizing the FDA for routinely allowing scientists with conflicts of interest to serve on influential advisory committees that make recommendations on drug policy."

"Well, I'm sure there are some honorable people in charge of the pharmaceutical industry, but it only takes one bad guy to do a lot of damage. I haven't had a chance to look through the whole stack there, but there's got to be over twenty-five different drugs represented there."

"Retranoin, Honuflex, Neolactin . . ."

"Did you say Neolactin?" asked Joe. "Where's that file you had? Those copies of the contents of Evie's file?"

"Here," said Michael, handing a file folder to Joe.

Joe opened it and flipped through the pages.

"Look at this," he said. "Neolactin was one of those trademark requests that Evie flagged for Paul as having been questioned by their client, Finley Regent. Apparently, those requests didn't come from who they appeared to. They must be from some nameless drug manufacturer that Alan was doing approvals for under the table. He had Evie securing trademarks for these illicit drugs without her knowing that they were going to be introduced into the American drug market before being properly vetted by FDA procedures. Evie said she didn't see the final forms filled out for these so she wouldn't have known the applications weren't really for Finley Regent."

"You're on to something here. I think we've got another dirty government official . . . and a nice little illegal drug pipeline."

"Hmmm. Wellvex, Bylinion, Interium." Michael continued reading from the bundle of paper.

"Bylinion is a drug my Dad's been taking," said Joe.

"And Wellvex I know is controversial. There have been calls for the FDA to revoke its approval. It's too addictive apparently."

"There've been quite a few news stories lately about drug side effects. I wouldn't be surprised if some of them are represented here."

"Selling drug approvals. An insidious little business. Sickening and killing how many hundreds . . . or thousands?" He began to dial Agent Weber's number, but stopped when his colleague, George, appeared in the doorway with a stunned look on his face.

"You've been tied up," George said looking over at Joe. "CNN is reporting that Senator Arbeson's been murdered."

"What?" asked Michael and Joe almost simultaneously.

"They're not saying much. His campaign manager said he was found this morning . . . gunshot wound. They don't yet have any suspects. There'll be a press conference, but they're not going to release many details for obvious reasons. The investigation is already in full swing."

Michael and Joe stared, first at George, then at each other.

"I thought you'd want to know," said George in Michael's direction. He nodded at Joe and left.

The two men stayed silent for a few weighty seconds, and Michael spoke first, "Joe, Evie's alive. I know it."

"God, I hope so. If she is, she's the last person alive who's named as a player in this Gerais Chevas deal and who's resisting its closure. I've got to find her."

"The FBI has a task force dedicated to her recovery. They don't like being impersonated and they don't like losing a witness, so they're pissed."

"If Senator Arbeson was murdered because of what he knew about Project Neon or what he threatened to do with that knowledge, Evie could suffer the same fate. Since we began putting the pieces together, I've been afraid that Levenger might decide he needed to—"

"Don't make yourself crazy. Senator Arbeson has many more enemies than just Levenger," said Michael.

"Another way Levenger could get Evie out of his way would be to frame her for murder. She'd be a natural suspect. He's already set her up as the Senator's mistress in the media."

"There could be any number of suspects—Levenger and his henchmen, ideological enemies, someone connected to Romez Nuevo, somebody who didn't want to pay up on a bribe, a political assassin, one of Arbeson's wives or lovers, their angry spouses. Everyone knows he had a hard time keeping his marriages on solid ground."

"I don't like the odds that there's anyone on that list who might have their sights on Evie."

Michael began re-dialing Agent Weber, but looked up to see the agent standing at the door of his office. The man was breathing hard and beads of perspiration were apparent on his forehead. He quickly glanced around the room, nodded at Joe and announced, "We've found Evie."

In the intensive care unit of New York's Saint Andrew Hospital, Evie was lying inert in a coma, her chart identifying her as "Jane Doe #2." She had responded to physical stimuli, but her movements had been essentially reflexive. In the last few hours, the nurses had reported increased responsiveness, but her eyes remained closed.

The doctor turned to a nurse standing next to him. "Keep her on oxygen and fluids. Continue the physostigmine salicylate. Contact me if there's any respiratory difficulty or change in heart rate."

The doctor was joined by two uniformed New York Police Officers who quietly approached the foot of the bed and waited for the doctor's attention. When the doctor turned and walked toward the officers, one of them stopped him and mumbled something in his ear. He smiled, reached for the chart at the foot of her bed, crossed out "Jane Doe #2" with his pen and wrote "Evelyn Sullivan."

As the policemen left the room to set up a post outside the door, Evie stirred. The doctor nodded to the departing men and walked back to her bedside.

"Look at me, my dear," he said.

Evie slowly opened her eyes and blinked away a blur. A giddiness and fog permeated her brain, but she was able to focus on a man in a white coat standing over her. After a few minutes had passed, she could see him clearly. He was balding and wrinkled; he wore wire-frame glasses over kind eyes. A doctor, but not one she remembered ever seeing before.

"I'm . . . confused. Where am I?" she said.

"That's understandable. You're in the hospital. Saint Andrew. You had a serious encounter with some narcotic analgesics. And an allergic reaction on top of that."

"What? I feel dizzy . . . like I'm floating."

"Just relax. Your body is purging itself of the poisons. You're going to be fine."

"Doctor . . ." Evie began.

"Hechman."

"Doctor Hechman, how did I get here?"

"I believe you passed out on Leonard Street in Soho. Someone called an ambulance for you."

∽

"I'm coming in," said Ariel.

"She's at Saint Andrew. We're headed there now," said Joe into his cell phone. "Meet us in the intensive care ward."

"Have they arrested Alan?"

"He's being questioned as we speak, flanked by some sleazy defense attorney." He looked over at Michael beside him in the taxi and smiled.

Michael nodded a look of resignation at the characterization of his profession.

"This is so unreal," said Ariel into the phone. "Did Alan orchestrate this?"

"That's the theory. I'm going to kill him." He glanced over at Michael who was now closing his eyes and holding his hands over his ears.

∽

"Good morning, *Evelyn*," said the doctor. It was good to address the patient by name. After coming out of a coma in the early morning hours of Wednesday, the 15th of September, Evie had slept a healing sleep and was now wide awake.

"I've been thinking about what you said before, Doctor. Narcot . . . what drug did you say was in my system?"

"Morphine laced with atropine and some additional substance we haven't identified yet. We do know that in the preceding days, you had inhaled methyl trichloride."

"When I was abducted, you mean." She licked her lips and took a deep breath. "Is that chloroform?"

"Yes." He walked over to a chair by the bed and laid the chart he was holding on the seat. He held an ophthalmoscope and leaned over her, examining her eyes. He told her to relax and with his thumb, gently lifted her eyelid while he looked into each eye. He finished and smiled at her. "Evelyn, your body didn't react in the predictable way, which was advantageous in some ways. You had an allergic reaction. The allergic reaction to the drug mixture caused your body to expel as much of the poisons as possible an quickly as it could."

"You can call me Evie, doctor. But, okay ... what were the disadvantages?"

He smiled at her reaction and inquiry. She was engaged. A sign of recovery.

"You were in a coma, but very briefly. Then you came around for a bit, yelled at the nurse and went back to sleep." He smiled. "It looks good so far. I don't think you're going to have any long-term side effects, but we'll watch you closely for a few days. Then we'll have to do some periodic checking for after effects."

"Oh. Please apologize to that nurse for me."

He nodded.

"Thank you, doctor. Everything hurts, and I feel absolutely exhausted."

"We had to stitch up a gash in your forehead and treat some cuts. You have some minor bruises, but they'll heal."

She reached up with her hand and touched the dressing on her head.

"We'll see what we can do for the pain, but I want your system to cleanse itself a bit more first. Just rest. See if you can sleep some more."

"How long have I been here?"

"Two days."

"I've been sleeping for two days?"

"Yes."

"Then why would I want to sleep some more?"

He smiled . . . *attitude . . . another good sign.* "Evie, you should just relax. Do you feel like trying to eat something?"

"Yes, something like . . . can I have soup? No, chowder?"

"Okay. We'll see what we can do."

After a bowl of clam chowder, she drifted back to sleep again. When she awoke, she felt much more clear-headed and alert. On doctor's orders, she was now breathing on her own. The nurse helped her wash, brush her teeth and pull her hair into a low bun. It was a glorious feeling to be awake, aware and cleaned up a bit. At her request, they turned on the television for her, but she used the remote to switch it off after less than an hour.

She was staring into space when Doctor Hechman re-entered the room, "Would you like a visitor?"

"Who?"

"There's been quite a collection out there, but there's one gentleman who has been most persistent."

chapter **37**

The doctor continued, "An FBI agent wants to talk to you."

"Okay. Send him in."

"Are you sure you don't want some more time?"

"No. Thank you. Really, thank you for everything. Could I have some water?"

The nurse disappeared and returned with a pitcher of ice water and a stack of Styrofoam cups. She poured Evie some water in one, announced that lunch would arrive soon and returned to the nurses' station. Doctor Hechman stood and watched her for a few seconds and left.

After several minutes, the hospital door opened again and a man who looked familiar walked in. He was speaking into a cell phone as he walked. ". . . taking a picture of the crime scene." The end of his sentence hung in the air. He looked familiar, but she couldn't pinpoint his identity.

"You're FBI, right?" she asked.

"Good. You're awake," he said. "I'm glad to see that you're going to be okay. Agent Weber. Do you remember me?"

"Yes, uuhhh, oh, Weber, Agent Weber."

"Yes, that's right."

"I was watching the news. Is it true that Senator Arbeson's been murdered?"

"Yes, unfortunately it is."

"Are you here to arrest me?"

He chuckled. "No, interview you." His grin broadened into a sympathetic smile.

The door opened again and Michael Scott entered.

"Michael," she said when she looked up. "Hi."

"Hello. God, you look great. You've got color in your cheeks. How's your head?"

"It's a little sore," she said. "But, I do like the drugs I'm getting *here* much better."

Michael smiled. "I'm so glad you're okay. It was so frustrating knowing you were somewhere in the city and we couldn't find you."

"Michael, where's Joe? Is he okay?" Is he here?"

"He's going to be fine. He'll be here soon."

"What do you mean? Did something happen to him?"

"He's having an x-ray. The doctor thinks he has a few broken ribs and they want to make sure there are no internal injuries."

"How did he do that?"

"I'll let him tell you."

Michael glanced over at Agent Weber and back to Evie. "Are you sure you feel up to talking for a few minutes?"

"Yes, I can do that."

Michael walked over and sat down on the other side of Evie's bed facing the agent.

"We were looking for you with every resource we could muster," said Agent Weber. "We found the apartment yesterday."

"What apartment?"

"The one where you were being held."

"Oh, yes. Whose was it?"

"Senator Winston Arbeson's, but we don't think he had anything to do with your abduction. At least, not directly."

"Alan."

"We're working on several theories."

"Why would those men go to the trouble to kidnap me and then allow me to walk right out of that apartment?"

"One theory is that whoever took you wanted to perpetuate the idea that you were having an affair with the Senator. Depositing you in his apartment was their way of planting your DNA in a place where it could support that allegation."

"Oh." She became lost in thought for a few moments. Then she asked, "Where's Alan? Is he one of your suspects? Has he been arrested?"

"Well, there was an initial interview. And, he's retained an attorney."

"Where is he?"

"Well, we don't exactly know."

"You don't know?'

"He, uhh. He disappeared. His attorney says he's trying to locate him."

"Isn't he under arrest?"

"No charges have been filed yet, but I imagine they'll be forthcoming."

"Do you have enough to indict?"

"There was reluctance to move forward with what we had until we saw the evidence that Michael gave us and the tie-in with some evidence we've retrieved from the Senator's apartment. There was enough for a limited warrant so we've started a search of his office and computer hard drives so we'll see what that yields. I think there will be enthusiasm for moving forward."

"You have access to the firm's computer system?"

"No, at present there are explicit restrictions on the warrant, but we can sift through what's on Alan's disks, stored in his computer and anything in his personal office."

"Is he the only one who's after me? Are there other people involved in the Gerais Chevas deal who want me silenced as well?"

"We will have the answers very soon. I don't think you're in any danger now, though."

"With all due respect, your colleague was supposed to be protecting me."

"Yes, point well taken. Our biggest problem is always the bureaucratic hurdles we have to jump through for warrants, interviews, evidence gathering. And we owe you a serious apology for letting that kidnapping succeed. Never should've happened."

"Apology accepted. Is the press still camped out in the lobby?" asked Evie. "The nurses told me."

"Yes, but I'll take care of them," interjected Michael. "There are armed NYPD officers outside your door. Just relax."

The hospital room door swung open again and an attendant brought in a tray. There was a second bowl of clam chowder, a chicken salad sandwich, a glass of orange juice, a cup of tea and a bowl of chopped fruit. Evie let the attendant adjust her pillows and arrange the tray on her tray table. She took a spoonful of the chowder and a sip of tea before she continued.

"Who do you think killed the Senator?"

"We've got a few different theories on that as well."

"He was shot? That's what the news reports were saying."

"Yes, that's correct."

"I wonder what will happen to all his legal files."

"They will become federal evidence, right?" Michael looked over at Agent Weber as he spoke.

"They will certainly be reviewed."

Evie spoke again, "Can I just say for the record that I'd never before seen the interior of that apartment, I never had an affair with Senator Arbeson and I had nothing to do with his murder?" she paused. "Nor did I have anything to do with initiating, arranging, negotiating or drafting the Gerais Chevas deal."

"Michael has already made a very convincing case on your behalf. May I ask a few questions?"

"Yes, sorry."

"This expense report you've identified as having a false hotel receipt attached—do you still have a copy of the Colonial Court receipt and the receipt from the hotel where you did stay?"

"It's in my briefcase, which was in the trunk of that car . . ."

"I've got copies," said Michael.

"We'll take them," said Agent Weber. "This handwritten note you received in the mail—the one questioning whether you'd had an affair with the Senator. Was there any subsequent contact? Or did you receive any telephone calls in that same vein?"

"No. No other personal contact. It's all just exploded in the media because of that photograph with that woman who looks like me. Do you guys know who that woman is?"

"Not yet. She hasn't been identified, but she does look a whole lot like you."

"So the people with Senator Arbeson that night haven't been found?"

"Yes, but no one recalls her name or background. No one seems to know her."

Evie let her gaze wander.

"We found a man's gold cufflink in the drawer of your bedside table," continued the agent. "It matches a cufflink owned by Senator Arbeson. Any idea how it got in your apartment?"

"Oh my God. I thought it was an old one leftover from my last boyfriend," she said thinking. "I remember coming home after shopping one Saturday morning and my apartment was unlocked. I never leave it unlocked. Then, when I saw those men outside my apartment, it occurred to me that they might have been inside my apartment. They could have planted it."

"Did you, at any time, keep a portfolio of newspaper clippings about Senator Arbeson under your bed?"

"No! I can't believe . . . NO! But, now that you mention it. Before that note was sent to me, I found one clipping of an article about his marriage in the drawer of my office desk. I thought my secretary had put it there. Just FYI, you know? It was when I was first assigned one of his matters."

"Probably came from the same source that put that cufflink in your drawer. There was quite a collection of articles found under your bed marked up in red ink."

"Red ink! There was red ink on that article I found, but I didn't put it there."

"Do you still have it? The article from your desk?"

"No. I threw it in the trash. I had no idea at that time that I was being set up for murder."

"There were also some notes written in red ink in the margins. Handwriting analysis will tell us more."

"What did the notes say?"

"Let's just say that they were designed to convince the reader that you were in love with the Senator."

"Oh, God."

"We think the men who entered your apartment were both employed by a 'security' company who does a little for-hire surveillance."

"How could that one guy have followed me into the offices of Bartlett, Warren and Ivy's that day?"

"We've done some inquiring and we think that man was also doing some private investigating for an estate attorney at that firm and just happened to be there that day."

"So, those guys were just spying on me? Who was the man who called me and threatened me over the telephone?"

"We don't know yet, but there were only two such calls, correct?"

"Yes, two."

"We have one occurring on the day you were abducted and the other one was on Tuesday, September 7th?"

"That sounds right. I'd have to check my notes."

"Is there anything else you remember about your conversation with Ms. Adelio?"

"She just said she had information for me. I told her that I couldn't talk to her because her company was on the opposing side of the transaction that I thought was being handled by my firm. She emphasized that the information was for me, personally. I asked her what kind of information, but she wouldn't tell me any details over the telephone. She said if the deal closed, she would lose everything."

"And she meant the deal involving Project Neon?"

"Yes, I asked her that and she confirmed that was the deal she was talking about."

"Do you remember anything else?"

"Only that she objected to being on speaker phone."

"So, she may have known someone *else* in your firm was in on this set-up and was presumably in conflict with you," said Michael.

Agent Weber was scribbling furiously on his note pad.

"Do you think the Senator's murder has anything to do with Project Neon?" asked Evie.

"It's possible," said Michael. "Although he's the one who was granting access to the prize. *Unless,* whoever he was splitting the payoff with lost interest in sharing." He glanced at Agent Weber who nodded.

"When I awoke from the coma and heard about the murder and what the press is saying about me, I had all these thoughts in my head." Evie looked over at Agent Weber as she spoke. "I thought you would think I was getting revenge on the Senator for having terminated our alleged affair. Or, perhaps I had conspired with him to arrange the GC Quadra government contract award and then decided I wanted to keep all the money myself. I figured Alan would just kill me and make it look like a suicide."

"Your mind has been active while you've been recovering."

"When so much is at stake, I guess the adrenaline superseded the toxicity of the drugs."

Agent Weber asked, "Will you come in and help us sort through some evidence we collected from Alan's office?"

"Yes, of course," she said. "Did the Adelio family provide any information?"

"The Adelios suspected that the purchase price was inflated to pay off a bribe and they had their suspicions about the government contract GC Quadra was to be awarded. They had already initiated legal steps to dissolve their partnership, but Emira tried to stop the deal to save her family's finances," said Weber.

"She and her family had invested their entire fortune in Romez Nuevo, and she apparently flew to New York to find you and solicit your help to crater the deal. Unfortunately, she was murdered before she could meet with you," added Michael.

"Who killed her?"

"It appears to have been a pro hired by the Adelios' business partner," said Weber.

"So, Alan wasn't directly responsible for her murder," she said almost to herself. "That drug they gave me—would it've killed me?"

"Apparently, because you had an allergic reaction, your prognosis would not have been good had you not gotten medical attention when you did," said Michael.

"You aren't the only person he was drugging, by the way," said Weber. "Jack Hanover's blood work revealed an interesting mix."

"Oh my *God*. Where did Alan get these drugs?"

"Apparently, Project Neon is not his only game. Alan has another revenue stream—peddling FDA approvals to the pharmaceutical industry," said Michael.

"So, he's got dirty FDA officials in his pocket, too?"

"Who knows what else he's into," said Michael.

"It appears that the drug pipeline has been going on for a while. Project Neon may not have been his first attempt at government-related fraud. Project Neon involves handing out government projects for money. This other scheme seems to be selling government approvals.

Whichever conspiracy preceded the other, I guess he was *diversifying*," said Michael chuckling.

"Wow. To think all this was going on as Alan kept up appearances in the firm and put himself out there as Senator Arbeson's spokesperson," said Evie.

She watched Michael take a sip of water from another Styrofoam cup before he spoke.

"Yeah. He apparently had numerous drugs on an accelerated approval plan. One of them was the last trademark in a series that you had printed out an email about—"

"Oh, yes! That email I tried to send Paul about that trademark search on Neolactin. Finley Regent's people apparently didn't request it."

"Alan probably did. Along with a list of others. Real arrogance to use a client's identity to have you do trademark searches for drugs he was trying to slip under the radar," said Michael.

"He did a pretty good job of using my identity," she said.

"Alan really did make a thorough attempt to steal your name and hijack your communications, and make good use of them, but he fortunately came up short," said Michael.

Agent Weber continued, "We've got a veritable dossier of information on these activities the firm was claiming ignorance of."

"They never did believe me. Only Hanover . . . so I guess that's why Alan tried to drug him to death. You know, there've been a lot of stories in the news recently about drugs with severe side effects and addictive properties. And calls for the FDA to pull approvals. I wasn't really paying attention, but now that I think about it, some of the trademarks we cleared may be associated with some of those—"

"There've been some articles lately in the *New York Times* questioning the FDA's procedures and some of its management," said Michael. "They're engaged in a feasibility study for a new electronic system. They've been looking into various technologies, but bureaucracy being what it is—they were sufficiently distracted. Alan and his facilitators took full advantage."

"That's true," added Agent Weber. "All internal resources have been focused on counterfeiting. Fakes that are marketed as legitimate drugs. Investigations of counterfeit drugs have increased to over 20 per year since 2000. Up from five per year in the nineties."

"Were some of those drugs that've been in the news ones that Alan pushed through the approval process?"

"We don't yet know if Alan was pushing counterfeits. It appears that he was primarily manufacturing the approvals for new, untested or failed drugs to get them on the market earlier so companies could realize earlier and larger profits."

"Gambling that not enough people would become ill or die from the dangerous ones for anyone to notice," added Michael.

Agent Weber nodded. "It will take some time to sort through the details," he said. "There will likely be some government officials that will soon be relieved of duty. The U.S. Attorney's Office is wading through all of it now." His PDA interrupted his thoughts and he held up the device so he could read the message.

"Okay. Good news," he said as he continued reading.

Evie and Michael exchanged glances and turned their attention toward Agent Weber.

"Alan's in custody," he said simply.

"Is it over?" asked Evie.

"Well, we hope you're still willing to testify," said Weber.

"I will."

"There will be a grand jury. An indictment is looking much more likely."

"Yeah? Did they find something else?" asked Michael.

Agent Weber glanced back at the screen of his handheld.

"Not to get too technical," he said, "but there were files on Alan's computer symbolically linked to core files. Files Alan probably didn't even know existed."

"A trail of his activities?" asked Evie.

"Apparently, a number of files have been deleted, but core files were replete with what are called file descriptors and a scorecard of attempts to create backdoors to other systems outside the firm," he paused. "Government systems."

"Alan was trying to hack into the computer systems of the *federal government?*" asked Evie.

"Well   "

"Maybe he had some underemployed hacker working for him," said Michael.

"It's unclear exactly what his purpose was, or the scope of his activities, but he was intercepting some electronic communications of the members of the Appropriations Committee of the United States Senate."

"The government contract award for GC Quadra!" said Evie.

"It appears Alan was making sure that the other members of the Committee were in concert with Senator Arbeson."

"So, even though Senator Arbeson was with him on the sole source arrangement, he wasn't confident the deal was going to go through unchallenged," said Michael. "He must've thought his twenty-five mil was slipping away." He glanced at Agent Weber. "This has to erase any remaining doubt about Evie's innocence."

"I probably shouldn't be telling you this," added Agent Weber, "but our IT investigation team found a reference to the timing of the Senator's demise." He paused and frowned. *"Pre-dating the event."*

"No way he's going to avoid an indictment now," said Michael. "Live by the computer, die by the computer." Michael smiled and patted Evie's hand. "Electronic pulses of ones and zeroes are going to put this guy away for a long time where he won't like the company."

Evie took a relaxing breath and her parched lips formed a smile. She shifted in her bed to try to get comfortable and took a bite of fruit.

The hospital room door suddenly opened again, and Joe stood in the doorway. Evie's heart skipped a beat. As he got closer, she could see that he had some bruises and cuts on his face.

"Hey Joe," said Michael. He invited Joe to take the seat he had been using by Evie's bed. Joe walked over to the bed and sat down next to Evie. Their eyes were locked on each other for several awkward seconds as Agent Weber looked over at Michael and beckoned him to join him in leaving the room.

"Well," said Agent Weber looking back over his shoulder. "We'll pick this up later."

"Yeah," said Michael nodding. "Evie, we'll have to . . ." he decided to finish his sentence later, when she might actually hear it.

"Yes, thank you," she said, her focus still locked on Joe as the door closed behind Michael.

Joe reached for her hand and kissed it. She thought she saw some moistness in his eyes.

"So," she said. "I have a feeling you met Alan."

"Yeah, but we didn't get along too well."

"Are you okay? They said you have broken ribs."

"I'm fine. They're just cracked. He got in a cheap shot or two."

"I have to say . . . I'm glad you hit him. Did he tell you anything?"

"No, but I didn't really expect him to. How are *you*? I looked in on you earlier, but you were sleeping." He smiled and rested her hand gently back on the bed.

"They say I'm going to be okay. What were you planning to do if I turned up dead?"

"I probably would've committed a murder myself."

"I tried to call you. While I was being kidnapped. I didn't realize at the time that they had removed the battery from my BlackBerry."

"I know. Your things were recovered."

"Do you think Alan had Senator Arbeson killed?"

"Well, I think he was pissed that his twenty-five million dollar commission was slipping though his fingers."

"Agent Weber said that there are lots of suspects, but they've got some pretty incriminating evidence against Alan."

"Maybe his fiery Latin wife put a hit out on him. Maybe she found the divorce laws unsatisfactory."

She laughed, but caught herself. "Joe, a U.S. Senator is dead. We shouldn't be laughing. Actually, you should avoid laughing altogether until your ribs heal."

"You're right."

"Joe, you don't believe all these reports in the media, do you? About me and the Senator? It started with a photo in *New York Magazine*. Senator Arbeson was with this woman who looked like me. Somebody sent me a handwritten note asking if I was having an affair with the Senator. I would never . . . I wasn't sure Alan was behind it because it was written in very elegant penmanship. And, I didn't tell you about it because I didn't want you to be upset."

"Somebody obviously got you confused with the woman in the magazine," he said. "It's just a note with a question that needs no answer."

"So you believe me? I never—"

"Yes, I believe you."

"Someone even went to the trouble to plant one of Senator Arbeson's cufflinks in my night stand. And, apparently a collection of press clippings under my bed. Who knows what other evidence has been planted."

"I just wish I could've been there when you needed me. I can't believe you were kidnapped right under the nose of the feds."

Evie forced herself slightly forward from the pillows, took Joe's hand and held it tightly.

"Joe, do you remember the first time we met? You joked about self-held illusions. I think you're an amazing man, but I don't think you could have changed the situation."

He smiled at her, warming the room. "So Eves, what are your plans?"

"This morning I had this dream. I dreamt I was packing up to move, and I was overwhelmed trying to figure out what to do with all my things. When I woke up, I had an epiphany. I realized that all the stuff I had accumulated was symbolic of the psychological baggage I've been carrying over the years. I think my subconscious was telling me to abandon it all, just let it go."

"So, you feel like starting over?"

"I got this interesting proposal from Roma Sori, one of my clients. It's a fragrance company. Adam Peyton, the president of the company, offered me a job."

"Eves, Michael's going to get you a settlement. He's even talking about defamation suits you could file with some of the tabloids. You don't have to work if you don't want to."

"Who knows what's going to happen if that merger with Newly, Boyce, Tate and Wells goes through. It may take years of legal battles to ever see any money." She paused and squeezed his hand. "I think I'm going to try something different. Actually, Adam's going to let me create and market my own perfume line. I think I'm going to call it *'Jurisprudence.'*"

Joe smiled. "That artistic soul I saw that hadn't yet found an avenue of expression. Well, maybe now you have."

"Maybe I have." She leaned over, wincing, and kissed him.

"Mmm," he said. "Listen, Eves, you have to promise me that from now on you'll be more careful. You can't keep taking drugs and getting into strange cars with people you don't know, okay?"

"Just because you beat up the bully in my life doesn't mean you can start giving me *advice . . .* "

"What if I were your husband? Would you listen to me then?"

"Don't count on it." *Yes, Joe I want to marry you.* The thought screamed so loudly in her head that she was sure he heard it.

"You're going back home to California?" she asked. "To Ajani and Ayoka?"

"Yes. I've neglected a few things out there."

She sat back against her pillows. "You know, Adam told me that I could set up my office at any of Roma Sori's facilities . . . New York, Chicago, Memphis . . . or *Los Angeles.*"

"And what did you tell him?"

"I said that I really want to see the sunset from a particular beach . . . and I . . ."

He smiled and leaned over the bed. He kissed her very slowly and softly on the mouth.

ATTRIBUTIONS

"Positive Illusions" study reference in Chapter 1:

Gamon, David, and Allen D. Bragdon. *Building Mental Muscle: Conditioning Exercises for the Six Intelligence Zones.* Cape Cod, MA: Allen D. Bragdon Publishers, Inc., 1998.

"Reading the Morning Paper" in Chapter 20 and other impressions of safari experience:

Ross, Mark C. *Dangerous Beauty: Life and Death in Africa: True Stories from a Safari Guide.* New York: Hyperion, 2001.

References to Operation Ill Wind in Chapter 25:

Pasztor, Andy. *When the Pentagon Was for Sale: Inside America's Biggest Defense Scandal.* New York: Scribner, 1995.

ACKNOWLEDGMENTS

I'd like to offer my gratitude to a number of people. Some of them, never seeing a word of my writing, simply offered timely advice or general encouragement; some read *portions* of my writing; and some read the *complete* manuscript and offered suggestions. These people include Deborah Hogan, Susan Griswold, Esslie Hughes, Brian Melton, Carol and Norwood Brenneke, Sharon Sholden, Gail McGlamery, Dr. Carsten Kampe, Nancy Kampe, Angela Saks, Deborah Haines, Karin Wacaser and Susan Ridley. I am also very grateful for the ongoing assistance of Vita Vlad and Mariette Roy.

A special thank you to my parents for their encouragement and assistance in too many ways to enumerate. I owe a special debt of gratitude to my mother, who eagerly read every version I produced. Tirelessly reading and critiquing numerous versions of a manuscript with limitless enthusiasm is something only she would do.

I will always be grateful to Susan A. Schwartz, my editor, who taught me so much about the writing process, as well as the publishing industry.

My lawyer, Bob Stein, was a terrific sounding board in addition to providing solid advice on the legal aspects of the publishing process. Additionally, Jeffrey Johnson and Teresa Lee provided input on specific legal issues, for which I'm truly grateful.

While I followed much of the advice of my editor, lawyers, friends and family, I want to stress that any mistakes, opinions, stupidities and the like reflected in this work are mine and mine alone.

Lastly, I would like to thank my beloved paternal grandmother who introduced me to the joy of creating stories.